The Fresno Incident

The Fresno Incident

Philip L. Rettew

authorHOUSE®

AuthorHouse™
1663 Liberty Drive
Bloomington, IN 47403
www.authorhouse.com
Phone: 1-800-839-8640

This is a work of fiction. Although this story contains references to certain historical facts, events, real places and real people, all behavior and statements attributed to those people are entirely a figment of the author's imagination. All other characters and most events and descriptions are fictitious.

Published by AuthorHouse 04/30/2012

ISBN: 978-1-4670-7305-9 (sc)
ISBN: 978-1-4670-7304-2 (hc)
ISBN: 978-1-4670-7303-5 (e)

Library of Congress Control Number: 2011919149

PREFACE

This story is about love, tragedy, good, evil, chance, luck, coincidence and the occasionally capricious and intense mysteries of life and human emotion, with the intention of provoking genuine human response, thought, and enjoyment.

Most of us go through life thinking we know what love is. Many are fortunate enough to find it in some form. Every once in a while, however, a man and a woman find love as an intense integration of two souls so far beyond expectation, fantasy and imagination as to defy comprehension and belief, but that does not mean that it is not real.

Chapter 1

Monday, September 10, 2007
Fresno, California

It's five minutes before eight o'clock. I should have just enough time to shower, change my clothes and get ready . . .

That's odd . . . . That police car has the flashers on and it's turning into the same street where I need to go . . . I wonder why . . . That big truck must be blocking the street . . . Come on people! Let's get going here . . . I don't have all day!

She was simply innocent. She was in danger.

"OH . . . OH . . . MY GOD! OH, NNNOOO! OH . . . MY . . . GOD . . . NNNOOO! OH! OWWWWW! OUCH! OH MY GOD, NO . . . NO . . . NO . . . OWWW! EEEEEEEAAAAGH!"

Jake? I . . . love . . . you . . . Jake? Save . . . me . . . Uhhh . . . Now . . . I'm . . . going . . . to . . . die . . .

What . . . is . . . that . . . white . . . light?

The beautiful young woman lay still, hanging out of the overturned and severely damaged van as utter chaos continued around her.

Their selfish and misguided beliefs masqueraded as compelling truth. The world still did not understand, so they felt compelled to act. His plan was born almost five years ago in a simple small teahouse on the other side of the world. His self-righteous intelligence would eventually lead to this tragic and delicate balance between life and death.

CHAPTER 2

Saturday, November 2, 2002
Mingora, Pakistan

Within sight of some of the highest, most inspiring and majestic snow-capped mountains on earth in the distance, two men in their mid-twenties huddled at a small table in the rear of a small teahouse, away from all the other patrons. They conversed in hushed voices, looking casually over their shoulders from time to time to assure themselves that no one was paying any attention to them.

Then Rasheed fixed his penetrating stare on the younger man's eyes and said quietly, "Khalid, you must soon take a wife and prepare for your mission against Satan in the United States. I will need you for important work in a few years. You can sustain yourself with your shoe business there just as you have here, and when the time is right, I will call you. We must be patient. You will need a period of several years to become a part of the local community and blend in with a minimum of suspicion so you can ultimately achieve your proper purpose on this earth and serve Allah as effectively as possible. The struggle will be long and difficult, but eventually, the rest of the world will recognize that serving Allah is the only destiny of all mankind."

Rasheed Shirani was fully comfortable with himself, the truth as he knew it, and was planning to make a significant contribution to the future, as he believed it should be. Only thirteen months had passed since the September 11 attacks upon the World Trade Towers in New York City, the Pentagon and an unknown target, probably the nation's Capitol building. Since that time, authorities throughout the world discovered and defeated several terrorist threats, but several other attacks succeeded. Some of the incidents received greater than average attention in the media, and others did not. Life would continue that way for most of the next five years.

Eventually, Khalid Kayani and his wife Farah moved to San Diego in late 2003. He developed his reputation as a skilled artisan as word spread throughout most of the Southwest about his fine custom-made boots and shoes. Farah was so excited about moving to the United Sates, that she could not see beyond her husband's words into his radical ideas. All she saw was an experienced artisan who could make anything out of leather to fit even the most unusual foot sizes and in any style that one could imagine or explain to him, even for children and people with foot deformities or other special requirements. She believed he was a good man and a hard worker. When he was not using his own ideas, he was working from rough drawings supplied by his customers, and sometimes from actual old or discarded shoes. Some of his customers' drawings were quite good, and others were relatively poor, requiring more of his artistic imagination to transform into the final product. If his customer did not like the finished footwear, Khalid would keep the returned shoes or boots in his shop, waiting for the unlikely coincidence of another buyer with the same size requirements and artistic taste. He could do this because he required a deposit of fifteen percent with each order. The customer would forfeit that deposit if he returned the product for any reason. Both men and women ordered shoes from him from as far away as Maine, Alaska, Mexico, Canada and Japan, and customer dissatisfaction was rather low. He did not advertise because it was not necessary. Word of mouth and internet traffic from satisfied customers spread sufficiently to maintain a steady flow of business and his acceptance in the local community, just as it had in Pakistan.

Farah cleaned three or sometimes four houses a week in the wealthier suburbs of San Diego. She earned $100 in cash per house. The rest of the time, she handled orders for footwear for her husband. She was happy and optimistic in her adopted country. They had money in the bank that she intended to use to buy their own house some day and live the American dream. She also looked forward to having a child or two through which she hoped to enrich their lives. Whenever she brought the subject up, Khalid always put her off.

He had other priorities that required dedicated work, patience and meticulous planning. Their marriage was proper and traditional, but devoid of the romantic passion in Farah's dreams. She had become accustomed to a life of only adequate happiness. That was her fate, given her limited upbringing and her current position in the most promising land of opportunity on earth. However, she carefully nurtured whatever hope for optimism she could find.

Almost four years later, his old friend Rasheed finally called to tell him it was time. They were ready to execute Rasheed's plan.

CHAPTER 3

Wednesday, September 13, 2006
Manhattan, New York

Eddie Barringer was in Manhattan at a restaurateur's convention for three days, trying to learn the latest ways to keep his mid-size Denver restaurant and bar competitive in the current tough and uncertain economic cycle. He was fortunate enough to keep his head chef, and he was smart enough to believe that people who liked his food probably would be willing to pay a little extra for good entertainment. For the last twenty-seven years, he had provided his patrons with a relatively inexpensive evening of delicious food that they did not have to prepare for themselves and usually good music at the same location without paying a small fortune.

He did not follow the entire schedule of events for the convention every day. He liked to walk around on his own and explore the entertainment districts in the late afternoon and evening for what he believed to be the additional benefit of exercise and the illusion of losing some of his 'extra' weight someday. He visited various entertainment restaurants, lounges and bars where he believed he had a credible chance of finding good talent, but he always hoped for something extraordinary. As a rather rusty musician himself, he still recognized good musical talent when he found it, and simply preferred to do his own research this time rather than rely exclusively upon professional scouts or entertainment agencies.

Shortly after six o'clock, he walked into The Bitter End in Greenwich Village, and not just heard, but also *felt* a woman's voice far superior to any other he had heard in many years. He was fifty-four years old, almost five feet, eight inches tall, somewhat pudgy and gradually losing his dark brown hair that was also changing to grey where he still had it. However, he was still young enough physically and mentally to appreciate a beautiful woman when he saw one. He sensed a winner for his bar in Denver, and waited patiently at his table for an opportunity to meet her and her backup musicians after their performance that evening. They were all talented men, one on keyboard, one on soprano sax, one on drums and one on electric guitar.

Quite an interesting group of instruments, he thought.

He was ecstatic as he approached the stage after their current number ended, and brazenly handed his card to the woman.

He announced with his most gracious and inviting smile in a voice loud enough to ensure that she could understand him above the background noise in the club, "My name's Eddie Barringer! I want to book your group at my restaurant and bar in Denver at your earliest convenience. I will wait until the end of your show tonight to talk further, OK?"

Nothing ventured, nothing gained, he mused to himself.

He discovered that she was just as beautiful at close range as she was attractive at a distance. He was doubly impressed because the latter circumstance did not always translate into the former in his experience.

To his complete amazement, she smiled and said pleasantly, "OK!"

Eddie returned to his seat and eagerly settled in for the rest of the evening, nursing a Budweiser as the world around him dissolved, leaving only the comforting sound of her voice. He did not need to explore any more entertainment venues. When it was obvious that they were through for the evening, Eddie returned to the stage, and true to her word, she spent a few moments with him.

"Hi Eddie," she said brightly as he approached her. "My name is Sasha. I'm more or less the business manager of the group."

"I'm more than pleased to meet you, Sasha!" he said with obvious and uncontrolled admiration. "How long have you all been performing together?"

"About three years," she said pleasantly, inviting further conversation with a smile.

"Have you ever been to Denver?" he asked without a strong preference for 'yes' or 'no,' but would have liked to hear 'no' so he honestly could claim to be the first to introduce her to the greater Denver area.

She unwittingly rewarded him with a friendly "No, I haven't, but I would really like to visit there, especially to see the mountains!"

"Well, you are most welcome to come out as soon as possible, which would be when?" he asked a little too directly in his excitement at the possibility.

He was completely prepared to rearrange his schedule if necessary to accommodate her.

She sighed briefly and continued, "We are booked rather solid for the next fifty-one weeks, Eddie, I'm sorry to say for your sake, but I would be willing to visit you after that if it's okay with you!"

Her response told Eddie that he was on the right track. They were good enough to be booked throughout almost a year, so they were good enough for him to pay whatever she wanted to perform in his club.

He continued with a hopeful tone, "I would like to have you perform at my club for a two-week period, or more, if you can manage that."

"I'm really sorry, Eddie, but we have another engagement after Saint Louis in Fresno that would eliminate anything longer than about five days in between those two in Denver."

The length of the potential engagement disappointed Eddie, but he decided five days was certainly better than nothing at all and effectively masked his disappointment as he continued with gracious acceptance of less than what he wanted.

"I would be simply *delighted* to have you at my club for five days, Sasha!"

She asked how large the restaurant was, where it was located, and how many people Eddie would expect to have as an audience, whether he had a performing stage and how big it was. She did not want to perform in some low-class dive or a small place with too few people. She wanted a certain minimum length of performance time, and a fair effort from Eddie to advertise their performance engagement in advance. After all, her group was still relatively new and she wanted to get as much exposure and free advertising as she could and as efficiently as possible. Even though her group had never been to Denver before, she wanted to have an audience big enough to make her feel comfortable with the expense and effort to get there, as well as to help spread the word about their music.

Eddie was quite happy to grant all of her requests and would do whatever was necessary to accommodate her and advertise her group at his place. He pulled out a simple contract form from his pocket to finalize the deal with The Autumn Dream, the name of her group. They exchanged all relevant particulars and contact information before Eddie returned to his hotel for the night feeling excited and optimistic, but dreading the long wait until she showed up in Denver. He felt like a fifteen-year-old again having to wait a whole year for his driver's license.

CHAPTER 4

Friday, September 15, 2006
Baltimore, Maryland

Eighteen-year-old Willie Jones was lying almost unconscious on a gurney in the emergency room at Sinai Hospital, bleeding from a gunshot wound of his right thigh.

His mother, Bertha Jones was a heavy-set, almost six-foot tall black woman with fire in her slightly bulging, blood-shot eyes, and a life full of enough disappointment to keep that fire burning. She raised three boys into their teens, but two were shot and killed in downtown Baltimore gang warfare before they reached the age of sixteen. She had not seen the boys' father for many years. He had abandoned the family when the oldest, Darien, was just three and the middle son, Damon, was only fifteen months old and the youngest, Willie, was merely an infant. Darien and Damon never finished high school. They succumbed to visions of a life of luxury and riches beyond the dreams of avarice from the sale of drugs, and fell into the world of Sigma, one of the most notorious drug dealers in the state of Maryland, or the entire east coast for that matter. He had no known first name or last name, by all official and unofficial reports. Everyone knew him only as Sigma. He was elusive, to say the least, both physically and legally. He brought in enough drug money from the most vulnerable along the eastern seaboard to keep a slick lawyer in his employ full time.

Benjamin Borglowski had a law degree. That was all he had in Bertha's opinion, from what she could read in the newspapers about him. He had no moral code. From his perspective, however, he was simply representing people in the complex legal system who could not represent themselves. His job was to protect Sigma, and he was rather good at it. He kept Sigma sufficiently distant from the original sources of his money through a variety of shell companies and associated 'business dealings' that effectively made Sigma's considerable income look like it had either spent a month in Clorox and boiling water, or came from a bevy of secret admirers and business deals. Sigma was on the hit list of criminals in the metropolitan Baltimore-Washington area, the list of people the police wanted behind bars, or dead.

Earlier that day, Detective Anthony D'Anatoli was having a late lunch at his favorite corner table at the Red Baron Bar and Grill before he went on duty for the evening. A disheveled old woman with straggly hair under a bandana and a flimsy brown dress that looked like it came from a homeless shelter was watching the street outside, because she knew D'Anatoli's routine. She saw him get out of his unmarked police car in front of the club and go inside. She waited for several minutes to be sure he was staying inside for his usual meal and not coming right back out to go somewhere else. She walked into the bar and looked around for any possible threatening people or situations. Then she saw him in the corner to her right after waiting for several moments to let her eyes adjust to the dark veneer wood and low light inside. She hobbled over to D'Anatoli's table and dropped a note on it with the subtle quickness of a street magician, turned, and then limped out of the club with speed uncommon among typical older 'injured' people. D'Anatoli had a virtual Ph.D. in 'street smarts.' He knew that was not a 'little old lady,' and he knew it would be pointless to pursue 'her.' 'She' was doing no harm to him or to anyone else and he had no immediate cause to detain 'her,' so he turned his attention to the note. The information was credible, interesting, and worth his time. It had the earmarks of a possible drug war about to heat up.

At approximately ten after eight that evening, he was sitting in his unmarked police car near the corner of Fulton and Pennsylvania Avenues, facing north on Fulton according to the instructions on the note, which was a tip from the 'little old lady' indicating he would see

Sigma in this area this evening. He wanted Sigma off the streets, and was sick and tired of battling the slick lawyers. He was going to settle this matter by himself. The more people who knew about the location, the more difficult his task would become, so he kept his information to himself, assuming the 'little old lady' had not told anyone else. He could not be sure, but he had good police instincts, and followed his intuition. He was not altogether sure Sigma was not getting 'help' from within the Baltimore police department to remain as elusive as he had. Sigma knew the Baltimore-Washington area better than the greatest majority of law-enforcement people in that part of the country, but not better than Detective Anthony D'Anatoli. He waited in his car with the window open, listening for any indication of trouble. He waited a lot in his job. He had been searching for Sigma for almost a year after he had suffered a minor gunshot wound of his right arm during a drug bust in the darkest shadows of western Baltimore, from which Sigma escaped and went deeper into the underworld of drug dealers along the east coast. D'Anatoli wanted him, and he wanted him tonight!

Then he saw movement halfway down the block. Two men standing on the sidewalk were apparently engaged in a conversation near a sparkling black late model S550 Mercedes with shiny custom chrome wheels. The men looked suspicious, but D'Anatoli could not see clearly enough to identify either one with certainty as Sigma. D'Anatoli got his binoculars out, squinted through them and whispered to himself with final recognition, "Sigma! You bastard, your time is up!"

Bertha had been uneasy during a conversation with her son just five minutes earlier in their home on Fulton Street. He had been evasive toward her, and said he had to go out for a while. She was suspicious, and feared that her only remaining son also would succumb to the ugly drug world of Sigma. She knew who he was, of course, as did almost everyone else in the drug-infested neighborhood. Several empty houses remained in the area as those with the means or opportunity finally moved away. Everyone in that neighborhood, including the police, knew Sigma owned that car, but all they could do was harass the owner in a cat-and-mouse game until he slipped up. Sigma was very careful. He never slipped up.

Then D'Anatoli saw a large woman appear from one of the houses just behind the two men and slowly move up just behind Sigma. She was holding something with both of her hands down in front of her. He did not recognize the other man, nor did he know the woman.

"Oh, shit!" he blurted out to himself.

He saw the large woman bring a baseball bat up over her shoulder and swing 'righty' for the fences, just as Sigma turned around with his pistol drawn. The bat struck him squarely in the face before he could aim his gun effectively. Sigma grabbed his bloody face with his left hand as the gun discharged in his right hand.

The bullet struck Willie in his upper left thigh near the femoral artery, as he yelled "No, Momma . . . No!" and slumped in agony to the pavement.

He was bleeding profusely and screaming for help as he fell and rolled onto his back, writhing in pain. D'Anatoli started his car and pushed the accelerator to the floor but kept his flashers and siren off. The tires squealed as his car almost flew down Fulton about a block before he jammed on the brakes sending another resounding screech down the mostly empty streets with the typical echo of yet another dangerous and tragic incident in the troubled neighborhood. He threw open the door, leaped out of his seat and ran toward them. He decelerated within fifteen feet of the shrieking woman, who was already through winding up for another blow with the aluminum bat and starting another swing. He was watching 'street justice' in action, froze, and said nothing because he could see instantly that her momentum was beyond both her control and his ability to stop it. This big woman was accomplishing what he had wanted to do for over a year, but could not because he was an officer of the law. She brought the bat down on the top of Sigma's head with the full force of 245 pounds of high-octane concentrated maternal wrath, placing a large dent in Sigma's head. His gun discharged aimlessly and fell to the pavement. Sigma moaned for the last time. The bloody bat fell from her grasp and clanked to the sidewalk, then rolled with a hollow repetitive metallic tune across the uneven pavement four feet before stopping at Willie's left foot. She huffed and gasped heavily, and urgently grabbed her chest with both hands, then slumped to the pavement in a sitting position with her legs out in front of her and her chin down on her chest, simultaneously panting and weeping uncontrollably.

D'Anatoli glanced thoughtfully at her for half a second, and then decided that the young man took priority. He raced up to him and immediately knew he needed to stop the bleeding from his leg, and then make sure the woman was not having a heart attack. He had to work fast, and he knew he was gambling with their welfare, but he did not want to call this one in. Besides, he was the only one on the scene who could help, and it would take too long to get more help that he really did not need or want. She accomplished one of his long-standing goals for him. As it was, he could not have prevented Sigma's demise anyway.

He thought to himself, *life is just not fair sometimes, is it?*

He quickly ripped another hole in Willie's blue jeans above the bullet hole with his Swiss Army utility knife, and widened the bullet hole in his jeans. He picked up the baseball bat, forced it through the two holes and then rotated the bat parallel to the bleeding leg above the wound, forming an effective tourniquet by increasing the pressure around Willie's left leg with his pant leg, slowing the bleeding to a minor trickle. He then cut a section of Willie's jeans from the other lower pant leg, folded it several times and placed it over the wound and told him to hold the wad of cloth on his bleeding wound.

He said firmly, "I don't know how long that's going to hold, kid so *make sure you hold that bat and don't let it move!* And you gotta keep that pressure on the bullet hole in your leg! Do you understand me?"

Willie was screaming with pain, but nodding rapidly at D'Anatoli with obvious fear in his wide-open eyes.

D'Anatoli spoke calmly, but reassuringly, "You're going to be OK, kid. I know it hurts big time, but just hang in there and stay as still as you can and don't yell! You're going to need all your energy to make it to the hospital with me without passing out! I'm going to check your mom real quick, and then get you both to the hospital. Remember, don't you dare let that bat loose!"

He went over to Bertha and made a quick assessment that she was in no immediate danger, but he asked anyway, "You OK?"

She was still breathing heavily between sobs of intense anguish, while pouring out almost a lifetime of tears, disappointment and pain. All she could do was nod as vigorously as she could, looking away from D'Anatoli with fear, shame and severe anxiety.

D'Anatoli quickly decided it was time to move. He raced to his car, and retrieved a large blanket from his trunk and spread it over the back seating area and secured it by jamming the edges between the seatback, rear deck, seat and both sidewalls and then spread the excess over the floor.

After he was finished, he raced back to Willie and said in his calm but clear and commanding voice, "I'm going to take you and your mom to the nearest hospital. Don't panic! Try to breathe easy, and hold on to that bat, or you'll bleed to death! We don't have time for an ambulance to get here! Do you understand me?"

Willie whimpered while nodding his head rapidly in agreement, and muttered, "Y-Yeah" and then succumbed to another torrent of tears.

With effort and uncommon strength, D'Anatoli got the injured boy, who was still holding the bat and the wad of cloth in place, and his mother into the back seat of his car with surprising strength and quickness. He wiped the blood from his hands onto the blanket and quickly got behind the steering wheel, slammed his door closed, turned his siren and grille flashers on, and raced through minimal traffic to Sinai Hospital, which was the closest one, leaving Sigma lying still on the sidewalk, essentially as Sigma had left so many others.

"What's your name, Ma'am?"

"Bertha Jones," she said with guarded fear.

"And you son's name?"

"Willie," she managed to blurt out before giving in to another rush of tears and sobs as she helped him keep the wound covered.

Within just a few minutes, he pulled up to the emergency room entrance at Sinai Hospital. He left his lights on, jammed on the parking brake, simultaneously rammed the automatic transmission shifter into the 'park' position, opened his door, took two steps to the passenger door on his side and opened it to grab Willie. He practically dragged Willie out of the car toward the emergency room entrance when a nurse and two orderlies appeared instantly after hearing the sound of the approaching siren and seeing the increasing glare of his red and blue LED grille flashers through the entrance. As he approached the parting large automatic glass doors, another huge beefy orderly seemed to appear out of nowhere and helped lift Willie carefully and deftly as if he were as light as a matchstick. With respect for the obviously makeshift tourniquet, he then helped place Willie gently on a gurney as a young male intern started to cut his left trouser leg. The doctor then removed the bat, quickly examined the wound and immediately applied pressure just above the renewed river of blood from an obvious laceration of the femoral artery. D'Anatoli rushed back to his car and motioned Bertha to get out, and led her into the emergency admissions room.

Bertha watched in utter horror with wide-open eyes, and then looked at the young doctor, then at the nurses, and then at Willie. He was not moving. His eyes were closed. A plasma bag already hooked to a tall metal pole attached to the gurney provided a life-sustaining fluid into a long tube inserted into a vein in his left arm. A slim young dark-skinned nurse in a light-blue uniform next to the gurney studied the flow of fluid from the bag with professional control and a furrowed brow, while she took a sample of his blood for typing and cross matching. Willie was fading. The nurses and orderlies were performing like a well-trained team. They had his clothes cut and removed and more IVs ready to run. Blood from an unknown donor would arrive as soon as possible to replace what Willie was losing.

"Open Surgery 'A' and get him in there NOW!" the young doctor ordered.

The flurry of activity disappeared with the gurney down the short hall and behind the large double-hinged doors with a big red 'A' painted over both them, as Bertha once again looked on with fleeting hope and increasing despair. Relative quiet resumed for a moment in the admissions area. Another son shot. She felt completely depleted as a human being, as a woman, and as a mother. She knew she would have lost Willie to the ugly world of drugs if she had not attacked Sigma.

"God, how much more will you take from me?" she cried out in painful agony toward the ceiling. She sat down heavily in abject surrender on one of the well-worn long oak benches next to the wall across from the admissions counter, put her face in her hands and sobbed uncontrollably.

D'Anatoli was filling out paperwork at the counter. The slim young clerk behind the counter was also filling out paperwork. She called out to Bertha in a firm but friendly business tone.

"What kind of insurance does your son have, Ma'am?"

Bertha looked up across the hall at the clerk with the bloodshot eyes of a spent woman. She was abandoned by her husband many years ago, had already given up two sons, and now appeared to be losing her baby, and yet they wanted money to boot?

"I . . . we don't . . . have . . . any . . . insurance," she said softly with resignation between sobs.

D'Anatoli glanced thoughtfully at her for a second and then reached into his left pants pocket for his billfold and removed a small leather credit-card holder, took out a plastic card, pushed it over to the admissions clerk and said quietly, "Use that."

She looked quizzically at him and said, "I . . . I can't use your credit card, Officer!"

He looked over at her with a calm, but serious and steely expression in his grey eyes, put his pen down, and said evenly, "Yes you can, and yes you will!"

"Sir, really, I can't do that!"

"Call the physician in charge, please."

"Sir, I can't . . ."

"If you don't call him, I will!"

She saw that Detective Anthony D'Anatoli was deadly serious and already looking over her shoulder at the list of emergency staff and phone numbers on the wall. She dialed the five-digit extension next to 'Physician in Charge' from a placard on the wall to her right and waited through only two rings with her head bowed slightly, but looked up warily at Detective D'Anatoli as she spoke.

"Doctor Goldstein, I have a small problem at emergency admissions. Will you please come down here? I would really appreciate it! Thank you," she said in evident controlled desperation.

In less than two minutes, the fifty-one-year-old Doctor Jacob Goldstein entered the admissions area from a stairwell between Bertha and the doors with the big red 'A' and strode with an air of professional pride and comfort to the admissions counter with his hands in the pockets of his long white hospital coat.

"What's up, Doris?"

"We've got a young man with a bullet wound in emergency surgery, and his mother over there says they have no insurance. This police officer gave me his credit card to use for the hospital charges. I told him I couldn't do that. He insisted that I call you."

Doctor Goldstein took his hands out of his pockets, picked up the card and examined it. It was indeed an ordinary credit card. The name underneath was 'THE CHANCELLOR ORGANIZATION.'

"So, exactly what is the problem?" he asked calmly.

"A policeman can't pay for patient treatment, can he?"

"That is not your concern, Doris. The paperwork you are preparing will be reduced to a stream of bits and bytes in a computer somewhere. The relevant credits and debits will end up at their proper destinations, and the personalities involved will eventually be irrelevant. The hospital doesn't care where the money comes from. I will take *full* responsibility, Doris. I can assure you that everything is in order."

That also meant that the police incident report and the official hospital and police records would eventually indicate a drive-by small caliber gunshot wound to the upper left leg of a nineteen-year-old black youth, with no suspects and no arrests.

Detective D'Anatoli and Doctor Goldstein looked into each other's eyes for only a second longer than necessary in silent understanding as Doctor Goldstein placed the credit card on the counter in front of Doris before turning to go back upstairs to his office. She sensed that she was within a whisker of learning something she would be better off not knowing. However, she dutifully picked up the card, entered the account number into her computer with barely controlled anxiety and then handed the card back to D'Anatoli, while her gut was unsettled and straining against her outward appearance of professional efficiency and business as usual. What Doris did not understand was that both Detective D'Anatoli and Doctor Goldstein were members of The Chancellor Organization.

After she entered the data into her computer, an infinitesimally small portion of the vast fortune of Duke Chancellor started to ricochet throughout cyberspace from one financial enterprise to another in an untraceable manner, eventually satisfying the financial requirements of Sinai Hospital for services rendered to a poor and unfortunate young man fighting for his life behind the 'A' surgery room doors.

Detective D'Anatoli finished his paperwork, and turned to Bertha.

"OK, Bertha. Let's go."

The prospect of being taken to the police precinct for booking on a murder charge frightened her terribly, and her heart started to race again. She had lost so much. She had absolutely no more fight and very little self-respect left in her. She stood somewhat uneasily with the assistance of D'Anatoli's right hand, and he escorted her out to his car and helped her get in the passenger side back seat away from the blood, and closed the door. He did not handcuff her. She was too distraught, confused and exhausted to pay attention. He went around to the other back door, opened it, and removed the blanket and put it in his trunk to discard later. Then he returned to get behind the wheel.

"Do you have good friends or relatives in the area, Bertha?" he asked her, looking directly into her bloodshot eyes in the rear view mirror.

"Yes sir. I have . . . a sister . . . across town. Why . . . Why . . . do . . . you . . . ask?" she said cautiously, still trying to control her tears, but slowly beginning to realize that something very unusual was happening to her.

"You may want to rest and freshen up, and you probably need to be around friends or family right now before you will be ready to come back to the hospital to see your son and help him get better. You can't do anything for him here right now anyway. I'll take you to your sister's place. What's the address?"

Bertha sat motionless with her mouth hanging open and almost crimson wet eyes wide open with profound disbelief. She absolutely could not comprehend what was happening to her. She thought he was going to take her to the local precinct for booking on a murder charge, and now he was going to take her to her sister's place to rest and refresh herself.

"But . . . what . . . what about . . . the . . . the charges?"

"What charges, Bertha?"

"I . . . I hit that . . . I hit that man with a . . . with a baseball bat!" she began to cry uncontrollably again.

"I never charged you with anything, Bertha. I didn't see any crime. I saw a young man who desperately needed medical attention. I saw a woman trying to defend her son. She also looked like she might have been having a heart attack. I did what I could to help him and her. That's not a crime, is it?"

She broke down again in uncontrollable sobs and cried out with the tiniest beginnings of new hope as she began to realize that this man was no ordinary police officer.

"Oh, God . . . Lord in Heaven!"

"That's close, Bertha . . ."

He turned his flashers off and pulled out into the street.

CHAPTER 5

Saturday, September 16, 2006
Las Vegas, Nevada

After graduating with honors from M.I.T., Sammy Chin held a variety of computer-related jobs with major electronics and technology corporations, but remained restless and unchallenged, until he met Joe Czarzhynenski at Caesar's Resort and Casino in Las Vegas during a computer hardware convention. Sammy was representing Intel at the convention where he was to promote the new dual-core processors Intel started introducing in May of 2005. Joe was at the poker tables, as was his habit once a year, every year, but was maintaining an uninspiring run of mediocre hands for about an hour, leaving him down a few hundred dollars, but that was insignificant to him. However, he watched the young Chinese man at the other end of the table add to his already considerable pile of chips.

Sammy knew how to play, and when to quit. After several more hands, the young man smiled at the croupier, tossed two $100 chips on the table in front of him, and calmly said, "I'm through for the night, folks!"

Joe recognized the young man's discipline, which piqued his voracious curiosity as he saw his opportunity to learn more about him and said casually, "So am I."

He followed the young Chinese man away from the table and eventually caught up with him in a long corridor of 'one-armed bandits' and introduced himself.

"Hi! My name is Joe! I noticed that you played a very smart game of poker back there!"

Sammy recognized the short, stocky, balding man from the table he had just left, smiled at Joe and said, "Thank you!"

The feeling developing between them was almost electric, as if they already knew each other or had met before. The atmosphere between them was not really 'Don't I know you from somewhere?' It was more as if they were continuing a conversation started long ago, interrupted by the urgency of life but now present, relaxed and familiar. Joe could have that effect upon people almost at will.

Joe continued with calm conviction without missing a beat, "I think I know a good card counter when I see one."

Sammy was not the least bit intimidated and betrayed no emotion or outwardly visible reaction whatsoever. He knew card counters were not welcome in Las Vegas or anywhere else gambling was legal, or illegal, for that matter. Joe recognized the remarkable calm in Sammy's demeanor—not a hint of emotional response, confirmation or denial. He especially admired and valued that trait.

Joe wanted to emphasize that he would not be a threat to the young man and said, "Let's eat! I know a special restaurant off the beaten path, but the food is excellent—my treat!"

Joe saw the makings of a new member of The Chancellor Organization.

Sammy realized with that invitation and Joe's demeanor that Joe was most likely not an agent of the casino business or any other potential source of trouble, flashed his special broad natural white-toothed smile and said, "Great!"

They walked out onto the street, where Joe immediately hailed a cab and instructed the driver where to take them and both men entered the shiny yellow late-model Chevy cab from the passenger's side back door. Twelve minutes later, they arrived at one of Joe's special places in Las Vegas. They exited the cab and entered the restaurant, where the hostess, Estelle immediately greeted the two men. She was still a shapely woman with residual visible hints of former beauty. At probably over fifty years of age, she could still easily catch a man's eye, even if for only a moment.

She looked slightly down at Joe and said warmly, "We have a table all ready for you, Joe."

That did not really mean that the table was already actually reserved for them. It meant that she was happy to see him again, and that by the time she escorted Joe and his guest through the spacious main room, she would have made eye contact with her assistant manager in a way that communicated that she wanted a particular table in the corner ready immediately! Sammy was very observant and noticed how she had made lightning-fast arrangements, and decided that he had better pay attention to this friendly, engaging and apparently well-known, or at least persuasive and influential gentleman. After she seated them, Joe wasted no time in expertly assisting Sammy in the process of spilling out his whole life story right there at the table, including explaining his impressive academic credentials and rather superior computer talents. That was one of Joe's many rare abilities. He could get anyone to relate even the intimate details of a first love affair. Even a short conversation with Joe easily led one to imagine that he could convince a state patrol officer to trash a speeding ticket on the spot, apologize and make him feel good about it. Joe had many other talents as well. After their lengthy discussion, Joe knew his next question was the right one at the right time.

"How would you like an exciting new job, Sammy?"

Sammy masked his intense internal excitement and fascination with this strangely familiar man and continued with his naturally calm, controlled and friendly demeanor.

"Of course! I'm always interested in new opportunities! What do you have in mind?"

"I am in the business of helping people and organizations who cannot always achieve their goals by themselves in certain circumstances, for one reason or another. I require the assistance of dedicated people from time to time, who are talented, smart, discreet, honest, effective and loyal. The world is not always fair, and tragedies abound. Justice is not always served. We all know that. However, we have choices in life. We can chose to be selfish, or we can give of our talents and abilities according to our hearts and minds where it actually means something positive to another human being, or, in some cases to our social structure and the future of us all. We can make the right decisions when it soothes the soul, restores a sense of fairness, or enables peace and eliminates suffering, in spite of all the 'rules' and misguided social pressures of one kind or another. We can do things in the best interests of the greater good for society as we all would like it to be, and in so doing, help ourselves."

"I will compensate you in a manner that assures me of your cooperation, loyalty and discretion. Either I or my employer, and absolutely *no one* else, will give you instructions. If at any time you chose not to take an assignment, you must honestly inform me of that in a timely manner, so I can make other arrangements. My work will proceed with you or without you. My commitment to my employer is complete, and I require the same of those who work for me."

"Above all, and I *do* mean above *all*, you *must* dedicate every cell, ounce and fiber of your being to secrecy and discretion. You will learn soon enough the importance of that requirement. Some of our work is dangerous or subject to 'legal challenge.' You *must* understand that! There is no future without risk. If you need assistance, then *ask* for it. My organization will provide consistent, effective and reliable support at all times. However, if you violate my requirements for secrecy, then you will forfeit the compensation and considerably effective network of protection and support that I provide my 'contractors' and an impenetrable wall of denial will forever separate you from my organization's people, who, by the way, are all over the world."

Sammy started to breathe again. He did not know how long he was not breathing, but he was hooked. He thought about his uncertain start in life. He knew life was not fair. He had lost his parents, either to the wrath of nature or to government corruption. He was never sure which. They must have suffered terribly after the earthquake before they eventually died in the collapse of their apartment building. Speculation about faulty cement used in the construction of the vast apartment complex where they lived in China surfaced shortly after the tragedy, but Sammy never knew that until many years later. He knew about separation, though. However, he also knew there was good in the world. Someone saved him from an uncertain life as an orphan in China. It seemed like a deed of grace and good will not typical of most people he encountered in life before or since that time. He would accept. He would look forward, and put himself at the cutting edge of the exciting reality he wanted. He would accept this unusual and challenging adventure in a manner uncommon among young people, with complete and sincere commitment to a cause he believed in, and to a strangely familiar man, to whom he could be steadfastly loyal.

Without hesitation, Sammy boldly replied with genuine sincerity and maturity slightly beyond his years, "I will honor your requirements to the best of my ability."

Joe had worked his magic once again. The Chancellor Organization just became one member stronger, and would become even more effective with his talents. He got his first chance to apply his own version of the effectiveness and power of The Chancellor Organization just six months later.

CHAPTER 6

Friday, March 30, 2007
New Haven, Connecticut

Jason M. Holloway, Ph.D. was a full professor of philosophy at Yale University at the age of forty-three. He was also a member of The Chancellor Organization. In common terms, he had connections.

He was in his office in Davenport College, one of the residential facilities of the University, reading the third philosophy papers of the spring term submitted by students in his 'Ethics in The Modern World' course, Philosophy 460. The 400 level had prerequisites, and was therefore not open to freshman, so he did not feel burdened by what he saw as the typical insecurity of even second-term freshmen and their struggles to grow up.

Well, this should be interesting, he thought to himself.

Janice Smith's paper was next on the pile of unread assignments from last Friday. He marveled, even at his age, experience and position, at how such an attractive young woman could have such a simple and common last name. He imagined that she should have had a more elegant, longer, mysterious, exotic or sophisticated name to match her physical beauty. All of the allure had to be in her first name, if, of course one did not have the pleasure of seeing her in person. Jason began to read.

It appears that our governmental culture is contaminated with selfishness at the expense of longer-term consideration for the betterment of people's lives. The nature of our governmental system allows lawmakers to make special laws that directly affect their financial security and well-being in a manner significantly disproportionate to that of the public. In addition, our social order is threatened by the eroding ability of elected officials to function in a governmental culture influenced by special interest groups with powerful financial incentives, specifically designed to mold public officials to suit the desires of special interest groups, whose techniques are designed to reach even the most dedicated and thoughtful members of our legislative and ancillary government organizations, including the military, the judicial, and the intelligence communities.

Jason sat up a little in his chair. There was obviously some feisty intelligence behind that pretty face. He continued to read.

The nature of our democracy is necessarily dominated by compromise. However, the nature of recent problems is such that compromise is not sufficient for realistic expectation of effective solutions.

Modern governmental behavior has the appearance of reactionary regulation, without enforcing relevant regulations and laws already on the books. Ted Kennedy is reported to have participated in about 2500 bills. Why is that good government? Why is more regulation better? It appears that we cannot earn a living or walk a straight line today without violating some kind of regulation or law. This appearance of continuing regulation merely teaches the population governed that behavior not explicitly forbidden is allowed. It erodes the essence of individual and social self-discipline, moral conscience and generally socially constructive ethical behavior. The constant cascade of legislation interferes with an entrepreneur's ability to plan . . .

Professor Holloway continued to read with interest. He eventually came to the end of page 4, flipped it over and found page 6 next. As if to check the order of the pages to see whether he had inadvertently turned two pages stuck together, he carefully separated each page from the adjacent page, only to find that indeed, page 5 was missing. The logic of her writing up to that point verified that her thoughts were discontinuous on page 6 and the beginning grammar and sentence structure on the page was obviously dislocated. Page 5 was definitely missing. Jason groaned to himself at this intrusion of evident incompetence upon his idealistic impression of the beautiful young Janice Smith. He dismissed the thought with effort as he put a large red check mark on the upper right corner of the front page of her paper without adding any written comments and tossed the paper on the floor next to those he had already read and on which he had written his comments. He read more papers until just after eleven o'clock, and then left for his home in Woodbridge, just northwest of New Haven, and went to bed.

Monday morning he was in his office before nine o'clock, preparing for his ten o'clock seminar, which Janice Smith should be attending, when he would ask her about the missing page 5 from last week's assignment. Then a rapid, but oddly gentle knock on his office door startled him.

"Come in! It's open," he said.

He looked up and watched the slightly tarnished brass handle turn slowly as the door inched toward his desk with only the slightest creaking of colonial-era hinges. Janice Smith stepped gracefully from behind the door into his moderate, cramped and cluttered office with tall bookshelves completely lined with books all the way from the well-worn wood floor to the ceiling and carefully closed the door behind her with barely a click of the latch. She was wearing a white silk blouse with one-too-many buttons unbuttoned down the front, over a bra that was obviously about two sizes too small to hold what appeared to be more than her fair share of feminine assets, and a simple plaid red skirt that was fashionably above her knee, but not far enough to set off a fire alarm. She held a printed sheet of text, which she waved in his direction with only the slightest coy, but self-conscious smile.

"This is page 5. I wanted to make sure you see it, and that *no one else* sees it, so I took the liberty of bringing it over here early to show you personally."

She put the paper on Jason's desk, placed her palms on the edge of his desk with her thumbs to the outside, forcing her elbows in toward her chest, and leaned slightly forward, and at the same time subtly squeezed her elbows together in a manner that made her ample breasts push higher above her undersized bra and into her already strained blouse where a strategic button was missing.

Jason fought her obviously sensuous and flirtatious behavior by not looking directly at her beautiful chest, although he gradually succumbed to using his peripheral vision to satisfy his undeniable innate male interest as best he could.

He picked up the paper without looking up at her and said to his cluttered desk, "Sit down please. I wanted to ask you about this before class anyway, but since you are here we will settle this here and now before class."

She slowly backed away from his desk, turned and walked over to an old wooden chair in the corner of his office and sat down as he paused for several seconds while he retreated into his academic persona and then continued.

"First of all, I do not tolerate immature jokes or clever little tricks at this level of education, and second, I do not appreciate provocative female behavior from students. You should know by now that University regulations . . ."

She interrupted him with an impatient, pleading voice approaching adolescent desperation, "Please read the page, Professor Holloway. It's *very* important!"

He looked at her with the beginnings of some confusion. Although she still wanted to make sure he saw what she had to offer in case she felt the need to be more persuasive, she had absolutely no idea what she would *actually do* if her efforts so far were insufficient to secure his cooperation.

He turned his attention back to the page in front of him as his natural curiosity trumped his half-hearted authoritarian effort, and began to read it.

Page 5

The following has nothing to do with my paper, but it has everything to do with political ethics and government, and my life. I apologize, but this unusual method of getting your attention was the best way I could think of to make sure you understand my painful predicament in complete privacy and secrecy.

Senator Richard Lamont Russell IV of Connecticut, chairman of the Senate Finance Committee, has been blackmailing my mother for the last several years because he says he has evidence of an indiscretion about 20 years ago that produced the form you see before you. I love the father I know, the man who has shown constant love toward me for my whole life, the wonderful man who married my mother. He knows nothing of this indiscretion because my mother never told him, and she has been paying this asshole of a senator several times a year with money from her inheritance, and from the sale of treasured family jewelry at his 'request' to keep quiet. She confided in me under tremendous stress and emotional pain a few weeks ago when my father was traveling in Europe on business. She is simply not capable of admitting to her husband that he is not my natural father as he has assumed for the entire marriage, because she cannot risk inflicting that much pain upon him or possibly losing her marriage and she is running out of cash. My parents have always had 'separate money' and never discussed their sources. They never felt they had to. They were both from wealthy families.

I am extremely upset, and I refuse to see my parents hurt in any way any more than they have been already, and I will do <u>anything</u> necessary to assure that this matter dissolves completely, so they can live through the rest of their lives in as much peace and harmony as possible. I have not gone to the police or a lawyer, nor has my mother because, as you probably know, they will foul up my parents' lives with inevitable investigations and associated publicity, and emotionally I cannot handle that, and I doubt that my mother can either. If I went to a private detective, my dad would see the payments and force me to reveal their purpose. I am not foolish enough to approach the Senator on my own, as much as I would relish doing so. He will simply deny everything, and shred my life into tiny little pieces.

I am coming to you because I believe you can make this ugly situation disappear and thereby restore my parents' lives, by eliminating this outrageous invasion of my mother's privacy and peace of mind before things really get out of hand. If this situation is not handled properly, then I have very good reason to believe that my father's business will suffer, and his rather substantial contributions to Yale, financial and otherwise, will diminish proportionately, if not cease altogether. Furthermore, I am not willing to endure my share of my mother's agony any more than I already have. Life is not fair, Professor. I know it, and you know it. However, I have come to terms with my life situation and intend to live with it to the best of my ability, and I absolutely refuse to see anyone else hurt because of it.

Please do not underestimate me! I am determined to fight for what I believe to be right, and in this case, that means eliminating my mother's pain, and making Senator Russell pay for his crimes, one way or another! If you cannot help me, then, as much as I absolutely dread the prospect, I will be forced to handle it on my own, regardless of the consequences. I am at the end of my rope.

P.S. I already sent the real page 5 for my paper to your e-mail address early this morning. Surely, you will allow me this slight departure from normal academic protocol without any unnecessary adverse consequences.

Professor Jason M. Holloway let page 5 drop onto his desk as he looked up at the attractive young woman sitting in the corner chair in his small and cluttered academic office. He felt competing emotions between admiration for this pretty and apparently unusually strong and mature young woman on the one hand, and anger at what could possibly be true about the Senator on the other. He taught ethics classes. He thought he was promoting valuable and important standards of thought and behavior appropriate for what he wanted the world to become. He held up real-life examples of ethical behavior as well as historical examples for his students to appreciate and debate in class—the good, the bad, and the ugly—and this was *ugly*. However, he would never hold this particular real life situation up to his classes as an example, obviously, because it would be a gross violation of confidentiality. He could see that this determined young woman was trying to recognize right and wrong, and make what she honestly believed to be a very difficult, but necessary compromise to promote the greatest peace and happiness for as many of the parties to this complex tragedy as possible, and yet she knows she has limited capability and influence.

She does not know what to do herself, so she is coming to me for help. I cannot in good conscience refuse to help her, given my position, connections and knowledge. She is obviously much more than just another pretty student. I also cannot in good conscience just teach. I must act ethically as well.

Professor Holloway remained still, looking down at his desk for several moments without apparent focus but with a thoughtful expression creased into his brow before speaking.

"Well Janice, I can see that you are much more mature than you might normally appear to be to most people. Tell me, why are you coming to *me* with this information? Is there no one else in your life that you trust? What makes you think I can actually help you?"

"Frankly, Professor, *no!* There is no one else in my life I trust enough for this task! Isn't that one of the major tragedies of life? We need to trust someone occasionally because life's hurdles and problems are sometimes unanticipated and many times insurmountable alone, but can be overcome with the right kind of help. The problem is that there are so few trustworthy people available, or we simply do not know who is trustworthy, or are afraid to ask for help for any number of valid reasons. Some situations require immediate trust. There is simply not always enough time or opportunity to 'earn' trust, or proof of friendship, which usually takes weeks if you are really lucky, or even months, if not years, and even then there are no guarantees. Immediate absolute trust requires a higher moral standard than we are provided in the modern selfish world. I trust *my dog* more than I trust most *people* I know! So you see, Professor, I am dealing with this horrible intrusion into my life the only way I know. I believe I am morally responsible to resolve this dilemma the best way I can or suffer, possibly forever, the consequences of doing nothing, or worse, of doing the wrong thing, possibly making the whole situation even worse. It may appear that I have a choice, professor, but I do not see it that way at all. *I have no choice!*"

"I see," he said thoughtfully.

He started rubbing his chin, shifting in his faded, and well-worn black leather chair in an effort to recover from her unusually sharp sincerity, but he remained unsettled. Professor Holloway considered the tragic plight of such a bright, forthright, capable and attractive young woman being subject to such intense personal torment. The scenario he perceived in her life was an insult to his vision of the way the world should and could be. He reasoned that her pain was just as real and harmful to her as any pain he had felt at any time in his own life.

"No, professor! With all due respect, you do *not* see! I have a brother who I love as a genetic brother, who believes with all of his heart and mind that I am his birth sister. I have a 'father' who thinks I am really *his* daughter, and who has worked very hard to see that I get the very best education and value system available upon which I can build a life for myself and try to improve upon what I find in this world. I have a mother who grieves constantly because she made a mistake a long time ago, but she has raised me and sacrificed for me the very best way she knows how, and I *will not* allow *anyone* to hurt her *any more!* I did not dress this way because I wanted to seduce you. I dressed this way so I could determine how capable you are of listening to me truly with your brain instead of your libido! Sometimes we can't address unusual situations in life properly or effectively through traditional or 'socially acceptable' means. You of all people should know that by now. You know ethics inside and out! Your reputation and position tells me so. I had to be sure you would understand the urgency of my message by doing something unusual that would get your immediate attention. My family and I do not have the luxury of unlimited time to find trustworthy people and an effective solution. I did what I did to find out as quickly as possible whether you are really and honestly willing to help me. If you cannot help me, then I will have to go on and find someone else to help me, or take my chances by myself!"

She finished without tears. She had no more tears left to shed. Yale Professor of Philosophy, teacher of ethics, Jason M. Holloway, Ph.D. had met his match. He sat still for several moments, obviously deep in thought. This situation had the earmarks of a difficult situation that The Chancellor Organization could easily eliminate without subjecting Janice and her family to unnecessary public exposure typical of the traditional police, media and legal circus. After a few moments of internal evaluation and reflection, he finally spoke.

"Janice, I know some people who I believe will be able to help you. I honestly cannot explain fully to you exactly who or what I am talking about right now, but you have presented a situation that you obviously believe requires an unusual approach, as you so effectively demonstrated, so you should understand if I do not offer you typical explanations. All I can promise you at this point is that I will present your situation to the people I believe can help you. This plan requires your trust, in spite of your quite eloquent and rather accurate cynical opinion of trust. Once these people respond, you and I will be out of the picture completely, and will be unable to control or even influence what happens. Are you prepared to accept that?"

Janice had never heard such a statement from anyone in her entire life, and was somewhat frightened by Professor Holloway's tone in spite of her most recent bravado. She thought for just another moment, realizing that it was *she*, and no one else, who had generated the momentum toward this point of no return. That is exactly what she was doing in Professor Holloway's office. The gravity of her situation and her decision to approach Professor Holloway suddenly became irreversibly real, and had definite consequences, which were also apparently unalterable. She swallowed imperceptibly, hesitated for just a moment, and then let go of her intellectual and moral inhibitions and committed herself with a daring and unaccustomed leap of faith.

"*Yes,*" she said after another brief moment of hesitation.

Janice Smith was a lucky young woman. She did not know about The Chancellor Organization or Professor Holloway's participation in it. She merely stumbled innocently into its vast web. Professor Holloway would see that Joe learned of her plight. He believed that her situation warranted special help unavailable through normal channels. He was not prepared to feel any responsibility for her fate without his help. After she left his office, he logged on to System 11, one of Duke Chancellor's many secure communications systems, on his laptop computer to contact Joe, present this latest problem, and look for a solution.

Joe Czarzhynenski was the owner of Joe's Restaurant on the north side of Franklin Street on the south side of Reading, Pennsylvania. Joe's was a little 'hole in the wall' with a sign smaller than most barber shop poles that belied its well-deserved five-star rating as a restaurant. Joe did not really need a bigger sign. Word of mouth was sufficient in itself to assure continued business. The sign merely served to make the location of the actual restaurant entrance a little more obvious from a distance. If one wanted to eat at Joe's, he had better bring plenty of cash or a credit card with room to spare. One person could not eat there for less than forty dollars, and that did not include dessert! Joe just happened to be a Yale graduate. He was also a high-ranking member of The Chancellor Organization, Duke Chancellor's main lieutenant. Joe's function within The Chancellor Organization was senior in communication and facilitation. He was a cell leader, a 'go to' guy, the equivalent of a military general. He read the necessary newspaper columns, or perused specific websites for instructions and facilitated communications and various projects through Duke's elaborate and effectively secret communications networks. He was at his computer when the message from Professor Holloway came through on System 11. He knew who the professor was.

Holloway: "Would like to meet to present a difficult 'business deal' that needs special resolution."

Joe: "When and where?"

Holloway: "Monday at noon."

Joe: "Understood."

"When and where" meant Mory's, which is a private eating club associated with the University on York Street in New Haven, Connecticut. Any other statement would have indicated meeting at the New Haven train station, where they would discuss other arrangements in person.

CHAPTER 7

Monday, April 2, 2007
New Haven, Connecticut

Joe did not mind driving on his various adventures. He treated himself to a brand new sleek jet-black 2007 Corvette Coupe as a 'travel vehicle' and kept his more serviceable Chevy van for more mundane daily personal and business tasks. He turned the restaurant over to Bart Lupold, his trusted friend and manager for the next few days and headed for the bypass north of the city onto U.S. Route 222 and up to Interstate 78 East. He was in New Haven within three hours.

Joe arrived early at Mory's, asked for his usual table upstairs and told Marcus, the manager, to send his expected guest to his table when he arrived around noon. Joe had sung at Mory's many times on Monday nights down on the first floor as an undergraduate member of the Whiffenpoofs. He enjoyed the current brief period of nostalgia and allowed a smile and reflection of his younger days. He ordered spring water and a cup of tomato soup, with the usual saltine crackers. He knew what was required to produce a good restaurant meal and preferred his own restaurant, but he knew that at least the tomato soup was very good at Mory's. Precisely at noon, at least by Joe's watch, Professor Holloway made his way through the richly nostalgic atmosphere of the first floor, where dark stained walls were barely visible behind scores of old photographs of various Yale athletic teams throughout its more than three centuries of history. He walked up the old mildly creaky wooden stairs, surveyed the small crowd on the second floor and immediately recognized the short, but compact, bearded, and balding Joe at his usual corner table. Joe looked over at the professor as he approached and smiled briefly as they greeted each other.

The two men sat in the corner eating very little and talking a lot about 'page 5' and the young woman who wrote it. Joe listened intently, absorbing the atmosphere as well as the facts as Holloway presented them. The professor handed Joe the original 'page 5' he received from Janice, so he could see it for himself and form his own impressions. Joe studied 'page 5' intently for several minutes, as if he were looking for signs of forgery, inconsistency or some other form of 'gamesmanship.'

Joe finished studying the paper, looked up and said, "What do you believe, Professor?"

"I believe she is exactly who she says she is, and suffers exactly as she says. She made a point in my office of discussing the concept of trust, and made her argument quite effectively, I might add, at a very basic biological level. She is very persuasive, Joe. Even you would believe her! I took the liberty of talking to several of my friends and other contacts around the country as well as looking up as much information on the internet as I could about the good Senator from Connecticut. He seems rather clean to me, but then that is what I would expect from public sources. I also looked up her mother's name, and found some rather impressive institutional, political and social connections. She is evidently a prime candidate for blackmail. I believe Janice as much as I believe you, Joe."

Joe looked into the professor's eyes carefully for several seconds, and then said softly, "I will go to Maryland this afternoon to present this to Duke. I have an idea about how to solve this problem."

The efficiency and effectiveness of The Chancellor Organization was based upon complete trust among all members, completely secure and disciplined communications, and the lack of burdensome political or bureaucratic 'structure' to impede efficient and rapid decision-making or covert and swift action.

Chapter 8

Monday, April 2, 2007
Laurel, Maryland

Joe drove his shiny brand new black Corvette coupe south on Interstate 95 from New Haven through New York, down the New Jersey Turnpike into Delaware, and on into Maryland, following his GPS to coordinates given to him for the meeting over the internet on his laptop computer via System 8, another one of Duke's many communications systems. It turned out to be a parking lot next to a public storage facility just outside Laurel. Joe marveled to himself that these gadgets were so precise! He pulled into the parking lot, turned off the rumbling eight-cylinder 400 horsepower engine and waited. Within five minutes, a big new dark blue Lincoln SUV with tinted windows pulled into the parking lot and made a wide circle around the perimeter of the vacant lot, and then disappeared behind the extreme east wing of the storage facility. Joe's phone rang through the blue-tooth. He pressed the 'talk' button and waited.

A male voice said, "Who won the Mets game last week?"

Protocol required a specific answer, or Joe would never see Duke.

"The Phillies, four to two."

"The Phillies" was Joe's pseudonym for the day as prescribed in the System 8 message with the coordinates. The score or anything else he said was irrelevant.

"Follow me to John's Pub."

"I don't drink" Joe replied.

With that phrase as further confirmation, Duke knew he was talking to Joe, and they would meet. Duke wheeled the big SVU around the storage facility, circled behind Joe's Corvette to stop at the exit from the parking lot, and waited for Joe to drive up behind him. The two cars then sped off toward Washington. Within several miles, Duke pulled off the highway and drove into an abandoned forty-acre factory lot, pushed a button on a controller in his pocket, and a large metal garage door opened near the corner of the enormous building. He drove into the warehouse about fifty feet, and waited for the Corvette to follow. After the Corvette came to a halt behind him, Duke pressed the close button on his controller, and the garage door slowly fell to the concrete floor and stopped with a loud metallic thud that echoed throughout the spacious vacant warehouse for a few seconds. He waited for Joe to get out of his car, and then Duke turned off the ignition and exited his Lincoln. They greeted one another with friendly bear hugs and smiles.

"Hi, Joe. I apologize for the unusual impromptu meeting place and extra security, but I've been on the road more than usual recently. I just bought this place last month. It has potential investment value, and is a convenient private meeting place away from my office, and I want to keep it that way. Now, what do you have for me?"

"It seems Senator Russell from Connecticut has been blackmailing a well-known Washington D.C. area lady, whose husband is a big contributor to the Yale General Fund, which has been engaged in paying for a massive reconstruction project among other things, employing a large number of people, as you might guess. She has a daughter, who is an undergraduate at Yale, from a so-called 'indiscretion' about nineteen or twenty years ago that the husband does not know about—thinks the girl is his as much as his real younger son within the current marriage. The woman has been paying the Senator for over a year to keep his mouth shut. She has no effective representative or realistic means of protecting herself and her family from this bastard, and the public connections and repercussions are far too complicated to keep out of the legitimate, let alone the illegitimate press and other tabloid media and, of course, the internet. The media types would pounce upon any effort by the family to seek help from law enforcement or the legal profession, which the girl believes would inevitably harm her father's business, which in turn would choke off his apparently considerable contributions to Yale. Her father was away in Europe on business recently when her mother broke down and told the entire ugly story to her daughter, apparently out of complete desperation. The Senator is too powerful, so the public will never see her side of the story for what it really is. The girl believes, probably rightly so, that there is no one she can trust, so she confided in her ethics professor at Yale, effectively putting him in a position to help her. He's one of mine, Duke—sheer coincidence."

"How'd she do that?"

"I'm given to understand that she is very pretty and can exercise persuasive feminine behavior."

"Oh. Is that it, Joe?"

"Pretty much, Duke. You want me on this?"

"Can you handle it?"

"Yeah, I can. I want this one! I feel this girl's anger!"

"What do you propose?"

"I think the honorable nutmeg Senator should get a strong dose of his own medicine!"

"Good idea. I'll set aside an account for your expenses and send you the identification number and access codes via System 2. Keep me informed on System 3."

"Will do."

Duke gave his good friend another warm big bear hug and then turned to his SUV. Joe opened the driver's door to his Corvette and disappeared inside. The huge garage door started to rise. Joe started the powerful engine and gave it a shot of fuel to express his anticipation of leveling the playing field for the Smith family. The big engine roared in response, as Joe let out the clutch and the big wide rear tires squealed in response for a second as he drove out of the garage and back toward Baltimore and Interstate 83 North to Interstate 76 East back toward Reading.

Duke drove in the opposite direction toward one of his office buildings in Glenn Dale, Maryland. After parking his car, he took the elevator to his top floor office to attend to a variety of business details and projects, as well as a few stock trading positions. Then he sent a message to an old friend who did local interviews around the country for prospective Harvard applicants.

"I believe Harvard would benefit from the admission of Michael Jepson from Linden, a small town west of De Moines, Iowa. Please give this young man an interview for this coming year's class."

Translation: *Accept Michael Jepson.*

CHAPTER 9

Tuesday, April 3, 2007
Reading, Pennsylvania

Joe sent a message via System 2 to a secure server in Maryland, which automatically encoded the message and rerouted it instantly through System 2 to another secure server in Los Angeles, which re-encoded the message and sent it to yet another secure server in London within a specific narrow timeframe. Duke owned those computers. He invented System 2 as well as several other systems of encryption and communication codes. This was one of Duke's inventions. Code the message in a manner that could be unlocked and decoded only within a certain timeframe with a character or series of characters from a specific computer. Duke had recorded the identifying addresses for about two dozen computers throughout the world to be used in this manner, and added several new ones and dropped old ones every month. It was brilliant, and completely untraceable, because the code 'swept behind itself' obliterating all evidence of its route, including the origin, and was constantly revised. The encoded message to commence the Smith operation made its way to Sammy's computer in Hong Kong.

CHAPTER 10

Wednesday, April 4, 2007
Hong Kong

Sammy was a hacker with a heart and considerable intellect, a professional computer geek with incredible cyber-savvy. He was a junior member of The Chancellor Organization, recruited last year. He was still young, and very idealistic. He did not care much for politics, and he had a soft spot in his heart for beautiful young women. His close friends believed that he had never met a woman he did not fall in love with instantly for at least five minutes. Joe chose him for this task precisely because he knew Sammy would put his best efforts into trying to rescue a 'damsel in distress.' Those best efforts were nothing short of astounding, as were his discipline, daring attitude and maturity beyond his age.

After his parents died in mainland China when he was just four years old, virtual strangers gave him a new life—a very rare second chance. His 'family' in Los Angeles eagerly adopted him shortly after they had heard the story of the apartment collapse and death of his parents from friends in China, and loved him as their own, because they were unable to have children for reasons that they could never understand, and gave him the security he had lost in China. He had very little memory of his first four years of life. As far as he was concerned, he was an American. He excelled in school and learned to play the violin. His musical ability was merely one portal for genius of a broader scope, which he discovered with his introduction to computers. His adoptive father had limited resources, but managed to keep two Chinese restaurants open and running at a profit, providing enough income to see that Sammy could have a real future. His adoptive parents instilled in him the values of honesty and hard work, which he parlayed into high academic performance and a scholarship to M.I.T. Sammy had imagination and dreams of a bright and happy future. His new parents never allowed him an opportunity to doubt that he could achieve those dreams, and they encouraged him in every effort to explore and learn.

Duke had sent Sammy to Hong Kong, with all expenses paid by The Chancellor Organization, including a brand new VISA credit card. He knew the city well enough to live comfortably there, and was culturally and individually inconspicuous in almost every way. Duke and Joe both believed it would be best for him to operate from outside the continental USA in this matter. He had found his new temporary home with no trouble at all. It was a comfortable furnished condominium owned by The Chancellor Organization with plenty of room for his few possessions. During the next few days, he adjusted to the time zone difference and bought some minor personal items and enough food to assure his comfort while he awaited the details of his next assignment via System 2. Occasionally, he would play his violin out on the street for his own personal satisfaction, and whatever change it might bring his way, although he did not actually need the money. Foreign tourists were particularly generous to him. He was young and had simple needs, and earned more than most of his college classmates. His work was far more interesting, significantly more exciting and personally satisfying as well.

Sammy was eating a hamburger at his computer table, which was also his dining table as well as his desk. However, he never risked letting any food or drink come into contact with his precious computer keyboard, which was his portal to the world. He kept a small window open all the time in the upper left corner of his large, high-definition monitor specifically for System 2 messages.

He was idly surfing the internet when the System 2 window flashed a message, *'Sammy, I have a contract for you.'*

Within several seconds, the image of a beautiful young woman with blonde hair and very attractive feminine features slowly rose from the bottom of the small System 2 window in the upper left quadrant of his large flat screen monitor. Then a typed message appeared just under the image.

'This young lady needs your assistance. Your task is to disrupt the financial world of Senator Richard Lamont Russell IV of Connecticut, who is blackmailing her mother. Your objective is to halt the blackmail permanently, and as soon as possible. That is all you need to know right now. Important details and communications protocol, including passwords will follow your confirmation. Confirm within five minutes per System 2 protocol.'

Sammy knew the drill. This was not his first 'job' for The Chancellor Organization. He was good. He had passed several of Joe's initial tests with Duke's enthusiastic approval during the prior three months. Duke and Sammy both knew computers extremely well, and Duke was impressed with the elegance and creative genius of Sammy's solutions. Sammy knew he was good, and they knew he was good! Others would soon discover how very good he could be. He concentrated to sear the image of the beautiful young woman into his memory, and opened a new window on his computer. He would soon open a new window in her life as well.

'Ketchup, no pickle, to go' bolted through cyberspace back to Joe's computer microseconds later. The authentication code followed, so Joe knew it was Sammy at the sending computer, and that he had accepted the contract.

Just two days later Senator Russell would meet Sammy in cyberspace.

CHAPTER 11

Friday, April 6, 2007
Washington, D.C.

"Margaret, will you please get me a fresh cup of coffee?"

"Yes sir."

"Thank you, Margaret."

"You're welcome, Senator."

Senator Richard Lamont Russell IV was studying a bill on his computer monitor about the latest regulatory principles intended to reform what senators knew as 'Wall Street.' Of course, their version of Wall Street was from a lawyer's perspective, and not that of a trader, investor or businessman since most legislators were lawyers. It was common knowledge among professionals in the financial community that lawyers were generally notoriously poor traders and investors, probably because they assumed incorrectly that legal logic and reasoning had something to do with understanding the financial markets. Congress believed that rules were necessary to restrain and contain the natural urges people have to cheat any system in any way possible to enrich their own lives. Of course, that principle did not apply to most lawyers, particularly those who ascended to the ranks of the U.S. Senate and House of Representatives. He kept a small window open in the upper right-hand corner of his monitor for e-mail and internet access.

Margaret entered his plush office and placed a fresh cup of coffee on the left side of his highly polished large mahogany desk, and then quietly left his office. The Senator was not watching his computer for several minutes, but a message scrolled up from the bottom of a new chat window in the upper right corner of his monitor.

'Hello, Senator. How are you today?'

Richard reached for his coffee, took a sip and sat back down in his chair to read further information about the proposed new legislation. Out of the corner of his eye, he saw the message. He looked at it and blinked a few times.

What the hell is this?

He ignored the message after a moment, and went back to his reading. The message remained where it was. The Senator looked over at the message again and pressed the escape key, then the delete key, then clicked on the little red 'X' in the upper right corner of the window to close the message window. Nothing he did removed the message. Then, another message flashed under the first.

'You really should respond, Senator. I do not like to be kept waiting!'

Senator Russell exploded with anger! "Who the hell do you think you are?" not realizing for a moment that he would never be able to converse verbally with the source of a message on his computer.

Margaret bolted into his office and said, "Senator, did you call? Is something wrong?"

Senator Russell regained his composure and sat down with carefully controlled effort to keep his voice normal.

"I'm fine, Margaret, and I did not call you. Thank you. Please do not disturb me for the next hour or so."

Margaret turned slowly away from the Senator with a quizzical expression on her face and quietly slipped back into her office and closed the heavy solid wooden door behind her without so much as a click. Russell stared at the message window again.

'Senator, you really should answer me, because I am withdrawing money from your bank account, and if you want me to stop, you should be polite to me and answer.'

Russell gasped and lurched upright in his chair without backing away from his desk, tried to stand up and pummeled his skinny upper thighs on the underside of the center drawer of his desk, then immediately fell back into his seat, wincing with pain.

"Who the hell are you?"

Margaret heard him virtually yelling through the wall, but knew there were no visitors in his office and hoped that he was not hallucinating. She called security immediately.

'Senator, you have been extorting money from a friend of mine, and I do not like that, so I am going to take money from you, so you can appreciate how it feels to have someone take what you have worked very hard to accumulate throughout your life.'

Russell gasped again and froze for a moment in his seat. He felt moisture on his leg and looked down at the dark spot on his trousers.

"Oh my God!"

'Your God is not going to help you in this matter, Senator.'

The Senator gasped just short of apoplexy. Sammy had just guessed that the he had certainly responded internally, took a wild flier at something to send next, and Senator Russell took it as a direct personal response to what he had just said.

The computer could not possibly have been listening to me, could it?

Tom, the uniformed security guard assigned to his office area burst into the Senator's office and saw him staring at his computer monitor in apparent disbelief and shock. His face was unusually red and highlighted what was left of his receding white hair. The veins in his neck and balding head were standing out much more than usual.

"You OK, Senator?"

Russell lurched out of his chair, regaining what was left of his dissipating composure, stood up and turned toward Tom to distract him from his computer screen.

"Yeah, yeah, Tom . . . I'm OK."

Tom glanced down slightly at the Senator's pants with a very brief quizzical expression on his face, and then looked back up without expression, acting as though he had not seen anything unusual.

"You sure, Senator?"

"Yes! Now please leave me alone! Margaret, I do not want to be disturbed again!" He glanced over at Tom—*"By anyone!"*

Tom relented and backed out of the Senator's office, turned around to Margaret just outside the Senator's door to her office and whispered, "What's going on?"

"I don't know, but I *do* know enough to leave him alone right now. I'll call you if I need you again."

Senator Russell was staring at the message window.

'You now have $543,440 in your savings account, Senator. Yesterday, you had $603,440. If you do not believe me, then log on to your bank's website and check for yourself!'

The Senator did exactly that in another window. After fumbling with his user ID and password, he was able to check his balance. Indeed, it was exactly $543,440. Sammy was watching the computer exchange between the Senator's computer and his bank's computer in another window on his monitor. He knew the Senator was checking his balance. Russell looked at the message window again, waiting for another message. He felt light-headed as an unfamiliar reality beyond his control invaded his life. For the first time, he had no control over what he assumed he had control over. He could control people, but computers and the internet were an entirely different matter.

Sammy continued, *'Now that I have established my credibility, Senator, perhaps we can have a reasonable discussion about the Smith family.'*

Russell slumped down in his chair, breathing rapidly, while staring at the message window as his heart started beating faster.

He typed 'What Smith family?' He was gambling out of desperation.

'I'm referring to the well-known Washington socialite, Eleanor Smith, who has been sending you money in response to your threats to expose her prior life to her husband if she did not 'help' you. I believe that is called blackmail, Senator.'

'I've done no such thing!'

'Senator, you do not know who you are dealing with.'

'Whoever you are, you do not know who *you* are dealing with!'

Sammy knew the Senator understood money.

'Check your balance, Senator.'

He did. Another $20,000 disappeared from his account.

"All right. All right! *All right!* I got your point!" he said to his computer with increasing emphasis while fuming internally.

His heart rate was irregular, and his breathing came in gasps while he typed the words 'Stop it!' He finally realized that he was dealing with someone he should take very seriously. The good Senator saw his life flash before him within the span of just a few seconds as he sensed a sickening helpless feeling in the pit of his stomach. He could not imagine getting any help from any of his considerable network of friends and recipients of favors. This was a very private matter. He had very carefully made it so. He simply could not afford to be exposed financially, personally, or politically. He quickly realized that he was completely out of his league.

He had no choice, so he typed, 'What do you want?'

'Senator, you must follow these rules. First, you will not alter this transaction, and you will never discuss this transaction or communication with anyone else—ever! I will transfer these withdrawals from your account in a completely untraceable manner to Mrs. Smith's account to compensate her for your unpleasant behavior. I realize that is probably more money than you took from her, but then, life is not always fair, is it, Senator. You must pay a penalty for your wrongdoing. And second, from this moment forward, you will never have any further contact with any member of the Smith family or any of their relatives for any reason whatsoever, Senator, or I will go public with my information about your behavior in this matter! Furthermore, I will withdraw more money from any account you establish anywhere in the world, and continue to look over your shoulder for the rest of your life. I suspect that the penalty I am imposing is significantly less than the one you would endure if I were to make your behavior toward the Smith family known to the public in the media, as well as to your neighbors, bar association, the Connecticut Attorney General, your local community and your entire home state of Connecticut. I assure you, Senator, that I can be very persuasive! DO YOU UNDERSTAND ME, SENATOR?'

He imagined that the typed message was almost shouting at him through the computer monitor.

'If you understand me, Senator, then you must indicate that by typing an affirmative response in this window. If I do not see an affirmative response within three minutes, I will continue to withdraw money from your account for eventual deposit into Mrs. Smith's account in a completely untraceable manner. Your choice is simple, Senator. Comply, or suffer the consequences I described.'

Senator Richard Lamont Russell IV moved his computer cursor to the message window and typed, 'I understand. I will comply.'

'Thank you, Senator. It has been a pleasure doing business with you. By the way, if any of your friends have similar financial arrangements, please let them know what I am capable of doing. Oh, and one more thing, Senator, I am very good at what I do. You cannot find me, but I will

always be able to find you, because you are an upstanding public official, and I am just a single very private citizen. That is a promise, Senator, not a threat. I have friends all over the world who hate blackmailers as much as I do. Some of them are not as nice as I am, however.'

Senator Russell was still hyperventilating. He felt real fear for the first time in his adult life. He had just been introduced personally to the extent to which computers and the internet were redefining traditional concepts of privacy. For the first time in his professional career, he realized that he was not the only one in control of his own life, his money or his own political future.

The message window disappeared. Senator Russell arose from his desk chair, grabbed his suit coat from his closet and left his office, visibly shaken.

CHAPTER 12

Wednesday, April 11, 2007
New Haven, Connecticut

Professor Holloway was in his office preparing an exam, and without looking up, he mumbled, "Come in."

Janice Smith strode into his office with none of her prior desperation and anxiety. She was wearing a thick high-necked dark blue wool sweater that camouflaged her figure, but accented her freshly combed contrasting long blonde hair, which fell in suitably collegiate fashion down both her chest and her back, straddling her shoulders. She wore somewhat faded designer jeans and unremarkable faded blue sneakers. There was no need for her to be particularly persuasive.

"Hello, Professor Holloway. Do you have just a few minutes?" she said softly.

Startled from his concentration, Jason looked up and saw a hint of peace in her pretty face.

"Yes, Janice, I do. Please, come in and have a seat."

She was obviously fighting back tears and smiling at the same time as she closed the door behind her, sat down and said, "Thank you! I knew you could do it! I have a letter from my mother that I would like to share with you."

"Seems like you have a habit of handing me papers to read, Janice," he said playfully with a smile in an impromptu effort to help her control her tears and put her at ease.

She handed an elegant tan obviously custom-designed letter-sized paper to Professor Holloway.

> *Dearest Janice,*
>
> *I want you to know that the awful situation I described to you when your father was away appears to have ended. I have found an enormous deposit in my bank savings account that I did not put there. I have not said anything to your father, and do not intend to. Furthermore, I have not heard from Senator Russell since the last time he demanded payment last month. I feel renewed and refreshed with the apparent removal of this awful and heavy burden, and I want you to understand that and go on with your life with freedom from this ugly concern to make your own future. I do not understand what happened, and I do not intend to look into it any further, but I am greatly relieved.*
>
> *By the way, I received a curious e-mail message from someone named Sammy. It said, "Your daughter is very pretty." Who is Sammy, Janice?*
>
> *Love,*
> *Mom*

Jason finished reading the letter, looked up, and handed it back to her as he said with genuine sincerity, "I'm very glad to know that, Janice. It was very thoughtful of you to share this with me. Thank you very much."

"Professor?"

"Yes?"

"Who is Sammy?"

Jason looked blankly at her and said, "I honestly don't know."

After she left his office, he contacted Joe to confirm that the blackmail had apparently been defeated.

CHAPTER 13

Friday, April 13, 2007
Linden, Iowa

In spite of the common superstition about Friday the 13th day of any month, the postal carrier stopped at the driveway entrance to the Jepson farm and deposited several envelopes in the black mailbox firmly anchored to a decorative sturdy support post made of various old wrenches of different sizes welded together and spray-painted with a dull silver color.

A handsome young man bolted outside through the front door and raced the roughly 100 yards to the mailbox, where he removed and rifled through the eight envelopes to find the treasure of his life up to that point. It was a rather thick legal-sized white envelope addressed to Michael Jepson, with a return address of Harvard University, Cambridge, Massachusetts, printed in the upper left corner in crimson, the school color. He tucked the other seven envelopes under his left arm and eagerly, but carefully ripped open the special envelope and then removed the topmost single official letterhead addressed to him:

Dear Michael,

It is with great pleasure that I extend to you this letter of acceptance to the Harvard College Class of 2011. Enclosed you will find information you will need to secure your acceptance

> *and register for your first semester courses, as well as register for housing and meal plans . . .*

He did not need to read the rest of it until later. It was a bittersweet feeling for a bright and talented young man at the promising frontier of the rest of his life. The only problem was that his parents made too much money for him to qualify for a scholarship, but they did not really make enough to pay for the total four-year cost of a Harvard education. Debts on farming equipment and poor weather had kept the family income at a modest level during the last several years, and Paul Jepson, Michael's father, was developing back problems that made it difficult for him to continue the farming operation without the extra expenses associated with hired help.

CHAPTER 14

Wednesday, May 23, 2007
Linden, Iowa

Paul and Sarah Jepson listened with anticipation as the bidding progressed.

"I've got two, two, two thousand and one hundred dollars . . . Hey! Hey! Bidda-bidda-bidda going for two, two, do I have twenty-two? I want twenty-two *hundred* dollars . . . twenty-two two two! I have twenty-one *hundred* dollars an acre! Gimme gimme twenty-two two two!"

Auctioneer Bob Baker was just tuning up. When he was hot, he could sound like a verbal Gatling gun spraying syllables around the auction crowd with ease and make sense doing it—a feat that would have astounded his high school English teacher even over four decades after he graduated.

"Who's bidding, Paul?" Sarah whispered to her husband on the far right of the crowd facing away from the auction trailer.

"I don't know for sure, but I'd guess Gerald Whitely is in there somewhere."

Jimmy wheeled around in a graceful pirouette that even an experienced ballerina might not have accomplished in cowboy boots without extensive practice. He thrust two weathered fingers high into the fresh Iowa air and bellowed in his slightly southern accent.

"HIP! HIP! Twenty-two! Two! Two! I got twenty-two here!"

He turned back to the crowd looking in one particular direction, but Paul could not see who was responding. The bidders were inconspicuous or incognito for any number of reasons. There were strangers in the crowd, probably from neighboring counties, and possibly neighboring states, including speculators, investors or farmers, but no one could ever be sure. No one wanted to let anyone else in the crowd know that he was spending his precious money on a farm, let alone how much money he was spending! It was a small town, and everyone knew everyone else's business, more or less, but this day was different. Of course, everyone would find out later who the successful bidder was, because it was a matter of public record eventually. Nevertheless, no one really wanted to be identified as a bidder at the auction itself. Anonymity was acceptable and expected custom. Jimmy turned around gracefully once more with excitement in his eyes while thrusting three fingers toward the scattered puffy clouds overhead.

Bob saw him and continued, "I got twenty-three, three, three. Twenty-three! Hey! Hey! Bidda-bidda-bidda I have twenty-three . . . Do I have twenty-four? I want twenty-four, twenty-four twenty twenty twenty four four four! Gimme four twenty-four *hundred* dollars! Now twenty-three, I want twenty-four! Gimme gimme gimme twenty-four four four!"

Paul was hopeful. Sarah was close to tears. The farm had always been a quiet and sturdy source of security for her for many years, so the impending sale tore at her heart, even though she and Paul would receive a hefty sum of money in compensation after paying off the mortgage and farm loan. They intended to keep their house on a relatively small ten-acre lot on the southeast corner of the farm. With that arrangement, they would still maintain essentially the same feeling of being at home. That would be enough land for their dogs to run around in if they wanted to, and where future grandchildren could run and play, if they were ever to be so fortunate to have grandchildren. Sarah and Paul loved their only son as much as any parent could and wanted him to pursue his dreams, even though they were giving up so much of their own lives to make that happen. Paul rationalized his difficult decision. He was getting older, and it was simply time to move on to the next stage of his life.

Michael really wanted to go to Harvard. It was the biggest dream of his lifetime. He received his acceptance letter, but they did not have the money for tuition, room and board, let alone all the other expenses that they knew would come up over the course of four years. No one in Paul's family or Sarah's family had ever gone to college, so Michael's dream was very special. He was exceptionally bright, academically at the top of his class of 285 and very popular in high school. All his teachers knew his potential was open-ended. He was the only middle linebacker on the football team, president of his class, and active in church. He was the only local delegate from the county to the state debating tournament. He did not win, but he left a very favorable impression good enough for second place. The girls could not keep their hands off him given the chance to be within arm's reach, either on a date, or many times not on a date. However, Michael had his sights set on the future implicit in a Harvard education, and he was not about to jeopardize that future by impregnating a local girl. He knew that would lead to the obligatory marriage and being bogged down in a small mid-western farming town for the rest of his life, so the girls inevitably discovered just how single-minded Michael could be when the date got hot. He played the game well, but never crossed the line of no return. 'The game,' as it became known among the girls, became a hidden challenge among a select few who were lucky enough to arrange some private time with Michael, but the 'winner' was always Michael.

Paul was running a 900-acre farming operation on land he inherited from his father, who had inherited it from his father, and so on back into the family history so far that Paul could not remember exactly how the farm was originally acquired or by which relative. Now he was selling, with tears in his eyes, because it was all he could do. Michael had never expressed any interest in farming or staying in rural America, and Paul and Sarah knew it would be terribly unfair to push him into continuing the family farming operations. Life had taken its toll on Paul. His body was no longer capable of responding to his every command without pain.

His doctor had told him, 'Paul, the pipes are getting rusty and the power plant is losing steam. You're not going to die anytime soon, but you are simply aging—it happens to everyone.'

As hard as they tried so many years ago, Sarah and Paul Jepson could not conceive another child. Life was not fair to them in that regard, or so it seemed. After all, everyone in the community knew that they were fine people, but for one reason or another, or for no apparent reason at all, they had fallen short of fully achieving their dream of a large family. Paul accepted their fate and worked hard—the only way he knew how to work. Full-bore effort and straight-ahead honesty and trust were the foundation for the only way he knew how to live. If life dealt him a card from the bottom of the deck, he simply studied it and tried to figure out how to play his hand the very best way he knew how. But God help you if you ever lied to Paul Jepson.

Carl on the left side of the crowd spun around mimicking Jimmy with one fist in the air and bellowed, "Twenty-four here! Four! Four! I got four!"

Sarah squinted toward the far end of the crowd. She did not see anything or anyone unusual. She worked it out in her head—$2.16 million and counting—and they had not gotten to the farm equipment or the outbuildings yet! She noticed that Jonathan Wiley, the local banker was in the crowd.

"Well doesn't that beat all?" she said just under her breath. "The old scrooge wants to know how he's going to get his loan back!"

"Hey! Hey! Bidda-bidda-bidda! Four! Four! I have four and now I want five! Gimme five! Five! Five! I want five *hundred* dollars! Gimme gimme gimme twenty-five! Five! Five! Now I want two thousand and five *hundred* dollars!"

Bob continued spraying syllables into the crowd and beyond, almost defying the normal urgency to breathe occasionally.

"Hey, folks this is cheap! *Cheap*, I tell you! You saw what happened to land in the seventies and eighties! Gimme five! And I don't mean a high five—just a normal five." He chuckled at himself even though no one else did. "Gimme five! Five! Five! I want twenty-five *hundred* dollars an acre!"

The sun slipped behind a large dark grey cloud, casting a shadow across the crowd and Bob's auction trailer as a cool breeze alerted the crowd to the increasing possibility of rain. Jimmy whirled around toward Bob Baker with his arms wide apart as if he were a proud eagle showing off his wingspan.

"Whoop! Five! I have five here, five here, five, five, five!"

Sarah turned to Paul as her jaw slowly fell, and she gulped with an effort to speak, but no sound came out of her mouth. Wiley smiled with a slick banker's approval that Paul imagined he had to have acquired in De Moines or some other major metropolitan area in the East.

"Hey! Hey! Bidda-bidda-bidda! Five! Five! I have five and now I want six! Gimme gimme gimme gimme six six six six! I want twenty-six *hundred* dollars!"

Bob knew that the incessant calling and repeating of any words at all, including even any common or senseless syllables and, of course the number he wanted, would eventually have its effect. It really did not have to make any sense other than the number he wanted. He had been at this game for over forty-one years and knew his craft well. His professional reputation throughout the Midwest was one of the best. 'Straight as an arrow' people would say about him. He worked for his clients, and no one else. He always got satisfactory or reasonable results. He worked hard, just as Paul did. Paul knew that, so he gave all his auction business to Bob.

Carl turned quietly away from the crowd again and back toward Bob without fanfare and pointed his thumb to the sky at belt level, but he did not indicate anything else. Another bidder was in the crowd with explicit instructions of anonymity beyond the normal practice. Bob was surprised, but did not flinch at all. He knew Carl well, and knew what was happening in the crowd. A new bidder was active.

"Six six six! I have six! Who's going to go seven? Seven! Seven! I want seven! Bidda-bidda-bidda! Seven! I want twenty-seven *hundred* dollars! Now six! Now six and I want seven! Seven! Seven! Six now! I want seven!"

Hushed sounds of surprise wafted briefly through the crowd loosely stretched along the line of cars and pickup trucks parked just off the four-mile long straight country road at that point. There were another fifty or more vehicles parked in a relatively orderly set of rows in a freshly mowed grass field adjacent to the barn between Bob's auction trailer and the distant darkening sky.

Mary Hertwig arrived at the auction scene with her well-used red 1984 Ford F-150 truck with an even more used second-hand metallic silver concession trailer hitched to the rear tow bar. Mary was somewhat of a local fixture, traveling from one outdoor event to another throughout the county and adjacent counties, delivering tasty treats of one sort or another—ice cream, hot dogs, hamburgers, French fries, candy, pretzels, popsicles, brownies, coffee, and whatever else she could find wholesale, retail or make herself. She catered to the inevitable crowds at auctions, high school baseball and football games, or on otherwise dull days, to motorists just a few hundred feet away from gas stations throughout the county without competitive convenience stores nearby. Winters were more difficult for her because she was a server in a local restaurant where she could not have as much freedom for 'creative fashion,' but she worked hard in her concession trailer during the rest of the year. She was pushing forty-six years of age, and was a somewhat weathered, but nicely made up former high school homecoming queen and cheerleader, trying to make her own way in life after three disastrous marriages during the last twenty-six years. She kept her long natural blonde hair with a few grey strands tied back with a dark blue ribbon in a ponytail that fell just below the waist of her tight blue jeans that she thought would create, or at least add to the illusion of youth. Her advertising was word of mouth, simple, and effective. Mary recognized the commercial value of an innocent friendly smile and her perfectly matched and well-preserved feminine assets with minimal or no support and 'showcase,' but legal upper attire. Today was one of her 'Hard Rock Café' extra large T-shirt days. She was expert at serving men coffee, hamburgers, hot dogs or other prepared items by leaning over the counter set in the side of her concession trailer at just the right angle to attract and fix the gaze of the closest male patrons. For those items requiring a little physical effort to prepare, like scooping ice cream into a cone or a cup from the interior freezer bin just below the counter, she had perfected just the right combination of innocent but vigorous shoulder action and simultaneous leaning forward to mesmerize any male customer. Since none of the men who knew about her wanted her to go out of business, no one ever registered a complaint and she always managed to earn a decent living by offering nourishment of the male stomach and imagination wherever she could find a crowd. Besides, that was the local men's way of being charitable. They knew she had struggled in life. Women never got any of the special 'creative' service. No one ever complained about paying her somewhat inflated prices. She usually did well at Bob Baker's auctions, and this one was a particularly profitable auction for her.

Bob was feeling a little uneasy. He knew the bidding was getting rather high, but he had a job to do. He was going to get Paul and Sarah the best price he could get, regardless of how insane it might appear to someone else. That was what he did. He was an auctioneer. He had a business to run, and he needed to keep intact his reputation for honesty and effectiveness, so he could garner the all-important referral. That was why he believed in advertising. He mailed his auction fliers to other states most of the time, because he wanted his name out there when someone wanted to have an auction and did not know an auctioneer. Fliers for the Jepson auction went as far east as New York, as far south as Alabama, west into Colorado, and north into Minnesota. He wiped his brow in spite of the cooling breeze that just arrived, and looked to his left far off to the west, beyond a large grove of trees at the ominous curtain of dark clouds pushing in from Omaha and Sioux City.

Gerald Whitely turned to the side and looked down, averting the glance from Jimmy. Everyone in town knew he wanted this property, but he had met his match. Jimmy knew he was finished. The bidding was above his limit. He was obviously bidding against someone with access to more money than he had. He was curious. He knew most of the folks in town, and he had a fair idea of what their financial capability was. He did not know of anyone in the area who could bid so high for the Jepson property. He just assumed he would be the successful bidder. He was wrong.

Bob called out "Seven! Seven! I have twenty-seven!"

He had authorization to bid to a certain limit by an unknown bidder who may or may not have been in the crowd. He had a notarized letter from a bank in Maryland authorizing him to bid to a certain price limit. What he did not know was that someone representing the source of that letter was in the crowd, and was signaling bids to Carl whenever necessary. No one could determine the exact location of the bidder Carl was watching. It did not matter to Carl one way or the other. He fielded bids and cajoled potential buyers with over thirty years of auctioneering experience. He knew a real bidder from a phony one, almost just by looking at him. He could 'smell' when the bidding was approaching an end, and he sensed that it was close. However, Carl did not know about Bob's instructions. That was not part of Bob's game. He was in charge of his business, and no one else was entitled to know how he would conduct the auction.

Bob called out, "Seven! Seven! Seven! I have seven, now I have seven! Do I have eight? Twenty-eight, twenty-eight! Do I have twenty-eight hundred?"

He knew that he was finished. His authorized limit was $2,800 per acre, and not a penny more. He stuck to his instructions.

"Twenty-seven, asking twenty-eight! Do I have eight? Eight, bidda-bidda-bidda, eight eight? I want eight! Gimme twenty-eight *hundred* dollars for this beautiful farm owned by Paul and Sarah Jepson. Gimme eight eight eight! I want twenty-eight *hundred* dollars!"

Silence fell over the crowd.

"Gimme eight, eight! I want eight, twenty-eight *hundred* dollars for this farm! I'm going to sell this farm *today*, folks! And *before* it rains!"

As if encouraging Bob, the sun slipped back into full view from behind the clouds, and instantly warmed the crowd once again.

"I've got seven now! Who will go eight? I have seven, folks, seven! Seven, seven, seven, seven, twenty-seven *hundred* dollars! Twenty-seven *hundred* dollars going once! Now let's go eight—I want eight—twenty-eight *hundred* dollars! Gimme gimme eight eight eight!"

Silence and quiet shuffling in the crowd absorbed Bob's urging like the dry earth soaked up a light rain. Heads bowed, or turned from one side to another as people looked for the other bidders without looking like they were looking. They never saw the bidder in Carl's crowd in the first place. Silence continued—not a good sign at an auction. Carl turned slowly and inconspicuously from the crowd back to Bob with his fingers interlaced and his left hand hooked over his old shiny silver belt buckle, but he turned his right thumb up.

Bob broke the silence and bellowed, "Eight! Eight! I have eight! I have twenty-eight *hundred* dollars! Do I have nine? Nine! Bidda-bidda-bidda! Nine! Nine! Nine! Nine! Do I have nine?"

Bob knew he was out of the bidding now, and felt somewhat relieved that he had done his job, and was no longer obligated. He felt charged up and renewed without having to participate any more in the bidding.

Jimmy was looking almost idly into the crowd. A middle-aged, rather fit man near the middle of the crowd with dark sandy hair, wearing a grey denim shirt and blue jeans was staring right back at him through what appeared to be a custom corridor of vision deliberately designed for eye-to-eye contact. Jimmy was somewhat taken aback by the man's stare, and he could not take his eyes off the man's face. Although he was wearing dark glasses, Carl could see the man's eyes to some extent in the bright sunlight. He had an almost imperceptible scar running down his right cheek from the corner of his eye almost to his jaw that was accentuated when the man silently mouthed the word 'NINE.' Jimmy kept staring at the man, who then brought his right thumb up to his face and then to his brow as if he were wiping sweat from just above his tinted glasses. A gentle breeze flowed over the crowd.

As if by instinct alone, Jimmy turned slowly back to Bob, and simultaneously raised his eyebrows and very subtly rotated his right fist at his belt buckle with an extended thumb from down to up. Bob Baker surveyed the crowd. He was looking at Carl. Carl was looking the other way. He turned back to Jimmy and saw the thumb pointed up. He swallowed uncomfortably. He had not seen anything like this in his forty-plus years of auctioneering.

He blurted out hoarsely, "Twenty-nine *hundred* dollars bid, folks! I have twenty-nine *hundred* dollars an acre bid on this farm!"

Now he felt like he had to pee. His shirt was absorbing all the sweat it could as the cool breeze from the west picked up again. He wanted this auction over before the storm hit. The clouds were almost black, with threatening but graceful, almost artistic swirls of white and grey, the kind that quite often brought tornados, but they were still off in the distance.

Jimmy turned back as if in a trance to look for the man with the scar. Jimmy was an actor when he had to be. No one knew where he was getting his bids. People looked around in casual polite efforts to survey the faces around them, but 'Scarface' was inscrutable and looked around with all the others. He could have been just another interested auction hobbyist, or maybe an investor from another state. He turned back and locked eyes with Jimmy after another moment of innocently glancing around.

Bob was aware of the two 'hot spots' in the crowd. He looked back toward Carl on the left. Carl briefly jutted his jaw upward, indicating he had the next bid up.

Bob squeezed his legs together as best he could and bellowed "Three *thousand* dollars! I have three thousand dollars an acre bid for this farm!"

He summoned every iota of gall he could as a professional auctioneer and firmly called out, "I want a hundred more! Gimme thirty-one *hundred*—thirty one one one one bidda-bidda-bidda-bidda. One! One! I want thirty-one *hundred* dollars!"

He knew it was high, but he had a job to do. He owed Sarah and Paul his best. He knew he was doing well so far, but he wanted to push his efforts to the limit. Every bid from now on was auctioneering paradise. This was simple capitalism at work in open competition. He knew from the town records he studied last week in preparation for the sale that the last auction farm sale in this county was for $2,750 an acre only two months ago. Bob Baker knew his business and did his homework. He knew land values as well as a physician knew anatomy. The river bottom adjacent to the far north end of the farm flooded a few times a year, depositing thick rich sediment over that part of the field, replenishing it annually for high-yield farming.

The soft 'whoosh' of incredulity swept through the crowd again as the breeze picked up and the faint rumble of distant thunder reached the crowd after a flash of lightning over ten seconds ago in the darkening horizon. The sky had become clearly delineated between the darkness approaching from the west, and the remaining beautiful summer skies overhead and toward the east, but Bob was going to finish the auction one way or another before it rained, and before he wet his pants.

'Scarface' was the only person in the crowd who knew about the bidder on the left. His real name was Chris Morrow. The other bidder was Jim Harley. They both worked for Duke Chancellor.

CHAPTER 15

Thursday, May 24, 2007
Ashton, Maryland

Duke checked his System 8 messages.

"Crimson Tide Green."

The message was the prearranged code for 'mission accomplished' regarding the Jepson farm. Sarah and Paul would now be able to afford a Harvard education for their son, Michael, hold their heads up and prepare for their own eventual retirement.

Duke smiled to himself and swiveled around in his chair to face an array of computer terminals that looked like the banks of professional traders' terminals in the major brokerage firms' trading floors, studied his charts for a few seconds and clicked his mouse on the 'sell' button. One thousand S&P call options left his options trading account, leaving him with a $660,000 profit.

He was fifty-five years old, but had a deceptively strong and solid six-foot frame. The meanest Chicago street gang soldier probably would not want to meet him in a dark alley, even on his own turf if he knew Duke's physical capabilities. Duke was a thoroughly accomplished expert in a variety of martial arts, including a black belt in Karate. He appeared mild-mannered and a little overweight, but could inflict significant damage to another human body if he wanted to, in spite of his age. This strength in addition to his genius-caliber intelligence and extraordinary wealth gave him an inordinate degree of self-confidence.

He could, would, and did run his life the way *he* wanted to, rather than sit back and 'let life happen' to him. Those days were over!

He was a complex man in many ways, but shaped by his parents, environment, experiences and the people he interacted with, as we all are. He attended the University of Virginia, where he maintained a 4.0 grade point average majoring in physics before he dropped out after his sophomore year and joined the Army. He endured the rigors of basic training at Fort Dix in New Jersey, after which he was assigned to an electronics school at Fort Devens, near Ayer, Massachusetts, which is about thirty-six miles from downtown Boston. That is where he started to learn the basics of electronics, which in turn formed the basis of his current very extensive knowledge of computers, systems programming, and the internet.

His overseas assignment was on a small mountain off the northern coast of Turkey that jutted north from an isthmus near Sinop. There were no trees to speak of to hinder the almost constant wind, which could reach at least fifty miles per hour in the winter. He spent most of his three years there in square buildings with no windows, maintaining the complex electronic equipment used to gather signal intelligence from Russian space, rocket development and satellite operations. Social interaction was minimal to non-existent with the locals, and activities on the base were limited, simple or boring. There were no American women on the base, and Turkish women were culturally, if not officially off-limits. This set of circumstances defined his tour of duty as 'hardship,' which had the benefit of qualifying an enlisted man for an early discharge five months earlier than his original commitment of four years. He applied for what was referred to as an 'early out' and through the rare and uncharacteristically altruistic conniving of a sympathetic master sergeant, qualified by only a few hours of 'bureaucratic delays and artful flight schedule bungling and contrived minor innocent snafus' for the early freedom for which he had mentally so carefully prepared himself.

After he was honorably discharged in 1970, he went back to school at the University of Alabama in Birmingham to finish his degree in mathematics instead of physics. Among the interesting people he met in college was a young man by the name of Cordera Alvarez, the only son of a wealthy Mexico City real estate developer. Cordera was an affable young man, majoring in economics and business. He easily formed a strong and lasting friendship with Duke.

Before he graduated, Duke had married a young woman who eventually turned out to be sexually insatiable. One day after classes, he returned unexpectedly to their apartment to find her in their bed with another man, who was remarkably lucky to escape with his clothes, let alone his life. Duke gathered what was left of his inner strength and sense of manhood and left for good. He finished his marriage and finished his degree in that order, and added to the heavy burden of cynicism and internal anger at the people he loved. Cordera was the one solid friend and sounding board who helped Duke through this difficult time and kept him from straying too far from his efforts to find happiness.

After graduating, he gained employment easily in various corporate programming positions and project management positions one after another, because they were essentially child's play for him. They were limited in time on a contract basis, usually one to three years in duration, but quite lucrative. Within a few years, he was an expert computer programmer and more than a very proficient systems engineer, with extensive experience in defense contract projects, communications systems and cryptography, facilitated by his top-secret military security clearance.

Duke Chancellor was well off, to say the least, due to a well-structured inheritance and some very perceptive trading in the securities markets.

His father had started working on the loading docks of a small dairy company in central Maryland fifty-six years ago, struggling to keep food on the table for his family of four. He worked his way up in the company to shipping supervisor, then vice president of sales, and then vice president of the company. Charles Chancellor was a very gifted man. He was intelligent beyond the capacity of most men in his position, or in any other position for that matter, and he won the truly loyal friendship of Daryl Chapman, the owner of Chapman Dairies. Daryl loved Charles as he would a son, if he had one. He learned through the years that Charles was competent, reliable, honest, trustworthy and loyal almost to a fault. If Charles said he was going to do something, then you could bet the farm that he would do exactly as he said, and the result would be both elegant and profitable. He was a man of few words, and developed a reputation for making people pay very close attention to the few words he did use when he chose to speak, contributing to his reputation for intelligence and having a dry sense of humor.

After a small dinner party with his wife and a few close friends who had arranged a small celebration in recognition of the end of his first year as vice president in 1979 Charles and Cheryl went home. Cheryl went upstairs to their bedroom, while he entered his private den on the first floor to relax for the evening and catch up on correspondence, reading and habitual personal reflection. Around eight fifty-five that evening, the doorbell rang unexpectedly. Charles rose from his burgundy leather reading chair, and walked briskly through the elegant teak wood foyer to the front door, opened it, and immediately sensed trouble. Standing before him in the portico was Jerry Franklin, the corporate counsel for Chapman Dairies.

"Hi, Jerry! Come on in! Have a seat! What brings you out here at this hour?"

Charles closed the front door and walked into the sitting room where Jerry found a comfortable chair, and sat across from his friend leaning forward with his elbows on his knees and his hands clasped in front of him. Jerry went straight to the point.

"There's no easy way to put this, Charlie. Daryl died earlier this evening in an automobile accident."

Charles managed his shock and sorrow as efficiently as he managed money and people—with unusual skill, remarkable poise and little outward display of emotion, but inside, he was devastated.

After several moments of stunned disbelief, Charles asked, "What happened, Jerry?"

"His automobile was struck by a drunk driver over on dead man's curve. The police said he never had a chance. The pick-up truck hit his car head-on travelling well over fifty miles an hour. There were no survivors in either vehicle. His funeral will be on Tuesday."

"Daryl wanted you to succeed him as President and CEO of the company, Charlie. We'll make it official on Monday at a corporate meeting at nine o'clock. It's really just a formality, you know. Everyone knows you are the next in line."

"Thank you for telling me personally, Jerry." He waited for his emotions to settle. "I'll be there on Monday. Can I get you something to drink or eat?"

"No. Thank you, Charlie. I really should get home. Nancy was expecting me over an hour ago as it is."

"I understand, Jerry. Thank you again for stopping by."

The two men walked slowly to the front door, where they parted without further discussion, and Charles closed the door slowly. With that simple motion as punctuation after Jerry's message, his world changed forever. Charles Chancellor was to be the President and Chief Executive Officer of a mid-sized dairy company with 142 employees and annual sales of over $188 million. He went to his bedroom and calmly whispered to Cheryl that Daryl died in an automobile accident earlier that evening. For the first time in decades, Charles Chancellor wept and lay down on their bed in an implicit request for comfort from his wife.

Charles managed the company with self-taught skill and remarkable business intuition, including experience at almost every level of the company. He enhanced his knowledge and management ability by taking several business courses at Princeton University. To Duke, his father was disgustingly right—always. Duke was very smart, but he saw his father as much smarter. His father could do no wrong. He led a charmed life.

However, Duke learned whatever he could from his mostly contentious relationship with his father. All Duke wanted from his father was evidence of his love, but all he perceived was instruction and the constant evidence of 'I told you so,' and the seemingly endless bits of confirmation of his father's brilliant business intuition. Duke never saw his father fail *at anything*. He was somehow superhuman and beyond Duke's ability to emulate, regardless of how much effort he applied toward that goal.

Before Charles died, he had sold his dairy company to Southland Corporation in Texas for a handsome $296 million. He sorted through the advice of his lawyer brother, Jack, as well as several business associates, made up his own mind, as usual, and put his money to work in Florida orange groves, real estate, some well-chosen stocks, and several other businesses, largely in the health care field that passed the tests of his unusually sharp business acumen.

Cheryl died in 1983 of leukemia, adding another weight of sorrow to Duke's inventory of personal pain. She was the soft and warm nurturing counterbalance to his father's unusually sharp business mind. After Charles died almost a year later, Duke inherited over $197 million in various forms, some of which were protected in trusts and other legally obscure arrangements his uncle Jack had contrived for Duke and his brother Nathan that generated a handsome income for each of them for a very long time to come. However, Duke was the one who learned how to invest his money wisely. Nathan did not.

Nathan spent all he could before his parachute and brakes failed in his expensive 1,000-horsepower dragster racecar and he died in the woods beyond the end of a Maryland racetrack after plowing through almost 5,000 cubic feet of baled hay into the final safety barrier at over 220 miles per hour. Nathan's wife Janet continued to raise their very pretty little six-year-old girl without remarrying, since she still had a respectable income left from the trusts she inherited from Nathan, which Charles had Jack design with certain controls to counterbalance what they both knew to be Nathan's tendency toward the high life. Janet managed to raise the girl with the same homegrown values of hard work and honesty her family had raised her with, in spite of her husband's undisciplined history with money. Although she did not actually have to work to pay her mortgage, utilities, and buy food, she chose to work in order to keep her daughter schooled in what she considered the proper traditional values of working for a living. She also needed to work for her own sense of self-respect. She taught her daughter by example. She knew there were very few, if any 'sure bets' in life. She kept herself busy with teaching at a local intermediate school, provided her daughter with singing, dancing and piano lessons, and kept her active in the local soccer league as well as the school swimming team. She wanted her daughter to be intelligent, fit, healthy and physically and psychologically strong—qualities she believed her uncommonly pretty daughter would certainly need in an increasingly threatening world, not to mention the presence of men, who would without any doubt whatsoever notice her in many ways.

Although Janet was an attractive woman, the men she met after Nathan's death never seemed to have enough of whatever it took to sweep her off her feet, given that she already had a good idea of what marriage involved. If she played her cards right, she could see all the way down the road of her life reasonably clearly with enough creature comforts to last well beyond her sunset years, and provide a significant financial cushion for her daughter after her death. Duke kept his eye on the family and became somewhat of a substitute father for his pretty niece during the early years after his brother's death. Eventually he saw her less often as his business interests took more and more of his time as she progressed through her senior year in high school, and eventually graduated from Smith College with highest honors.

Duke learned how to trade stocks and options, as well as futures and other exotic financial instruments. He was self-taught, but was smart enough to learn from others as well as his own mistakes. He parlayed his inheritance income into his own personal fortune. His father would have been proud of him, he thought, but his father was no longer there to appreciate him. No one was there to appreciate him. He lived alone. He vowed never to marry again after his devastating first experience. However, for the rest of his life, he would arrange for others to appreciate him, even though they most likely would never really know him.

Since his father died, Duke's life was full of unresolved tensions based upon his love for his father and his sense of never having been able to earn his father's love in return. What Duke never understood completely is that his father loved him very much. He just could not express that love the way Duke could understand it. Duke harbored anger within, but maintained honesty and sincere respect for other people. He also developed a strong sense of fairness in spite of living with an insufficient sense of measuring up to what he thought his father's expectations of him were. He knew the world was not fair, to say the least, but he vowed to do whatever he could to make it more tolerable for those who could use a little help.

Duke Chancellor would challenge the limits of human determination beyond the imaginations of the most hardened criminals, the greediest politicians, or the most determined corporate executives, or whoever else appeared to violate his understanding of decent human conduct, fairness and the purpose of life, which he believed was the creation of freedom for the individual to strive to achieve his dreams and full potential. He believed that it was primarily through the pursuit of individual excellence, education and freedom that the human race as a whole stood the best chance of surviving the effects of even its own worst elements, collective incompetence and frequently overstated social and political sophistication and competence, let alone the ravages of the inevitable forces of nature.

The process of helping others was sometimes complicated. Duke Chancellor kept his distance from any named group other than The Chancellor Organization in order to assure his anonymity, privacy and effectiveness. He employed a ring of 'communicators' around him, who in turn operated 'cells' of operatives, with members throughout the world, somewhat like Al Qaeda, only with a higher standard and noble purpose from a western cultural perspective, and with far superior organization and information capabilities. Duke tended to believe that the social order either appeared to be or actually was corrupt, and officials at almost every level were too often selfish, untrustworthy, ineffective, incompetent, weak, or outright criminal in their behavior and conduct of official, if not personal business. They appeared to act with impunity and flagrance, even beyond and often in spite of daring anyone to call them out. Members and operatives of The Chancellor Organization were unique in their sincerity and dedication to helping those oppressed unnecessarily by 'the system of government or social order' according to Duke Chancellor and his staff of communicators and advisors. He perceived his organization to be the counterweight to the inequities of the nature of man as practiced in the official order, most commonly found in government, but also in the corporate, diplomatic, political and criminal worlds.

To accomplish his goals, Duke had to work with and within law enforcement organizations, including the military. Sometimes he operated outside even those boundaries where the ends appeared to justify the means, where the law or social custom was simply inadequate, and where otherwise, people simply did not care. Although he put enormous effort into keeping his admittedly threatening influence in perspective, he had learned that he certainly was not alone in his quest for a better world, and that there were like-minded people everywhere. High-ranking officers in military organizations around the globe who recognized that the existing social, religious and governmental tools were not always adequate to achieve enough progress toward universal peace for the greatest portion of humanity in an increasingly complex world were attracted to The Chancellor Organization. Quite a large number of police forces also had sympathetic members.

In simple terms, Duke's world order consisted of four main groups. First, countries with traditional national geographic borders of diminishing effectiveness, relevance and value, and associated historical interests evolved separately through decades, if not centuries of shortsighted and mostly selfish governmental or religious views. Second, governments and political groups not currently in power existed within those geographical borders with their own equally selfish or otherwise misguided agendas. Third, multinational corporations and other groups evolved, which for the most part do not recognize or respect any borders. And fourth, The Chancellor Organization existed throughout the world regardless of corporate, religious, geographic or governmental functions or influences because most formally organized social groups kept pushing their own agendas, simultaneously trying to justify their continued existence. However, he believed that those groups many times kept making the same mistakes and could not actually solve many of the problems they felt entitled to tackle. Duke knew his work would ruffle the feathers of many people, to say the least, but he was prepared to act according to his convictions. He also knew that secrecy was paramount to his continued effectiveness. He was not so naïve as to believe that he recognized the ultimate truth. He was simply smart enough to realize that among social groups, religions, governments, or any other group of people with common beliefs around the world, struggles for dominance would be inevitable, including efforts by some to insist upon their views as the only correct views and that all others should be eliminated. He knew that survival and peace was the optimal goal, not ultimate total world domination. As long as he had the means and the will, he would continue to work for as much peace, balance and fairness as possible through individual justice, freedom and education according to his best understanding of human nature and the history of civilization. He knew the limits of idealism and practicality, as well as their strengths.

CHAPTER 16

Friday, August 24, 2007
Mumbai, India

Raj Sampat was the only son of a wealthy Indian merchant. He had known only comfort in his twenty-seven years, and was educated at Oxford University. He worked for his father, handling international shipping of silk goods from factories within India and a few surrounding producers. While at Oxford seven years ago, he studied economics, and took an interesting elective course during his last year taught by a man named Teodor Michalik. He was so impressed with the professor's passion for teaching and the subject matter of his course that he decided he would turn his efforts in life toward those who needed help. He would use what little influence he had, which was more than most, but not with the impact that his father had, to try to help his fellow man. His inheritance would increase his influence considerably later in life. His father built his fortune from nothing, working eighty hours and more a week for decades out of constant fear of becoming poor like his parents had been when they were growing up. Raj idolized his father for what he had accomplished, and for giving selflessly to him and to others.

System 17 was dedicated to the recruitment of new members of The Chancellor Organization. It was usually inactive, but Duke always checked for messages every Friday. The system had been dormant for several weeks, but last week he received the information about the only son of a wealthy business executive in India who had many of the qualities Duke was interested in, according to his informant. He was educated, creative, energetic, smart and loyal.

Duke was in his office on the seventh and highest floor of the Plymouth Building. He typed his message into his computer on the secure System 8.

Joe, I want you to go to India and evaluate a young man we should consider as a member of our organization. I would like you to do this for me personally.

'*I have to be at a convention next month. Sorry, cannot help,*' appeared across Duke's monitor.

'*Thank you. Contact later.*'

Even though the system was electronically and cryptographically quite secure, Duke kept all of his important personal messages obscurely encoded with different language and syntax, using familiar techniques unique to each of his main cell leaders or other contacts he preferred to keep secret. That exchange meant that Joe would go to India in September.

CHAPTER 17

Friday, August 31, 2007
Cambridge, Massachusetts

Michael Jepson arrived in Cambridge, Massachusetts and started to settle into his dorm for the most exciting challenge of his life up to that point. The temperature was an inviting seventy-six degrees, and the sky was clear. He was optimistic and full of anticipation and energy, relishing this exciting and wonderful opportunity to be on his own away from home for the first time, and to begin preparing for the excitement and rewarding challenges of his future. He loved learning, but he was still young and had yet to learn how ugly life can become. That ugliness would resume in his country in a very subtle manner in just three days.

CHAPTER 18

Monday, September 3, 2007
Miami, Florida

Rasheed Shirani arrived at Miami International Airport after a long journey on Qatar Airways from Rawalpindi International Airport in Pakistan to Doha, Qatar, then from Doha to Washington Dulles International Airport and from Washington Dulles to Miami International. He was a tired, but determined young man of twenty-six years. He knew right from wrong, and was absolutely determined to do what was right and best for the world with the help of Allah.

He had a valid Pakistani passport. He was 'clean.' He had no known ties to terrorist or criminal organizations anywhere around the world. There was no record of his name anywhere in the FBI, CIA, Interpol, Mossad, British, French, Canadian, Italian, Swiss, German, Indian, Chinese, Japanese or Russian intelligence databases. He was a well-trained, but also self-taught explosives expert. None of the major criminal or national security organizations around the globe had yet identified him as a person of interest. If he had a part in any prior terrorist activities, no one in a position of authority ever knew about it.

He hailed a taxi outside the airport terminal and told the driver in almost perfect English to take him to Rivera Brothers Service Station at 999 West Flagler Street in Miami, not far from the airport, where he had arranged to meet his first contact. He had developed and memorized the entire plan in Pakistan, down to the smallest detail, including the names, locations and contact information of sympathetic extremists inside the United States who would assist him along the way. By design, they were ignorant of the entire plan, and therefore just in case they were discovered by police, honestly could not provide details if they were apprehended and interrogated. With only limited or partial knowledge of the entire plan, they could sincerely claim genuine ignorance persuasively without revealing enough information that could be useful to police in the very unlikely event of their apprehension and capture.

After he got out of the taxi at the service station, he paid the taxi driver and walked toward the U-Haul rental lot, where he was to wait for Mohammed, his first contact. He dialed the first number on his personal cell phone to notify his contact that he had arrived. Within seventeen minutes, a large U-Haul two-axle box truck pulled up to the curb near the rental lot. The driver looked out at Rasheed, held his left fist up to his face, waited for Rasheed to look his way and then nodded when they made eye contact. Rasheed looked around carefully as he casually walked to the truck and stood next to the driver's door looking up at Mohammed through the open window.

The driver said as quietly as possible, "What is your name?"

Rasheed recognized the expected phrase and responded, "Rasheed. Do you have the package?"

"Yes. You have 4,000 bricks of C4 back there. It was very difficult to obtain, so drive carefully."

"Open it up so I can see," Rasheed said, not wanting to take any chances or make any foolish assumptions.

The driver got out of the truck, walked with Rasheed to the back of the truck and unlocked the cargo door while he looked around the area carefully. He lifted the door just enough to allow Rasheed to see the cargo for himself. Rasheed saw at least three layers of identical light-brown paper-wrapped bricks spread neatly and evenly across the entire floor of the cargo area. He reached under the door and opened one of the wrappers to see for himself the off-white clay-like substance inside, the powerful C4 explosive. Inside the cargo area was significantly more, perhaps fifteen to twenty times more and purer C4 than what created a large hole in the U.S.S. Cole on October 12, 2000, killing seventeen U.S. soldiers and injuring at least another thirty-nine. No one was watching them. The two men then closed the door and Mohammed fastened the lock on the door. They embraced briefly as Mohammed pressed an envelope containing $5,000 in cash into Rasheed's hand between them, handed him the truck keys and then walked away from Rasheed down the street. He turned into a side street to blend into the city and, for all practical purposes, disappeared forever.

In his frequent dreams during the last several years, Rasheed had imagined driving a large tractor-trailer rig for this mission. However, he eventually decided that it would be far too difficult to complete the mission due to the necessary operator training and special licenses he would be required to obtain and produce on demand for such a large commercial vehicle. In addition, he would have to stop at the periodic personal and sophisticated electronic inspection and weighing stations, particularly in the new era of official 'anti-terrorist' vigilance and suspicion associated with large commercial tractor-trailer rigs in the United States since 9/11. Besides, it would have been too suspicious to drive such a rig through a medium-sized city as he had planned. He would be satisfied with the two-axle, twenty-six-foot rental truck, appearing to be just another normal citizen moving his household goods from one place to another, immune to possible irregular checks most likely required for larger trucks without the U-Haul 'seal of innocent approval.' Appearance was his ally. He believed that the cultural attitudes of the southern states were much more relaxed than the more sensitive attitudes around the northeastern areas where the September 11, 2001 attacks occurred, and that American memories were relatively short if not devoid of passion, in his assessment. Official vigilance outside the airports was generally lax and overseen by relatively careless 'politically correct' bureaucrats with a profoundly naive and mindless aversion to 'profiling.'

The greatest threat to the success of his mission was that he did not have a valid driver's license, and therefore could not take any chance whatsoever of being stopped by the police. All he had was a 'good' counterfeit Florida driver's license created by underground experts in producing such very expensive documents from previous visits to the United States, but it did not have all of the special embedded security features developed after 9/11. He could not count on police officers being stupid or not keenly observant. This weakest element of his plan would gnaw at him like a stomach ulcer throughout his journey until he arrived at Wheeler Ridge.

Rasheed stepped up into the truck cab and settled in for the long drive to California. He retrieved his Garmin Nuvi 360 GPS from his backpack and mounted it on the dashboard. He checked the fuel level, fastened his seatbelt, took a deep breath and started the engine. He drove toward I-75 and entered the highway on the westbound ramp. He continued west on I-75 to I-10 just north of Lake City, Florida, from which he would continue the long trek west toward Los Angeles, where he would turn onto I-5 North to Exit 219-A at Wheeler Ridge Road. From there he would find the designated meeting place with his old friend, Khalid nearby at the Travel Centers of America truck stop just off the highway. He started to drive with the windows down, enjoying the fresh warm air, which energized his resolve and determination to complete his mission. He did not fully appreciate how very big the United States of America really is.

After driving for almost seven hours, he decided to rest at Live Oak. He had planned to divide the long journey into relatively even segments, bearing in mind he had a lot of work to do along the way to meet scheduled stops to pick up 'merchandise' from specific locations that were secretly arranged through obscure coded messages via phone and the internet during the preceding twelve months in northern Pakistan. He dialed the second of several phone numbers on his cell phone to arrange for the first pickup just outside Mobile, Alabama.

Among hundreds of thousands of other people traveling west across the United States at that time was a strikingly beautiful young female vocalist and her four male backup musicians on their way to provide musical joy and excitement to the residents of Denver, Colorado.

CHAPTER 19

Monday, September 3, 2007
Denver, Colorado

As she had promised fifty-one weeks ago in Manhattan, Sasha and The Autumn Dream arrived in Denver at Eddie's Place for a five-day engagement. The lovely lead singer entered Eddie's Place around two in the afternoon, much to Eddie's delight. He had been waiting for this moment all day with unaccustomed impatience and the rich anticipation of a young child on Christmas Eve. He had already polished the entire elegant dark brown frontier-era bar surface six times.

"Hi, Eddie! Remember me?" she said cheerfully as she entered the building and walked through the empty main dining room toward the shiny bar, where Eddie was idly still polishing the antique wood finish for the seventh time just for something to do in his excited active anticipation of her arrival. She was wearing faded blue jeans and a loose-fitting white denim shirt with a light blue sweater vest that obscured the outline of her figure.

"Like Romeo remembers Juliet!" Eddie blurted out in enthusiastic joy but obviously without a nanosecond of thought.

Sasha sometimes had that effect upon men, briefly disconnecting their otherwise sound judgment, poise and intelligence from appearances of maturity or sophistication. He was simply overjoyed and simultaneously flustered by the approaching realization of his own 'autumn dream' of presenting this beautiful woman and her marvelous group of musicians to his patrons, even though it would be for only five evenings, which he decided was better than nothing! He had spent more than four months advertising The Autumn Dream engagement at his bar on the local television and radio stations, in the local newspapers and on the internet. He hinted regularly in his bar with announcements throughout that period that he would have a very special treat for his patrons in early September, and that his regulars should mark their calendars and invite 'all of their friends and relatives, and even their in-laws' during the week of September 3 through 7.

"I hope you and your boys are rested, because I have been pumping you up big time for a large crowd this week!"

She responded with a generous dose of her uniquely feminine charm and social grace, "Thank you, Eddie! We've really been looking forward to this visit because it is our first time in Denver, and we want to leave a good impression!"

"You already have!"

She continued with a refreshingly spontaneous and genuine laugh as she reminded him, "But we haven't done anything yet!"

Eddie walked to the open end of the bar and out into the main floor to greet her with a warm hug, and said, "Thank you for coming all the way out here. I really appreciate having you and your group here!"

She artfully allowed a polite hug from the shorter man without compromising her business demeanor. Eddie managed with some concentration not to show his delight at the 'close encounter of the breast kind.'

"It wasn't a difficult decision," she said. "I just love the Rocky Mountains, so it's a real treat for me to be here, and I know my guys enjoy the fresh mountain air as well. It happens to be a convenient time after our gig in Saint Louis and before our next engagement in Fresno, so time and location worked out very well for us."

"Even though today's Labor Day, I'm going to open at five o'clock. Can you be ready by five?"

"Sure! It will take only about a half hour to set up, so we will be ready by five!"

Sasha turned to leave the bar to get her group ready.

Eddie mentally clicked his heels together in anticipation after a brief study of her retreating figure, clapped his hands together in childish glee and smiled broadly as he stepped two stairs at a time all the way back up to his office above the bar. Eddie worked on his books for a while, and for once was blissfully ignorant of the evils of the world.

Sasha returned shortly before four o'clock with her band members and equipment, and set their instruments up on the stage in ample time before the first of the crowd would enter the bar at five o'clock. The world appeared to be at peace that evening in Denver. The patrons at Eddie's Place forgot their troubles as The Autumn Dream transported them with their music to special places of peace and tranquility in their past or in their imaginations.

CHAPTER 20

Tuesday, September 4, 2007
Mobile, Alabama

Rasheed was awake and showered before six o'clock in the morning, and ready to drive the next leg of the trip that he estimated to be about 325 miles to Mobile, Alabama. He ate a small breakfast across the street from the motel at a convenience store and then returned to the truck and started the engine. So far, everything was in order. He prepared himself mentally for the possibility of unwanted attention by the police, but he kept driving. He concentrated to force himself, one minute at a time and one mile at a time to complete the long journey. With this measured passage of time, he gained a little more confidence that he would accomplish his goal without detection. On the west side of Mobile, he turned off I-10 onto the Michigan Avenue exit, and continued to Eagle Drive and pulled into the Exxon station on the southwest corner for fuel. After refueling the truck, he went inside the convenience store to find the men's room to relieve himself. Shortly after he came out of the men's room, he stopped at the counter to pay for the fuel, a Snickers candy bar, a bottle of water and No-Doz to help keep him alert on the long drive ahead. Roger Benson, the manager of the store, took Rasheed's money for the three items he placed on the counter.

"Pump number two, right?" Benson said as he looked into Rasheed's eyes.

"Yes," Rasheed said politely.

In the process of ringing up the sale on his cash register, Roger looked casually out the window and saw another two-axle box truck, almost identical to the one Rasheed left next to the pumps, but it had no markings on it at all. A man was sitting in the passenger seat. Roger did not think much of it at the time, but he registered a minute question of coincidence of the two identically sized trucks and looked back carefully at Rasheed as he handed him his change. He experienced a fleeting moment of unfamiliar dread, as he thought his heart skipped a beat, but he tried to shake it off. As Rasheed left the store and returned to his truck, he noticed a man standing next to the driver's door. Roger noticed as well. What Rasheed could not know was that this smalltime businessman with wrinkled trousers, dirty Nike shoes, an open shirt collar and equally open soiled red tie, had an eidetic memory. Rasheed continued to approach the man near his truck.

He said in almost completely unaccented English, "What do you want?" which was the 'identification, friend or foe' sign he was to initiate at the first pick-up stop.

The other man answered quietly, "I am from Peshawar and I have 1,000 bricks to ship west."

He looked slowly and inconspicuously over his left shoulder at the almost identical, but unmarked truck parked across the street, and then just as slowly looked back toward Rasheed.

"I will take them," Rasheed answered quietly.

The other man continued in a hushed voice while looking slightly away from Rasheed, "You must follow me. It will be almost a seven minute drive from here, where we can transfer the load."

With that exchange, Rasheed knew the contact was good. He turned around and entered his truck and started the engine, as he waited and watched the other man walk across the street to the other truck, and looked around casually but carefully for anyone nearby who might appear suspiciously interested in his activities. Unnoticed by either Rasheed or the other driver, Roger Benson watched as well. After the other driver entered his truck cab, he looked back at Rasheed and pointed south with his thumb. He pulled into the Exxon station to turn south onto Michigan Avenue, proceeding slowly until he knew Rasheed was following directly behind him. Roger Benson watched the two trucks disappear from view as they continued south toward 9th

Street, where the 'man from Peshawar' pulled into a large parking lot near the air center and drove to a medium-sized abandoned industrial garage. There was plenty of room in the building for the two trucks, so they would not appear suspicious in transferring merchandise from one truck to the other in the garage as they might out in the open, even for the relatively brief time they would be there.

After parking the two trucks with their rear doors as close as possible, the three men proceeded to transfer identical unmarked boxes of what Rasheed knew to be C4 from the other delivery truck to his U-Haul truck. They carefully finished the top layer of C4 bricks and added another layer on top of that, and then finished with part of a fifth layer. They left the discarded boxes inside the truck so there would be as little residual evidence of their activity as possible. By the time the three men were finished almost ninety minutes later, only a little less than six percent of Rasheed's truck cargo space was now occupied by the 5,000 dense C4 bricks, each roughly two inches by one and a half inches by eleven inches long, weighing about one and a quarter pounds each.

After they closed the U-Haul cargo door, the 'man from Peshawar' surreptitiously and carefully handed Rasheed a fully loaded .44 caliber Magnum revolver and a box of fifty rounds of ammunition, and said, "Good luck. It's fully loaded."

He then quickly returned to his truck with the other man, stepped up into the driver's seat and started the engine as the other man entered the truck on the passenger side. He backed out of the garage carefully and then drove away to disappear into the city traffic en route to an abandoned factory parking lot where he had left his car. After he turned the engine off, the other man got out of the truck and walked away. The man from Peshawar left the truck and got in his 1997 Chevy Malibu, drove out of the lot and then followed a circuitous route back to his motel. He knew that a gang of 'street thieves' would be at the factory lot within an hour of his phone call on a prepaid throw-away phone to disassemble the abandoned truck and cart it off in three flatbed trucks to deliver automotive parts to various scrap dealers in southern Alabama and Georgia, effectively making the truck disappear permanently.

Rasheed placed the weapon and box of ammunition under the driver's seat and found his way back to Interstate 10 West with his

Garmin GPS, and headed for Houston, Texas. He was extremely tired from the exertion of loading the truck, and he deliberately reminded himself to stay awake and avoid mistakes that could cost him the success of his sacred mission as he guzzled down two of the No-Doz caplets with some of the bottled water. After the eight-hour drive, punctuated by several more fuel stops where he also had to buy food and relieve himself, he found another motel just east of Houston, paid for the room in advance with cash, and checked in for a much-needed rest. The air was warm and humid, but Rasheed slept soundly, in spite of the humming and occasional buzzing and rattling of the air conditioner in his room, at peace with his righteous and necessary mission.

CHAPTER 21

Friday, September 7, 2007
Denver, Colorado

Jake Lewis finished a long day at the Veterans Administration Hospital counseling center listening to other people's problems and trying as best he could to assist them in gaining insights into their difficulties. He wanted them to learn to manage their own paths of adjustment to civilian life, and hoped they would not become dependent upon him or others for recovery from perceived impediments to working toward more fulfilling lives. One particularly troubling client was Richie Barlow, a twenty-three-year-old former enlisted man Jake had been working with for over six months.

Richie had developed an unshakable guilt complex due to three separate unusual incidents of unspecified premonition in Afghanistan. On one occasion, he became agitated on a Humvee patrol near Kandahar during Operation Medusa in 2006. Shortly thereafter, the vehicle triggered a roadside improvised explosive device. Richie recovered from his relatively minor wounds, and returned to duty a little more than a month later. The second incident was almost identical, and because of his intense anxiety, the driver of the patrol vehicle stopped to calm him down as an IED detonated less than 100 feet in front of them. The explosion rocked the vehicle, but no one was seriously injured. Shortly thereafter, however, they encountered light enemy gunfire and returned fire, killing all but a few of the small band of Taliban fighters apparently responsible for the IED explosion. The third instance involved a suicide bomber in Kandahar almost two months later. While on foot patrol, he again succumbed to intense anxiety just before others on his patrol noticed a young Afghan man approaching them from the front on the same street, smiling in what appeared to be an oddly forced manner. Richie yelled to warn his buddies, who apparently had been completely unaware of any immediate danger. Because of his alarm, they instinctively aimed their weapons at the young Taliban man approaching them, who immediately detonated his bomb, killing himself and injuring two of Richie's buddies. After that incident, his commander sent Richie home to the Veteran's Hospital on Clermont Street in Denver, where Jake had been trying to diffuse the chronic unspecified anxiety, but with only mild success so far.

After his rather exhausting one-hour session with Richie, Jake cleared off his desk and returned several files to their proper cabinets, and left for the day. He left his silver 2005 Acura TL in the nearby parking garage and walked several blocks down the street to Eddie's Place for a light supper and some desperately needed relaxing entertainment. He was early enough to find a small sturdy round table for two with a cream-colored tablecloth on it near the right side of the stage, sat down, placed his elbows on the table and put his face in his hands for a brief period of stolen quiet and relaxation.

After just a few minutes, a server startled him from the very beginnings of sleep as he said, "What'll you have, sir?"

Jake looked up at the wall to his right, completely disoriented, saw a sign indicating 'Occupancy by more than 250 people is illegal' and suddenly realized the voice came from the other direction.

He turned toward the server and said, "Excuse me?"

"Would you like something to drink?"

"Uh . . . Yes. I'll have the biggest glass of ginger ale you have, please . . . with lots of ice."

The server responded smoothly with a friendly voice, "Yes sir, coming right up!"

The entertainment for the night was slowly organizing on the small stage representing much of the corner of the room nearest Jake's table. An average-looking man, in his forties, Jake guessed, seemed to be looking for the perfect spot for his wooden stool, settled on a place on the right side of the stage and put it down exactly where he wanted it. Another man, somewhat younger in appearance, with long and apparently not recently washed dark brown hair with blonde streaks came from behind the right side curtain, also with a stool, and set it down on the right half of the stage toward the back. Two other men lugged a very sophisticated looking professional electronic dual keyboard into place on the left side of the stage, and set up all the wiring connections to the floor pedal and the speakers, including the ones for the electric guitar. After they finished, 'Streaky-hair' returned with another stool, set it down toward the front of the stage in the middle, and then disappeared behind the stage curtain again.

Jake closed his eyes once again and put his face back in his hands, with his elbows resting on the table. After just a few minutes of oblivion, which seemed to him to be an hour, he opened his eyes to find a large glass of ginger ale in front of him, just as he wanted, and yet he did not remember seeing the server put it there. The stage was already set up, including the drums centered toward the rear of the stage, with the bass drum bearing a bright blue script title, 'The Autumn Dream.' The room was almost full of people and a mild cacophony of their fragmented conversations and periodic laughter appeared to ricochet throughout the main room.

"Anything to eat tonight, sir?"

The same server once again seemed to appear out of nowhere, since Jake was still recovering from another episode of incipient sleep. He had no idea how long it had been, but it could not have been very long, because he thought the band could not have taken more than fifteen minutes to set up to be ready for the evening's musical entertainment.

"Yes please . . . A big hamburger, well-done, ketchup, no pickle, no tomato, on a well-toasted Kaiser and no fries please, and a house salad. No, wait . . . Make that just hearts of lettuce with French dressing."

"Will that be all?"

"Yes. Thank you."

The server quietly disappeared once again as the PA system just barely overcame the level of customer noise that allowed 'news' and 'secrets' to pass from one person to another without special notice or unwanted intrusions. Eddie's voice originating from some unknown location in the bar filled the room through the PA system.

"And now, ladies and gentlemen, Eddie's Place presents for the fifth and final evening this week, a wonderful new group for your listening pleasure! Please welcome 'The Autumn Dream' all the way from New York City!"

Brief polite applause rippled through the room with diminishing conversation for about seven seconds, while Jake mulled that over for a moment.

The Autumn Dream? From New York? That's interesting. I hope they're good, because I'm right up here in front of them!

He noted the four musicians already on the stage, but the center stool toward the front was still empty. The drummer started a mesmerizing pace of soft strokes and introductory fanfare, as the forty-something guy started caressing the keys of a soprano sax and put some wind into it. With the sound of the sax, Jake was fully alert and started to concentrate on the music as 'Streaky-hair' put his guitar to work with a pleasing melodious strumming and fingering that Jake thought had to have come from many years of experience. The musical pace and tempo announced real music to come from real musicians, and not some blaring amateur 'wanna-be' small time pop show. He did not recognize the music at all, but he smiled in anticipation. It was a good start for the evening.

Eddie also smiled from the far corner of the bar for the fifth consecutive evening. He knew a winner when he heard one almost a year ago in Manhattan. He was a businessman who had an ear for music. He played the piano since he was nine years old through high school, but never really worked hard at it. He knew word about this group had spread since Monday and he would have a packed house tonight, probably even more customers than his usually large Friday evening business. His advertising had already been effective with the last four days of larger-than-usual crowds. He paid a moderate premium for The Autumn Dream to play in his place whenever they could get there, but he could not get more than the five-day commitment. He surveyed the crowd, thankful that he had these five performances, yet wished for another week or more of The Autumn Dream. He savored the refreshing anticipation of the joy he already knew his patrons were about to experience.

Jake sat up in his seat a little and guzzled down half of the ice-cold ginger ale to make sure he would be able to stay awake and enjoy the rest of what appeared to be the beginning of an exceptionally good show. The charge of carbonation did its work, and Jake concentrated on the music, letting it set him up to appreciate whoever was going to occupy that last stool.

After less than two minutes of introductory music, the third stool at the front of the stage remained vacant. And then the remaining crowd noise disappeared altogether as a woman's rich mezzo voice joined the sax a third interval lower, sometimes a fourth, as dictated by the harmony from 'Streaky hair' on the guitar and the tall guy with wiry dark hair and a thin face on the electronic keyboard. Jake thought he looked a little like he thought Ichabod Crane should look. The musicians on the stage looked around casually at each other, smiling with the knowledge of what would happen next. Sasha's voice matched the volume of the sax, and trumped the superior quality of the forty-something guy's efforts on the guitar as she parted the black curtain and instantly drew the breath out of every man in the audience. She stepped slowly and smoothly toward the empty stool at the front of the stage, climbed gracefully up on it and into the white cone of light from the overhead spotlight, and crossed one perfect leg over the other without even a hint of Jerusalem. Her smile was alluringly effective as almost every attached woman in the audience soon looked inconspicuously with at least some apprehension at the man she came in with for evidence of infatuation, or possibly worse! Eddie smiled his big flashy 'maximum-teeth' smile as he looked appreciatively around the room from behind the bar for the fifth consecutive evening of genuine pleasure and profit.

She was no pipsqueak, and filled all of the necessary room in her one-piece white sequined suitably form-fitting dress, which accentuated her very feminine figure against the black curtains. She was not 'Hollywood made-up beautiful' according to Jake's scale of pulchritude, but she was 'wholesome middle-America beautiful.' He imagined she could attract a man's stare and hold it without flinching or changing colors, regardless of where his focus began or ended on her very well-proportioned five-foot nine-inch frame. Her long, wavy dark brown mane had natural auburn highlights and invited touching, even from a distance. She was fantastically radiant with apparently the barest minimum of makeup, and had dominant, unusually alluring, flashing clear blue eyes.

However, Jake did not see all of this clearly for long, because his eyes were slowly filling with the moisture of joy. Her voice reached his soul immediately as he involuntarily inhaled and bit his trembling lips.

He quickly breathed in and out a few times to gain control of himself, and took another long swig of his cold drink. He listened intently as her voice poured forth with almost unbelievable range, duration, clarity and power. She was more than just mezzo or alto. Jake was marking her range in his head, and estimated that she had covered three and a half octaves so far in that one song alone, even stretching into the soprano level. She was in complete control of a variable tremolo, and made her voice sound like it came from a source larger than her earthly form. She held notes as long as, or longer than Jake had ever heard the best professional opera singers hold them, and with at least equal quality. She had obviously had *significant* voice training at some point in her life.

The 'stealth' server appeared from behind Jake and placed his hamburger and salad in front of him from his left. He was smart enough not to obstruct a male patron's view of an attractive woman on the stage. It was bad for business, and occasionally became a very serious personal or public relations problem. Jake continued to focus upon the young woman on the front stool on the stage before him, as if drinking from her the essence of life itself. He had the best seat in the house, and was oblivious to the rest of the crowd and the rest of the world.

She was a performer in her own universe, giving to her audience what they could get nowhere else—her unusually rich crystal-clear smooth voice, her smile and her stunning beauty. Smiles and rhythmic taps of fingers on tables and thighs and slight head nods and light foot-taps on the floor throughout the bar joined with the well-tuned beat from the drummer. The music flowed together with enchanting harmony from the electronic double keyboard and the periodic dominance of the guitar melody, alternating with the warm cry of the soprano sax in duet with her voice, still entwined at thirds, fourths, fifths, sixths and octaves. Her music brought smiles of joy from all, especially from Jake, who was falling hopelessly in love as the next shift in harmony to the complementary minor sixth over her endless voice sent a shiver of pure excitement down his spine. Almost everyone in the bar was hearing unusually good music for the first time in recent memory, but Jake was hearing *heaven* for the very first time. Then the instruments stopped, as she continued solo with a refrain, practically whispering her melody, looking into the eyes of each and every person in the place, one by one, delivering real human emotion to them with her voice and her eyes. She unmistakably rested her gaze on Jake's eyes for just a moment and then continued to survey the rest of the crowd. Her backup musicians watched her as they always did, usually just as mesmerized by her performance as the audience even though they had heard her hundreds of times before. She had a rare talent for making each performance fresh and exciting.

Jake tried to control his emotions, but tears welled out from his eyes again, and fell obediently down his face. He literally got a grip on himself by squeezing his thighs with his hands under the table, trying to keep his emotions under control. His big hamburger on the toasted Kaiser roll was still untouched on the plate before him. His hunger had changed from that of the body to that of the heart and the soul. He did not remember the last time he cried out of sheer joy. He did not remember the last time he cried, period. He could not remember ever having felt such musical excitement. He did not remember the last time he had seen such a beautiful woman.

And this was to be her last night in Denver?

Jake questioned everything he had ever thought about fate, realizing that he could very well have missed her altogether had he not decided to come to Eddie's Place for a bite to eat! He could have eaten somewhere else and would have missed at least the experience of a lifetime.

The instruments rejoined her voice as she sang the final verse and brought the song to its expected close as the audience had already begun an enthusiastic shower of applause that brought Jake out of his private reverie as he belatedly joined in the applause. He was the last one clapping after everyone else had stopped, but quickly returned to reality with everyone else and sat back down in his chair. He forgot having stood up in the first place during the applause. The usual rattle, clatter and buzz of the bar resumed as everyone released whatever tension and thoughts had accumulated during her first song. The group took a well-timed, but very short break before starting the next number. She briefly looked his way again. Then she worked her magic once more, giving her audience a slightly longer period of anticipation than they most likely expected. Just raising the microphone near her lips quieted the crowd instantly. She looked to 'Streaky-hair' as if to coordinate the exact start of the next musical number. All was quiet. Then somewhere in the kitchen behind closed doors a knife dropped on the tile floor and sent a brief but very faint metallic clatter into the main dining area that normally would not have been audible. The bar was unusually still with palpable anticipation. A few people put their sandwiches or utensils back on their plates, preparing to devote their full attention to the beautiful woman in the white dress. Others held forks, but remained motionless, not eating. No one was lifting a glass or a bottle.

The keyboard started with a very soft slow rhythmic deep bass tone complemented by a very light two-octave range of a staccato string-like arpeggio over three octaves above middle C from the second keyboard. The musical result set the stage for what could have been the crystal clear night-time sky of middle America, far from any city lights, revealing millions of stars overhead visible only with perfect atmospheric conditions, opening up the night sky and beyond to the imagination. She began with an almost inaudible soprano whisper that seemed to fall directly from the slow reverberating staccato tinkling at the high end of the keyboard, as she blended her voice smoothly into harmony with the arpeggio. She was pushing the envelope of her range beyond the three and a half octaves Jake had estimated before and yet with perfect control and quality! It sounded like she was singing with a completely different voice! Jake was beyond transfixed. He easily slipped back into his private focus of joy.

He wondered to himself, *who is this woman? What is she doing here when her voice obviously qualifies her for bigger and fancier clubs, if not Broadway or beyond? Where did she come from?*

After she finished that song, the audience was still quietly contemplating wherever she had led them, and then they slowly recovered to offer another extended round of standing ovation.

'Stealth' was in perfect form, periodically gliding almost imperceptibly from table to table from parts unknown behind the bar serving sandwiches and drinks as well as larger meals. He and the other servers noticed that everyone seemed to be unusually hungry. Eddie was still smiling, inside and outside, watching the entire action on the stage and throughout the restaurant from his customary perch at the far end of the bar.

She sang several more numbers. Eddie was very pleased. Everyone in the bar was pleased. Jake was *beyond* pleased. He was now completely hers if she wanted him, and there was *nothing* he could do about it.

He was responding to a woman in unfamiliar ways beyond all of his psychological education, knowledge of human behavior and personal experience. He felt himself being drawn to her irreversibly, as though he were being absorbed rapidly into a black hole as he lost track of time.

The music ended over half an hour ago, and the unusually large crowd at Eddie's Place was thinning out as Jake picked up his slightly warm hamburger and started to eat. He knew he would not last through the evening without nourishment, and would need to get another meal one way or another, so he ate the one on the table in front of him. He closed his eyes and tried to replay the evening, savoring the incredible joy he felt, as he munched on his surprisingly tasty hamburger that still released the inviting odor of charcoal preparation and only mild residual evidence of the Kaiser roll having been nicely toasted. He decided he had to meet her—win, lose, or draw—before she left the bar forever. He thought about 'forever' in a new way. It was well beyond an opportunity passed by. It was a distinct and everlasting meaningful fork in the road of his life. After three bites and associated chewing, he opened his eyes with a start and stared across his table at the beautiful singer in the white dress, just as striking outside the spotlight as she was within it.

"Hello!" she said with a warm, confident, but not quite sultry, gentle voice. "Do you mind if I sit down? My name is Sasha. What's your name?" she asked softly with a smile and an undeniably inviting tone while she gracefully sat in the other chair across from Jake without waiting for either his permission or an answer to her question.

He swallowed politely, dabbed at his mouth with his napkin, managed to smile a little and moved his mouth with the elements of 'Jake,' but no sound came out. He swallowed and subtly cleared his throat to try again.

"My name is Jake Lewis."

He decided not to embellish his response with further efforts, because he knew he was emotionally off balance at the very least, and he did not want to say anything more complicated than his name, lest he put her off or embarrass himself with heroics like a compound sentence that he might fumble, or expression of his true feelings. Now within touching distance across the table, and within the effective range of her very alluring scent, Jake summoned every ill-practiced form of male courtesy he could remember from his mother's 'school of how to behave in the presence of a lady.' He inhaled a little more as subtly as he could, to take in her unusually alluring scent as well as a desperately needed fresh supply of oxygen.

"I . . . I enjoyed your music very much," he ventured after gathering some confidence and self-control, while exhaling as inconspicuously as possible.

"I know," she said in a very soft and gentle reply without changing her extremely effective visual grip on his eyes.

Jake's mental, emotional and biophysical alarm system was firing, misfiring and short-circuiting throughout his entire body.

"How . . . How did you . . . know?" he muttered in obvious unchecked astonishment.

"I have more than a woman's intuition, Jake. I have a *musician's* intuition. Everyone in this place was smiling during my performance, except you. I was watching. You had tears in your eyes. I'm very curious . . . Why?"

She punctuated her question with an alluring tilt of her head, while maintaining that incredibly inviting smile. Jake was not accustomed to such blatantly direct conversation and behavior from a woman, particularly a very beautiful woman and at close range, but he shifted his mental and emotional gears as rapidly as he could under the circumstances. He was in survival mode. He was still falling in love, and had no intention of continuing his life without at least her phone number.

She detected his intense mental maneuvering for a second, and brought her hands to the top of the table from her lap and placed them where she surely knew they represented a deliberate invitation to be touched. She tilted her head slightly to the left, which had the effect of causing her long naturally wavy brown hair to flow to one side and down her arm, while her clear blue eyes never left his. Jake responded by shifting in his seat, just enough to brush accidentally against her leg under the rather small round table.

Jake blurted out, completely flustered, "Oh! Please excuse me . . . I'm . . . Sorry, I didn't mean to . . . I mean . . ."

She smiled in complete acceptance of his erratic attempt to apologize for what could have happened to anyone. But it did not happen to *just anyone!* It happened to *him!* Her mesmerizing eyes never left his as she waited patiently for him to speak. She knowingly parted her expertly lightly colored red lips with an inviting, yet polite smile, exposing either God's beautiful creation in perfect white, or the result of a really good orthodontist's expertise.

"They're really mine . . . all natural," she said.

"Oh? Oh. OH! No, I'm sorry! Was I staring? I didn't mean . . ." Jake was in trouble. He felt his face heat up. He was blushing! He was definitely mentally off balance. This whole scene really was not going according to 'Plan A: Male in control' mode!

"The teeth—they're really mine—natural teeth, and no cavities. I have really good genes," she said playfully to put him more at ease, and tilted her head a little more to bring her eyes more into his slightly diverted field of view. "I noticed that you were looking at my mouth. I'm very observant."

She chuckled with a broader smile as she turned slightly in her seat and 'accidentally' brushed her leg against Jake's thigh again according to the mental map she had made of their proximity under the table from the first contact just a few moments before. She watched him very carefully, noting that his nostrils flared a little more open and he immediately inhaled, and sent him a message through her smiling eyes into his slightly widening grey eyes, attractively set into his masculine and somewhat chiseled face.

I know you liked that!

She continued innocently, "You know I sing, but I know nothing about you, other than that you are very handsome."

Jake felt another rush of heat throughout his body as his heart raced in preparation for . . . *for what?*

My God, she is gorgeous!

"I want to know all about you, from day one!" she said softly, but confidently.

Jake got the message. He knew he had time—a heavenly privilege at least to talk with her, to get to know a little bit more about her, to bask for a little longer in the astounding luxury of her very feminine presence. But how much more did he need to know? *Everything,* he decided.

She raised her index finger on her left hand, attracting Jake's attention via his peripheral vision. He glanced at both of her hands—relatively large for a woman, artistic hands, rather short fingernails artfully polished and smooth with minimal pink color and no rings on any fingers, or anywhere else he could see. She had relatively small, tastefully simple jeweled silver earrings hanging less than an inch from her pierced ear lobes. He could see them sparkling through the parting of her lovely dark brown hair in which at this range he could see her natural auburn highlights much more clearly.

This is good, he said to himself. *This is very good!*

"Well!" he said, mentally racing for the right way to continue. He started again. "I was born in Boston, lived most of my 'growing up' years in Pennsylvania through high school. Went to college and graduate school, and now work as a research counselor at the V.A. Hospital here in Denver. I'm a Psychologist."

"That does not tell me why you had tears in your eyes," she said in a coy conspiratorial tone and the most devilish and inviting smile Jake had ever seen, starting with alluring dimples just beyond the corners of her tastefully glistening red lips.

"Well!" Jake swallowed as inconspicuously as he could. "I am an amateur musician. I play the piano, and . . . and, well, I love music! Your music was just beautiful! Music is much of my non-professional life, actually. I have an antique baby grand Steinway piano at home, and I play almost every day . . . my own stuff, mostly. I think it keeps me whole and stable most of the time, instead of drinking or taking drugs like some of my clients. Music just comes to me rather frequently—at work, at night, on the road. Some of it I like, and some I don't like at all. Sometimes I feel like I'm cursed! Well, not really cursed, but, you know . . . like I have this incurable 'condition.' It's not unpleasant, mind you, but it is rather persistent. Sometimes it's almost as if a radio is on all the time in my head and I can't turn it off. Other times, I'm not conscious of any music at all. I've been that way since I was about four years old, when my parents first started piano lessons for me with one of my great aunts."

"That's wonderful!" she gushed enthusiastically, with shining wide blue eyes without a single blood vessel visible that Jake had not really noticed before.

Probably evidence of very good total health, he thought to himself, as she 'involuntarily' captured his right hand with her left and looked down at his as she coaxed him with her subtle touch to bring his hand up with hers in mirror image, fingertip to fingertip, palm to palm.

It was a way for her to touch him in a playful, but rather innocent and non-threatening, socially acceptable manner. His hand was strong, warm and rather large, with slender expressive fingers, and slightly more reach than hers, but that was to be expected. He was taller—almost six feet tall, and she could not have been more than five-nine, although she was wearing heels. Jake thought he was feeling fire in his hand.

Was she actually communicating with him physically?

"How far can you reach?" she asked innocently.

"An octave plus four with consistency," he said. "Plus five is a stretch, and I dare not try it very often without a roll."

He felt the warmth of her hand as if it were practically searing his, and looked again at his hand only slightly larger than hers and realized that hers were definitely the hands of a musician. He let his gaze drift up her arms, observing their smooth and relatively firm feminine muscular tone. She played an instrument of some kind, probably a keyboard. He was sure of it! Probably a piano! His heart leaped with joy enough for him to wonder whether she noticed.

"Yes, I do play the piano," she admitted as if reading his mind. "I'd like to hear *you* play," she said softly with a conspiratorial lift of her eyebrows and another subtle version of her captivating smile. "Eddie has a Yamaha six-footer backstage. I saw it there before we set up on Monday. It's only fair. I sang for you, now you must play for me!" she said with the subtle but effective pleading and simple compelling sense of logical fairness of a five-year-old child.

"Really?" *You sang for me?*

Jake felt like a schoolboy on cloud nine with his very first female admirer. He thought of Jeanie, the girl who kissed him for the very first time when he was in fourth grade, and wondered what Sasha looked like at age nine.

"Yeah," he said, "but I paid to get in here," picking up on his part of the game with some creativity and a little more confidence.

"Well, if I like what I hear then I'll pay *you*, but not before," she parried playfully with a subtle mischievous glint in her eyes.

She held his gaze for a few moments, as they arose from the table together and then she turned and walked ahead of him toward the black curtain to the left of the stage, knowing she was giving Jake another angle from which to appreciate her very well-proportioned figure, even though she camouflaged it somewhat with her dress.

Eddie called from the bar, "You need some help, Sasha?"

"No, Eddie. I just want to hear some music. This guy says he needs a job, so I'm going to audition him right here."

She glanced back at Jake with a playful smile and a wink to draw him into her analogy.

Jake took careful note of the phrase 'audition him.' He reveled for a moment in the unmistakable excitement of being at the center of her attention. She could have been pointing a camera at him, spilling coffee on his lap or accidentally bumping into him on a subway or in any other innocent normal social encounter. He imagined it would have had the same exciting effect.

"OK. Let me know if you need anything. I'm not leaving for another hour or so," Eddie said.

"Thanks, Eddie!" she called over her shoulder while again fixing her bright flashing eyes on Jake's.

Together they pulled the curtain back to let in enough light for Jake to see. He touched the instrument with admiration, as if to introduce himself, to let the piano know he meant no harm, like a stranger approaching a waking dog cautiously looking up for affection. He gently lifted the top, and propped it up with the shorter wooden support rod. He did not feel the wide-open concert position was appropriate. He smiled in irrepressible joy as he rotated the height adjuster at the side of the bench to the position to which he was accustomed. As he prepared to lower himself onto the bench, he gestured with the hand motions of flipping an imaginary pair of tuxedo tails out from under him before he sat down and looked over at Sasha with the self-conscious smile of an amateur comedian after a wasted joke.

"I must warn you, Sasha, I really don't know what is going to come out of this. I mean, I don't have anything in my head right now."

Jake felt like a schoolboy again with the thrill of actually addressing her by her first name for the first time, and at the same time, his mature intellectual self recognized the very fringes of confirmed, rapidly accelerating and irreversible total physical and emotional attraction.

"I'll bet!" she said coyly just to his right.

What did she mean by that?

"Here, you get me started. Pick a key. Start a melody—anything to prime the pump."

"*Prime the pump?*" she murmured slowly and softly.

She then glanced slowly and deliberately down at his eyes with an intentional and unmistakably flirtatious grin. She moved behind him and leaned purposefully into his back, reached around his arm with her right hand, and started playing with middle C, followed by F, G and A ascending in even cadence. Jake picked up the progression with the next higher solo C and then a simultaneous soft base C and added a C-major arpeggio resolution an octave higher, shifted to an F-major interlude, which in turn dissolved into a seven-note phrase with a G-major continuation inviting yet another resolution into A-minor. The music was coming freely now, right from his soul. Jake quickly adjusted to the piano's responsiveness without first having tested its quality as he usually did with an instrument he had never played before. The keys responded to a light touch with brilliant sound, perfectly in tune as well. He could not have continued with an instrument out of tune. He had perfect pitch, a dubious blessing, so anything that sounded off-key would have been like fingernails across a blackboard to him—virtual inhumane treatment, almost psychological torture. Oddly enough, he had no more control over that response than he had over any other biophysical or biochemical reflex or response.

Counseling other people was how he earned a living. Playing the piano was his life. It was real. He was making it up as he went. The present flowed along as he continued to play in real time. The music was not prepared or otherwise rehearsed. It was not a matter of politics, business, clients, or someone else's sorrow. It was not the evening news. It was not the folly of humanity. It was not yesterday, or memories, or fears and apprehension about tomorrow. It was neither right nor wrong. It was the 'here and now' Jake, concentrating on the joyful, live and very real and exciting present with one note either demanding or begging for another, anticipating or pleading for harmony and resolution. It was his *life*.

Sasha very quietly brought a chair from the main dining floor and placed it slightly behind him and to his right. She sat down and leaned forward to rest her chin between her hands, with her elbows on her knees in rapt attention. He never saw her move to get the chair and return. He was completely absorbed in his music. Eddie stopped wiping down the bar, put his towel down and leaned on it with both forearms, listening with fascination to Jake's music.

This is my lucky night for music. I could have played like that if I had worked at it, Eddie thought to himself.

Music not common in a bar poured out of the Yamaha, prompted by the emotions of an unknown talent, coming from some mysterious source, yielding breath-taking crescendos and heart-stopping shifts of harmony, repeated with several different shifts in complementary harmony demanding resolution, lifting the music to another realm, and then carefully setting it back down in the original musical phrase. It seemed that he had not left a key without expression. Black keys, white keys—it made no difference to Jake. He made the instrument sing, as was its only destiny, in stark contrast to its former dormant state hidden in dark silence behind the black curtain of Eddie's stage. After more than twelve minutes of this adventure in music, Jake wound it down to a soft and melodious return to the introductory musical phrase Sasha had started him with, and a final soft statement from the bass range with his left hand to complement the final resolution to C-major with his right hand. He kept his fingers on the keys until the music faded into complete silence. Then he slowly put his hands on his lap, closed his eyes and effectively held back emotional tears of joy once again.

After about fifteen seconds, Eddie clapped from the bar, breaking the tranquil spell of Jake's music throughout the entire restaurant and said, "You want a contract?"

Sasha rose slightly from her chair and turned around toward Eddie with an impatient and dismissive *'NOT NOW!'* wave of her right hand, and then turned back to Jake.

He felt Sasha's warm soft hand on his, as she said, "That was beautiful! Really *beautiful!*"

She studied him for a moment, looking directly into his eyes, and then said very carefully in her softest, most gentle voice, almost whispering, "Where have you *been?* Where is your music? Who *are* you . . . really?"

He inhaled deeply and regained his composure with some effort. It was now or never. The inevitable truth would either save him or sink him, but it was inescapable, regardless of the outcome. He had absolutely no choice. The truth was welling up inside him and demanded expression.

"That was from you, Sasha. That is what you have done to me. That is how *your* voice and *your* music have affected *me*. That is the sound of how I feel after having heard your beautiful voice—after having been immersed in your presence. I simply don't know how to explain it any better."

She paused for several seconds as if trying to comprehend what he had just said.

"How long have you been playing like this?" she said carefully, searching his face with her eyes, as if she were digging into family secrets that might destroy the delicate beginnings of an urgent and promising mutual attraction.

"As long as I can remember," he responded softly after evident reflection.

She continued with an increase in her special confidence. "Well, I would like to have that music, Jake. Will you please play it again for me when I can record it?"

"No . . . I can't, Sasha. I'm really very sorry. It's gone. I cannot play anything exactly the same way twice. It comes, and then it's gone—like the present becomes the past. Sometimes I don't know from one phrase or note to the next what I'm going to play, and after I play it, most of the time I forget what I did even just one or two minutes before."

She sat back on her chair with her beautiful lips slightly parted in an expression of disbelief and wonder, just looking at him, almost dumbfounded as her heart rate increased.

Jake looked into her eyes playfully with a smile and said, "Does that mean you're going to pay me, like you said?"

Within several seconds, Sasha stood gracefully with the self-assurance of a woman who knows *exactly* what she wants, and said softly, "Please walk me to my hotel—it's just a few blocks away—are you married?"

It all came out as one coherent thought. She just wanted to confirm her intuition with absolute certainty.

"No . . . I'm not . . . married," he managed to say with some hesitation but perfectly clearly in spite of his racing heart, sudden flush of internal heat and his body's intense but still mounting urge to process massive amounts of oxygen very quickly.

They held hands eagerly as they walked out of Eddie's Place with simultaneous brief recognition of Eddie's knowing smile from behind the bar. They walked side by side in the cool evening air down the four blocks to her hotel, saying little of substance. She laced both her arms around his left arm and leaned into him gently in order to maintain her balance and shield herself from the cool night air, and yet not make him lose his balance. The result was an occasional gentle, incidental bump from her solid and shapely hips against Jake's upper thigh, which he enjoyed immensely, but said nothing, lest she stop doing it.

She disengaged her embrace of his arm as they walked through the revolving door into the hotel lobby and guided him to the right, where he saw the elevator bank. He pushed the up arrow as if he knew exactly where he was going.

She looked up slightly into his eyes as they entered the elevator and said softly to him, "Six, please!"

For just an instant, Jake wondered whether she had said, *Sex please!*

The elevator door slowly started to close without a sound as he stole a few seconds to admire her beautiful hair. He pressed the 'six' button.

Then an urgent voice said, "Hold it please!" and a hand reached between the closing doors, interrupting the photoelectric sensor, as well as his developing anticipation.

The closing mechanism automatically reversed and allowed an older couple to enter the elevator, much to Jake's dismay and frustration as he and Sasha made room for them, effectively cooling some of their urgent desire for privacy. Sasha merely glanced sideways and slightly up into Jake's eyes without turning her head, but with the slightest smile at the corners of her mouth. The apparently septuagenarian couple stood near the side of the elevator car watching Jake and Sasha with unabashed stares of disapproval, knowing, of course, that she must be a hooker, and he must be a john. They were the triumphant invaders, protecting society from sin!

Jake just stared at the white plastic successive number forms above the shiny brushed metallic doors as the elevator moved much too slowly for him on its ascent to heaven. Sasha reached behind Jake with her right hand deliberately in full view of the other couple and squeezed his buttocks. She could scarcely suppress a giggle as she imagined their ever-widening eyes and dropping jaws! She liked what she felt. Jake got her message and could not hold back his smile. He knew she was putting on a show for 'the odd couple.'

The number '3' illuminated above the door.

Jake reached down with his left hand and caressed Sasha's firm and perfectly shaped ass and murmured just loud enough for the other couple to hear, "How much for all night?"

Sasha sensed his intent and responded in a soft sultry voice intended for their understanding, "You can't *afford* me for that long, honey!"

She smiled and stifled another giggle with great effort.

'4' lit up.

Jake was about to let out two lungs full of suppressed laughter, but held it firmly inside with intense concentration and self-control, which only had the effect of making the whole scene even more hilarious to him. Sasha raised herself up next to him on the balls of her feet and kissed his ear, but did not move away without letting a soft, long suggestive groan of anticipation from deep in her throat hang in the air for his enjoyment and the 'odd couple's' further shock.

'5' lit up.

Sasha then turned and looked directly at the older man and flashed her brilliant white-toothed smile at him with slightly parted lips and room for her tongue to slip out and wet her red lipstick, which, of course, she did—*with emphasis.*

The 'odd couple' woman looked over at her husband with a sharp expression of anticipation, as if to say '*Don't you DARE smile at her!*'

He looked down at the floor and cleared his throat, while inside he smiled all the way to nirvana. Sasha won the game, as she expected. Invaders vanquished!

'6' lit up.

In less than a second, the elevator slowed to a stop and the doors finally parted. Jake finally burst out laughing and left the elevator as quickly as possible. Sasha followed, accentuating her naturally alluring hip sway as she turned around and blew a kiss to the older man, looking directly into his eyes as if to assure him that it would stay in the elevator as the doors moved together. Then she quickly caught up with Jake in the hallway and joined in his full laughter.

He turned to her, wiping his eyes, and said, "Did you notice? They never pushed a floor button, and they didn't get out with us!"

She fell into him laughing from deep in her chest even harder, as he wrapped his arms around her for the first time, to keep her from pushing him over or falling herself. The sensation of her very feminine contour against him was electric.

They both steadied themselves and worked their unabashed laughter to a halt in fits and starts until she regained her composure and whispered in his left ear, "six-one-four."

She then licked his ear and lightly nibbled his earlobe as punctuation for just a moment longer than necessary to make her point, and then started to walk down the hall with his left hand clasped in both of hers.

Jake barely whispered to himself, "So heaven is on the sixth floor."

Sasha showed no recognition of having heard him as she released his hand, took her key card from her purse, and slipped it into the electronic lock to room 614 and then withdrew it. The small LED above the card slot changed from red to green, as Jake imagined the announcement, *'Ladies and gentlemen! Start your engines!'*

Indeed, he mused to himself.

She pushed the door open and turned to Jake as if to make sure he was following her. He was right behind her, followed her in and closed the door behind him, and then quietly turned the lock on the handle, rotated the dead bolt knob until it answered with a spring-loaded clear metallic 'thud' into the door frame, and slipped the security chain latch into its brass restraining channel on the back of the door. She flipped the wall switch near the door that turned on the small table lamp beside the king-sized bed, illuminating the comfortable room just enough to allow them to move around without stumbling and possibly injuring themselves. Sasha immediately removed her high-heeled shoes, making her a few inches shorter and padded to the window occupying almost the entire outside wall, and drew the thick room-darkening curtains from the opposite walls together, each to a point slightly beyond the center of the window and overlapping to assure privacy.

Jake was sitting on the edge of the bed watching her carefully, actually admiring every motion of her body. He was alive with intense anticipation! She moved with uncommon grace away from the curtains and directly toward him. She approached him and pulled her white dress up high enough on her thighs to allow her to straddle his lap on the edge of the bed, but revealed nothing other than panty hose.

However, he caught her unmistakable female scent as she leaned into him, knowing she was setting off a subtle chemical arousal that he would be powerless to resist. He fell backward onto the bed and she carefully lowered herself on top of him, pressing her pubic bone against the hardening bulge in his pants, moving slightly over it from top to bottom and side to side. Of course, she was enjoying herself as well as she rotated her hips into him.

She finally said, "Yes, Jake. Heaven *is* on the sixth floor."

She moved her head to make sure most of her hair fell into his face, and she moved from side to side, caressing his face with her hair.

Jake started to get out from under her, but she said, "I'm just getting started, Jake, so *don't move!*"

"But I need to go to the bathroom and shower. *Really!* I've been up all day, and that didn't start very well."

"OK" she said, adjusting to him instantly. "I'll wash you! I wouldn't mind a shower as well, so let's save water and do it together!"

She drew her shapely legs up on either side of Jake's thighs and pushed herself to a sitting position on his thighs. She put her hands on his lower abdomen and pushed up toward his chest, pulling his shirt out of his pants in the process. She slipped her hands under his shirt as her smile widened when her fingers reached his chest where she encountered his pectoral muscles and played with the hair on his chest. Then she removed her hands, and started unbuttoning his shirt from the top and took her time at it. Jake was on his way to heaven, so he could not resist. After she removed his shirt, she drew her relatively short fingernails through the hair on his chest again, ever so slightly, barely touching him at all. She was doing to him what she had seen and felt him do to the Yamaha. She was making music out of his body and soul. Jake had no choice but to respond with utter joy, whenever and wherever and however she touched him. She worked her feather touch down over the bulge in his pants, never taking her eyes from his. She wanted to play every note on him, and hear and see every response.

Jake had been around the block a few times, but he had never been to heaven on the sixth floor of a Denver hotel, or any other hotel, for that matter. She continued to run her nails over his pants, which had the effect of a slight vibration against the fabric that Jake felt very clearly, and she knew it. She was still 'playing' him, and had a long way to go to the end of the concerto. This was just the first movement.

She grasped the tab of his zipper and pulled it down ever so slowly, releasing a minute amount of pressure against his fully engorged organ with each minor point of resistance in the zipper, until she had it completely down. Jake was watching her face, content to see her beautiful smile and beautiful hungry eyes as she played with him. Then she backed off from him to stand at the side of the bed, where she unlaced his shoes, pulled them off, and easily removed his socks as well, then pulled his pants off with his assistance as he lifted his hips at the appropriate time. She took his trousers over to a chair and draped them carefully over the back. When she returned, Jake was already entering the bathroom to start the shower. She pulled off her panty hose. That was not going to be part of the thrill for either of them. She wanted the pleasure of feeling him undress her, but he got ahead of her.

"Jake. Will you please come here and help me?"

She needed help like her uncle Duke Chancellor needed help. She was a twenty-eight year old talented musician and worthy entertainer. She could reach any man's soul with her voice regardless of his age, culture, nationality or social position, or with her hands, or with any other feminine asset that comprised her perfect body. She knew herself very, very well.

Jake left the water running and padded back into the room to see her faking a reach behind her back as if trying to undo whatever fastener was keeping her dress on.

He said, "I can get that," while listening to the little voice in his head saying, *you idiot! Do what she wants you to do!*

He easily pulled the zipper down a few inches, and then suddenly remembered what she had done to him, so he slowed his effort to a crawl while surreptitiously looking around the room to make sure there were no mirrors positioned to reveal to her his delight in turning the tables. He had at least another foot to go, but carefully moved the zipper one catch at a time, smiling to himself.

"Can't you go any faster?" she pleaded urgently.

"I can go as fast as you can," he replied, sensing a slight advantage in the game they were playing.

He was getting soft again with this mechanical diversion.

"All right," she said. "Have your fun!" she conceded playfully, but with some genuine impatience.

Internally, she was enduring increasing and unaccustomed anticipation with impatient effort, challenging her capacity to remain under control on the surface. She urgently wanted to feel his hands removing her clothes. Jake noticed the wide back of her bra pressing into the soft skin of her back and ribcage. She was far from skinny, but certainly not fat by any stretch of the imagination. The band was almost three inches wide, suggesting that it was holding considerable weight in place in the front. Her contour was remarkably smooth and well proportioned, with perfectly clear skin, and the widespread firmness of muscle everywhere he touched her.

She had to be physically coordinated, perhaps an athlete, like a skier, or a swimmer or a soccer player. He glanced at her legs—*NO, definitely not a soccer player! Had to be a swimmer.*

He finally reached the bottom of the zipper, which she took as a signal to turn around to give him the planned full frontal attack. She did not want him just to *see* her beauty. She wanted to *present herself* to him with direct, full and bold deliberation, so he would have absolutely no choice but to admire her. She pulled her dress up over her head with his mild assistance, as he started to appreciate for the first time a hint of what was under her dress. In the relatively dim light from the bed lamp, he could see that her bra was completely full, and there were no pads, since he could see the faint hint of pink nipples straining against the delicate, fancy, partially transparent feminine fabric. She reached behind herself to unhook her bra, and faked another difficulty for several seconds longer than necessary, so Jake turned her around and easily unhooked the four wire hooks that released the pressure around her chest. He briefly took note of the faded bra tag but could see in the limited light only that there were four characters, and the first one was probably a '3.' She turned back toward him and without removing her special vibrant gaze from his, reached down to grasp his manhood. She felt its warmth and the pulsating strain against her grip as it quickly became fully engorged again. Jake hooked a finger under the center of her bra and pulled it slowly away from her body. The cups remained full for almost a second longer than he expected, as her breasts followed her bra away from her rib cage before suddenly giving way to gravity. They shook only briefly into their unrestrained freedom, indicating their weight, but steadied instantly in obedience to her toned muscular body. He had no idea how beautiful they would be, because she kept her curves camouflaged with the relatively tight bra and dress that did not cling to her figure to a provocative extent. He had never seen a more perfectly matched pair on any woman except the ones represented by ancient statues in Italy and Greece, which he believed to be man's imagination of female perfection. Jake was not up to speed yet. He knew she liked him a lot, and she liked what he could do with a piano. He had no idea that she was falling in love with him, just as she had no idea how much he loved her. She had a beautiful face, a body to die for, and a voice from heaven, right here on the sixth floor of a Denver hotel.

She was going to have him tonight, and forever after. She pointed down to her panties. Jake hooked a finger inside the waistband on each side of her perfectly shaped hips, and pulled down slowly on the light blue, laced panties with a small white bow to the left side. They followed easily down her shapely muscular legs, and he let them fall to the floor, as she stepped out of them with as much grace as he would have expected. He felt almost intoxicated as he rose slowly back to a standing posture, deliberately brushing his face against her skin on the way up and inhaled her 'acquired' scent—some kind of body lotion not as strong as perfume in his naïve opinion, but very, very nice! She was 'programming' him to know her by scent, as well as by sight, feel and sound. He was fully erect now, in both senses, and looked only slightly down into her face. Her full frame at five feet nine inches brought her glowing eyes within easy sight. She appeared even more beautiful in the dim light of the single lamp beside the bed six feet behind them and to the left. She felt him pulsing at her pubic bone, lifted herself up on the balls of her feet and expertly parted her legs to grab and hold his member firmly between her thighs next to the hottest part of her uniquely feminine charms. She drew even closer to him watching his mouth, as she tenderly grasped his lower lip with her moist red lips. She easily sucked it into her mouth ever so gently and then carefully eased her tongue between his lips, slowly exploring them, and then continued to massage his lips with hers in soft gentle nibbles.

Steam from the shower was wafting into the bedroom as they simultaneously drew apart in sudden realization of the shower and their desire to clean up. She quickly tied her long hair in a knot over her head, and then led him into the bathroom and stepped over the edge of the bathtub, away from the hot water, as she leaned forward and away from the direct water spray that hit the back wall and turned the temperature knob around to something less than 'HOT.'

"Your turn," she commanded gently. "In the shower!"

She grabbed a washcloth from the rack above the adjacent commode and a bar of soap from the soap dish on the shower wall and lathered it up thoroughly, positioning him between her and the shower spray. Then she began to caress his face and around his ears with it, and worked her way to his neck and strong shoulders and down each arm pressing firmly around the strong piano muscles in his upper forearms that controlled his powerful fingers. She squeezed his wrists and then worked her soapy massage along each individual finger and his thumbs all the way to the ends. Jake shut his eyes in utter pleasure at her attention. She then lathered up the washcloth again and started down his athletic, but not bulging thigh muscles 'accidentally' brushing against his manhood as often as she could within the credibility of 'accidental,' knowing that the effect would be quite pleasurable. She needed to bend down more to reach his calves and ankles and slid her face along his erection, pushing it to one side in the process as it hardened against the wet softness of her cheek. She coaxed one foot off the floor of the tub and massaged it with the soapy washcloth, including each toe, set it back down, and repeated the process with the other foot. She wrung out the washcloth and lathered it up with soap yet again, and knelt down before him and gently lathered up his genitals, thighs and everywhere else she could imagine would produce pleasure as she glanced up at his face to look for signs of her success.

Then she stopped washing him and stood up while rinsing out the washcloth, and announced, "OK, your turn!"

She reached for a fresh washcloth from above the toilet. Jake admired her form with delight as she reached out and then returned to the warmth of the shower. She tried to keep her hair out of the direct spray of the showerhead, but could not avoid the water completely. She was going to teach Jake to know every square centimeter of her body, just as she had started to learn about his. Jake took his cue from her techniques with him, and started with her face, gently caressing her with the warm soapy washcloth, being ever so careful not to get soap in her eyes, nose or mouth. He shifted his attention to her tender neck and across her chest and rubbed from left to right, fascinated by the response of her breasts as they swayed ever so slightly in fluid response to his gentle pressure from side to side. He was mesmerized by their seemingly contradictory weight and softness, and the contrasting hardness of her erect nipples, which he dutifully massaged with the washcloth as well. She groaned ever so softly and pressed his hand against her, encouraging him to continue. He turned her around and worked on her back with his right hand, while holding her to him from the front so he would not push her away with the pressure from his right hand rubbing the washcloth against her back.

Even his large piano hands and wide finger span could not contain all of her, so he grabbed as much of her soft flesh as he needed to steady her against the pressure from his right hand. He scrubbed her back with more pressure than she expected, but she moaned in response to his firm strength expertly massaging every muscle in her back and down her thighs and gently between her legs. He released his handful of her breast and turned her around to face him. She held on to his head with both hands and moaned softly as he continued to rub gently around her most sensitive area. He was playing *her* piano now. He took his cues from her hands on his head, as she continued to rub her fingers through his wet hair, down to his temples, into and around his ears, and back up to the top of his head, and back down to his ears again as he continued his rhythmic massage.

Within a few more minutes, Jake had seen and touched almost every square centimeter of Sasha's exquisite form, and had not noticed a single blemish, scar, body piercing or tattoo of any kind. He had never believed that such a perfect body existed outside novels and little boys' imaginations. He wondered whether another man had seen this beauty before him, but quickly dismissed the thought as irrelevant. He was with her now, and that was all that mattered. He had grown up believing that nobody is perfect, as his mother had always told him.

Well, guess what, Mom!

He wondered what else he thought he knew about women that Sasha would prove to be wrong or inaccurate about her.

She removed her hands from his hair, and Jake took her cue as 'enough.' It was time for them to get out of the shower and dry off.

"Wait a minute," she said, as she lathered up her hands with soap. "I want to make *sure* you are perfectly clean," she said mischievously with a devilish smile.

She knew, of course, that he was already 'perfectly clean,' and so did he. She just wanted to see how long he could withstand her intimate and playful erotic attention. She was mapping his male responses to her natural inclinations into her female psyche, learning what to do and exactly how to do it in order to give him maximum pleasure as she would soon teach him to give her. She began stroking his shaft from the base back up to the head, as she paused there and rotated her hand around the whole head as though she were squeezing oranges. She was playing his 'piano,' watching carefully in anticipation of the 'music' she wanted.

After several minutes of this attention he gasped, and virtually yelled, "NO! Wait! WAIT!"

She simply responded with 'squeezing more orange juice' as she took him beyond the threshold sensitivity of his organ in a way he had never felt before. She adjusted her stimulation when he moaned loudly and reached for the wall for support as his hot seed shot out of him in several long sequential spurts. She could not appreciate the sheer intensity of the feeling she was generating within him, and the fact that she had taken him beyond his normal threshold for the first time in his life, effectively disconnecting his self-control completely. She had done what only *she* could do to him.

Jake was completely 'spent.' His original plan born in the elevator of enjoying seducing her evaporated as he slumped in the tub, and sat limp before her.

"Do you have any idea what you just did?" he asked somewhat disappointed, and yet as kindly as he could.

"Yes, Jake, I know *exactly* what I just did," she said coyly with her special self-confidence, and looked deep into his eyes for just a second before continuing. "I took you to the basement of the Empire State building. And now . . . *we* are going to start at the beginning . . . and take the stairs . . . one step at a time . . . stopping briefly on each floor . . . as we climb back to the top *together* . . . where we will jump off . . . *together*."

Right! He said to himself, as he understood her analogy perfectly, and wondered where he would get the energy.

He just did not understand that she could 'recharge his batteries' with remarkable ease as they had never been 'recharged' before. They toweled each other off playfully, and then Sasha led him out of the bathroom to the end of the bed and gently pushed him back onto it. He took the hint, and moved up with his head on the pillow and stretched his arms out and away from him toward the headboard.

Sasha got on the bed and lay right next to him and said softly into his right ear, "I've been watching you very carefully this evening, Jake. I know how to play your keys. Later, I will teach you how to play mine. I will guide you, and we will fly together. Heaven is on the sixth floor . . . right here with me."

She lingered close to his ear so he would feel her warm breath, as she succumbed to her body's demand for faster, deeper breathing. Then she moved her right hand slowly down his abdomen aiming for the inevitable target. It was still rather soft, of course. She had completed the first movement. It was now time for the second. She started kissing his face, and then his chest, while playing with his hair. She raised her right leg over his abdomen and rubbed her pubic bone against his hip. He felt how wet she was. She tongued his nipples, and then started to move farther south, grazing her soft lips against his skin. She paused to tease his limp penis with her erect nipples, as he stirred with a moan of pleasure with his eyes closed concentrating on what she was doing to him. She continued this light stimulation as she grazed his thighs, and then suddenly he felt gentle wet warmth around his most sensitive area.

CHAPTER 22

Friday, September 7, 2007
Houston, Texas

After he stopped very early in the morning for food and fuel, Rasheed called the next phone number on his list, and got new instructions. He was to take Interstate 610 South around Houston to the Sam Houston Toll Way north, to Clay Road west, to Route 6 south to Groeschke Road west for a few miles, where he would see another U-Haul truck 'broken down' off to the side of the highway, with its engine hood raised. The last-minute change in details was designed to keep the mission obscure to possible prying eyes. He was to call back when he turned west onto Groeschke Road so the next delivery man could raise his engine hood and not allow too much time for some unwanted help to arrive from a 'good Samaritan' in a passing vehicle before Rasheed showed up. The transfer of the contents from the 'disabled' U-Haul to the newly arrived U-Haul truck would very likely not arouse suspicion. It would look like a logical procedure to maintain timely delivery of merchandise temporarily disrupted by 'engine trouble.' Within five minutes, Rasheed pulled up next to the 'disabled' truck with two men in it, sufficiently off the road to allow passing traffic to proceed without difficulty or attracting unwanted attention.

"Do you have merchandise for transfer today?" Rasheed asked the driver through the open window on the other side of the cab.

"I have 1,000 bricks," was the reply, as expected, confirming his identity.

Rasheed then turned his truck around, and drove past the waiting truck and pulled off the road on the same side as the first truck. He slowly backed up to where the two cargo doors were close enough to minimize visibility of their activity in transferring the load to Rasheed's truck. The three men worked quickly and efficiently to transfer the C4 from the first truck to Rasheed's truck, but it still took well over an hour to complete. After the transfer, Rasheed found his way back to Interstate 10 West and proceeded on to Ozona, Texas. The other truck would eventually disappear, as had the first one. This part of the plan also worked without any unexpected disturbances. Rasheed's truck was now loaded slightly above its stated full capacity by weight. Technically, he had 100 pounds more weight in C4 than the U-Haul specifications allowed for that truck. In spite of his meticulous planning, he had underestimated the weight of the C4 somewhat, but he rationalized his minor miscalculation with the satisfaction of anticipating a greater explosive force. He noticed that the handling characteristics of the slightly overloaded truck definitely had changed, and reminded himself that he needed to be all the more careful. He had always known that it would be a long trip, but he was still amazed at the sheer size of just the state of Texas alone and the time it would take him to drive from one end of it to the other. Texas was in fact about eighty-seven percent of the size of Pakistan in total area, and was almost as hot at this time of the year. The maximum north-south and east-west distances from one side of Texas to the other were both significantly greater than the maximum northwest-southeast width of Pakistan, but significantly less than the maximum northeast-southwest length of the country.

His plan included stopping frequently to top off the fuel level, since he knew that the farther west he went in Texas, the less populated the area would be, and the greater the distances would probably be between gas stations. It was important for him to be on time, so he could not risk any damage to the truck or running out of fuel. If he did not show up within a specific period at Wheeler Ridge in California, Khalid had instructions not to wait for him, and either the last leg of the mission to Fresno would have to be abandoned, because he, Rasheed, was unwilling to die, or he would have to drive the final leg to Fresno himself. In that case, he would have to park the truck in

Fresno and leave it, and then take the time to reach a safe distance on foot before detonating the device, assuming no one would discover the contents of the truck before he could do that. After that, he would have to be lucky enough to avoid the police, and still escape into Mexico about 317 miles away without his planned transportation—Khalid's Kawasaki motorcycle. As a last resort, he would simply abandon the truck wherever it was along the planned route, escape into Mexico and detonate the device with a phone call from there. This was assuming no one would be curious enough about the abandoned truck to open it up and possibly disarm the device or call the police during the time it would take him to get to Mexico. A stranded U-Haul truck with a locked cargo area would certainly attract the attention of the state highway patrol or local police, if not unwanted travelers, and he could not allow that to happen. He was also concerned about what he had heard about the Texas Rangers during his planning—that they were some kind of super-police force he definitely did not want to have to deal with. The fewer people he encountered on the trip the better. He was prepared to shoot a police officer or, if circumstances threatened completion of the mission, he was prepared to detonate the C4 with the cell phone if necessary. However, he had not yet armed the device, so this was becoming the most vulnerable part of his trip. There was simply no other way to detonate it, so the need for caution was paramount until he could arm the full load after his next stop. All he had to end his life quickly if necessary until then was the pistol. He vowed not to be captured alive, with or without the C4, with or without the planned explosion, in spite of his intense desire to live to plan more missions to fulfill his destiny. Rasheed's anxiety intensified as he balanced his innate desire to live against his determination not to be arrested, which he could assure only by killing himself. Perfect execution of the plan was absolutely necessary.

Allah requires the success of my plan. I must not fail!

CHAPTER 23

Saturday, September 8, 2007
Denver, Colorado

The early morning sun crept into her room with a soft warm glow around the curtains, but was enough to awaken Jake from the deepest sleep he could ever remember. For an instant, he was clueless about his location, what day it was, or the time. He gently whisked away some hair from his face and suddenly realized it was not his, but Sasha's. He smiled in a flash of joyful recognition. She lay next to him facing away toward the curtain, still completely nude and only partially covered by the king-sized white sheet still covering him. He dared not move because he did not want to awaken her while he reveled in admiring her beauty even in that rarest and most intensely private moment of her sleep, however long or short it might be. He was her imaginary protector, even if it would be for only a few minutes. He lay still and moved only his eyes, starting with a glance at her long strands of disheveled hair, which was simply pure beauty to him. He followed the contour of her flawless skin farther south to the inviting valley of her waist and then up the accentuated small hill where her figure flared out and disappeared under the sheet to the powerful lower torso and thighs that enveloped him in so many different and profoundly delightful ways last night. She stirred slightly and pushed herself closer to him, maintaining her approximation of a fetal position. Jake thought that she might wake up, interrupting his enjoyment of this most precious moment and the greatest sense of peace he had ever known, but he felt her succumb to her deep sleep again. Her beautiful voice was singing in his head while she lay quietly, breathing so close to him. He continued to devour her image and intoxicating scent uninterrupted by the rest of the universe.

Only time was moving, and he savored each passing second, but wished time would stop immediately at his command so he could hold and continue to relish that moment. He watched life itself in the simplest visible form of her slowly rising and falling ribcage, which every few seconds would halt to a perfect stillness before her reflexes demanded another breath. Mother Nature was keeping her alive for him. Although he could not see from his angle, his imagination gave him a perfect recollection of the astoundingly beautiful fleshy mounds cradled in her arms in front of her. His mind was devoid of everything but his intense awareness of Sasha. His heart rate was increasing. She was working her way into every nuance of his body, mind and soul, and he was powerless to stop her, even if he wanted to.

What is this force that draws me to her—so common and natural, yet so powerful and so precious?

Jake was 29 years old. He had his share of girlfriends over the years, and maybe a few more than his share. He thought he had actually been in love once or twice. He knew he had been completely infatuated a few times. He definitely knew he had felt pure unadulterated lust from time to time. Now, however, Jake was in heaven. Jake Lewis, Ph.D., psychologist, researcher, facilitator of lost souls searching for wholeness and meaning, and amateur musician was completely and hopelessly in love, really in love for the first time in his life. His life would eventually change in ways he could not even begin to imagine. Sasha opened her eyes and smiled confidently to herself, still facing away from Jake, but knowing that he was staring at her.

"Why are you staring at me?" she asked softly with a coy curious tone in her voice.

Jake was astounded and quickly jolted back into reality. He did not even know she was awake.

How does she know?

As if reading his mind, she said, "I know you are staring at me because I love you. I can feel your eyes on me. I can feel your soul within me. I can read your body, heart and mind."

Whatever Jake had planned for his life, whatever the future held in store for him, he had to include Sasha. He had absolutely *no choice.* He almost literally had fallen in love with her. He was as completely obedient to that fall as he would have been to the force of gravity had he jumped north from the south rim of the Grand Canyon.

He had never believed in fate, but this was the closest thing to predetermination that he had ever experienced. It was a shock to his prior intellectual and scientific understanding of human behavior and the universe. However frightening the prospects, and however unsure he might have been, he had to take whatever risks and make whatever sacrifices were necessary to have her by his side. He was at another major crossroad in his life. He was absolutely convinced that it would be better to have loved her and lost, if that were to be his fate, than never to have loved her at all.

Where had he heard that before?

One night with her was simply not enough. He needed every second of a lifetime with her. They lay quietly next to each other for another several minutes. Then she turned around slowly to face him and gently kissed his lips. Although intensely aware of the passage of time, they continued to lie there quietly, trying to hold the moment, trying to keep it from slipping away from them, but knowing that they both had commitments for the day, and could not linger.

She broke their intimate silence first with a gentle whisper, "I have to get going."

"I know. So do I," he answered, with reluctant effort.

They arose from the bed and went to the bathroom together and moved around each other silently as necessary, but with occasional deliberate 'accidental' rubbing or playful teasing and bumping against erogenous zones, which seriously challenged their resolve to continue to prepare for the normal part of 'outside' life in clothes and with friends, clients, associates, and new strangers.

Fully dressed, but before they were ready to reenter the normal routine of 'regular' life, she stood before him locking his eyes in her special gaze and draped her arms over his shoulders as he reached around her waist and pulled her to him. She assisted his intention by dropping her arms down and encircling his chest, squeezing him with surprising strength in a manner that maximized the unmistakable pressure of her chest into his as she rotated her pelvis into his. She was a little off the mark, but close enough to feel him becoming engorged against her. She flashed that profoundly effective smile at him, and looked directly into his eyes, inviting his soul to enter hers.

She started humming the melody from what he played on the piano last evening before Eddie closed for the night. Her voice was clear, strong and smooth as pure silk from deep inside her. Even though he knew he could never play *exactly* the same thing again the same way, he recognized the melody completely, which he knew he could reproduce for the most part in another effort. Jake was still mesmerized by her voice as a tear fell from his right eye in response. She was watching him intently, never missed a beat and gently raised herself up to lick the tear from his face with her warm tongue as if to take more of him into her, while still humming from deep inside her body. He moved his hand up and gently held her head against his to feel the softness of her hair on his face. She never stopped humming, so he started to feel her voice as well for a while. Then, she stopped humming.

Again, Jake wanted to suspend time. What he could not know was that she did also. They disengaged simultaneously but reached for each other's hands between them after another few moments and asked the age-old lover's question at precisely the same time.

"When will I see you again?"

They both smiled, and then threw their heads back in uncontrolled laughter. They stopped laughing simultaneously after a few moments and looked deeply into each other's eyes with singular serious recognition of what they had just done. They spoke *as one*, with *one* meaning, and *one* desire to each other about *their future* together. After another haunting moment, Jake spoke first, dissipating the magic up to that point.

"I have a meeting in Colorado Springs today, and I have to be back at the V.A. hospital on Monday. I won't be able to get away until next weekend. I'll make it a point to see you at Eddie's Place on Saturday evening, OK? Will you be back on Saturday? We'll have dinner together!"

She looked down for a moment and said with obvious disappointment, "OK, but I probably won't be able to get back here until Sunday."

She had given herself to him completely and wanted to see him again well before next Sunday, but also recognized that he had a life without her before she met him, and she had long ago made the commitment in Fresno, which she would never break.

"We have to start the trip to California today. We'll spend the night in Las Vegas, and then leave for Fresno on Sunday so we can be rested by Monday for our next performance."

She gathered herself together and looked back up into his eyes with a 'normal' smile, and said, "We'll finish up in Fresno on Friday the fourteenth, so I could start back to Denver the next day and make it back sometime late Sunday. We have that week off before we head back to New York. I want to spend most of that time with you, Jake."

"That will be absolutely *wonderful!* I won't be able to take the whole week off, but I can manage to take several days off during the week, or go home early. You can stay at my place the whole time!"

He lit up with the promise of being with her again at a specific time and place. It was the future defined! It gave his life meaning, purpose, and renewed hope and joy!

"I'll be looking forward to seeing you then! We'll meet at Eddie's on Monday evening at six for dinner. There are nicer places in the city of course, but Eddie's now has a special meaning for me. Is that OK? Then we'll go back to my place, and I'll play for you, or we could take a nice walk, see a movie or do whatever we want. You can stay with me as long as you would like! OH! I almost forgot! I need . . . I mean I would like to have your phone number before you go."

"You were right the first time, Jake . . . You *need* my phone number!"

He smiled in silent agreement as she removed a slip of paper from her purse, and wrote her cell phone number on it very clearly, so there would be no mistake, and handed it to him. He felt like she had just given him the key to heaven.

She said, "That's the key to heaven, Jake, *so don't lose it!*"

He looked at her with absolute astonishment. *She did it again! How does she do that?*

She looked deeply into his eyes with her special knowing smile. It was an eternity for her, but she would honor her commitments to her backup musicians and The Autumn Dream engagement in Fresno, even though she wanted to stay with Jake in Denver. She could not act any more. She broke into tears and put her arms around him again.

"Hold me, Jake! Just . . . hold . . . me . . . tight!"

He did.

"Tighter!"

He did.

She could feel his heart pounding. He could feel her shaking with sobs. Less than fifteen hours ago, they had met each other for the first time by sheer chance, and were drawn into profound intimacy and love by the mysteries of music and the human voice. They had experienced rare and intense joy together, and momentary deep disappointment. Two former strangers on different paths in life, one looking for temporary relief from the work-a-day world and in need of food, the other performing as she had for years in front of another sea of strangers. She elevated quite a few heart rates in her audiences. It always happened that way. He was simply another guy in another crowd with another heart, until she heard his music.

Chance? Was that the nature of love? Of life?

Sasha had a beautiful face and a very eye-catching figure. Any man could see that and respond in a completely natural masculine way, as anyone would expect. To Jake, however, she was uniquely attractive beyond what almost any other man would appreciate. Her voice *electrified* him, whether she was whispering in his ear, or belting out a ballad with all of her considerable musical might before a full audience. She could have been singing 'Three Blind Mice,' 'Jingle Bells,' 'Scarborough Fair,' or 'La Boheme.' It did not matter to Jake, because the quality and sensation of her voice excited him well beyond what everyone else experienced, regardless of the music. Where most men would see her undeniable raw sex appeal, Jake felt the presence of a musical goddess in addition to that. Her voice was her life force and enriched him beyond all of his academic, personal, intellectual and professional understanding. She was vitally and aurally *intoxicating* to him. They were not teenagers wrestling with hormones, identity, 'image' and insecurity. They were both adults experiencing what had to be a uniquely intense integration of two souls including, but also well beyond physical attraction.

Jake remembered that his mother had once told him that 'there is a lid for every pot.' What she apparently had not realized is that one of those 'lid-to-pot' matches would be constructed of pure gold, with the almost unbelievable frictionless precision fit and perfect finish that defies imagination and prompts belief in a super-human power and grand design at the source of it all. He wondered. She wondered. What would the future hold for them?

It's always about the future, isn't it? he thought to himself.

"I have to go," she said as gently as she could, almost whispering.

As they left the room hand in hand, they both looked back at the bed one more time, and then into each other's eyes, etching the memory of a lifetime permanently into their souls.

They could not know that about 773 miles to the south and slightly east of them in a small town in Texas and far removed from the sensuous excitement of love, a younger man from another country had dreams of a different kind of excitement and personal fulfillment.

CHAPTER 24

Saturday, September 8, 2007
Ozona, Texas

Early the next morning, Rasheed checked out of the Hillcrest Motor Inn on Avenue E and drove down the street to a Subway store, where he bought a western egg and cheese sandwich for breakfast, and took it to his truck. After he finished eating in his truck, he started the engine and drove south to turn right on 14th Street, which he followed all the way to the western end of town, where it became Avenue J going north. He turned into the vacant dirt lot at the corner of 14th and J Streets, where he found the expected red Ford Explorer parked at the far perimeter of the lot with a U-Haul trailer hitched to the tow bar.

A man was sitting in the driver's seat of the Explorer. He had been waiting for Rasheed for the last eighteen minutes. Rasheed drove to the far end of the lot and parked near the Explorer. He got out of his truck and cautiously approached the driver's side of the Explorer as the driver saw him in the side-view mirror and opened the door.

Rasheed said, "Do you have cargo to take west?"

The other man responded "Yes. You can take the whole trailer."

Rasheed recognized the expected identifying conversation and replied, "I will take the trailer."

"I could not get C4. My supplier gave me 2,000 bricks of PE4, which is more powerful by about two percent. I thought you would not mind the substitution. I also put eight electrical detonators in the trailer, along with the two telephone receivers and plenty of wire, just as you required. You will also find boxes totaling about 35,000 two-inch box nails for added effect. That was my idea. I felt inspired!"

"It is Allah's wish, my friend. Thank you! I would like to see the merchandise, please."

He went to the rear of the trailer with the other man to raise the cargo door and verify the size of the load. The PE4 was stacked neatly in over five and a half layers of thirty bricks across the width and twelve bricks front to back in the trailer, with the half layer toward the front for the best balance. Boxes of nails were set evenly across the middle of the load in several layers. Rasheed took one of the bricks from the pile and opened the paper cover to see for himself that it was indeed sufficiently similar to the C4 in appearance, texture, color and weight. Then he picked another brick at random and examined it in the same manner, and satisfied himself that it was exactly like the first one.

Rasheed nodded with his approval and said, "You have done well, my friend. We cannot fail in our sacred mission!"

With that exchange, the two men were satisfied that they were secure and free to make the trailer switch. After they looked carefully around the vacant lot one more time, they wasted no time realigning the two vehicles to facilitate the switch of the trailer with minimal effort, allowing for forward vehicle movement and room for the large truck to back up to the U-Haul trailer after they unhitched it from the Explorer. After they unhitched the loaded trailer, they set the tow bar down on a block of wood from Rasheed's truck, keeping it at roughly the same height for easy re-hitching to the truck. The other man then entered the Explorer and drove it out of the way. Rasheed entered his truck and maneuvered it backward as close to the trailer hitch location as he could so the two men could attach the trailer to the back of the truck with minimal effort.

Rasheed turned the engine off, exited the cab and joined the other man at the rear of the truck. The two men lifted the tow bar of the fully loaded trailer with some difficulty, but eventually slipped the end of the tow bar over the truck's ball hitch, let it drop into place as the truck's suspension gave in slightly to the added weight and a loud metallic 'thud' indicated the proper placement of the tow bar. They secured the hitch and reconnected the tail light wires to the truck tail light circuit. Rasheed's part of the mission was approaching completion with the addition of this final load of explosives. Now all he had to do was arm the device and then deliver it to Wheeler Ridge. The other man retrieved eight blasting caps with ample wire length for each from his Explorer and handed them to Rasheed. Rasheed had already had extensive training and practice in northern Pakistan assembling the final detonating mechanism, which Khalid would trigger with a phone call from Rasheed's special cell phone. As before, the two men had minimal final exchanges beyond what was necessary, and the other man returned to his Explorer after the transfer was complete. He started the engine and slowly departed the vacant lot with a final glance at Rasheed. His Explorer would disappear completely in much the same manner as the first and second transfer trucks, leaving no trace of its involvement in the mission.

Rasheed stepped up into the cab of the truck and closed the door, fastened his seatbelt, and started the engine. He drove the fully loaded vehicle and trailer toward the vacant lot exit, and immediately noticed the increased weight. The total load for both the truck and the trailer was now over the total maximum recommended limits for each, but he did not know that. Nevertheless, he maneuvered the truck back onto 14th Street, and drove back toward the entrance ramp to Interstate 10 West.

He had a long drive to his next planned stop near Tucson, Arizona. It would take eleven or more hours to traverse the next roughly 665 miles without stopping, under normal conditions. He had to stop periodically to refuel, rest, and eat, so it would take him much longer than his prior estimate of eleven hours. He became increasingly anxious as he noticed the truck engine and suspension straining under the excessive load. He knew that pushing the truck to and beyond the maximum speed limit would not be wise, not only because of the risk of being stopped by the police, but also because he would thereby risk damaging the truck, and possibly destroy the mission. He had come too far successfully to deviate from his deliberate plan designed to avoid any traffic violations. There would be no turning back. Although his cargo most probably would not explode upon impact with another vehicle, it would surely be discovered, unless he detonated it with the cell phone. He had to make sure he avoided any possibility of a traffic violation, mechanical breakdown or vehicular accident. He recommitted himself to the original plan to detonate the device in Fresno. If he were discovered before he reached Wheeler Ridge, then he would have to detonate the device immediately wherever he was discovered. An explosion in the middle of nowhere was better than no explosion at all, and death was far preferable to arrest, interrogation, incarceration or personal failure. However, he still harbored significant anxiety about the prospect of personal injury in an accident to an extent that did not kill him or allow him to use his cell phone, leaving him perhaps incapacitated, or vulnerable to arrest, interrogation, torture, or worse before he arrived at his destination. His anxiety increased even more as he realized that he had yet to arm the device.

He drove back onto Interstate 10 West, and gradually brought the truck speed up to sixty-five miles per hour and then approached seventy miles per hour, the posted limit around Ozona. He turned the truck radio on and found KYXX FM, broadcasting Chris Knight's special version of Texas country music, which he could scarcely tolerate, but he needed to have some kind of distracting noise in the truck to help keep him alert while crossing the apparently endless mildly rolling expanse of west Texas.

He glanced at his side-view mirror as his heart rate accelerated and he started to panic. Far behind him in the open plains of Texas, he could see a small cluster of bright flashing red and blue lights and the alternating glare of the high-beam headlights that had to be on a Texas Ranger Patrol car in the left lane, obviously traveling faster than he was. He checked his speedometer. He was going sixty-eight miles per hour—under the posted speed limit. The police could not cite him for speeding.

Why are the police chasing after me?

He instinctively decelerated to 60 miles per hour.

No! I cannot act as though I am guilty of something!

He was fully alert, and did not need the radio on any more and turned it off to concentrate on the developing, and possibly threatening situation with the police car. It was gaining on him rapidly, only about a mile behind him. He sat upright in his seat, and grasped the steering wheel firmly, making sure the truck would not weave from side to side. He checked his side-view mirror again. The police car was still approaching rapidly, and then sped past him, apparently not interested in him, but hurrying to some other location. He was *sure* the ranger had looked over at him as he passed the truck. Rasheed exhaled heavily and wiped fresh sweat from his brow as he checked his speedometer one more time. He continued to breathe heavily for more than a minute to calm his racing heart, trying to regain his concentration.

This must be perfect! I cannot make any mistakes!

CHAPTER 25

Saturday, September 8, 2007
Denver, Colorado

The Autumn Dream headed west in their dark blue 'pre-owned' 2001 GMC Savana on Interstate 70 on what would be roughly a 750-mile, thirteen-hour trek through the Rocky Mountains and down into the vast beautiful expanse of the southern Utah desert, all the way into the sparkling metropolis of Las Vegas. They would spend the night there before continuing on the next 400 miles in about seven hours from Las Vegas to Fresno. The Savana was adequate for their traveling comfort and had just enough room for their bulky musical instruments and electronic sound equipment. After they arrived in Las Vegas, they booked a cheap motel and stayed in three separate rooms, as they always did. Sasha stayed in her own room that evening, ignoring the occasionally exciting atmosphere of the big gambling center, while the men took the Savana downtown for a night on the town to look for their minor fortunes at various casinos. She wanted to start saving more money for her future life with Jake and was not about to spend any of it needlessly at a casino. Besides, she was tired, and wanted to be at peak performance in Fresno. She needed her beauty rest. She missed Jake intensely.

Jake had gone back to his condominium for fresh clothes, dressed, and left by nine-thirty for Colorado Springs, where he had an afternoon meeting at the University of Colorado. He would return the next day to relax at home before another busy week. He *wanted* it to be very busy so he could keep his mind thoroughly occupied and hopefully make the week pass more quickly in his eagerness to see Sasha again on Monday, the 17th at Eddie's Place.

CHAPTER 26

Saturday, September 8, 2007
Tucson, Arizona

After a little more than twelve hours of traveling, Rasheed slowed the truck and took Exit 275 North onto South Houghton Road east of Tucson, and drove about a mile north until he found an unpaved and nameless road to the right. He turned there and drove several hundred yards to an area off the road where he was satisfied that no one could observe his activities. The sun was now approaching the mountain peaks to the west, reminding him of the northern Pakistan mountains where he practiced arming various explosive devices. The mountains in Arizona were not quite as majestic as the snow-covered peaks in Pakistan, which comprises the densest array of the world's highest peaks. However, they had their own classic southwestern beauty, and the approaching dusk would still provide enough light for him to accomplish his task just as he had practiced so many times in Pakistan.

He stopped the engine, got out of the cab and opened the cargo door of the trailer and then the truck cargo door. He crawled up onto the load of C4 bricks in the truck and carefully inserted one of the eight prewired blasting caps into each of four C4 bricks at the front and rear top corners of the main truck cargo load. Then he carefully attached those wires to one of the two electrical detonators, which he placed near the rear of the cargo area. He then attached the telephone receiver to the detonator with electrical tape, and attached the output signal wires from the telephone receiver to the electrical detonator, effectively arming the device to explode with the signal from the proper phone call from the special cell phone. Then he got out and walked back to the trailer and pushed the other four detonator caps into the upper four corners of the trailer PE4 load in the same manner, and repeated the same electrical connections to the second electrical detonator and telephone receiver delivered with the trailer, which he placed near the door of the trailer. The entire device was now completely armed. It would translate a specific phone call into a signal to each of the two telephone receivers at the same time, which would send identical signals immediately to each of the two electrical detonating devices, which would in turn simultaneously send the necessary electrical charges to each of the eight blasting caps. Immediately thereafter, the enormous and devastating explosive force of the entire C4/PE4 cargo would expand initially at more than 18,000 miles per hour within microseconds. He then tossed roughly a third of the supply of nails into the trailer over the PE4 bricks and the remaining two thirds into the truck cargo area over the C4 bricks. Then he gathered up all remaining materials, unused wire and tools, and placed them in a plastic bag and put them behind the driver's seat.

Overhead and slightly to the north, a blue United States Air Force F5-G aircraft was flying in from the east for a landing at Davis Monthan Air Force Base near Tucson to the west after a routine training mission. The pilot, Major Thomas R. Henderson had not yet shut down his complex photographic camera arrays. He was still running high-resolution visual and infrared camera recording equipment from his training mission. He would belatedly shut them down just prior to his final approach. The sophisticated cameras recorded high-quality images of Rasheed and his truck and trailer, but no one would learn the significance of that for days. Rasheed looked up, and grimaced at the shrieking roar of the jet engines overhead and slightly to the north as the plane rapidly traversed the distance between him and the air base to the west.

He spent a few moments reviewing everything he had done, and made sure the cargo doors for both the truck and the trailer were properly closed and locked. He looked slowly around the mostly empty Arizona desert landscape for any evidence of unexpected visitors for the next minute. Satisfied that no one had observed him, he decided that everything was ready. In spite of his careful planning and all of his prayers, he could not know what kind of aircraft just flew overhead. He checked the truck and trailer cargo locks one more time and returned to his driver's seat. He took a deep breath, started the engine, and retraced his route back to South Houghton Road and then to Interstate 10 West, toward Tucson. His mission now had a significantly different feel since the device was now actually armed and profoundly deadly. Rasheed was effectively traveling with certain death for the first time in his life, but it was not quite as comforting as he had always imagined it should be.

He found a Red Roof Inn just off Interstate 10 to his right at 3704 East Irvington Road, and exited the highway. He drove to the motel, pulled into the parking lot and looked for enough space to park his truck and trailer near the end of the lot. After parking along the edge of the lot behind the motel, he turned the engine off, and stepped down out of the cab and locked the door. He was mentally exhausted and physically tired from driving. His arms and shoulders had started to ache from the constant tension of practically choking the steering wheel for hours on end.

He entered the motel office and approached the front desk to register for a room. Juanita Morales greeted him cheerfully and typed his personal information into her computer. He offered her five twenty-dollar bills with soiled and dusty hands from arming the device and his contact with the truck out in the desert. She lost her smile immediately and looked carefully into his eyes for just a moment, and felt uneasy. Nevertheless, she finished the transaction quickly and gave him a room key with a completely bland facial expression as her body betrayed a chill in spite of the late summer desert heat. He said nothing, but nodded slightly and left to settle into his room. His heart quickened to the possibility of a rogue phone call detonating the device unexpectedly. There were many more than four billion cell phones in use in the world, and yet he had not taken the precaution of assuring that he was using a unique number.

How could I? It is impossible! But Allah surely will not permit such a coincidence!

This new imagined threat interfered with his sleep, so he needed to pray to manage his ever-increasing anxiety until the device was no longer his personal responsibility at Wheeler Ridge. He had never planned to be a suicide bomber. That job was for others. After all, *someone* had to make the plans and supervise their proper execution according to Allah's will, as well as learn from each experience to perfect future methods and devices.

CHAPTER 27

Sunday, September 9, 2007|
Las Vegas, Nevada

Late the next morning, Sunday, The Autumn Dream started the final 400-mile journey to Fresno on Interstate 15 South from Las Vegas. They drove almost two and a half hours to Barstow California without much conversation. From there they turned onto Route 58 West for the next two and a half hours through the mountains to Bakersfield, where they stopped for fuel and then turned onto Route 99 North to Fresno completely oblivious to the evil role that road would have in their lives. Two hours and twenty minutes later, they took the Fresno Street exit from Route 99 and drove north to the Fulton Mall and turned right into the next one-way alley behind the Holiday Inn Downtown where they had planned to stay until the following Friday. 'Thin face' had been driving the last leg of the trip into the early evening. He turned into the parking garage, pulled into a parking spot and turned the Savana engine off. The five musicians got out and stretched their arms and legs to work the long trip out of their bodies while they walked around near the vehicle. After a few minutes, they locked the van with their instruments in it and walked to the lobby entrance. They were all tired, hungry, and wanted to get a good night's rest before their first performance at eight thirty on Monday evening.

Rasheed awoke very early and not completely rested. He showered and dressed in the same clothes for the final 575-mile leg of his delivery mission from Tucson to Wheeler Ridge. He ate a light breakfast at a nearby convenience store, and purchased enough food to take him through the day. He could not afford to stop for anything other than fuel, because it would increase the risk of discovery in a much more populated area of his route, possibly also with increased risk of inspection by the police. He would have to drive to Pomona, California on Interstate 10, where he would take Interstate 210 to the outskirts of San Fernando, from which he would take Interstate 5 North to Exit 219-A onto Wheeler Ridge Road. If traffic was as heavy as he had learned it could be, it might take him well over eleven hours. He had to be rested and refreshed. He could not afford an automotive accident without detonating the device in what promised to be heavier traffic conditions. Unlike Khalid, Rasheed was unwilling to die in this mission. He had many more missions to plan, develop and execute.

A single rented U-Haul truck with legitimate Florida registration plates, towing a properly licensed U-Haul trailer, each loaded to slightly more than its specified weight limit with two of the most powerful non-atomic explosives known to man was making its sinister meticulously planned journey carefully across almost the entire southern span of the continental United States. Rasheed drove with the same freedom cherished by almost all who have lived here, the freedom earned and preserved by millions of soldiers and more than a few unknown heroes throughout its history, many of whom made the ultimate sacrifice. For all appearances, he was just another person moving household goods west, probably to a new apartment or condominium and a new job. He and his helpers were certainly far less conspicuous in the 'melting pot' of the United States than either Joe or Duke would have been in Pakistan.

The final driver would wait patiently in complete freedom in a truck-stop parking lot for the connection that would lead to the completion of their plan. After Rasheed accomplished his part of the mission, he would leave in complete freedom to disappear into the everyday world of life in southern California only for as long as it would take him to reach the Mexican border. He would then ride across the border in complete anonymity all the way to Mexico City to board a flight back to Pakistan. The abandoned motorcycle at the airport would become an attractive target for someone with less than honorable respect for Mexican law and general human decency. No doubt, someone whose acquaintance with evil paled in comparison to that of Rasheed's imagination would steal the motorcycle and innocently continue his life, probably with smug satisfaction, completely ignorant of its evil role in history.

CHAPTER 28

Monday, September 10, 2007
Cambridge, Massachusetts

Michael Jepson was taking an elective in Philosophy called "The Individual and the Social Order." In addition to his medical school preparation requiring biology, among other subjects, he would eventually take organic chemistry, physical chemistry and physics, but he wanted to explore the humanities as well. He was in a small classroom with eight other students, as the elderly but physically very fit Professor Teodor Michalik arrived at precisely ten o'clock.

"Good morning!" the professor announced brightly in only slightly accented English. "As you know from the title of this course, we are going to study the nature of human beings as individuals and within what passes for social order. Toward that end, each of you will prepare five papers during the semester, each twenty to thirty pages in length, in which you will present and defend your ideas about the nature of the individual, and the individual's relationship with a specified element of the social order as follows: Religion of any kind or the lack of it, government, education at any level, international relations, and any other similar subject that I will have to approve. You will get the most out of this course if you submit your papers on time, because we will be discussing them in this room every week and I will reduce your grade five points for every day your paper is late. During these discussions, you will gain insight into your own ideas from others in the class, and gradually come to a better appreciation of the world we all live in, and hopefully you will have enhanced your ability to think critically as well as to deliver and receive thoughtful and constructive criticism. You will benefit by reading from the assigned books, which we will also discuss in class. I will question you and provoke you in an effort to stimulate your appreciation of the reading assignments as well as our discussions and push your minds to and beyond whatever limits you brought here to Harvard with you, so don't take it personally. OK?"

He knew he had the full attention of nine very smart young people who already knew everything.

So far, so good, he thought to himself.

"Well, then, let's get started. Since this is our first meeting, we will start by introducing ourselves, clockwise around the table, including a brief personal history, please, as a start in understanding ourselves and others as individuals and members of the larger social order."

He checked his class roster before him, and looked up, slightly unsure of which student would respond to the name 'Martin.'

"Martin, please. You start by telling us a little about yourself."

He expected the introductions to enhance familiarity from the start and enrich the course by eliminating many preconceived impressions, thereby allowing everyone in the class to get right into the subject matter on an equal footing without unnecessary anxiety or false impressions, commonly known as 'breaking the ice.'

Almost ten feet across the large rectangular antique wooden table from Professor Michalik sat Martin Joseph Willoughby, III.

"I'm Marty. I'm from Minnesota, where everyone plays hockey, so it's no surprise that I play hockey." He smiled, but felt a little foolish. "I'm going to be a lawyer like my dad, and his dad, but first I have to graduate from college so I can get into law school. If that doesn't work out, then I can always play hockey."

He smiled at his own weak sense of humor, but provoked friendly smiles around the room. He set the tone for the rest of them and looked to his left at a delicate, pretty girl.

"My name is Susan Wong, but everyone calls me Suzy," she said in perfect, unaccented 'American' English, in spite of her dark almond-shaped eyes and long straight jet-black hair that might have prompted anticipation of a far eastern accent from strangers. "I play the cello, and intend to pursue a career in music eventually, but I also want to get a well-rounded education. I'm from Los Angeles, where it never snows, so I'm looking forward to experiencing winter and learning to ski, believe it or not!"

Her smile was simply infectious. She turned to her left, took a deep breath and let it out with measured control as she eagerly anticipated the next introduction. A dashingly handsome young man spoke next. She was watching him with eyes a little too wide open to hide her infatuation.

"My name's Michael Jepson. I come from Linden, which is a small town west of De Moines, Iowa you probably never heard of, played football at my high school and did pretty well in the national debate contest. My parents sold the family farm at auction so they could afford to pay the tuition here, so I owe them, big time. All I can do to honor their sacrifice is to do my best here at Harvard and beyond. I would like to become a physician, hopefully with a well-rounded education and not just science."

To his left was an attractive girl with wavy mid-length dark hair who was almost as tall as Michael. She took note of Suzy's eyes as Michael introduced himself, and felt equally well-positioned sitting on the other side of Michael for the inevitable pursuit of his attention.

"My name's Gaye Getman. My dad is a four-star Army General, so I've been all over the world, but never really stayed in one place more than two years, I think. I have met many people, and speak five languages in addition to English but, as you can guess, the friends I have been able to stay in touch with over the years are all over the place. I want to go into medical research, eventually."

Michael took note of that and concluded that she probably did not have a steady boyfriend. He knew he usually had his pick of the ladies, and he wanted *her*. He glanced appreciatively for just a moment at her ample chest.

This is good, Michael thought to himself. *We have something in common already besides prospects for sex.*

Next was an athletic male specimen if there ever was one. At all of six-feet, four inches tall without an ounce of fat evident, he was a muscular light-skinned African-American with a handsome chiseled face, and penetrating, but kind, intelligent light-colored eyes and closely cropped hair.

"My name's Cecil Jackson. I'm from Jackson, Mississippi, and no, I don't own the town." Chuckles echoed around the room. "Everyone calls me 'CJ,' and I've never been able to stop that, so y'all might as well keep up the tradition. I played sports in high school, and I enjoy photography. My mom raised me and my four sisters by herself, since my dad died unexpectedly of a heart attack when we were all very young. I want to get into politics and make a positive difference somewhere."

Actually, he played whatever sport anyone would chose to name, and lettered in football, baseball, and basketball, but he did not want to admit that to the class, because he thought it would sound disgustingly egotistical. He had already produced two prize-winning photographs that had appeared in galleries across the south. For a moment, the room seemed to fill with silent respect for CJ's progress in life, without his father.

To his left was an uncharacteristically beefy young man with a deep, clear and commanding voice with no accent.

"My name is Samson Shen. Everyone calls me Sam. I was born in Shanghai, but my family moved to New York City before I could ever remember anything about China. My dad is a business broker. He represents businesses all over the world who want to buy or sell other businesses. I would like to enter the business world as well, but I'm not sure I want to be up in the air for half my life like he is. I'll probably do something in the securities industry where I can at least stay in one place."

Everyone chuckled for several moments. CJ imagined how effective Sam could be on the floor of the Chicago Mercantile Exchange, out-muscling others for position and out-yelling them, as well.

A heavy-set teenager with thick 'coke-bottle' glasses spoke up next.

"Hi! I'm Fred Hampton, from Dallas," he said with a proud and smooth friendly drawl, as if everyone knew where Dallas is. "I was the state billiards champion last year for the second straight year, and I play cards—all kinds of card games! I am pretty good with computers, so I expect to major in computer science and then work my way into systems design, and then see what happens. My parents never went to college, but my dad owns a small machine shop, and manages to get along well enough, but I got here on a full scholarship, probably because I aced the college boards."

Frederick M. Hampton was only sixteen years old. He cruised through high school all the way to graduation as valedictorian after having skipped from fifth grade to seventh and then again from eighth to tenth. His teachers felt they were wasting their time with him. He was way beyond the curriculum at most age levels, and frequently drained his teachers' genuine efforts to challenge him. School officials decided that their best compromise was to put him in a higher grade until they thought he was actually working for his grades. He struggled with brainpower far beyond his social maturity, which gave others the impression that he was personally and socially awkward or simply a little strange. He grew up as fast as he could under the circumstances with constant, genuine and loving encouragement from his parents. He had never been physically attractive to the girls, and his razor-sharp intellect intimidated even many adults, including a few of his female teachers. However, it also served as a magnet for certain women recently who admired the power of male intelligence regardless of age or maturity, drawing him into often very uncomfortable social and occasionally intimate personal situations with them.

To his left was Tiffany Louise Brentworth. She spoke with a soft but confident alto voice with a clear, clipped British accent that stirred Michael, as both Gaye and Suzy surreptitiously glanced at him.

"I'm from England, as I suppose you might have guessed," she said playfully while cocking her head to one side and looking directly across the table into Michael's eyes for just an instant.

"My parents are both scientists, and teach at Cambridge University. My dad does consulting work for major corporations when he has the time. I want to be a teacher as well, because I believe education is a necessity for world peace. I am interested in literature, but I also hope to try my best at acting some day. I am here partly because I have always admired the American experience and want to become a part of it, and my dad told me to 'aim high,' so here I am!"

To her left was Max Delaney, from Chicago—South Chicago—where life can be short, but it was certainly tough where it was relatively long. He was over six feet tall, and weighed a solid 200 pounds with battle-tested muscle. Max was a very alert, tough kid with unusual class and brains for where he grew up, and who stayed just to the right of the line throughout his life, encouraged by hard-working parents who did not spare the whip when they felt that he might slip away from them into the unending darkness of South Chicago street life. They wanted the best for their only child, their gift from heaven, and so did Mr. Adam Jones, his math teacher in his junior year in high school. They saw potential in Max, and although his parents had not attended college, they had always told Max he should go to college some day.

"Hi! I'm Max. I'm here because I'm lucky. I heard this was an interesting class, so I signed up. I grew up in Chicago, where it snows a lot and where I learned how to get things done. My junior year math teacher threatened me with extinction if I did not apply to Harvard, and stayed on my butt and in my face through the whole goddamned—Oh! Sorry!—darned application process. I told him my parents did not have that kind of money, because they had all they could do to keep the family laundry business going, and he said I shouldn't worry about that. He said it with a look in his face that I will never forget for as long as I live, and beyond that. He said he would see that I got to Harvard, or die trying. He said it like a man who knew people. He said it as if I would go straight to hell if I did not make Harvard my goal. Believe me when I say you know to take a man like that *very* seriously, particularly in Chicago. Because of him, I began to believe in myself, really believe for the first time in my life, and here I am!"

Everyone in the room, including Professor Michalik was staring at him in rapt attention, admiring what he had accomplished from his unusually challenging background, imagining how they all would individually watch over Max and make sure he would succeed. He was one of *them* now, in spite of his tough life up to this point, and they would *not* let him fail. Professor Michalik knew *exactly* how Max had been admitted to Harvard and who Mr. Adam Jones was.

Professor Michalik would no longer need his roster in class. His students had etched their initial identities firmly into his memory. This was going to be an exciting class indeed, and the world would eventually be a better place because of their talents.

"Well, then! Thank you all for your introductions. I noticed that all of you mentioned your parents. I suspect that is further evidence of what I have believed for a very long time. Our parents are critical to our personal and social development and survival. We learn from them about the world in which we find ourselves. They teach us right from wrong, good from bad, and they generally try to encourage behavior and values that they believe will enhance our success and happiness in the real world as they know it until, of course, we determine that we are smarter than they ever were. Interfering with this learning, however, is the inevitable learning from our environment, the information media, our individual experiences and other people. That is an important point to keep in mind as we progress through this course. Most parents have a strong, sincere and powerful emotional investment in their offspring, regardless of which culture you consider. It includes the most genuine of all forms of love and trust, and usually tends to perpetuate cultural values and beliefs, often in spite of the competing lessons of life outside the home and family. We will return to this topic frequently throughout this course."

"Although I know that you are all young adults, I am obligated to inform you that what you are about to see could be shocking or unsettling, even though I suspect many of you have already seen it. Regardless, we will see it together as a basis for opening our dialogue about the nature of life and the individual. You will understand this presentation as it relates to this course in due time, so try not to prejudge or dismiss it out of hand."

Professor Michalik activated his laptop computer on the table before him from its 'sleep' state, and clicked on the 'start' button on his laptop internet window, which the class could watch on the large flat-screen television monitor on the wall farthest from the table.

'Battle at Kruger' was an amateur video recording on the internet obviously made by a safari tourist at Kruger Park in South Africa. The viewer's vantage point was from a safari vehicle, looking across a small lake or pond, and included voices of apparently German, Scottish and American origin. It started with a scene showing a herd of black water buffalo to the left on the far side of a lake, including a huge horned bull marching to the right away from the herd. The video panned to the right ahead of the bull, revealing a group of lions crouching several hundred feet ahead of the bull in the tall dry grass. The bull kept advancing ahead of the heard, toward the lions. The voices in the safari vehicle began to describe and speculate about what appeared to be an inevitable confrontation between the two animals. The bull approached a little too closely, apparently, as one of the lions charged toward him. The bull turned and started running back toward the herd to the left, as the rest of the closest buffalo including a small calf also turned to run away from the charging lions. The much faster lions snarled and charged after the buffalo and two lions caught the calf on the slope down to the water in their powerful paws and jaws and dragged it farther to the water's edge with the momentum of their pursuit. Three or four other lions joined the brutal catch as the water buffalo disappeared from view. People's voices from the vehicle expressed concern about whether the young buffalo was still alive. The lions all had a firm grip on the calf as it slid partially into the water, but a crocodile suddenly appeared from under the surface of the water and grabbed the calf as well, creating essentially a vicious tug of war against the lions with the calf in between. The voices in the narrative were expressing obvious shock and fear for the calf. The lions won the tug of war after the crocodile thrashed its powerful long tail out of the water and slid back under the surface, while the lions dragged the wounded calf up on the dry grassy mound on the far side of the lake. The scene widened to include a very large herd of water buffalo returning from the left, vastly outnumbering the lions. One bull swatted and kicked a lion, driving it off to the right as he gave chase in an apparent effort to discourage at least that one lion from returning. The herd of buffalo kept milling around with threatening behavior, gathering closer and closer around the besieged calf, still in the firm grip of at least two lions. Suddenly, a bull gored a lion with his horns, and tossed the large cat several yards into the air. After it returned to earth on all fours, several bulls chased it away to the left, keeping that lion at bay and far away from the calf. The scene panned back to the calf, which was now standing on its own, but wobbling slightly toward the protection of the herd of water buffalo, with two lions nearby, but no longer immediately threatening. The buffalo surrounded the lions and chased them away to the right. One of the lions stopped as if to threaten another attack, but the bull chased that lion away and down the far side of the grassy mound and out of sight.

The video ended. The class exhaled in unison as if each one of them had apparently suspended breathing for a while. Suzy was wiping her eyes with a tissue. Tiffany was staring down at her hands on the table.

The young men looked around the table at each other with an implicit expression, *Wow! I wonder what's next!*

Professor Michalik started the discussion.

"The internet gives us incredible reach and facility to access vast amounts of information immediately, and can affect our life experiences in ways unimaginable to your parents' generation and all of human history prior to that. That represents a social force unique throughout human history. It facilitates widespread awareness of the nature of human beings and 'reality' in ways that were inconceivable only twenty years ago. However, we will get into that a little more, later in the course. There are other such scenes of natural life and death encounters available on the internet, but this one will serve as a reference point for some of our purposes in this course. I presented this video clip as an introduction to what I call the 'law of the jungle,' or evidence of pure life and death and the struggle to survive at its most basic level, without a human sense of right or wrong. It is one thing to know intellectually that animals often fight each other for survival, but it is quite another to see visual evidence of exactly how vicious that reality can be. An old saying, 'a picture is worth 1,000 words' comes to mind here. I trust that this video has spoken the equivalent of millions of words, if not billions. We will discuss some of these 'words' and their implications for the human community throughout this course."

Everyone in the class was still recovering from personal visceral reaction and intellectual upheaval, as each of them suddenly realized that Professor Michalik was no 'pushover' and this was not going to be a 'gut' course for an easy grade.

CHAPTER 29

Monday, September 10, 2007
Anchorage, Alaska

Hector Johnson roared to his wife Sheila, "I ordered those damn boots two months ago! That's plenty long enough to make a pair of boots that cost $1,200! I'm gonna call that son of a bitch and get either my boots or my money back!"

Hector was a large truck driver and handy man, all of six feet, six inches tall with about 330 pounds of mostly bone and muscle, but also some minor family fat. Over fifteen years ago, he used his size and weight to advantage as a wrestler in high school, and won several state championships. He had worked on the oil pipeline for a year or so several years ago, and most recently drove a tractor-trailer rig for whoever needed to haul something in Alaska. He never bothered to comb his curly blond hair, because he was accustomed to hats and hoods that made such vanity ridiculous and irrelevant. He knew the roads in good weather and bad, and he knew when to drive and when not to, so his driving record included very few accidents, which are almost an inevitability in the mostly unpredictable winter weather, and earned him a reputation as a reliable driver. He wanted the boots because they were practically a necessity, particularly in the cold Alaska winter when he had outside work.

He picked up his cell phone and dialed the number he had for the boot shop in San Diego. After several seconds, the connection was successful. He heard the usual ringing, and waited for a voice to answer. After fifteen continuous rings, there was still no answer. Hector was not going to let that stop him. Sheila knew enough to stay out of his way.

"Dammit! I'm goin' to San Diego myself as soon as I get off this job! To hell with the phone!"

Hector drove almost everywhere, primarily because he was simply too big to fit comfortably in a typical airplane seat, and he simply refused to pay the higher prices for first class seats. He had done it once as a much younger man, and swore he would never do it again. He hopped in his 2006 Chevy Silverado and transferred his full-bodied determination to the accelerator. The powerful 345 horsepower V-8 engine responded through the transmission to throw several dozen stones from his crude gravel driveway straight back from the double pair of rear tires into his old metal storage shed in the back yard, creating a resounding clatter that echoed briefly throughout the otherwise quiet and serene Alaska landscape. The neighbors who heard the noise knew that Hector was pissed off about something or someone, and at the end of the line, wherever and whenever it was, there would be sheer hell, if not blood to pay!

CHAPTER 30

Monday, September 10, 2007
Denver, Colorado

Almost six years to the day had passed since the attacks upon the World Trade Center, the Pentagon, and another target, probably either the nation's Capitol building or the White House, on September 11, 2001.

Jake turned his computer on and started his web browser Monday afternoon after leaving his office early, completely unaware of many events around the world. He was concentrating only on searching for recording studios in Denver. He found several, but none had a grand piano, which he needed—not wanted, but *needed*. He simply would not play anything smaller than a baby grand for this occasion, and preferably one larger than a six-footer. He wanted a concert grand. Not only that, but it had to have been specifically tuned for him ahead of time to validate the purity of his purpose and to satisfy his perfect pitch. He finally found one at FTM Studios, LLC in Lakewood on the west side of Denver. The internet home page included a picture of a plain, but relatively modern, rectangular one-story building.

This place looks promising, he thought to himself.

He clicked on the tab at the top of the page marked 'Studio A' and immediately discovered that the studio had a nine-foot Steinway concert grand piano! He was bubbling over with joy as he reached for his cell phone without watching what he was doing and started juggling it as though it was a wet bar of soap in his excitement to call for an appointment to see the instrument. He finally grasped the phone firmly enough to dial the number and waited through four rings.

Good! They're not really busy!

"FTM Studios, this is Rocky. How may I help you?" he said in a clear, brisk and welcoming baritone voice.

"Hello, Rocky! My name is Jake Lewis. I'm an amateur pianist. I noticed on your internet site that you have a nine-foot Steinway grand piano in your studio. Do you provide individual amateur recording sessions?"

"We sure do, Mr. Lewis! We sure do, indeed!" he responded pleasantly.

"That's *great!* Can I stop by your studio this afternoon to see your piano, and maybe play a few keys to get a feel for it?"

"Sure thing, Mr. Lewis! I have an open slot 'til about seven forty-five this evening, when I must set up for a session booked for that studio at eight o'clock."

Jake looked at his watch. It was eighteen minutes after two. He could get there by three o'clock and have enough time for a 'touch and feel' session before he had to return to his office to finish up for the day, and still have time for his doctor's appointment.

"Is it OK if I get right over to your place? It'll probably take me 'til three to get there. It would really mean a lot to me if I could do that!"

"No problem, Mr. Lewis. I'll see you around three o'clock!" He was after all operating a business, and welcomed any new interest in his studio.

Jake left his office, and walked briskly to the parking garage and got into his silver Acura TL and headed toward the mountains with almost all green traffic lights and the excitement of his budding plan for his 'homecoming' gift for Sasha. He arrived at FTM Studios just before three o'clock, parked his car in front of the building, got out and walked quickly to the front door. Just as he rang the doorbell, the door swung open and Rocky extended his right hand to greet him with a firm and hospitable handshake.

"Jake Lewis? I'm Rocky Mason. Welcome to FTM Studios! Come on in! Come on in!"

"I'm very pleased to meet you, Rocky!"

The 'M' of FTM Studios closed the door behind Jake and took him immediately through the main room to Studio A.

"Here it is!" he announced, as though he was proudly presenting the original Mona Lisa.

Jake walked slowly into the large recording room to the majestic glistening black instrument highlighted with several narrow spotlights from the ceiling, and surveyed its form from top to bottom and end to end, outside and inside. The glistening surface was in nearly perfect condition, and the entire instrument was obviously polished and very clean. Someone was apparently taking very good care of this very expensive piano, so he assumed that the inner heart of the instrument was well cared for also. Rocky smiled and watched, shifting his eyes from Jake to the piano and back again several times. He saw a true musician about to fall in love with his beautiful Steinway piano. Jake marveled at the instrument. The top was already up and fixed in the wide-open concert position. He looked inside at the array of steel piano wires, each firmly anchored to its special tension on a massive bronze-colored cast iron frame bearing the Steinway name on the right side in raised letters, 'STEINWAY & SONS NEW YORK' along with the 'Model D' designation.

"When was the last time it was tuned?" Jake asked with a hopeful look at Rocky.

"Yesterday morning," Rocky replied.

Jake's heart started beating faster. He could not help himself. He was drawn to the piano in almost the same way he was drawn to Sasha.

"May I?" He looked at Rocky as he gestured with his hands with his fingers waving in succession toward the keyboard.

"Of course! Take your time! I'll have plenty of time before I need to set up for my next session."

"That's great, Rocky! Thank you very much! I'll discover what I need to know in just a few minutes."

Rocky turned to leave Jake in the privacy of his sealed and sound-proof recording room 'A' and entered the adjacent control room filled with what appeared to be hundreds of dials and sliders, with a wide variety of switches, monitors, computer keyboards and two Alesis ADAT HD24 professional-quality digital recorders.

In distinct contrast to the almost imperceptible soft humming of a fan in the control room, Jake was alone in the specially designed acoustical silence of Studio A with the Steinway concert grand piano. He knew that the instrument was a product of a 160-year-old company. He guessed that it would have cost about $150,000 or more, brand new. He gazed into the heart of the instrument, knowing it weighed almost 1,400 pounds, and marveled at the many thousands of man-hours and precise attention to detail by the hundreds of people necessary to assemble its nearly 12,000 parts. The combined pull in the tension of all 230 strings was about thirty tons. He sat on the cushioned bench looking from left to right, admiring the perfectly clean, glossy white and black keys. He reached for the lowest 'A' key and pressed it firmly, but without force. A deep and rich vibration roared from the longest and thickest wire-wound piano wire and the large carefully crafted wood soundboard beneath it. Jake smiled with his lips, with his mind, with his heart, and with his soul. Reaching to his right for the upper keys, he played a rapid chromatic scale for two octaves all the way to the highest 'C' key. The instrument sang obediently with a consistent, crisp, bright and even voice for every individual key all the way up. He struck a series of octaves, fourth and fifth intervals with both hands and varying degrees of force, listening for the perfect consonant harmonic agreement among all of the key sounds as well as consistent attack sensitivity throughout the key and hammer action for each key he struck. A chill raced down his spine. He was very pleased. The instrument was ready for him. He placed both hands over the keyboard not knowing what would happen next and glanced at their reflection in the glossy black raised keyboard cover. He let his mind open and whispered 'Sasha' quietly to himself, as his hands pressed softly into the array of keys before him.

It started. The music poured from his heart, down his arms through his fingers onto the keys through the hammers and out of the strings in progressions of instantaneous creativity and unconventional shifts in harmony leading from one musical phrase to another with a smooth overlapping flow of harmonic consequence and anticipation. In the past, sometimes Jake liked what he heard, and sometimes he thought it was trash. This time it was very pleasing, at least to him. He was lost in his music and continued to play with absolutely no concept of where the music would lead him.

Rocky watched him from the control room. He had heard musicians of all kinds over the years, on all kinds of instruments. He could not recall the last time he had actually seen someone become one with his prize piano, as he was witnessing now. He knew he had gained a new client.

About twelve minutes later, Jake felt the music approaching an end. He returned from wherever he was mentally and emotionally, back to the studio and opened his eyes. His hands stopped with a final harmony, holding the keys down until the sound faded into silence, and then he let them fall to his lap. He sat there, motionless, admiring the instrument for another minute. He did not dare to start again. He had discovered what he needed to know, and wanted to preserve his initial comfort and satisfaction with the instrument for the next time without risking contamination of that pleasure with another effort. He stood up from the bench just as Rocky opened the door from the control room and strode over to the piano.

"Did you write that?" Rocky asked with genuine interest.

Jake had anticipated the question and had already decided to give him the short answer, because he did not want to take longer than necessary for the complete answer. It certainly was not the first time someone had asked that question.

"No, I didn't. It just came to me. It's not written down anywhere."

Rocky was stunned for a moment, although he had heard of improvisation before. However, he had not personally listened to such a piano improvisation in years, and certainly never on this particular instrument.

"How much will it cost me to record?" Jake asked.

"We charge a flat rate of $100 an hour for just the piano," Rocky replied in a friendly business manner, "plus $100 for tuning, if you want that."

Jake did not flinch at all, as he said, "How soon can you fit me into your schedule?"

"I can give you any time after one tomorrow afternoon, Tuesday," Rocky offered.

"How about six o'clock tomorrow evening then, freshly tuned?"

Jake wanted the instrument to be as ready and as pure as its creators intended it to be for his special gift to Sasha.

"No problem! Everything will be ready before you get here. I'll see you then!"

The two men shook hands as Jake thanked him again. He left the studio, and returned to his car and drove back to his office to finish up for the day and get to his appointment for his annual physical. Before he left his office, he noticed a note on his desk in Jenny's handwriting.

'*9/10/07—Richie Barlow called today while you were out. He said he is very worried about something, but he would not say what—wants to talk with you soon.*'

CHAPTER 31

Monday, September 10, 2007
Southern California

Khalid shifted the wheel of his sky blue seven-year-old Toyota van with a dull grey driver's door obviously from another similar Toyota van as he maneuvered the vehicle into the exit lane from Interstate 5 North to Route 99 North, 205 miles north of San Diego, about halfway into his six-hour drive toward Fresno. Fresno is almost at the geographical center of California, with a population of more than 900,000 people. He was going to switch to a larger truck, with a special cargo just off the Wheeler Ridge exit on his way. Behind the van, he was towing his prize possession, a bright green 1999 Kawasaki ZRX1100 motorcycle that he rode throughout southern California for pleasure.

He took the exit from Route 99 onto South Wheeler Ridge Road to a Travel Centers of America truck stop at the intersection of Laval Road and then drove to a relatively deserted area near the back of the large truck parking lot, where he saw the big U-Haul truck and trailer. He continued driving to within about 200 feet of the U-Haul, and parked his van and waited. He remained in his Toyota, rolled down the window in the eighty-six-degree heat and watched the U-Haul truck for several minutes. A man was sitting in the driver's position in the cab. No one got in or out of the vehicle. After about ten minutes, he got out of his van and walked over to the driver's side of the U-Haul truck as his heart started beating faster. He knocked firmly on the door with his knuckles to wake up the driver. He could not see the man's face completely, so he continued with the planned inquiry.

"Excuse me! Are you Rasheed Shirani with a shipment of leather for Fresno?"

Rasheed sat upright in the driver's seat with a start and looked out at Khalid for two seconds, as the two finally recognized each other.

"All the way from Miami," he said with a smile.

The plan would proceed. Khalid would have his 'leather.' Rasheed got out of the truck and went around to the back of the trailer to prepare the hitch for Khalid's van. Khalid would be driving the big truck illegally for the remainder of the journey to Fresno, with the trailer and his van in tow. Since he was not the registered lessee, he could not afford a traffic stop by the police. Khalid walked back to his van, unhitched the small motorcycle trailer, and drove the van back to the truck and parked behind the trailer. The two men secured Khalid's van to a towing bar behind the trailer, connected the tail light wires and tested them, and checked carefully to make sure the hitch to the van was secure.

As they finished securing the hitch, Khalid asked, "Is it ready?"

Rasheed handed him the special cell phone, and said, "Dial 1-468-643-2836 or '1-g-o-t-o-h-e-a-v-e-n' for heaven. After one or two rings, you should not hear anything at all, because by the time the signal goes out, you will already be in heaven with Allah's blessing. There is a loaded pistol under the seat with a box of extra ammunition, just in case you encounter unforeseen difficulties. Allah Akbar!"

Khalid closed the cell phone and put it in his shirt pocket to make sure he did not inadvertently press any buttons from the pressure of putting it in his blue jeans pocket. He climbed up into the cab of the big U-Haul truck and closed the door, as Rasheed walked over to the motorcycle trailer. He checked the fuel level in the gas tank and concluded that he had enough to ride far away from Wheeler Ridge without stopping for more fuel. Then he released the tension ratchets on each of the two dirty heavy canvas straps securing the Kawasaki motorcycle to the small slightly rusted black metal trailer bed and carefully steered it off the trailer. Khalid waited to be sure Rasheed started the bike, and then wistfully watched him ride out of the parking lot with his favorite toy, leaving the small trailer behind, further ratcheting up his commitment to their sacred plan. More than ever, he knew he could not change his mind and turn back now. Rasheed accelerated down the road away from the truck stop as the big engine whined sequentially through the gears into the distance and disappeared into the peaceful silence of the late afternoon central California warmth. Khalid was completely alone, burdened only with the purpose of his life at the threshold of its predetermined ending. He fastened his seatbelt. With a sigh of determination, he started the big truck engine with almost automatic habit, adjusted his mirrors and checked the fuel level. Rasheed had apparently just recently topped off the tank, as the fuel gage indicator was just slightly below 'Full.' He had more than enough fuel for the rest of his life.

Someone would eventually see the abandoned motorcycle trailer in the parking lot and innocently or 'justifiably' take it, not knowing its relatively minor but sinister role in Rasheed's meticulous evil plan. Some unknown trucker or biker, perhaps someone who flunked out of society, or maybe even a businessman who took advantage of dumb luck would pick up a cheap bike trailer, a 'bargain,' and would live with this apparently innocent automotive accessory, 'someone else's trash,' without ever knowing its evil role in history. The conspirators moved in opposite directions. Rasheed proceeded to Interstate 5 South on the motorcycle, and would follow it all the way through Los Angeles, and farther south into Mexico. Khalid drove back onto Route 99 North, toward Fresno. From Tulare north, Route 99 was called 'Pearl Harbor Survivors Memorial Highway.' Somewhere north of McFarland, Route 99 was known as 'Veterans of Foreign Wars Memorial Highway.' Khalid would soil those memorials with his very presence on that road.

He would be in Fresno in about three hours. He would take his time, and stay within the posted speed limits and obey all of the rules of the road. He had come too far to risk detention by the police even for a minor traffic violation. The plan was almost complete. He would not take any chance of ruining its final execution. He checked his running lights and his headlights one more time to make sure they were in proper working order. If the police stopped him even for the most trivial traffic reason, they would most certainly also search a U-Haul truck towing a U-Haul trailer and a van. In that event, he would plead his innocent story of moving all the way across the country to start a new life. If the policeman were to discover the cargo, he would have no choice but to make his one legally permitted phone call, and dial '1-g-o-t-o-h-e-a-v-e-n' on his cell phone. It would not be his ideal plan, but the traffic inconvenience, chaos and damage would be quite severe on a major highway. He wondered with a jolt of fear whether the phone would actually work, but he did not dare to test it. Nevertheless, he had to consider the possibility that he would not survive a traffic stop by a police officer.

He had told his wife he needed to pick up a shipment of special leather in Fresno. He said it was a bargain he could not ignore. The mountains of Sequoia National Park stood gracefully in the slightly hazy distance to the east. The twelve cartons of 'boots' were securely fastened to the bed and walls of the van with ropes and bungee cords. He did not know that the truck and trailer were each loaded beyond their stated weight capacity. Khalid breathed in the warm summer air, much warmer than it was in San Diego when he left, enjoying his final day of freedom from the burden of his wife and her petty earthly needs and desires. He glanced to his right to admire the mountains for the last time, as he continued to count almost obsessively through his memorized checklist.

As one unknown man drove his hidden deadly cargo north on Route 99, life around the world continued with its myriad normal characteristic rhythms and periodicity of small human events as the earth rotated through space around the sun. That single star was only a miniscule spot in the Milky Way, which in turn was hurtling through the outer limits of human imagination and beyond in the infinite universe. From that distant perspective and at any one moment, the entire human life experience on earth could appear to be evident simultaneously in its many stages at different locations all around the globe. Khalid's mission was, from that infinite perspective, so incredibly insignificant, as if the entire earth were on the scale of a single neutron within a universe represented by the size of the sun. The explosive force he would unleash was miniscule compared to the energy elsewhere in Allah's infinite universe. However, Khalid fully believed that his current role was part of Allah's grand plan. It was so obviously self-evident to him. No one other than Rasheed knew where he was going or what he intended to do, and nobody cared. That was, in part, why he knew he would succeed.

While Khalid was driving north on Route 99, a fisherman near Vladivostok once again cast his net in the middle of another day of trying to earn a living from the sea. Just off the California coast, a fishing vessel returned to port for the day with a modest catch in its hold, and a crew anticipating their paychecks. Human life renewed itself as babies were born in Tokyo, Birmingham, Tulsa, Sydney, Montreal, Cairo, Tashkent, Santiago, Ankara, Nairobi, and Boston, and many other cities, towns and villages around the world within just minutes of each other. A heavy rain fell in Beijing as a delivery boy made his way on his bicycle through the busy mid-morning stream of small Chinese cars punctuated every several hundred yards by either a late-model black Mercedes or a black Buick. He was focused only on not being injured, and getting his package to its destination intact and on time. In Lhasa, Tibet, a monk prayed for peace in the depths of the old Potala Palace, high above the city. In Boston, a recidivist, lost young man robbed an unemployed middle-aged man sitting on a park bench of his last twenty dollars, and then clubbed him to instantaneous death with a tire iron. In Mingora, Pakistan, it was early morning where a room full of young boys nodded their heads repeatedly in obedient memorization and acceptance of the madrasa version of 'the only truth.' The town could not afford the best teachers, so they had to settle for those with perhaps some rather extreme ideas. In Prague, a baker awoke in the small apartment above his bakery shop, and started to prepare for another day of baking delicious breads and cakes, almost all of which would be sold by the end of the day, providing untold gastronomic pleasures to his 'regulars' and the occasional tourists. In Moscow, a pretty, young blonde bride gently kissed her sleeping husband in the crisp cool early morning of their first day of official marriage. In Gdansk, a middle-aged woman stuck in an uninspiring and mundane marriage once again yelled at her husband for staying out all night with his friends drinking at a bar, and once again, he ignored her. In Reykjavik, a few mourners bid farewell to a former local politician under a cool grey sky, as they lowered him into his earthly grave, taking untold secrets with him. In Berlin, a handsome young university student arose early to cram for a few hours before taking his chemistry exam, which was only one more hurdle in his conscientious effort to make something admirable and useful of his life. The nightlife was still going strong in Buenos Aires at the

Kika Club on Honduras Street, providing small evidence of humanity's periodic need for fun, self-indulgence and relaxation. It was just starting in Mexico City, where Rasheed was going. In Johannesburg, traders were arising in preparation for another hectic day of trading at the stock exchange, like so many gnats in the world's economic fabric. The moon was shining brightly over Pittsburg as dusk had finally given way to what otherwise would be darkness. But it was bright and noisy in many bars, where dozens of sixty-inch wide flat-screen televisions showed the contest between the Cincinnati Bengals and the Baltimore Ravens on Monday Night Football. To some it was just a game, but to others, it was much of their lives. The setting sun painted the cliffs east of Albuquerque, New Mexico in a beautiful bright orange, in sharp contrast to the darkening blue sky to the east, as the earth continued to rotate on its axis, resulting in regular periods of darkness and light, as it had for hundreds of millions of years. Life continued with new births every few minutes. Death in one form or another marched on as well across the globe. Man's inhumanity and carelessness continued to snuff out life, happiness and hope. Joy appeared from time to time throughout the world's population like the periodic brief glow of each of thousands of fireflies in the vast expanse of a warm summer evening across the flat farmland of northwestern Ohio, and then disappeared for a while before reappearing somewhere else. No one knew or cared about what Khalid was doing, or where Rasheed was going, or what they had so irreversibly set in motion.

A dark heart was now traveling north about one hour driving time south of Fresno, and another headed south for the Mexican border. Khalid had plenty of gas—240 gallons of it, to be exact—in forty-eight individual common red plastic five-gallon containers with yellow spouts sold in just about every hardware store throughout the country, packed in groups of four in each of the twelve cartons labeled 'shoes' in his van. He had spent the last six weeks inconspicuously purchasing the containers at different major chain hardware stores throughout southern California, paying for them with cash. He then filled them with high-octane gasoline one at a time and paid in cash, at different times at various gas stations similarly spread throughout the southern part of the state so no one would notice his unusual accumulation of fuel. He also had plenty of C4 in the U-Haul truck and trailer as well as a load of PE4 in the trailer behind the truck. He checked his side-view mirrors frequently to assure himself that his van was still securely hitched to the trailer and that the trailer was still firmly hitched to the truck.

The engine was straining and the temperature gage needle was moving ever so slowly into the red area under the 'HOT' label on the temperature gage. Khalid knew he had to stop soon and unload all of the gasoline from the van and leave the van behind, or he would never arrive at his destination. Everything had gone almost perfectly until this moment, but he had complete faith that Allah would allow him to complete his mission. He pulled off the road behind a small grove of trees that provided just enough cover from Route 99 traffic to obscure his activities and circled the truck around counterclockwise toward the van behind the trees in a way that put the truck between him and the road, also partially shielding the Toyota van from view from the highway. He stopped the engine, which would allow some degree of cooling while he worked to unload the gasoline from the van and place it in the truck and the trailer on top of the high explosives and the nails. It was not the best solution, but it would have to suffice. He could not take the chance that the truck engine would break down under the strain of the extra weight of the van.

One by one, he lugged eight of the twelve cartons of gasoline from the van to the truck, and started sweating profusely. He worried constantly about someone stopping to see what he was doing. Each of the twelve cartons of gasoline weighed about 130 pounds, which he could handle one at a time, but lifting one after the other twelve times would become extremely exhausting. He did not have the means to lift the cartons and place them all the way toward the front of the cargo area. He had to set each one down near the end of the cargo area, carefully avoiding the detonators, wires and the telephone receiver, and then push it over twice on top of the layers of C4 bricks, possibly risking spilling the gasoline. He was not concerned about a leak ruining the explosive character of the entire cargo, but he was concerned about the definite gasoline odor that would develop, possibly arousing suspicion from a following driver, or possibly by the police. He was sure he had securely tightened all of the caps to the gasoline cans, but relentless doubt nagged at him anyway as he tried to keep up the pace he needed to finish transferring the boxes of gasoline containers and be on his way again. He felt he did not have the time to open all of the boxes to check the container caps to see whether he had screwed them on properly and had not cross-threaded them, and had tightened them securely. He was already wasting time at an unscheduled stop in a relatively exposed area as it was. Every second before completion of his mission was another second of possible discovery. Intense and increasing anxiety would plague him until he brought the truck back up to normal traffic speed on the highway. After he had finished pushing the first eight cartons into the back of the truck, he closed and locked the cargo door, and then turned his attention to the remaining four cartons he had yet to put in the trailer. He was still sweating profusely. The trailer door was lower than the floor of the truck cargo area, so he could lean into the trailer more easily to dump each carton farther toward the front to distribute and balance the load better and not have to place one carton on top of another. It was also easier to avoid the detonators and the telephone receiver.

He did not realize that he was now increasing the load for both the truck and the trailer well beyond their stated recommended weight capacity, but he absolutely could not leave any cargo behind. It was bad enough that he had to abandon his van, but he took the time to remove the license plates and anything else inside the van that he thought would easily contribute to identifying him as the owner, even though he knew his identification would be essentially useless after he arrived at his destination and left earthly life. He was simply obsessed with this interruption of Rasheed's perfect plan and the rather remote possibility that someone could catch up with him and stop him before he arrived at his final destination. He started praying feverishly as he hastened his efforts to get the final carton into the trailer and close the door. He finally locked the door and glanced one more time at his abandoned Toyota van, satisfied that it would not give up its secrets, looked up and down the highway through the trees for any stopped vehicles possibly with people watching him, decided that there were none and stepped back up into the driver's seat of the truck. He started the engine and noticed that the temperature gage indicator was down only slightly from where it had been earlier, but he had to continue. Every minute in the truck was a risk of possible discovery that ate at his resolve like the flame of a burning candle consuming its own source with each passing second.

Automobile drivers, truck drivers and motorcyclists on Route 99 were too busy to notice or care about what was going on behind the small grove of trees just off the east side of the north-bound divided highway. It was none of their business. Stopping to satisfy even the slightest curiosity would delay them too much during another normal day of hectic movement from one place to another in the process of ascending to the perfect earthly life. It was almost six o'clock local time. Khalid pulled out onto the highway, and resumed his drive to Fresno as his heart raced and he continued to breathe heavily from the exertion of moving the cartons of gasoline. The temperature had been rising all the way from San Diego, where it was in the low seventies, to the current eighty-five degrees farther inland. The temperature inside the truck cargo area and trailer was rising as well. The engine and transmission continued to heat up with the strain of the excessive cargo weight.

His destination was the alley behind Casino One, at the corner of Van Ness Avenue and Tulare Street, next to the downtown Holiday Inn. The Fulton Shopping Mall was across the alley behind the hotel and casino. He wanted to approach the greatest concentration of people he could find in an area representative of what he considered to be the 'American heartland' away from the 'trophy' sites, such as San Francisco or Los Angeles.

His target could not be a small farming village because the concentration of people would be minimal and too widely dispersed for maximum death rates and physical damage. He wanted to destroy a place of common popular congregation. He wanted to make a statement. He wanted to attack freedom at a deeper level than just damaging the popular, well-known iconic structural symbols of history and daily life in the United States. He wanted to punish and inject fear, pain and death simultaneously at a level that made the maximum number of people fearful of the very real possibility that *no one* was safe anymore, *anywhere* in the country. Surely Allah would reward him in heaven for punishing the infidels in this most ingenious, efficient and effective manner! After all, he was following the one universal truth of all mankind since the beginning of time that he had learned as a boy many years ago in the northern mountains of Pakistan.

A California Highway Patrol car with flashing red and blue lights on the roof pulled into that same area behind the grove of trees twenty-three minutes later, and stopped about twenty feet behind the abandoned Toyota van. Trooper Vince Robertson got out of his patrol car to investigate. He noticed the fresh tire tracks of what appeared to be another vehicle with double tire mounts near the Toyota resting in its own fresh tire tracks. He also noticed quite a few fresh shoe prints, most likely all from the same shoes, implying recent activity between the van and the other vehicle tire tracks, probably by only one person. He also saw the fresh tracks of relatively narrow tires, probably from a trailer, but not behind the van. By examining the tire tracks thoroughly, he reasoned that the truck was towing a trailer, and possibly also the van behind the trailer. He noticed that all of the tire tracks described a semicircle, which he thought was rather peculiar. He definitely smelled the faint odor of gasoline, which he thought was odd because the Toyota vehicle apparently had been abandoned.

Why would this vehicle still be here if it needed more fuel? Maybe someone was taking fuel from the van and putting it into another vehicle, he thought to himself.

He could not be sure. Someone obviously had removed the registration plates. That person deliberately did not want this vehicle easily identified, apparently recently. He became even more suspicious as he returned to his cruiser and then continued to drive north on Route 99, keeping his flashers on to provoke anxiety or a misstep by someone who might be trying to avoid the police. He looked with even greater interest for anything out of the ordinary along the way. He called in to his dispatcher to report that he was going off his normal patrol schedule to search for an unknown suspicious vehicle, probably a two-axle truck leaking gasoline and perhaps towing a trailer. Given the possibilities of drug trafficking in that part of the country, a vehicle with no plates would be of interest to the FBI, so he made a point of telling his dispatcher that the FBI might want to examine that van, and reported the van's location.

CHAPTER 32

Monday, September 10, 2007
Fresno, California

Sasha slept late and awoke well rested. Since she had most of the day open, she decided to visit her former college roommate, who she knew lived in Fresno. The men unloaded all of their equipment from the van, and moved all of it into the club, where Sasha caught up with them.

"I'm going to take the van for a while to drive out to the suburbs to visit with an old college girlfriend I haven't seen for years. I will be back in plenty of time for the show."

'Thin-face' said, "Please drive carefully, Sasha and don't get lost! We need you back in one piece!"

"I *will* drive carefully and I *won't* get lost! I have the GPS! You know that," she said with a reassuring smile, thinking briefly of Jake.

She returned to the van in the Holiday Inn parking garage, got behind the wheel and entered the address she had in her cell phone contact list for her former college roommate at Smith College into her GPS. Tanya Theisman, now Tanya Wilkinson, lived on North John Albert Street. Sasha dialed Tanya's phone number on her cell phone, and simultaneously cursed her failure to get Jake's cell phone number after their torrid love session at the hotel in Denver.

Tanya picked up after three rings. "Hello?"

"Hi, Tanya! This is Sasha!"

"Sasha! My gosh, it's great to hear from you!"

"I'm here in Fresno for a performance at Club One over on Van Ness this evening, but I have some open time during the day, and I wanted to give you a call to see whether you were home before I drive all the way out there. You're still at the same place, right?"

"Yes! I'll be here all day, and I would love to see you! Come on out, and bring your bathing suit!"

"I don't have a bathing suit with me, Tanya."

"So? That never stopped you before, did it?"

Sasha giggled and admitted that it had never stopped her before.

"According to my GPS, I should be at your place in about twenty minutes or so!"

"Great! I'm looking forward to seeing you! It's been too long! I'm by myself right now, but Randy and the twins should be back from soccer practice while you're here. I'd really like you to meet them!"

"I'm on my way! See ya!"

It was almost two o'clock in the afternoon by the time Sasha drove the Savana in front of a palatial home on North John Albert Street as Tanya raced out from the front door. Sasha noticed that she still had her basic college figure, only slightly altered by the birth of twin girls and about eight years since graduation. Her long blonde hair had given way to a shorter, more manageable style, but still attracted men. She was wearing light tan Bermuda shorts, sandals and a white blouse tied around her midriff. Sasha was wearing equally casual attire with a tucked in light blue blouse and pale yellow shorts, a little shorter than Tanya's, with white sandals. The two embraced as they had so many times at Smith, sharing the many secrets, triumphs and tragedies of female collegiate life.

They parted and held each other at arm's length, as Tanya gushed, "Let me look at you! You are just as gorgeous as you were in college! Let's go into the house and talk! It's been only eight years since we last saw each other!" She led Sasha into the kitchen, where she took a prepared plate of various cheeses out of the refrigerator, grabbed a basket full of a variety of crackers from the spacious cream-colored granite counter and asked, "What would you like to drink? I have just about everything—juice, milk, water, Coke, Pepsi, Orange Crush, Fresca, or I can pour some wine."

I can see that you have just about everything, Tanya. "I think I had better stay with the soda right now, Tanya, because I have a show tonight. I'll have a Fresca, please."

"Tell me about your life, Sasha!" Tanya said in a friendly command as she handed Sasha a can of Fresca from the built-in refrigerator with a door that blended perfectly into the entire custom-built stained maple wood kitchen décor.

"Well, after college, I bounced around for a few years, trying to figure out what I wanted to do with my singing, but didn't find anything promising until about three summers ago in New York, where I was in one of those 'talent' night clubs. A guy came up to me after the show and asked whether I would like to be part of his group. I had heard him earlier in the evening on a soprano sax, and really liked his music and style, so I thought 'why not?' As it turned out, we clicked on a musical level, but nothing more than that. He introduced me to the rest of his group, three other guys, one on guitar, one on keyboard and one on drums. As coincidence would have it, they had a girl singer at one time, but for whatever reason, she apparently decided to quit several weeks before I met them. We called ourselves 'The Autumn Dream' and started doing the Manhattan scene, and gradually got some recognition. It was obvious they needed someone with a business mind, so I gradually took over that job, and basically managed the group. They were glad to let me do that, because we all started to earn more money shortly after that point."

"That's obviously because of your superior voice, Sasha, and not necessarily your business acumen! You always sang beautifully in college. I'm so happy that you have chosen to share your voice this way!"

"What about you, Tanya?"

Sasha took a cracker from the plate, and placed a sliver of cheese on it and made it disappear in two bites.

"Well, after college, I also bounced around for a couple of years, doing unrewarding corporate work, but then met 'Mr. Right' on one of those infamous stupid double dates with my roommate in Boston. As it turned out, he was a Harvard Law student. We fell hopelessly in love, married, and eventually moved out here, where he got a really nice job in a large law firm. We have two beautiful little five-year-old twin girls, Marsha and Melissa."

She reached for a set of photographs from the table next to the sofa they were sitting on.

"These are my two little angles!"

"Oh! *They're soooo adorable!* Is that your husband?" Sasha motioned to another photograph on the table.

"Yup! He's the responsible party of the first part!"

"He's cute!" she lied politely.

"Hey! Let's hit the pool, Sasha!"

"I told you I don't have a bathing suit with me, Tanya."

"And I said it doesn't matter! Let's go take a dip before Randy gets back with the girls!"

"Oh, all right!" Sasha admitted, almost willingly.

The two women pranced out through the open sliding glass doors to the pool in the fenced-in back yard and stripped down to their panties and bras, and jumped into the pool with the renewed glee of their college days.

After coming up for air, Tanya faced her friend and gasped, "My god, Sasha! Your boobs! Jesus, Sasha, you didn't, did you? Tell me you didn't have surgery!"

Sasha threw back her head in uncontrollable laughter. "You can't tell can you?" she said, teasing her friend.

"Please tell me!"

"I'll show you!"

Sasha grabbed the front of her bra and pulled it up, letting her gorgeous breasts fall free, floating just near the water's surface in contrast to sinking like implants would. Tanya gaped at them with envy—pink nipples, no stretch marks, no scars, no cuts, no tattoos, no blemishes and no red spots—no surgery! She grabbed one playfully with each hand as Sasha yelped in surprise. She felt nothing artificial, just pure natural premium all-American mams! Sasha pulled her bra back down and stuffed her treasures back into her bra cups and wiggled them into comfortable form and symmetry.

"You weren't that big eight years ago, Sasha . . . were you?"

"What can I say? I wasn't through growing up then!" she responded, trying to deflect the conversation to something else.

They splashed each other playfully, as Tanya asked directly, "Do you have anything going with any of the guys in your group?"

Sasha gave her an especially generous splash of water with both hands and said firmly, "NO! I Don't!"

"Is there *anyone* special in your life right now?"

"Actually, yes! I have met the man I will marry," she announced with calm confidence.

Tanya shrieked, and then caught herself, clasped her left hand over her mouth and looked around to see whether anyone had heard her, although she was in her own generous and private back yard lined with tall fir trees and a substantial fence.

"Tell me all about it!" She insisted almost hoarsely.

"Well, last Friday, we were still performing at Eddie's Place in Denver, which is an entertainment dinner bar. There was this cute and handsome guy sitting . . ."

Tanya interrupted with unbridled maternal urgency, "*Wait* a minute! Hold the phone! Wait *just a minute!* You met the guy *three days* ago? And you have already decided you are going to *marry* him? Sasha, have you *lost* your *mind?*"

"I have never been more sane! He was sitting near the stage. He was not like all the others in the room. I could tell that from the stage, and I really wanted to meet him. It was quite a strange situation, almost compelling. So, after the show, I went down to his table and introduced myself!"

"You *didn't!*"

"Indeed I did! We talked. Turned out he is a psychologist at the Denver V.A. Hospital, and an amateur musician. I coaxed him to play for me on a rather nice piano hidden backstage. I liked him a lot up to that point. After he played for me, I knew it was going to get serious—*very* serious."

"Sasha . . . Let me get this straight! You fell in love with a *total stranger* in just *one night?* Is that what you're telling me?"

"Yes! How long *should* it take?" Sasha parried with her special confidence.

"Oh, I don't know. I guess I always thought true love took *time* to develop."

"Well, I don't believe it does, necessarily. When it happens, it happens, with or without intention, preparation or planning. I fell in love with him, and then I asked him to walk me to my hotel room, where I . . . well . . . I seduced him. It was then that I knew it had to happen, and that it was real! It was the most *natural* feeling I could ever have imagined!"

"You're putting me on, right? You're just trying to wind me up and then bust me!"

"No, I'm not! Remember the time we got a willing guy from Yale at a mixer at Smith to go up to the attic of our sorority house in Northampton, where we undressed him and teased the holy living daylights out of him for over two hours?"

"Oh *my god*, Sasha! You *didn't!*" she screamed with unabashed lascivious glee.

"I did to him by myself what the two of us did in two hours to that guy in college, plus variations that I will never reveal to *anyone,* for almost the entire night!"

Tanya stood stone still with her mouth open, staring at her former college roommate with friendly envy and amazement, slowly beginning to realize that Sasha was not making this up.

"You're really *dead serious*, aren't you," she said seriously and not as a question, as she studied Sasha's face with a suddenly much more sober attitude.

"Yes . . . I am."

After several seconds of complete silence, she said, "When are you going to see him again?"

"After we finish here, I'm going back to Denver to meet him for dinner at six o'clock next Monday evening at Eddie's Place, where we first met. After that, I'm going back to his condominium to listen to him play again, and probably stay with him for several days before I return to Manhattan. I have that week open, and I intend to make the most of it with him."

"Sasha, *listen* to me," she said firmly in her newly-acquired maternal tone of wisdom. "How in the *world* are you going to make this work if you are traveling all over the country singing, and he is working in Denver? Explain that to me!"

"I'll quit traveling with the group. I can live without the guys in the band, but I can't live without Jake. I have become comfortable with my decision. I know I can't have everything in life, and love is not a guarantee. I have had a relatively short, but wonderful professional singing career and I honestly love it, but now I have an opportunity to experience true love for as long as it lasts, hopefully forever. That opportunity may never come again if I stay with the group. I can always sing. I can't always find love. I'm not getting any younger, and my biological clock is ticking. I have some money coming from my mother some day, so I'm not worried about having to work forever for long-term security."

Tanya listened with concern but without a viable objection and punctuated the silence with a simple "Oh, I see."

"Well . . ." Sasha said with a hint that she should start back to her hotel, and then made it clearer, "I should probably get back to the hotel and get a shower and get ready to sing."

"But you haven't met Randy!" she said as she picked up a large bright orange beach towel from a plastic lounge chair nearby and handed it to Sasha.

"She has now," he said, suddenly walking out onto the patio after sending his two little girls upstairs to take their dirty soccer uniforms off and take their baths.

Sasha casually wrapped the towel around herself without any indication of embarrassment or juvenile urgency to hide herself. Obviously, he had already seen her beautiful figure soaked to the skin through her underwear, and she was not about to apologize for her beauty and sex appeal by freaking out just because her best college friend's husband happened to stumble into the scene. He saw what he saw—end of story. *Let him suffer*, she thought to herself.

The two women walked past him into the house, as Tanya lagged slightly behind Sasha and gave him a silent, but persuasive elbow to the ribs on the way. Sasha entered the small dressing room just off the living room, dried off and put her dry clothes on without her wet underwear. She would change into other clothes later at the Holiday Inn for her performance anyway. She came back out into the living room where Tanya conducted a more formal introduction to her re-chastised husband.

"Randy, this is Sasha, my best friend from college. She's a singer with a group playing at Club One on Van Ness for a few nights. We should go over there and hear her while she's still in town."

Randy was still reeling from the eye-full of amazing feminine beauty that invaded his mind just a few minutes ago, but said ironically, "It's indeed a pleasure to meet you, Sasha."

Tanya turned directly toward him with an unmistakable fiery glare that said, '*that did not come out right!*'

This exchange was not lost on Sasha, who managed to keep an indifferent composure with only the smallest hint of a smile beginning at the corners of her mouth.

Then Tanya turned back to Sasha and said, "Hey, Sasha! Let me show you around the area, if you have the time! Randy and the girls will be fine until we get back!"

Sasha looked at her watch, hesitated slightly and rationalized staying a little longer, and said, "OK. Sure, but I can't lose track of time!"

The two women went to the garage and got in Tanya's bright red 2003 Porsche 911 convertible and left for more 'girl talk' and a tour of the Fresno area, secure in their well-ordered lives and completely unaware of how the city would change before the end of the day.

While they were riding around Fresno, Khalid's U-Haul truck was approaching the town of McFarland on Route 99 North like a vicious virus traveling through a vein toward the heart. It was just another vehicle in busy traffic. Anyone driving past it would pay no particular attention. It was none of anyone else's business. Seeing the truck was an unremarkable event—just another tiny fiber almost unnoticeable in the vast fabric of busy California life.

By the time they got back and walked into the house, it was twenty-five minutes after seven o'clock.

Sasha said, "I really enjoyed seeing you again, Tanya, but I really should get back to the club. I'm sorry to have to rush off like this, but I do have a commitment tonight."

"It was great to see you again, Sasha!" Tanya called after her as Sasha walked briskly down the driveway to the van parked on the street.

By that time, Randy had reappeared at the front door behind his wife, waved to Sasha, and wisely kept his mouth shut, as he silently studied Sasha's retreating beautiful form without underwear. It was almost seven thirty that evening when Sasha started the Savana engine and drove away on North John Albert Street, and headed back toward the downtown Holiday Inn.

CHAPTER 33

Monday, September 10, 2007
Denver, Colorado

At three thirty in the afternoon, Jake was catching up on reading some professional journals when he heard Richie Barlow outside his office, talking to Jenny in obvious agitation. He was seeing Richie on an outpatient basis, and he did not have an appointment today, so he knew Richie was having another episode of intense anxiety. Jake got up and went out to Jenny's office to calm him down. He took a cup from the cup dispenser next to the water cooler in Jenny's office, filled it with water and handed it to Richie to give him something else to concentrate on as soon as possible.

"Thanks, Doc!"

"Hello Richie. Would you like to come in and talk?"

"Yeah, Doc, I'm really upset. I think somethin' awful's gonna happen, but I don't know what. It's like Afghanistan all over again."

They entered Jake's office, and Jake closed the door behind him, as Richie sat upright on the front edge of a black cushioned leather chair while rapidly bouncing his legs with the toe ends of his shoes on the floor.

"When was the last time you took your medication, Richie?" Jake said calmly, as he sat across from Richie on another identical chair, leaning forward with his elbows on his knees.

"I always take it in the morning with my breakfast, Doc. I never forget. Never!"

"OK, Richie. Now tell me what you can about this feeling you are having."

"Well, Doc, it's like I said before. I get this feelin' every once in a while that somethin' really, really bad is gonna happen, but I don't know what it is or when it's gonna happen. I don't know whether I'm gonna be involved or not, and sometimes I don't know who else is involved. I jus' don't know! It's really uncomfortable. If I'd said somethin' earlier to my buddies when I was in Afghanistan, maybe they wouldn't have been hurt, ya know? And now I feel the same way I felt then, but I jus' don't know who to tell, so I'm tellin' you. I know I'm gonna feel really awful when it happens, though, whatever it is, I jus' know it! I'm really, *really* upset, Doc, and I don't know what to do about it!"

"Richie, I want you to think about something. Everyone on this planet has feelings of impending danger at one point or another during his life. Many times, those feelings are false alarms, but sometimes they actually are unusually prescient signs of actual danger. Sometimes we call such feelings intuition or subconscious warnings or premonitions. Apparently, you have experienced more than your share of such real danger warnings, but you were also exposed to unusual potential for danger just by virtue of having been in combat zones as part of dangerous military missions. Most people don't ever have that experience. However, that does not mean that you are actually responsible for every nuance of subsequent reality. You are not in a war zone now, Richie. You are home and safe. I want you to think about where you are right now. I want you to think about everything you see and hear, and evaluate it in terms of whether it really and honestly presents a danger to you or the people around you. I don't care whether you are looking at a traffic light, or a bedpost. I want you to look at it carefully and evaluate what you see, and honestly determine whether it represents a threat to you or someone around you. I want you to get into the habit of experiencing calmness and safety, instead of apprehension and dread. If you do not make an effort to change your behavior, then I strongly suspect that these feelings will continue. Talk to yourself if you have to. You have to take important responsibility for controlling your reactions and understanding these feelings. I cannot do it for you. I can help you do it, though, if you are willing to work at it and let me help you. I also strongly doubt that these feelings will vanish all by themselves without your sincere efforts to stop them. Next week, we will talk about all of the experiences you have between now and then, so I want you to remember all of them. Write them down if you think you will not remember them. Keep a diary. Will you do that, Richie?"

After a few seconds, his legs stopped vibrating, and then he said, "Yeah, Doc. I'll do that."

"There is something else I want you to think about. You were no more responsible for the injuries to your buddies in Afghanistan than they were. You were all *equally* exposed to the *same* danger. That is part of combat."

"OK, Doc. I think I get your point. I'll see you nex' week!"

He sat still for several moments, apparently thinking about something, and then stood up and looked briefly into Jake's eyes. He thought he saw sadness for just a moment. Then he turned and left the office a little more relaxed than when he entered it, but not much more.

Although Jake was finishing up at the V.A. Hospital, he was far from finished for the day. He had scheduled an evening appointment for his annual physical. He cleared his desk, turned off his computer and replaced several case files in the large tan metal filing cabinet behind him. He left his office, and walked outside and down to the College Inn on East 8th Avenue for a bite to eat before going over to the doctor's office at Aspenwood Internal Medicine one block over on 9th Avenue. He had already left urine and blood samples during a brief office visit early in the morning the week before, so he indulged in another well-done hamburger without concern about distorting his blood tests.

It was seven minutes before eight when Jake was lying on an examining table in Doctor George Stevenson's office having his annual physical exam in a rare evening appointment. The EKG continued as Doctor Stevenson watched the rhythmic trace of the electron beam across the monitor while a sensitive stylus was tracing out the same pattern on a continuous flow of paper coming out of the machine from a slot in the lower front side.

CHAPTER 34

Monday, September 10, 2007
Fresno, California

Meanwhile, over 830 miles to the west, Patrolman Vince Robertson continued north on Route 99 through Fresno without seeing anything to arouse his suspicion further. Patrol Officer Larry Manchester picked up the radio traffic about a suspicious truck, possibly leaking gasoline. He was just leaving Fresno southbound on Route 99 and radioed his location, as he turned on his flashers and crossed over the median strip to head north back into Fresno.

North of the city limit, Robertson felt a compelling intuitive urge to turn back into Fresno. At seven fifty-five, Manchester was already driving north on Fresno Street, with his flashers still on, still looking, as Robertson approached the same location, and saw Manchester's cruiser with the lights flashing almost six blocks ahead of him. He continued to follow his intuition, but with a heightened sense of apprehension and increasing anxiety. As Manchester passed by the Fulton Mall, he looked to his right and saw the big U-Haul truck and trailer slowing with the brake lights on almost a block away. It looked out of place, but his intuition was unsatisfied. He jammed on his brakes, quickly looked in his rear-view mirror and backed up several yards to a point where he could more readily negotiate the sharp right turn into the alley.

At seven fifty-five, Khalid slowed the truck to a halt between the Holiday Inn and Club One in the alley behind both buildings, shifted the transmission into park, but kept the engine running and mumbled a prayer to Allah for about ten seconds, while sweating profusely. He saw the flashing red and blue lights on Manchester's cruiser in his side-view mirror. A few pedestrians walking across the alley from the Fulton Mall toward Van Ness looked down the alley at the unusual combination of the U-Haul truck with a trailer in tow parked carelessly in the middle of the alley, but saw nothing out of the ordinary beyond that until the police patrol car appeared. It might have been just a minor traffic violation.

By seven fifty-five, Sasha was heading northeast on Fresno Street, a block northwest of the casino at Van Ness and Tulare Streets. She was planning to turn right just after she saw the police car with its flashers on about fifty yards ahead of her turn into the same alley now blocked near the far end closer to Tulare Street by the big U-Haul truck and attached trailer. She could 'read' Jake with uncanny accuracy almost at will, but she did not have Richie Barlow's almost pathological but remarkable sense of premonition. She was simply innocent. She was in danger.

Khalid reached into his shirt pocket for the special cell phone. His clothes were soaked with sweat and his heart was racing. A middle-aged businessman on his way to the mall was walking toward the truck and away from Tulare Street. He happened to look through the windshield, and saw the driver making a telephone call and felt an uncomfortable, unspecified intuitive sense of apprehension. His brain stalled in a futile effort to understand, to find equilibrium. The businessman continued to walk toward the walkway to the mall and past the big truck, which was still radiating extremely unusual heat from the long and mechanically strenuous journey that put enormous stress on the engine and transmission. He glanced at the truck, as he smelled gasoline. He thought it was odd that a big U-haul truck towing a trailer was parked in this particular alley. He just could not put it all together while he was 'multitasking' with plans for his business schedule for the next two days. He saw Manchester's police car with its flashers on slowly approaching behind the truck. He still did not perceive anything around him as a threat. It appeared to be just another minor traffic violation. None of the hundreds of pedestrians within the five-block area, guests of the Holiday Inn, or patrons of Casino One and the many shops in the Fulton Mall understood that danger was rapidly mounting near them.

Their worlds were normal. They continued their mundane efforts to find entertainment or some form of excitement to make their lives more interesting and rewarding. They were oblivious to the presence of evil.

Every muscle in Khalid's body contracted to the point of pain as he started to press the number '1' button on his cell phone. In spite of his life-long indoctrination, he still had a residual innate desire to live, but that desire was not strong enough to overcome his constant early exposure to extremist convictions with no counterbalancing education or breadth of knowledge of any consequence. He finished pressing the buttons for 'g-o-t-o.' It was all he could do to aim his fingers toward each key on the small phone accurately before pressing it, because he knew any further delay would bring him face to face with the police officer in the patrol car behind his truck, and possible failure if the officer confiscated his phone or somehow restrained him. He still had just enough time to finish the detonation sequence if he did not make any mistakes with the keypad. He just realized with a sudden jolt of fear that he had no contingency plan. He continued carefully pressing the series of buttons on his phone, 'h-e-a-v-e.' His inventory of life choices was rapidly approaching zero, as he assumed that the device would actually work, and followed Rasheed's instructions to the letter. The police officer was at his window. Rasheed turned toward him for just a second, and then concentrated on his phone again. He inhaled rapidly as he pressed the final 'n,' quickly pressed 'send' and again looked directly into the officer's face with an expression of defiance, and then final resignation. He had just crossed over the last line of his life. The laws of physics now completely controlled his fate. The officer knocked on the window, saying something that Khalid could not hear completely. He drew his Smith and Wesson 4006 pistol and aimed it directly at Khalid's head, again saying something to Khalid. Khalid turned away from the officer and defiantly stared straight ahead at . . . nothing. The officer was watching him carefully, and then suddenly sensed immediate and shocking danger. From sheer habit, Khalid raised the cell phone to his right ear to listen to the final sounds of his life—one ring . . . another ring . . . another ring . . . then a click. His eyes, mouth and nostrils widened to their limits as he inhaled involuntarily and his heart raced way beyond its prior maximum fear response in a final moment of intense doubt. Nothing happened. Again, Khalid inhaled deeply and involuntarily . . . for the last time. Then all his thoughts ceased along with his final image on this earth—a small telephone in his hands. For just that one final instant, he existed with absolutely no control over anything. His final sensation was simultaneous intense heat and enormous concussion.

At precisely seven fifty-six, Khalid's earthly life ended but the evil that he embodied continued. Most of his body simply disappeared into billions of disassociated molecules in the intense heat, leaving only a few small and very widely scattered charred bone fragments interspersed among those of his innocent victims from the enormous explosion. There was nothing left of him to enjoy the ingrained lifelong promise of virgins in heaven.

Patrol Officer Robertson was still almost four blocks from the mall when he saw the explosion that all but vaporized Patrolman Manchester and demolished his patrol car beyond recognition. Robertson suffered only relatively slight injuries, as the blast rocked his cruiser, slammed him against the side window, bruised his left arm and shoulder and dulled his hearing, but he would live to help sort through the carnage, looking for survivors. The events of this day would remain with him forever. His ears still hurt, but he was alive.

He called out on an open radio frequency in plain English, with no codes, "Emergency! Emergency! Large explosion behind the Downtown Holiday Inn! Repeat, Emergency! Large explosion behind the Downtown Holiday Inn!"

Although still somewhat shaken by the blast, he drove another few blocks toward the rising smoke, then left his cruiser and raced to the scene of the greatest devastation he had ever seen to investigate and render help. He was a professional. He was also *very* angry.

At precisely seven fifty-six, several hundred people in the casino, in the hotel, along the mall and on the nearby sidewalks and in vehicles traveling in either direction on Van Ness Avenue on the other side of the buildings and on Tulare Street and Fresno Street perished instantly in the intense heat and devastating shock wave. Many more suffered injuries within seconds from the enormous concussion and flying debris, including significant amounts of glass, steel, concrete, automotive parts, 35,000 nails and burning gasoline propelled outward at initial speeds greater than 18,000 miles per hour, channeled to some extent northwest and southeast between the buildings on either side of the alley, but everywhere else as well. The channeled northwest concussion knocked The Autumn Dream's Savana off its wheels and rolled it several times into the parking lot behind the Bank of the West across Fresno Street from the Holiday Inn, tossing Sasha around inside the van as if she were merely a rag doll.

At precisely seven fifty-six, FBI field agent J. Davis Harrington, was traveling in coach class from Seattle to Los Angeles International Airport, and was currently just west of Fresno. He looked out the window as he always did to admire the view and appreciate what he still regarded as the very odd accomplishment of human flight. He noticed a flash of light in the distance to the east. Then he saw what looked like an enormous bubble expanding into the air for several seconds, and then it collapsed.

He then saw a cloud of dark smoke rising from near the middle of a distant metropolitan area, and wondered to himself, *what was that?—Looks like an explosion of some kind in downtown somewhere—has to be Fresno.*

He was thinking of Oklahoma City, but he was wrong. This was not 'domestic terrorism' in the sense of a deranged or disgruntled citizen with a perverted sense of freedom acting out against the federal government that he as a federal agent was sworn to serve and uphold. He could not hear the inevitable screams of agony and pain tens of thousands of feet beneath him to the east. He could not know that a very special, talented and beautiful soul was among many others suspended in the uncertainty of unconsciousness, precariously near death. He could not know that the evening's entertainment at a nightclub would not occur as planned. He could not know that scores of people had made their last bets at the casino tables in Club One. The plane continued on to its destination in Los Angeles. The laws of physics did not change just because of human suffering, sorrow or someone else's religious convictions. He was uneasy for the remainder of his flight, unable to quell his budding professional and personal intuition that something very, very evil had just occurred.

At precisely seven fifty-six, Khalid's wife Farah was watching a television game show at her home in San Diego, simply oblivious to the tragic lie of her life, still looking forward to owning her own house someday and having her first child.

At precisely seven fifty-six and about 830 miles to the east, the ultra-sensitive EKG pen registered an arrhythmia and fluttered unevenly for three seconds. Doctor Stevenson looked immediately at Jake with concern and saw that his eyes were closed and his brow was furrowed as he drew a deep breath, held it for a few seconds, exhaled and then resumed normal breathing. He looked back at the monitor, mildly relieved. The bouncing bright green point of light had resumed its prior normal pattern across the same distance represented in the diminishing residual green glow at the left side of the monitor. Doctor Stevenson could not know that he had just witnessed a subtle, controversial but possibly very real sign of distant tragedy. All he saw was a relatively minor clinical aberration in Jake's otherwise normal heart function.

Chaos ensued from the burning gasoline and the collision of metal, glass, chunks of cement, nails and human flesh, causing the immediate and instantaneous termination of common thoughts, hopes and dreams, simple pleasures, and smiles of anticipation. It left a crater roughly 4,000 square feet in area, and about eight feet deep, contributing to the collapse of much of the Holiday Inn and almost the entire casino, and virtually all of the buildings on the north side of the Fulton Mall. Flying glass and fragments of twisted construction metal and nails from the truck and van became devastating shrapnel comparable to that of any battlefield since the Battle of Gettysburg. The devastation was the result of Khalid's fervent but distorted belief that he was doing the proper and necessary work of Allah to punish the infidels. His calling was far superior to that of any of his victims. The devastation was the mindless effect of the laws of physics unleashed by one who thought his beliefs should be the beliefs of the world simply because it was self-evident to him that they should be. After all, his early life was full of such conviction from his elders. It was the inevitable proximity of the intense C4 and PE4 explosion and 240 gallons of high-octane gasoline from the cartons in the truck and trailer. The ignition of the eight blasting caps responded to the perverse application of man's technological creativity in a convenient means of innocent communication that evolved from the early invention commonly attributed to Alexander Graham Bell. The electronic signal from a simple small cell phone commanded the electric charge that energized the blasting caps, causing the immediate and powerful release of nitrogen and intense heat. The result created enough force to savage several nearby buildings and damage, completely mangle or incinerate at least 196 vehicles either moving in nearby streets or parked alongside its curbs or in the Holiday Inn parking garage. Some initial reports indicated that over 373, later revised to 419 innocent people perished in the blast immediately, and dozens more suffered potentially fatal injuries. Fourteen survivors would never walk again. A half dozen would never see again. Many suffered permanent hearing loss. At least 128 people would face physical or mental rehabilitation expenses well beyond their financial capacity to manage. The living relatives of the dead and injured suffered as well, altering plans and hopes for the future, ripping apart the bonds of affection and love formed over a lifetime, or perhaps only within the last several days or weeks, suspending many of them in the cruelest uncertainty. The blast was audible as far south as Porterville, about seventy-five miles from Fresno, and at least as far north as Merced, fifty-eight miles away.

Over 200 miles above the western United States, the crew of the International Space station on the 25th NASA Expedition was forty-three minutes into their scheduled lunch period, when forty-eight-year-old Flight Engineer Fyodor Yurchikhin happened to look down at the earth below. He saw the outline of the western border of the United States against the Pacific Ocean. East of the coastline, and west of the mountains, he saw a very peculiar flash of light and subsequent smudge of dark smoke from one specific location in the otherwise remarkably clear atmosphere.

He felt an unexplained intuitive jolt of fear and thought to himself, *that was not normal!*

"Did you see that?" He asked Doug Wheelock, the commander of the expedition.

"See what?"

"A flash of light, like an explosion, down there, somewhere in your country, in California, I believe!" he said in only slightly accented English.

Commander Wheelock looked out the window, and saw the smudge of dark smoke. He turned to Yurchikhin with a pale hint of apprehension in his face. He knew that what he was seeing as a relatively small smudge of what was probably smoke at a distance of well over 200 miles above the earth had to be a much more significant event at ground level, most likely causing many deaths and horrific destruction. He had never seen anything like it since 9/11, and feared the worst.

He activated his microphone, "Mission control, we just saw somewhere in the middle of California what looks like a large explosion. We can see dark smoke. Will you check this out?"

"Roger . . . am checking now . . ."

The space station floated along in silence through space, high above the earth, with only the regular humming of its vital complex equipment, and a silent but very apprehensive crew.

Seven long minutes later, the voice responded, "We have no information about an explosion at this time . . . will check later and advise . . ."

Shortly before eight o'clock, Ramon Raphael was having a late supper of spaghetti and meatballs in downtown Fresno at The Old Spaghetti Factory on East Shaw Avenue when he heard the tremendous explosive sound, and looked down to see his plate jump briefly off the table and immediately lost interest in eating. His eyes dilated instantly as he became intensely alert. His Emergency Medical Technician training overtook him without his consent. At the same time, he felt fear. Something unusual had just happened, and he would be involved somehow, whether he wanted to be or not.

Not even twenty seconds later, a voice chirped from his pager, "Code 33, Code 2! Code 33, Code 2! Code 33, Code 2!"

The combination of codes meant essentially that all prior communications traffic was to stop and that an emergency had occurred. There was no formal code for a bomb explosion or an act of war, but after hearing the explosion, he did not need an exact code to respond. He jumped away from the table and threw some money on it to pay for his food, almost knocking over his chair and losing his balance in the process. He was six feet, two inches tall, and weighed about 187 pounds, but he was only twenty-four years old, and still extremely fit and unusually agile after an active athletic life in high school, where he played varsity basketball and baseball. He caught himself on the balls of his feet with one palm on the floor of the restaurant, regained his balance and was set to run out the door and down the street to his car. He did not have to think much about where he was going. He saw the cloud of black smoke rising less than two miles to the west and slightly south of his location into the fading blue early evening sky in stark contrast to a few orange puffy clouds overhead. He got in his car and put the blue flasher on the dashboard of his shiny customized dark blue 1998 Ford Mustang as he started the engine and pushed the accelerator to the floorboard. The car screeched out into East Shaw Avenue from the curb and headed west as the engine roared through the lower gears, propelling him toward the Yosemite Freeway southbound entrance as he used his inadequate siren and horn liberally to part traffic and gain speed. Still estimating the street location of the smoke from the freeway, he exited quickly at Route 180 West and immediately turned south onto North Fresno Street, where he saw people all staring in the same direction toward the smoke with facial expressions of fear and concern. The Mustang roared south on North Fresno Street toward the smoking chaos. Some men on the sidewalks started to run toward the smoke as well. People were lying on the pavement the closer he got to the center of the devastation. Women clutched their small children. It was indeed becoming 'all hands on deck' for the city of Fresno. The sounds of more sirens and the periodic deep blaring horns of emergency rescue and fire vehicles filled the warm evening air from all directions.

Ramon wheeled around the corner onto Van Ness, but immediately had to hit the brakes as he saw the debris from the former Holiday Inn blocking Van Ness Avenue, and complete destruction along that side of the street preventing any further vehicular approach. The smoke was rapidly billowing toward the few clouds outlined in the typical soft warm colors of early California evening as the sun sank lower in the sky toward the horizon.

His brain was half in 'hyper-think' mode and half in trained reaction mode. His eyes were wide open as he immediately turned his head to look out the back window while ramming the floor gear shifter into reverse, and let the clutch pedal fly out while turning the steering wheel to force the car into a virtual partial pirouette facing the opposite direction. The mustang was responding true its namesake, and vaulted forward again, as he rammed the shifter back into first gear and roared back onto Fresno Street. He turned left looking for the next side street behind the Holiday Inn to find another way to get closer to the main source of the smoke. That is when he saw the overturned blue GMC Savana on the street just off to his right in the Bank of the West parking lot across the street from the damaged Educational Employees Federal Credit Union building. Several people were milling about the overturned vehicle. Ramon jammed on his brakes, and the powerful steel horse came to a screeching halt as he threw open the door and raced over to the gathering crowd around the van. He saw other overturned vehicles, but without people around them, so he focused on the one that appeared to suggest the possibility of life first before checking the others.

"EMT, people! Please make way! Out of the way, please!" He yelled in his only slightly accented English. He was working toward eliminating his accent altogether, and was determined to succeed in his efforts to become just that much more of the ideal citizen he wanted to be in his beloved new country. He was taking evening college courses in computer programming at Fresno State to prepare himself for an independent livelihood and to be a more productive member of society, while working as an EMT for the city fire department rescue squad and working odd jobs of all kinds as they became available.

The small crowd parted quickly, and Ramon saw the beautiful young woman with disheveled, but striking long wavy brown hair with auburn highlights hanging out the driver's window of the overturned damaged vehicle. She was deathly still. Her top was ripped open, partially revealing her left breast. She had several abrasions and cuts, but they were rather minor, considering that she was in an overturned vehicle.

Ramon knelt down next to her and gently pulled her ripped top back over her and said, "Can you hear me?" and then reached out to feel for a pulse from her carotid artery in her flawless neck.

Her facial color was not indicative of breathing problems, but he checked anyway, and found only shallow breathing. He felt a slight pulse as the faintest glimmer of hope seeped into his brain, and asked again, "Can you hear me?"

He looked around carefully for further signs of bleeding, but other than the array of relatively minor cuts and bruises, he found no major blood stains anywhere on her clothing or other evidence of sustained blood loss.

He called on his pager for an ambulance with lights on for an emergency, but would have appreciated God's presence as well, as he virtually yelled into his pager, "Code 3, 11, 41. Code 3, 11, 41 at Bank of the West near Fulton Mall on Fresno!" Then he holstered his pager and yelled, "Oh God, please don't let her die! OK people, give this lady some space and some respect! If you're not a doctor or a nurse, please move away . . . *now!*"

He looked carefully at the young woman with his intelligent dark eyes, but perceived no immediately obvious vital signs. She still did not respond. Then he saw the slight expansion of her chest. At least she was alive! He was shocked by what he saw immediately before him as the most tragic sight in the whole universe—completely innocent and profound female beauty, obviously hurt or damaged in some way by unknown forces, and possibly near death. He wanted to scream out at the top of his lungs in raw anger.

Why has God permitted this?

Nevertheless, he wrestled his emotions back under control with extreme and concentrated effort, and immediately lurched back into his professional 'EMT mode.' He looked briefly for some kind of identification, but found nothing. If she had a purse or a pocketbook, he could not find it anywhere around her or near the van. He did not know whether she had any broken bones. He did not see any obvious evidence of fracture, but he decided not to try to move her. In spite of the catastrophe, she appeared to be in relatively good condition just for having survived with even a thin thread of life, at least up to this point, but he could not be sure how long she would last. He desperately wanted her to live. He called his dispatcher again on his pager, praying for her at the same time. Her eyes remained closed.

An ambulance arrived within three minutes since it was already on the road and in the vicinity from the first alerts. The ambulance crew stepped out onto the parking lot and moved toward the van with grace and remarkable speed. After another cursory examination, they handled the young woman with the intuitive coordination of years of training as if she were a rare statue made of fine crystal. They quickly placed her on the ambulance gurney, and gently secured her to it with apparently brand new white canvas straps and then pushed it to the rear ambulance door and carefully slid it into the back of the ambulance, locked it into place securely, and closed the doors.

Ramon crossed his chest and wiped tears from his face with his sleeve as he watched the ambulance start to leave, slowly at first, with its siren blaring and bright red LED lights flashing, and then moved on to search for others he could possibly save. He found another woman not far away in the mall walkway under a huge piece of concrete. She was sobbing softly, moving her lips as if saying something. Ramon approached her quickly, and saw that he could not move the concrete slab and immediately called for help to lift the concrete section. He did the best he could to assure the woman that help was on the way, and knelt down beside her.

Then he heard her softly praying . . . "For Thine is the kingdom, the power, and . . ."

Ramon shrieked almost with madness, draining his lungs into the empty evening sky not obscured by the smoke. "NO! NO, GOD! Please leave her with me! O God, please, *leave her with me!*"

He immediately checked for her pulse. He felt none, but he kept his fingers on her neck, to make sure, waiting, willing her heart to beat again. Then the woman expired quietly in stark contrast to the sheer hell that had brought a piece of the Holiday Inn down upon her, as Ramon touched her face in desperate simple hope, willing some life to flow to her from him. She lay completely still before him, crushed by the weight of the broken concrete slab. He fought back tears yet again, and looked for some kind of identification. It was the first time he had actually seen someone die right before his eyes, and it shook his entire being to its very core. It made no sense. She never really had a chance. It was so obviously and undeniably *final.*

The chaos continued around him as if nothing special had happened, and yet another life ceased to exist. He had to tell a loved one or a relative that he was there when she died, to convey some kind of closure that almost everyone needs. He also needed his own closure in telling a loved one that he was there at the end. After a brief search, he found a purse next to her under the concrete, wrenched it free from the rubble and opened it to look for a name. Her ID tag on her key chain indicated that she was a registered nurse. Her name was Amelia Johnson. She lived in Fresno.

Ramon kept the purse and its contents to give to her family and then continued searching for other survivors, carrying the pain of watching Amelia die, but also harboring hope for the beautiful young woman with the long wavy dark hair with auburn highlights. He went on into the evening fighting against his emotional upheaval, attending to others where he could help, and found still others who were beyond all help. Death continued to roll over the area, instantly in some cases, slowly in others. Some people knew their fate and felt it approach either quickly in just a few seconds or gradually over many minutes, while others simply perished with absolutely no chance of recognition.

Later that evening in his apartment, in spite of his exhausting day, he found the nurse's name and professional association on a Google search on the internet. She worked at Community Regional Medical Center at 2823 Fresno Street, not far from the center of the explosion. She must have been either going to work, or leaving when the explosion occurred. In spite of the late hour and his profound exhaustion, he needed to tell the next of kin about Amelia's death. It was well after midnight, but he drove to the slightly damaged hospital anyway and inquired at the front desk, explaining who he was and why he needed to know where Amelia's family lived. The desk clerk sensed his urgent sincerity, given her awareness of the day's events nearby and specifically the emergency activity at her hospital, and found the emergency contact information he needed and told him Amelia lived alone, but had a brother who lived in Anchorage, Alaska, and gave him the telephone number. He left the area to find some privacy, and, in spite of the late hour dialed the number on his cell phone, and awoke Sheila Johnson from a deep sleep.

"Hello?"

"Hello. Is this the residence of Hector Johnson?"

Sheila responded wearily, "Yes it is. Who is calling?"

"My name is Ramon Raphael. I am an Emergency Medical Technician in Fresno, California. Is Hector there, please?"

"No. He's out working. What is this all about?"

She was suddenly much more alert as her heart rate increased rapidly.

"Listen, I'm really sorry about calling at this late hour, but . . ."

"Yes?" She said cautiously.

She was rapidly developing a sense of dread that energized her entire being into a completely alert panic in seconds. She did not like getting this kind of phone call when she was alone. Hector was out on a tractor-trailer rig somewhere, and she needed to talk to him.

"I was witness to the death of Amelia Johnson just after a catastrophic explosion in Fresno yesterday evening. It's all over the news. I have her purse with me, and found her emergency contact information, which led me to call this number. I'm very sorry to have to tell you this, but I just had to. I couldn't save her. She died as I felt for her pulse. I'm so very, very sorry! There was . . . nothing I could do to save her! I can tell you, however, that she was . . . talking to God when she died."

Sheila was shocked by the news that her sister-in-law had perished in the blast, but she managed to say with obvious difficulty that she would tell her husband as soon as she could reach him, and thanked Ramon for calling, and then broke the phone connection. She immediately dialed Hector's cell phone number and waited over half a minute for him to answer.

"This better be good!" he bellowed into his phone.

"Hector! *Listen* to me! I just got off the phone with an emergency medical technician in Fresno. He told me Amelia has passed away. She died in the explosion that's all over the news. I'm watching the news on television right now. It looks awful!"

"Oh! My God! Noooo!"

The connection was quiet.

"Hector? Are you there?"

After several seconds, he responded. "I'm . . . I'm sorry, Sheila. I shouldn't . . . I shouldn't have been so abrupt. I'm really, *really* sorry. I've been having a really bad day, and I'm still angry about the boots I ordered not being ready. I was going to go down to San Diego in a few days anyway to see about the boots, so I will drive up through Fresno on the way back to take care of at least some of her final affairs while I'm there. I'll be leaving in three days after I finish this job I'm on. I'm sorry, Sheila. I'm *really* sorry . . . I gotta go . . . See you soon . . . Bye . . ."

CHAPTER 35

Monday, September 10, 2007
Los Angeles, California

J. Davis Harrington was in his hotel room watching the late evening news, as he usually did even while on vacation, when a special report interrupted the regular newscast.

A familiar voice said, "We do not know what happened in Fresno at this point, other than an extremely powerful explosion most likely not of natural causes. We simply have no reliable information yet. However, I can assure the people of Fresno and all of California that we will ultimately discover who caused this disaster, and will take appropriate action to apprehend and punish whoever is responsible for this dastardly act. I have nothing further at this time."

The television cameras lingered on the aging but still somewhat handsome Arnold Schwarzenegger for a moment as he left the dais. Then they switched to several dozen talking heads, depending upon the location of the broadcast stations throughout the country and around the world, who repeated what the Governor had just said. They added their own obviously ill-prepared comments about the event, which spoke eloquently for itself, just in case the listening audience did not understand what the Governor had just said in only slightly accented, but very clear and plain English. Most stations offered a split screen with the Governor speaking on the left and a view of the devastation near the blast obviously from an amateur hand-held camera on the right. There were only two loops of about twenty seconds of repeated exposure each from two distinctly different vantage points, but they hinted clearly that emergency workers and police had made a serious effort to keep the media out of the area because of the human horror strewn about the entire blast area.

Harrington continued watching the broadcast as questions flooded his mind.

How do you 'punish' someone for mass murder on the scale of war? The marines at Okinawa did not 'punish' the Japanese soldiers or seek to incarcerate them. They killed them! The British did not look for the pilots of the German bombers who pounded the city of London unmercifully in an effort to 'punish' them. Where do you draw the line? When one man kills one other man, you call it murder, and you apprehend the offender and enforce the applicable laws of society. At what kill ratio do you stop calling it civil murder, and start calling it an act of war? How many innocent lives lost equates to an act of war? Three? Ten? Surely 200 or more! How do you deter a suicide bomber from repeating his 'crime'? Is a suicide bomber a 'soldier' in an 'undeclared' war? How do you 'punish' a dead man? Obviously, you don't, at least not in western culture, unless there is some kind of 'after-life.' Do you find his supporters and try them in a court of law in an effort to 'discourage' further similar behavior? Do you round up a bunch of people you suspect think the same way and summarily shoot them, like Hitler, Stalin or Pol Pot did? How do you persuade someone of something contradictory to a cause to which he is completely committed and for which he is willing to die? How do you 'educate' an extremist culture dedicated to the constant sacrifice of individual lives as a means of destroying another culture or life philosophy? Certainly not in a court of law! What 'law' governs the behavior of a field commander responsible for the lives of his men when he believes they are threatened? What 'law' governs the behavior of the lion in search of food? What 'law' guides the reaction of the water buffalo when his offspring is attacked? Should we just resign ourselves to the periodic brutality of life and thank our lucky stars that we are still breathing? How much religious freedom do we need to tolerate in order to assure our children and their children of a future worth working for? Is there no difference between one person killing another, and one extremist culture trying to wipe out a peaceful, constructive social order?

Harrington had questions—so many questions—many more than he had answers to.

CHAPTER 36

Tuesday, September 11, 2007
Maryland

One of Duke Chancellor's offices was on the top floor of his seven-story, 150,000 square-foot office building nestled in the Maryland woods in Prince George's County a few miles west of Interstate Highway 95, which he leased to various corporations usually involved with government contracts on the first six floors. The building was relatively new, with all of the modern office amenities including a cafeteria and four floors of underground parking, which kept the surrounding wooded area as natural as possible by eliminating typical acres of asphalt or concrete beyond that needed for the foundation, main entrance and a road out to the highway. Duke knew the property would only appreciate in value eventually in spite of the lousy economy.

He was in his private office, reading as many accounts of the Fresno incident as possible. He had his network wide open, waiting for information from around the world. Pictures of the devastation in Fresno were increasing by the hour, appearing on various websites, feeding the voracious human appetite in every country for high drama, controversy and the misfortunes of their fellow human beings. Nothing new and unique of any substance was coming in yet from his network. He picked up the headline New York Times story on the internet about the explosion in Fresno.

> *'The sudden devastating explosion near Van Ness Avenue in Fresno, California last evening appears suspicious because police and FBI investigators have found evidence of an accelerant and an extremely powerful explosive as well as a significant number of nails in some of the charred remains of the Holiday Inn Hotel and the adjacent Club One Casino. Many of the stores in the Fulton Mall behind the hotel and casino also showed unusual evidence of nails and gasoline. The death toll has risen to 419 from the originally reported 373. The current estimate of injuries is 1,633, but that number might increase. Police have been questioning local business owners and patrons of undamaged establishments just beyond the major blast area and have set up a hotline for phone tips, as well as an internet site with updated information and an e-mail address for people to provide information that could possibly be useful in the investigation (www.fresnocahelp2007.gov). Fresno Chief of Police Donald F. Buckingham said that there was no evidence supporting or denying any particular responsible source, domestic or foreign, of what appears to be an act of terrorism. However, he admitted that it was especially unusual that the explosion occurred in Fresno instead of a higher-profile location like San Francisco or Los Angeles, or any other big city anywhere else in the country. The FBI has joined the investigation with their special terrorism unit, but they have not released a statement at this time.'*

Duke was angry, and he did not suffer fools easily.

"*Appears* to be suspicious? That's all they know? This has got to stop!" he muttered to himself.

Duke Chancellor knew more than most people knew about a great number of things. However, he did not yet know that his beautiful niece Sasha had left for Fresno from Denver three days ago. In addition, he did not know that she had truly fallen in love for the first time in her life, well beyond any prior infatuation or relationship of any kind that she admitted at the time even to her mother or closest girlfriends as pure and true love. His private telephone rang somewhere on his huge custom-made mahogany combination desk/workspace/wall cabinet with countless compartments. It almost looked like a modern version of the old style post office with letterboxes and over a dozen small cabinets. He reached over piles of papers to answer it.

"Yes?"

"Mr. Chancellor, General Murray is on line three."

The gentle, melodious voice came from 'wonder woman,' his devoted assistant, secretary, gatekeeper and protector from deliberate or accidental intrusions into the inner world of The Chancellor Organization at the Plymouth Building.

Stephanie Paris would gladly lay down her life for Duke Chancellor because Duke had personally paid for her mother's cancer treatment during her final months of constantly recurring symptoms, because she could not afford treatment after her health insurance payments were exhausted. Because of Duke Chancellor, she enjoyed her relationship with her mother a little longer than circumstances would otherwise have allowed, before she finally succumbed bravely and defiantly to the relentless onslaught of the disease. Absolutely no one in his right mind would ever *dare* to challenge Stephanie Paris about Duke Chancellor.

"Duke, this is General Richard Murray. I met a man today who needs work. I would like to discuss it with you."

"I'm having lunch today with a business associate, and can't see you today. Will tomorrow work for you?"

"That's fine. I'll call you tomorrow."

They both hung up. That exchange did not mean what anyone listening in might have thought it meant. It was a pre-arranged code between just the two of them to meet at their favorite restaurant at six o'clock that evening. The CIA had used Duke's services before, and kept it at the highest levels of security clearance. The CIA was not eager to admit that they did not always have the proper resources to accomplish every mission either explicitly or implicitly assigned to them. They usually had to bow to congressional insistence upon 'high standards of conduct,' meaning no torture, no murder, and none of the other 'uncivilized' methods of clandestine service behavior that Congress habitually insisted be forbidden so they could claim 'the moral high road' in a dirty world and enhance their prospects for re-election by a naive populist resurgence. The significance of 'The Battle at Kruger' was lost on them. General Murray knew that the world was not an entirely civilized community where everyone played by the same rules. He knew his history well, and he had no illusions about the nature of man. He believed that if the revolutionaries of the struggling new nation he now served had stood in straight lines dressed in bright red coats and big silly black hats to do battle with the British hundreds of years ago he would not be standing here today. His understanding was that the revolutionaries focused upon the goal and not upon the folly of traditional 'correct military formation and tactics' at the time to accomplish their objectives. He believed that current western culture had deluded itself into believing that the world is much more civilized than it actually is. He also had no illusions about what highly motivated people are capable of achieving, and a system of western ethics had very little to do with how far people of other cultures and religious persuasions would actually go to accomplish certain ends. The Islamic extremists involved in the 9/11 attacks had made it perfectly clear that they do not respect western cultural, philosophical or religious values, and are quite willing, if not eager to exploit any innocent facet of common social behavior, custom or human nature for their own purposes.

General Murray's body was fifty years old, looked like it was thirty-nine, and housed the mental and physical alertness of a twenty-five-year-old, and he had the wisdom of an alert octogenarian. His neck still showed evidence of his having played linebacker at West Point. He was one very high-powered and deadly serious gentleman with a Ph.D. from M.I.T. in physics. Murray knew that things happen in the course of human existence that are unanticipated, not fair, too expensive to correct, or too unpopular to receive proper attention, or are just plain wrong by the most basic universally accepted moral values around the globe. He knew that the police and military forces throughout the world were unable to respond effectively to all of the tasks assigned to or expected of them. In some of those circumstances, he looked to Duke Chancellor for 'assistance.' General Murray respected the rules, but one of his rules was that the rules do not cover all of the requirements for action, especially in the new world of terrorism where the other side had no rules, at least as were commonly known in western culture. He was prepared to take responsibility in many instances when others would freeze in the bureaucratic hierarchy or forge ahead with false bravado or less than full conviction.

The old rules divided domestic and foreign investigative behavior and covert action between the FBI and the CIA, but the two organizations were gradually working together more and more since 9/11. However, General Murray saw the world in terms of problems and solutions, regardless of whether they were domestic or foreign, and he was going to attack the problem with whatever means he had at his disposal, which included The Chancellor Organization. He saw the traditional line between 'domestic' and 'foreign' becoming increasingly obscure with the tremendous influx of people from other countries, both legally and illegally, into the United States. The increasingly interconnected character of global organizations, commerce, politics, finance and social movements across traditional national borders justified in his mind the necessity to emphasize results over 'territory.' His experience taught him that results trumped politics every time, so he had absolutely no reservations about applying his resources within the United States, or anywhere else where he believed there was no acceptable alternative, thereby often challenging what the establishment had distinctly forbidden. He believed that 'policy' was too frequently a compromise between right and wrong.

Duke provided 'assistance' from time to time, as needed, with the assurance that his network would not be penetrated or exposed in return for his silence about helping the CIA. That code of trust had never been broken, and it never would be if General Murray had anything to do with it. He knew that the effective use of secret or special information was entirely contingent upon trust between at least two individuals, and once that trust was broken, the information and its effectiveness would be worthless or seriously compromised, and sometimes people would die because of it. He trusted Duke and his organization as much as he trusted his wife or his closest aides. Murray had already committed to himself that knowledge of The Chancellor connection would die with him. He never could break Duke's communications codes. General Murray strongly believed that Duke accomplished too many good things for him to risk destroying or weakening The Chancellor Organization for the sake of 'political correctness' or any other human folly. He would be a fool to do so, and worse, he would be a hypocrite and a failure in the eyes of his father and his Virginia family's long tradition of service to humanity and to the country he served, that dated back at least to the beginning of the Revolutionary War.

From that point on, General Murray knew that he would have the cooperation of The Chancellor Organization in his pursuit of those responsible for the Fresno incident.

CHAPTER 37

Tuesday, September 11, 2007
Reading, Pennsylvania

Joe was busy reconciling his business checkbook on his computer upstairs above his restaurant when he noticed the flashing System 9 indication in the lower right corner of his computer monitor. He quickly closed down all of his open applications and activated his end of System 9. The message was from Duke.

He knew about the Fresno explosion. He knew that Duke was getting involved. His instructions on System 9 were to get as much information as he could about the original source of the Fresno bombing and look for a 'solution.' He inhaled with determination. This was going to be interesting, indeed! Joe was very competitive, and loved a challenge, all the way back into his high school wrestling days. He was the smallest man on the wrestling team at the Hill School, an all-male private prep school at that time in Pottstown, Pennsylvania, about twenty miles southeast of Reading and about forty miles northwest of Philadelphia. However, he also had the best match record, with only one loss and no ties in his last two years out of thirty-four matches.

Joe studied the information carefully, and then booked a flight leaving in two days with an open return from Philadelphia International Airport to Mumbai to meet with the young prospect Duke had told him about. He called his head chef, Oscar, and told him he would be away for about a week, and to hire a temp if he needed help during that time.

Oscar and Bart Lupold would handle the restaurant quite well by themselves, even though it took both of them to approximate the smooth effectiveness of Joe's engaging personality with their customers. Joe's personal touch in the restaurant would have to wait. Oscar was always gracious. He felt fortunate in life because he knew he was a good cook, and he worked for the owner of the most expensive restaurant in the greater metropolitan Reading area, if not probably all of southeastern Pennsylvania, including Philadelphia. He was accustomed to running the restaurant when Joe was off on some trip. After all, the customers were eating mostly *his* creations, not Joe's, and he took great pride in his cooking. Joe had provided a special touch with mushroom recipes, however, that others simply could not duplicate.

CHAPTER 38

Tuesday, September 11, 2007
Mexico City, Mexico

Rasheed was eating a burrito at a sidewalk café in downtown Mexico City, effectively hiding in plain sight in the depths of the world's largest city, with the third largest population after Tokyo and Seoul. He was looking at a Spanish newspaper, which he could not read, but he could see the pictures of the horrific aftermath of an explosion, and the name 'Fresno' in the headline above it. He firmly believed that Allah was already rewarding Khalid in heaven, and praised Allah for this sign of his success and his righteousness. He would put more of his great plans into action after he returned to Pakistan. He would stay in the vast urban expanse of Mexico City for just a short while longer, allowing whatever trail the American or Mexican authorities might decide to follow to grow cold. He was confident time would be his friend and his savior on his journey back to Pakistan.

Unknown to Rasheed, a certain Mexican private detective, Cordera Alvarez was watching him at the café for no particular reason other than that he was obviously not a native Mexican, and he had arrived on a bright green Kawasaki motorcycle. The fifty-five year old Alvarez was still a bachelor, and plagued with intense curiosity about other people all the time, both innocent and guilty, clients and subjects of his clients' interests, corporate mavens, hoodlums, politicians, gangsters and aristocrats, movie stars, public and private figures. He was never without his broadband laptop computer because it gave him efficient access to information, communication and potential clients. Rasheed just happened to attract his intuitive curiosity for the day, and he had nothing else to occupy his time other than spider solitaire.

He easily followed Rasheed's bright green motorcycle in his grimy, unwashed white 1997 Jeep Cherokee for more than an hour in the city, because the rider obviously did not know the city as well as Cordera did. He eventually followed the bike to the Mexico City Airport, where they both parked their vehicles. His interest was not quite at the level of informing official agencies, but it was very strong and persistent, so he went over to the motorcycle and quickly wrote down the model and manufacturer's serial number in his notebook and then continued to follow his subject into the main terminal. Cordera watched him apparently checking in with a ticket agent, and shortly thereafter, he verified with that ticket agent that Rasheed was booked over ten weeks ago on a two-leg flight leaving that day for Rawalpindi Airport in Pakistan. This development piqued Cordera's voracious curiosity just a little more, since he had already heard about the Fresno incident on the radio and various televisions in public places, as well as the internet on his laptop. His curiosity was far too general to associate specifically or entirely dismiss his new subject from association with any particular event. He had learned over many years of experience to keep his attention to a specific subject as simple as possible and with as little bias as possible until he had hard and clearly convincing independent evidence to use as a reason for dedicated pursuit and more intensive research or informing law enforcement or governmental agencies.

For the time being, Cordera was simply following his nebulous, unspecified but very strong intuition. He had no evidence. He had no reason. However, he loved a challenge. He loved 'the game' as he called it. All he had was a non-descript 'detective's feeling.' He had lots of time. He had no current paying clients. He then contacted his old friend Duke Chancellor on System 17 from his laptop to see what else he could learn. He also told Duke all the details about the man he tailed and where he went, and included the motorcycle description and serial number. Duke urged him to go back to the ticket agent and see whether he could get on that same flight. If necessary, Duke was prepared to have Sammy 'bump' a passenger from that flight. This was Cordera's lucky day. He got a seat the 'normal' way. He started the longest surveillance episode of his career, because he had the time, he was intensely curious, and his suspicion was mounting.

CHAPTER 39

Tuesday, September 11, 2007
Denver, Colorado

Jake checked his biorhythms on an internet site just before he left his office for a bite to eat before he left for the recording studio. As a psychologist, he was especially curious about biorhythm theory. He entered his birth date and then smiled to himself in satisfaction after the results appeared within a few seconds. According to his physical, emotional and intellectual biorhythm patterns, he was at a higher total personal peak now than he had been in well over a year. He was theoretically as intensely and completely 'alive' as he could ever expect to be. Physically, he felt younger, stronger and athletically in peak form, such as his form was. Emotionally he was optimistic, carefree and excited. He felt mentally alert, with his entire life experience, superior intelligence, intuition and education at his instant command. He felt vigorous and ready for anything, and left his office to walk down the street to his favorite sandwich shop. He made short work of a fresh turkey sandwich on an Italian roll with lettuce and light mayonnaise, and a diet ginger ale for a chaser, paid the bill, and left to get his Acura from the parking garage.

He arrived at FTM Studios early for his six o'clock recording session. Rocky was not there, but Tommy, the recording technician greeted him at the door. Tommy was over six feet tall, thin, and dressed in faded blue jeans with no belt, faded Hard Rock Café T-shirt with some kind of faint rock-band image on it, and old scuffed-up formerly white Nike sneakers. He had short, uncombed blue hair and a simple circular gold earring in each ear lobe.

"Good evening, Mr. Lewis. My name's Tommy. I'm the recording technician here. I've been expecting you!"

He spoke in a polite and oddly contrasting cultured business voice that could easily have belonged to an experienced FM radio classical music station personality. The professionally rich and pleasant voice surprised Jake, since it obviously clashed with his blue hair, earrings and apparently very comfortable faded 'casual business' attire and other evidence of an 'off-culture' individual.

At least the earrings are symmetrical, Jake thought to himself.

"Please come in!" Tommy said as he closed the front door behind Jake as he entered the building.

"Thank you. I've been looking forward to this!"

They walked over to the door marked 'Studio A' and into the special soundproof room.

"Make yourself comfortable, please, and I will be ready in just a few moments," Tommy said as he headed for the control room.

Tommy closed the entrance door to Studio A as he left the room. Jake walked over to the freshly tuned instrument and stood motionless, admiring it once again in the special acoustic stillness of the studio.

He marveled to himself, *this beautiful instrument is actually hand-made, and it probably took about a year to make it!*

He leaned over the keyboard and played a few chords with both hands at different intervals in matching octaves, fifths and fourths from the lowest notes to the highest to verify that it was indeed tuned to his 'perfect pitch' standards. He smiled with utter joy and anticipation. The beautiful Steinway piano was ready for him, and he was more than ready for the musical adventure it would provide, both for him playing it and for Sasha when she heard the final professional quality digital recording. He sat on the comfortable cushioned black leather bench that was just a little more familiar to him now, and adjusted the height until he was as comfortable as possible. He removed his wallet, keys, loose change and cell phone from his pockets, as well as his Rolex watch, and placed them on the carpeted floor to his left. He made sure his phone was off. He did not want any unusual sounds, sensations or other intrusions during his recording, and he wanted to feel as comfortable as possible.

"Any time you're ready, Mr. Lewis."

Tommy's smooth 'FM radio' voice came through the 'Studio A' internal intercom system somewhere in the ceiling near Jake. He turned to look at Tommy through the control room window and nodded in acknowledgement while raising his right hand with an 'OK' sign. Tommy then turned the PA system off and got comfortable in his 'captain's chair' at the control desk, placed headphones over his blue hair and decorated ears, and gave Jake a 'thumbs up' through the window.

Jake took a deep breath and let it out slowly to try to relax as much as possible. He pressed his hands together, interlaced his fingers and squeezed them together several times to relax them and 'get the blood flowing,' and then wiped his slightly moist hands on his pants legs for a few seconds. He brought his right hand up to the keyboard and started with the melody Sasha first played back at Eddie's to 'prime his pump.' Whatever happened from this point forward in the recording session was his gift to Sasha. It would be real and unique, especially for her, never played before, even though he would try to include and embellish the main melody of what he had played for her the very first time at Eddie's. It would be from him alone. There was not another person in the world who could give her this pure and very special gift. He would give her this little token of his heart and soul to keep forever.

As he played, he became lost in his music. The studio disappeared from his awareness. Only the piano existed. The beautiful craftsmanship was quite evident in the response of the hammers against the strings and the closing action of the dampers, according to every nuance of Jake's varying touch on the keys. They whispered in response to his lightest touch, and cried out with brilliance and clarity with the firm and commanding strength of his fingers and forearms. Sasha was spiritually near him. His heart fluttered in arrhythmia for a moment, but he knew it would pass. He took a deep breath and continued to play, not missing a beat. Fully seventeen minutes later, Sasha disappeared, and his music was heading to a close. Jake brought Sasha's melody back to give the piece final closure, balance and completeness. The piano obeyed his commands precisely as he reduced the tempo and volume into a peaceful and consonant harmonic ending.

How is this possible? Jake wondered. He did not understand his own talent. *Is there really a greater force in the universe beyond my comprehension? Why does she affect me this way? How does my love for her become music?*

He sat on the bench in silence for a minute, pleased with his effort, but he had no idea what he had just played. He leaned over and picked up his loose change, wallet, keys, cell phone and watch from the floor next to the bench, and replaced them all in the same pockets where they were when he walked in, and then left the piano bench and headed for the control room.

Tommy opened the door for him as Jake entered the room, walked to the comfortable and well-used tan leather chair in the corner and sat down. Tommy proceeded to eliminate electronically all initial and post-performance incidental noise from the sound track with a 'fade-in' at the beginning and 'fade-out' at the end and prepared to create the master CD of Jake's performance. Jake listened to the recording of what he played as Tommy adjusted the controls. He actually did not remember most of it, but he liked it. He was *actually listening* to it for the first time as he watched the visual representation of the sound dance across the computer displays. He hoped with all his heart that Sasha would like it as well. He felt like a lovesick teenager. He just could not wait to see her again. A full half hour later, Tommy finished the master recording, and pulled the CD out of the main recording CD tray. He took a black magic marker out of the desk drawer behind him and printed neatly 'JAKE LEWIS' on the front of the CD, with the date '9/11/07' underneath. He handed Jake the completed CD of his recording in a plastic jewel case. Jake wrote out a check for $200 and handed it to Tommy.

Tommy said, "That was really nice, Mr. Lewis. It's been a long time since I heard anyone make love to a piano like that."

Jake said, "Thank you very much." *Was it really that obvious?*

CHAPTER 40

Wednesday, September 12, 2007
Langley, Virginia

General Murray was in charge of the satellite surveillance division of the CIA. His select staff of highly trained analysts were examining literally tens of thousands of computerized images produced by the highest quality electronic photographic equipment in the world from various satellites circling the globe, leaving not even one square mile per twenty-four hours unrecorded in standard untasked mode within the entire satellite system. All he needed was a single piece of evidence in either time or location in order to focus his sophisticated satellite imagery system and build a story about the past.

Samantha Billings was the first to see the top view of the twenty-six-foot U-Haul truck with a large trailer in the truck stop parking lot at Wheeler Ridge, California. She had confirming evidence from the extreme corner of an image from a surveillance camera mounted on the main building of the truck stop. It showed the distinctive U-Haul logo and the identifying twin axle design of the six-foot by twelve-foot trailer, and just a portion of the rear of the truck with the trailer hitch clearly visible that could easily have been part of the twenty-six-foot U-Haul truck. Her instincts and intuition forced her to believe she had found the truck they were interested in. She was sure of it!

"I've got the U-Haul truck!" She called out across the room.

General Murray instinctively shifted mentally into 'high gear hunt mode,' and ordered his staff to focus upon the image sources covering the field of view represented by that location and all roads leading to or from it in any direction, but particularly north toward Fresno.

"Put that up on the front monitor, Samantha!" he said with calm command.

The room full of twenty-three highly experienced CIA technicians buzzed softly as they all studied the image carefully for a few moments, and then went back to their own computer terminals, eliminating groups of images outside of the geographical travel area and timeframe described along the bottom border of the image on Samantha's computer. Murray paced in anticipation. He knew his crew was good, and that this was the undeniable link to what would lead to further evidence and a 'kill' as he was fond of describing 'results.' The actual truth on occasion was that 'results' could lead to an 'unfortunate' termination of life. It happens sometimes.

Life isn't fair, is it? Murray thought to himself.

The general continued to pace with controlled patience from station to station in the large windowless room, taking a personal interest in this search more than he had in any other in his long and productive career. He made suggestions to each person in his group, one by one, directing each of them in a particular geographical direction of search according to his intuition and experience, trying to make the entire effort as efficient and coordinated as possible. They all renewed their searches in silence, as General Murray recalled the 9/11 terrorist attack in Manhattan.

He had been in southern Manhattan with his wife Ginny on September 11, 2001 on a brief vacation from the demands of his intensive occupation. They were looking out over the peaceful Hudson River under the clear, bright blue sky from the marina immediately south of the World Financial Center North Tower and adjacent to the Hudson River. The crisp, clear early morning September weather boosted personal energy, a general sense of well-being, optimism, purpose and enjoyment of life across the entire southern Manhattan spectrum of humanity from the financial mavens and corporate chiefs to the traders and other Wall Street types, as well as the street vendors, tourists and taxi drivers.

He heard the rapidly increasing roaring shriek of powerful jet engines somewhere overhead and behind him to the north, much, *much* too loud to be 'normal.' The sound was as loud as he remembered it to be from a jet taking off at full throttle. He turned around and looked up and slightly to the north. Within a fraction of a second, the plane came into view, casting its large sinister shadow onto the Hudson River behind him. He knew what was happening immediately. His training, experience, military intuition, and every fiber of his body told him a terrorist disaster was at hand. No experienced pilot of any aircraft, let alone a commercial airliner, would be flying that fast at that low altitude over a densely populated metropolitan area in obvious violation of every conceivable aviation regulation, let alone common sense, by mistake or due to mechanical malfunction. This aircraft was deliberately guided on a death vector! He knew he was witnessing the final seconds of one of the most sinister and deliberate single tragic events in the history of the United States, if not of western civilization itself. He thought of Pearl Harbor. He felt the rage from what he knew about December 7, 1941 as a military man, as a student of history, and as a human being. He also knew that somewhere in the world, someone with an entirely different view of the universe would soon be basking in the personal and ideological pride and comfort of evil success. The thought tore at his intellectual, moral, military and personal fiber, almost to the point of crossing the line beyond his considerable training and self-control into the absolute and total madness of animalistic rage.

He watched in helpless awe and anger as the American-built Boeing 767 airplane, belonging to an *American* company, American Airlines, certainly with many American citizens aboard, roared ahead taking deliberate and direct aim at the north tower of the iconic World Trade Center. There was no doubt in his mind that he was witnessing a vicious attack upon the United States of America. He shifted his eyes slightly to the second tallest buildings in the country and then immediately back to the speeding plane. He knew what was coming less than a microsecond later. He could not avert his eyes! He could not redirect his attention! He was transfixed in horror. His wife shrieked and grabbed him with both arms and buried her face in his muscular chest, and jumped at the sudden rumbling explosive sound of the impact and immediate ignition of well over 19,000 gallons of extremely volatile jet fuel.

The plane crashed into the north face of the north tower, and disappeared entirely inside the huge gaping impact hole roughly the shape and size of the total rear view of the large airliner at a slight angle, left wing down, right wing up as seen from the north and facing south. Even the vertical tail section left its mark in the building. The explosion was relatively brief but deafening, as a huge fireball erupted, leaving an unstoppable intense inferno of jet fuel raging at an unreachable height above street level.

They'll never put that fire out, he thought to himself.

He could not hear the screams of the people inside the tower over 100 floors above him, but he already knew the sound of human fear and desperate anguish at the approach of certain and inevitable death. He seared that thought into his heart and mind to serve as a reminder of why he would do everything in his considerable professional and personal power to avenge the suffering of innocent people he did not even know—people with talent, intelligence, goodness and value to family and the social order. He promised himself that he would work deliberately toward eliminating terrorism wherever and whenever he found it, for the rest of his professional career and beyond, if he could.

Ginny slowly disengaged herself from him and turned to look up at the 'towering inferno,' the likeness of which had been only a story in December of 1974, considered one of the greatest disaster movies of its time. Now it was very, very real, but with an extraordinarily evil twist.

How had man's innocent imagination in the world of make-believe film entertainment been transformed into a real-life horror in southern Manhattan almost twenty-seven years later? Could the terrorists have based this evil deed upon that fiction?

General Murray was a hardened career military officer, and witness to countless tragedies, from the death of the lowest ranking soldier in Viet Nam to the selfless sacrifice of the most highly decorated soldier of any rank. He had seen the last breath of an innocent child caught in the mindless tragedy of war. Now he was witnessing the unimaginable choices made by people tangled in the deadly crosscurrents of evil events completely beyond their control or comprehension. These were choices between certainly being incinerated alive in the intense inferno of burning jet fuel raging within the north tower, and jumping through an open window to their certain deaths so far below. Perhaps some were too weak to break a window. Maybe they hoped for some kind of extraordinary biophysical malfunction of the body, or simple fright, to cause death mercifully during the first five to seven seconds that would elapse before they hit the pavement far below them. It was real life, and real death in real time.

How do you say goodbye to your wife, husband, children, parents and other loved ones before you make that choice? How could even the loneliest not think of a recent friend, acquaintance or even a pet before perishing? What is it like to focus instantaneously, suddenly, involuntarily and exclusively upon the almost immediate and certain end of your life?

Surely, they all tried to reach out to someone, while reflexively steeling themselves so inadequately for the rapidly approaching, inevitable end. Undoubtedly, many tried to communicate urgently with the Almighty of one religion or another. To General Murray, these choices were an insult to the individual, the culture and the species well beyond the intensity and magnitude of a super-nova.

Richard and Ginny stayed and watched in awe, as papers periodically fell from the open tower windows, catching a variety of winds generated from the sea and the high-pressure area coming in from the west, and from the temperature differentials developing at different heights around the towers from the fires. Important papers, insignificant papers, little remnants and details of the major economic machinery of the world scattered throughout southern Manhattan. Some were rising, some falling, some seemingly levitating in one place, like the financial markets themselves and the lives of the people trapped inside the towering inferno. The stock market had been struggling for months, setting lower highs on rallies and lower lows on subsequent declines.

Did the 'smart money' actually suspect or anticipate this event and start preparing for it months ahead of time?

That sickening possibility almost made him nauseous with rage, as he put the earpiece from his portable radio into his left ear, and searched the entire frequency spectrum for a news broadcast. It did not take long for him to find commentary about how 'a small executive jet, or possibly an errant passenger airplane' had apparently 'accidentally' crashed into the north tower of the World Trade Center. Almost every radio station was broadcasting the same story. Reports could not confirm the size of the aircraft. Some said it was a large passenger jet, and others claimed it was a smaller executive jet.

Damned idiots don't even know that no normal pilot is going to fly at that low altitude at full throttle into a densely populated area deliberately, against all flight regulations! If he is having mechanical difficulty, he will put the plane down in the Hudson River! Flying a large airliner into a tall building is absolutely not an accident in the year 2001! It is a deliberate and sinister effort! This is obviously a terrorist attack, and we're all in bad shape in this country because we have overpaid talking heads with no imagination, responsibility or common sense, and even less intelligence and judgment telling us what the hell is going on in the world!

It had been a little over sixteen minutes since the big jet hit the north tower. General Murray looked idly to the south still seething with inadequately stifled rage, and saw with intense alarm another large airplane descending ominously from the southwestern sky and turning slightly to the north, heading directly for the world trade towers. His eyes widened with resurging fear and anger beyond any he had ever experienced before that day. He knew more danger and death were approaching, and he could do absolutely nothing about it! He could not warn anyone effectively and he could not stop it. Within fifteen seconds, the second large passenger jet slammed into the southern face and southeast corner of the south tower. Now the whole world knew. There would be no more 'maybe' or 'by mistake' or 'accidental' crash mentioned in the media. The official broadcast discussion shifted toward the 'apparently' shade of truth promoted by the media lawyers. It was now 'apparently' a terrorist attack upon the United States.

General Murray watched a total of eighteen people periodically jump from the windows of the highest floors of the north tower. He saw them falling, but he could not, and did not want see their deaths on the pavement below while he and his wife Ginny were waiting for a half hour for space on one of the many river taxis crossing the Hudson River. The disaster had obviously prompted the spontaneous assembly and remarkably coordinated transport efforts of hundreds of private and public boats from all over the greater metropolitan area. She happened to see one person jump from above the flames and then turned to hide her face in her husband's chest and never turned around again before they boarded the next river taxi from lower Manhattan to the Jersey

City river taxi terminal on the west side of the Hudson River. The river traffic continued with all kinds of watercraft in well-organized apparent chaos.

The man in front of General Murray offered money for the taxi fare out of habit, but the taxi pilot refused and said simply, "Watch your step sir, Ma'am. Get on the boat!"

People continued to file onto the water taxi in an orderly and respectful manner until it was loaded to its maximum official passenger limit plus a few at the discretion of the crew. As that taxi pulled out into the Hudson River, another taxi was either already there or would be at the marina bulkheads within half a minute, and more people left Manhattan for Jersey City directly across the river, while many others walked or jogged north in Manhattan in search of transportation out of the city. This procession continued throughout much of the rest of the day. By evening, literally hundreds of watercraft had evacuated much of southern Manhattan, including more people than the British rescued from Dunkirk during World War II from May 26 through June 3, 1940. General Murray marveled at the spontaneous selfless behavior and efforts of so many individuals helping others in the face of this disastrous evil.

When the Murrays' water taxi was about half-way across the Hudson River, the section of the south tower above the fires started to tilt ever so slightly and then collapsed vertically, pushing the floors below it down with one floor 'pan-caking' down onto the next one below it at an accelerating pace. The south tower continued to collapse vertically with a fantastic, deep rumbling roar that intensified until a huge cloud of dust and smoke from the pulverized cement, wallboard and other building materials enveloped much of lower Manhattan. The pervasive cloud filled the air from street level to half the height of most other tall buildings, leaving an eerie partial skyline visible above it. The collapse took only about ten seconds, with the highest downward velocity that he would later learn had approached 200 miles per hour. He would never forget that sight. Had he and Ginny not boarded the river taxi when they did, they certainly would have had to flee the dusty smoke and debris, and quite possibly could have suffocated. About a half hour later, still fixing their attention on the sight of the collapsed south tower, they watched the north tower collapse from the Jersey City river taxi terminal in another cloud of dust compounding the smoky effect and devastation of the first collapse. The once proud and majestic twin towers were gone—completely destroyed into a pile of rubble.

Then he heard on his radio about the same kind of obviously deliberate airliner crash into the Pentagon building approximately forty minutes after the second jet hit the south tower of the World Trade Center, also hitting him a little closer to home. Many of his friends and colleagues worked in the Pentagon. Then he heard reports about yet another airliner apparently forced down in Shanksville, Pennsylvania about twenty minutes after that.

He wondered aloud, "What the hell is happening?" Then he partially answered his own question. "The law of the jungle!"

Ginny asked, "What did you say?"

"I said this is the law of the jungle at work. Man is viciously attacking his fellow man for the supremacy of ideas, religious truth and a way of life without any regard for centuries of principle values of civilization. It is one of the most profound single violations of western, if not any civilization that I know of, turning centuries of relatively positive human development, progress and ingenuity for good into an act even less civilized than war that even the word 'evil' fails to describe."

He recovered from his reverie and again concentrated upon his current task. He believed he could not afford *not* to find and punish the people responsible for the Fresno explosion. He accepted his self-imposed task as if it were predetermined, and privately committed himself.

I will identify them through the physical evidence and reconstruction of their activities, or by any other means necessary, even if it takes me the rest of my earthly life, and beyond that to do it.

CHAPTER 41

Wednesday, September 12, 2007
Denver, Colorado

"Doctor Lewis? There's a Doctor Buckwalter on the phone for you from Reading, Pennsylvania?" Jenny said with cautious questioning anticipation.

"Thank you, Jenny."

Jake was catching up on psychotherapy research first thing in the morning, and had no appointments for the rest of the morning, so he took the call. He picked up his desk phone with an uneasy sense of foreboding.

"This is Doctor Lewis."

"Doctor Lewis, this is Doctor Ronald Buckwalter at the Reading Hospital in Reading, Pennsylvania. Your mother has been a patient of mine for the last five years or so. I'm very sorry, but I'm calling to tell you that she was severely injured in an automobile accident last night, and is in intensive care, but resting as comfortably as possible. She is still unconscious, and in reasonably stable but guarded condition. I got your phone number from her address book in her purse that the EMTs brought to the hospital with her. I thought I should let you know as soon as possible."

Jake almost lost his grip of the phone as his body flushed with sorrow and anxiety, but after several seconds, he managed to utter,

"Thank you, Doctor Buckwalter. Can you tell me more about what her condition is and how this happened?"

"She sustained multiple leg and pelvic fractures, a concussion, and some internal injuries. Had she not been wearing her seatbelt, however, I strongly suspect she would have perished immediately upon impact or very shortly thereafter. She lost a significant amount of blood, but we have that under control. According to the state police, a tractor-trailer rig lost control on U.S. Highway 222 northbound north of the city and slammed into your mother's car on the southbound side. She was apparently returning home from somewhere. To the best of my understanding from the EMT and police reports, the truck driver had been on the road longer than he should have been, coming from the mid-Atlantic coast area, and apparently lost his concentration or fell asleep at the wheel. We will probably never know exactly, because he died, either immediately upon impact or perhaps shortly thereafter. It was a horrible, horrible and tragic catastrophe!"

Jake felt as though he had just hit the mat face first, and the only other person in the ring was Mike Tyson. There was no referee. Life was not fair, again.

"Doctor Lewis?"

After a few moments of disbelief, intense sorrow and aguish at what he perceived as a series of blameless, random tragedies, Jake gathered his senses.

"Yes. I'm sorry. Thank you for calling, Doctor Buckwalter. I am the only remaining family member, as I'm sure you must know by now. I will be in Reading to see her as soon as I can get there, probably sometime this evening. How can I contact you?"

"I will give you my private cell phone number, 610-667-8231."

Jake made a note of the number and said, "Thank you again for calling, Doctor Buckwalter. I appreciate your consideration."

"Please don't hesitate to let me know whatever I can do to help, Doctor Lewis."

"Thank you."

Jake replaced the phone gently in its cradle. A few seconds later, Jenny knocked on his door. Jake waited several seconds before responding.

"Come in, Jenny."

"Is everything OK, Doctor Lewis?"

"No, Jenny, it isn't. My mother is in intensive care with injuries from a truck accident. I need to go see her tonight. Please rearrange my schedule for the next three days, and move everyone into next week the best way you can, and call me if you have any trouble with that. Ted Sommers can help with some of the caseload if there is a real emergency. I will be leaving within ten minutes."

"OH NO! Doctor Lewis, I'm *so sorry!*"

He said with obvious effort, "Thank you, Jenny but life gets this way . . . every . . . once in a while."

"I'll take care of *everything* here. Don't you worry about a thing! You just go do whatever you need to do!"

"Thank you, Jenny. You're a gem!"

Indeed she was. She was also a secret admirer of the handsome Jake Lewis.

Jake went to his computer, opened up an internet window and made a reservation on U.S. Air, the only non-stop flight he could find. He felt lucky to get the last available seat on an eleven o'clock flight from Denver International Airport that morning, arriving at Philadelphia International Airport at four fifty-four that afternoon, where he would rent a car for the roughly one-hour drive to Reading, west on Interstate 76, the old Pennsylvania Turnpike, to Morgantown, and then north on US-422. If he hurried, he could make the flight out of Denver with only a few minutes to spare.

CHAPTER 42

Wednesday, September 12, 2007
Reading, Pennsylvania

Jake drove around through the sprawling campus of the Reading Hospital in what he feared would be an endless search for a place to park his rented white Chevy Cobalt as he cursed this time-consuming inconvenience competing with his urgency to see his mother. With a stroke of whatever remaining luck he thought he was entitled to, he saw a car pulling out of a space just five car lengths ahead of him, and he quickly slipped into that space with a quiet 'thank you' to the driver of the other car.

Eventually, he found his way from the large entrance foyer of the huge landmark colonial style main building to the Intensive Care Unit, and entered the main control area in the center of a modern large room with a central nurse station and several banks of electronic monitors suspended from the ceiling. The faint sounds of soft voices occasionally overridden by the hospital intercom system mixed with the electronic beeps from the monitors that filled the sterile atmosphere.

"Doctor Shipley . . . Code 7 . . . Doctor Shipley . . . Code 7."

"Doctor Weinstein . . . Call 4428. Doctor Weinstein . . . Call 4428."

Jake walked up to the center console and drew a professional 'smile' from a large middle-aged female nurse in a white uniform with a brass nameplate pinned to the upper part of her uniform indicating her name was 'Judith Downing, R.N.' Jake thought she looked like a retired linebacker for the Philadelphia Eagles football team.

"Can I help you?" she said in a contralto voice obviously without any training.

"Doctor Wesson . . . Call 4475. Doctor Wesson . . . Call 4475."

Jake looked up with controlled impatience at the public address speaker in the ceiling just to his left, and then back at the 'linebacker' in the white nurse's uniform.

He said, "Yes, my name is Jake Lewis. I understand that my mother arrived here last evening with injuries sustained in an automobile collision with a truck. I just came all the way from Denver, and I want to see her as soon as possible."

Beep . . . Beep . . . Beep . . . BEEEEEEEEEEEEEEEEEEEEEE.

Downing immediately looked to her left at the bank of monitors and called defensive signals evenly into a red hand phone, "Code 4 ICU. Code 4 ICU. Code 4 ICU."

Another nurse was in room seven within seconds.

Jake got out of the way as the resuscitation team arrived less than twenty seconds later and ran into the main ICU room pushing a wheeled cart with what appeared to be a resuscitator and a few other electronic devices on it and disappeared through an open door under a large number '7.'

He heard a man call out "Clear!" and then heard a noticeable dull 'thump.' "Clear!" Another 'thump.' "Clear!" Another 'thump.'

Jake was apprehensive.

"Doctor Weinstein, call 4428. Doctor Weinstein, call 4428."

Weinstein, get your act together! Jake said to himself in a futile childish urge to lash out at someone to vent his frustration.

He was obviously not a priority in the busy intensive care unit. The antiseptic silence of the hospital continued to flow through the main ICU center. Jake tried surreptitiously to peer into room seven, but could not see anything without appearing to be a profoundly rude voyeur, so he reluctantly kept his distance. He was apprehensive because he did not know which room his mother occupied. The 'linebacker' made some notes on a sheet of paper on her desk, and then called over to Jake.

"Mr. Lewis, you may have some time with your mother in room three. Please remember that she is unconscious," she said almost kindly.

Jake wheeled around with a jolt of relief as if *he* had been resuscitated.

"Thank you," he said. "Thank you very much!"

He walked cautiously into room three, and immediately inhaled involuntarily at the first sight of his once very attractive and vivacious mother lying perfectly quiet and still in a hospital bed with a tube running out from under the bed sheet, one in her right arm, and a ventilator tube in her nose. She had swollen bruises and cuts over her once strikingly beautiful facial features. Her left arm was resting at her side. A young nurse, definitely not on the football team, but looked more like a very pretty dancer was sitting by the bed making notes on a clipboard. Her nameplate indicated 'Jennifer Roth, R.N.' She looked up at him immediately with obvious genuine empathy.

"I'm Jennifer. If you need anything, please let me know. I'll be right outside at the nurse's station."

She stood up and smiled with enough sincerity to ease Jake's sense of 'hospital business as usual.'

"I'm her son, Jake Lewis," he offered.

Jennifer said pleasantly enough, "I know. I heard you come in."

Jake smiled sheepishly for just a second as she turned to leave him with his mother. He just stood at the foot of her bed for a minute, and then walked up to the side of the bed away from the tubes and pulled up the nearby chair Jennifer had been sitting in, and sat down as close to his mother as he could. He watched carefully for evidence of life. Her chest was rising and falling ever so slightly and not very often, but that was about all Jake could see as evidence of life. He started talking to her in a soft voice.

"Mom? Mom, I know you probably can't hear me, but I need to talk to you. I believe you're going to come out of this OK, Mom. It's not your time yet. You need to live. There is so much more for you to live for!"

"Mom, I have to tell you something. I've met the woman I am going to marry. I met her in a nightclub in Denver last Friday evening.

I know you don't think very highly of nightclubs, Mom, but if I had not had an intense hankering for a charcoal-fired hamburger, I probably would not have been there on that night and I never would have known true happiness. She's a singer, Mom. I know you probably think this is way too fast for a proper relationship to develop, but I have never been more sure of anything else in my entire life. You would absolutely *love* her voice! I *know* you would! And, someday, you will have grandchildren—beautiful little grandchildren! I want you to meet her as soon as you are able. I just know you will love her!"

"Remember those girls I used to talk about, even some of the ones I brought home to meet you and Dad when I was in college and grad school? How sure I was that I was in love? Well, I was really an idiot, an ignorant fool! I had no understanding at all about what love really is. I had no idea about how fantastically great life could be! I don't know whether she can cook or not, Mom, but I really don't care, either. I may not have the ace and jack of spades Mom, but I *do* have the ace and jack of hearts, and I'm going to bet the farm! I wish Dad could have lived long enough to meet her, but somehow, I believe he will approve of her, wherever he is. I know I have enough of him in me to believe he would love her as well. Mom?"

Jake sat quietly in the chair, watching his mother carefully for signs of consciousness or recognition of his presence. He looked at her closed eyes and lips for evidence of movement. He was trying to energize her hope and determination to live if there was any chance at all that she could hear him, any chance that she could know that he was right there next to her bed. If he said nothing at all, she would definitely not know of his hope for her life. If he assumed the improbable, that she could at least hear him, or somehow connect with him psychically, then it was worth the trip, so he talked to her as though she could hear him. He was pushing the limits of every medical, psychological or psychic 'fringe' theory he had ever even heard of, desperately wanting to believe she would sense that he was there next to her. Nothing changed. The sterile hospital air was still. The quiet sounds of her monitoring equipment continued to hum softly, as if not to disturb anyone.

"Mom?"

He watched her silently for several minutes. He thought he saw a finger move. Maybe that was wishful thinking. He waited hopefully. She was quiet and still.

Fifteen minutes later, Jake wiped a single tear from each cheek, left the ICU and the hospital, walked to his rental car, and drove away to find food and a motel for the night. He was physically and mentally absolutely exhausted.

CHAPTER 43

Thursday, September 13, 2007
Reading, Pennsylvania

Jake returned to the Intensive Care Unit at the hospital around nine o'clock in casual slacks and a sport shirt. The 'linebacker' was no longer on duty, but an apparently equally competent middle-aged woman Jake thought might have been a graduate of the Rockettes some three or four decades ago, was on duty. She still had the general appearance of a woman who had been quite shapely earlier in life, had not lost much of it and still carried herself with poise and self-assurance in what must have been her sixth decade. Her hair was relatively short, and showed small evidence of grey under her nurse's cap. She obviously used makeup, but kept it simple and efficient without looking like a clown or detracting from her friendly deep blue eyes. She smiled at him immediately upon his entrance to the ICU, revealing the early elements of facial wrinkles in her still attractive face. She greeted him by name, much to his amazement.

"Good morning Doctor Lewis. Your mother's condition has not changed. Doctor Buckwalter was here just after eight o'clock this morning to see her for about ten minutes. He asked me to tell you that he apologizes for his hectic schedule this morning without time to see you personally, and that her condition is pretty much in God's hands from this point on. He said that he will be back again before noon, so you can speak with him then."

The public address system reminded Jake that he and his mother were only a very small story in the vast hospital complex.

"Doctor Sampson, call 4428 . . . Doctor Sampson, call 4428 . . ."

None of this information really surprised Jake. Nevertheless, he felt his heart sink in disappointment as he glanced at her nameplate, 'J. Sheffield, R.N.'

She noted his attention with a smile, and offered, "My name is Jessica."

"Thank you, Jessica. I will stay until he returns."

Jake entered her room and looked at his mother in essentially the same condition she was in the last time he saw her. He inhaled deeply and then sighed as he sat down in the chair next to her bed and waited. He had been sleeping for over two hours when Doctor Buckwalter entered the room and awakened him with a start.

"You must be fighting emotional exhaustion, Doctor Lewis. I'm Doctor Buckwalter." Jake stood up and greeted the shorter and slightly overweight man with a handshake.

"Please call me Jake. Yes, I've been pretty busy these last few days. Thank you for stopping by. I would like to know your latest prognosis for my mother."

"We've done everything reasonable within the limits of her expressed wishes in her living will and emergency directives, Jake. Her internal injuries were severe, and there is no way we can estimate how long she will survive, nor how long she will be unconscious. I have seen cases like this in which complete recovery has been nothing short of miraculous, and I have seen cases with every justifiable real medical hope for recovery end in rapid and unexplainable death. We simply do not know anything more at this point."

"I understand. Thank you. That's about what I expected, but I wanted to hear it from you."

"I understand. She is getting the best care we can provide."

"I know."

"You are welcome to stay as long as you would like, Jake. I will check back with you in about two hours."

"Thank you very much for all you have done."

Doctor Buckwalter nodded, smiled briefly and then left the room to complete the rest of his rounds. Jake sat down in the chair again. He dozed off and then easily fell into a deep sleep right there in the chair. Images of his evening with his beautiful Sasha kept playing in the theater of his dreams. He could not get her out of his mind. She was as much a part of his life as the uncontrollable music that came to him almost constantly. All of his psychological education and training was useless in this raw emotional clash between beautiful memories of Sasha and intense awareness of his mother's fragile thread of life just a few feet away from him.

The Intensive Care Unit was located well within the depths of the large hospital structure, and had no windows to an outside view, so Jake had no immediate idea whether it was day or night. He was tired. His body gradually succumbed to sleep against his will. After only about ten minutes of sleep, the sudden soft rustle of fabric and gentle air movement nearby awakened him as people and hushed voices suddenly seemed to fill the room.

"Doctor Lewis?" Jennifer Roth said gently as she lightly touched his shoulder. "Doctor Lewis? Your mother has passed away."

Jake felt like he had just been hit by the truck himself as he slumped deeper into his chair. He had stayed with the path of hope out of his own choosing, and now his hope ended. The nurse's kind and gentle voice did nothing to blunt the sharp and profound finality of her message. He wanted to hit life's 'replay' button, to make time to go back immediately so he could at least have been awake to see her go. The nurses and orderlies quietly and quickly disconnected the tubes and electrical equipment from his mother's body. Jennifer Roth looked into Jake's eyes with her special nurse's intuition and saw more than the agony of a man who had just lost his mother. She turned around and quietly ordered all the other hospital personnel out of the room. She left as well, but remained just outside the entrance to the room, just in case he needed her.

Jake stood up with effort, and walked to the edge of the bed and looked down at his mother. He knew that she had long ago established a living will with emergency directives, stipulating that no extraordinary means would be permitted in the event of a life-threatening medical emergency to maintain her life beyond the most basic procedures designed to assure only her comfort and assist her natural recovery. There would be no 'Code Red,' 'Code 7' or any other 'Code' as she left the stage of life. There would be no theatrics. There would be no racing down the halls. There would be no blame. She would submit to her God when He called her. Jake knew that. He took a deep breath and let it out slowly. Now he had lost the one person who had given so much of herself to bring him into this world, taught him to be his own person and through loving him, showed him how he should love others. She had given him an appreciation of what a good woman is. She had unknowingly enabled him to love Sasha with all of his heart, mind, soul and unique musical talent.

CHAPTER 44

Friday, September 14, 2007
Maryland

Duke's private cell phone rang.

"Hi Joe! How is your vacation in Mumbai?" (What have you learned about our prospect?)

"The weather is beautiful, and the winds promise to bring more good weather." (He is well qualified, and has a genuine interest in working for The Chancellor Organization.)

"That's good! Are there many American tourists there?" (Have you contacted our representative at the embassy yet?)

"Yes, there are, and I have met a few of them." (Yes, I have already met with him.)

"When will you be able to return home?" (How much longer do you anticipate you will need to be there?)

"Within a week or two, I would guess." (Within a week or two.)

"What have you learned about the culture?" (Do you have a plan?)

"Quite a lot, actually. It is very interesting here. I will discuss it with you after my return." (I do have a plan. I will tell you in person after I return.)

"OK! Call me when you get back!"

"I'll do that!"

Duke ended the connection and then closed two open trading positions, one for a loss of $45,000 and the other for a gain of $347,000.

CHAPTER 45

Friday, September 14, 2007
Langley, Virginia

This time, General Murray himself was going to do something about the terrorist attack, rather than be just a spectator as he was in 2001, and the rules of engagement would be the rules of the jungle if he had anything to say about it. He ordered his staff to organize a timeline for the U-Haul truck, from the first appearance of the vehicle in the surveillance images to its last known appearance. This painstaking effort resulted in identifying the Miami area surrounding the airport where Rasheed had apparently first entered the country as the most likely start of the deadly plan.

He sent two of his best field agents to Miami to investigate the beginning of the U-Haul truck part of the story by interviewing as many people as possible to find out where the vehicle came from and who was driving it. Steve Markham and Lou 'The Bishop' Bischov scoured the general area around the Miami International Airport, interviewing all automobile rental and used-car dealership employees but could not come up with any useful information. They did get the manifests of all incoming flights for the prior four weeks from the airline supervisor, however. Lou called General Murray on his cell phone.

"General, we haven't found anything immediately useful about the truck in Miami, so we're going to follow the most obvious routes to Fresno, assuming stops at any Interstate highway locations with fuel, food, and motels, according to the most probable route from the satellite images. We will forward the last four weeks of all flight manifests for inbound flights, however. They should contain at least some information about something or someone of interest."

"Damn it!" General Murray muttered in obvious frustration. "That means we are dealing with at least one domestic accomplice in addition to the driver! We know the driver did not rent the truck in Miami, so someone else must have rented the truck and then drove it to Miami to pick up the driver or that driver drove to Miami from somewhere else. We don't know whether the truck was delivered with the explosive device on board, or whether it was assembled en route, or what! We should assume that whoever took the truck to Miami did not stay with the truck across the country, because we have already figured out that the timing of our satellite images of the truck so far suggests strongly that there was only one driver. We have to look for the person who provided the truck as well! We're going to have to contact every one of the approximately 15,000 U-Haul rental agencies in the country if necessary, but we're going to start with the ones in roughly 324 Florida cities and those in the immediately contiguous states, and then work our way out as necessary. The FBI should be able to handle that part. You two just stay with the truck route and identify the driver! I'm going to call the FBI to see whether we can get more people on the route and the U-Haul locations immediately."

He expected the new culture of cooperation among the federal clandestine and law enforcement agencies since 9/11 to make this task easier and more efficient. He also had to think about who might have financed this attack and how they did it. If the explosive material was indeed C4, then it most probably had to have come from a controlled source, and that meant significant money was probably involved on top of the typical logistical and transportation needs and support of at least two people, probably more. C4 is a very carefully controlled explosive substance, and is manufactured and stored primarily by the United States military. General Murray was completely incensed at the possibility of U.S. military collusion, either deliberately or unwittingly in this disaster although he had to consider that foreign military organizations could also have been a source, since Iran also has been a source of C4. The British were the only known source of PE4, and that was not a welcome fact either. However, he simply could not dismiss completely the possibility that some evil genius was bright enough to have re-invented C4 or PE4 without any collusion from the United States military organizations or the British.

They had satellite images of a large U-Haul truck on Interstate 75 North toward Live Oak, Florida, so they continued to follow what they believed to be the most probable route taken by the U-Haul truck across the southern states. The FBI spent many hours, even with the assistance of local police scouring the area, interviewing gas station employees, looking for any hint of the origin of the truck, but came up empty again. It was not until Markham and The Bishop got to Mobile, Alabama that they found someone who remembered the truck. After visiting two dozen other gas stations within logical proximity of the freeway, the two CIA agents entered the convenience store at the Exxon station where Rasheed had stopped for fuel, and identified themselves as federal investigators to the man behind the counter.

The Bishop said, "We're looking for a man, possibly of Iranian or Pakistani heritage who was driving a large U-Haul truck through this area. Do you have any recollection of such a truck or a driver of that description around Wednesday, September 5 of this year?"

Roger's antennae went up as he sensed immediately that this fit-looking man with a permanent five o'clock shadow and penetrating dark recessed eyes was deadly serious. He was not accustomed to having two men in suits show up together at his counter for any reason other than to cause trouble. He assessed the situation for a moment, and decided it would be best to maintain a friendly rapport for the time being.

"I do indeed remember that. Why do you ask, sir?" he said with only mild betrayal of his concern.

"What is your name, sir?"

"Roger Benson." He thought it would be unwise to elaborate or offer anything further out of fear of becoming involved in something he sensed he did not want to be a part of.

"Mr. Benson, we would like to learn everything you can recall about that occurrence, because we have good reason to believe that U-Haul truck was used in conjunction with the Fresno incident."

He did not like giving reasons for his inquiry, but he decided it was best in this case to accelerate cooperation and get to the meat of the matter as quickly as possible and move on.

"*Jesus, God Almighty!* You mean the explosion in Fresno several days ago?"

"That's right, Mr. Benson. Now, can we go somewhere private to talk about this?" he asked with obvious impatience.

"Oh! Of course! Come with me to my office, right over there."

He gestured to a small room on the far side of the building with an immediate mental shift to complete cooperation. He called out to his assistant Tricia to take over the counter. Roger led the way, with Steve and the Bishop trailing close behind with the feel of anticipation, and possibly success in their step. The three men entered the small office, and Roger sat in the well-worn brown upholstered chair behind his messy grey metal desk, and gestured to the two agents to sit in the two wobbly grey steel chairs on the other side.

The Bishop took the lead again. "Mr. Benson, I would like you to tell me everything you can remember about that man and that truck."

"Well, Mr.—Sorry, I didn't get you name . . ."

"Bischov," Lou said tersely.

"Well, Mr. Bischov, I can do a little more than tell you, because I have just about perfect recall—photographic memory, actually. I don't draw very well, but if you can find a sketch artist, or whatever you call them, I can describe the man who came into this store from a truck just like the one you described, so the artist gets on paper what I have in my head. How's that?"

The Bishop turned and nodded to Steve, who rose from his chair and walked through the main store as he retrieved his cell phone from his pocket. He called the Mobile police department on his cell phone from just outside the store building where he had sufficient privacy away from other people and asked for the Chief of Police. After being shuffled from a receptionist to the duty officer, Markham was connected to the chief of police who spoke with an obvious southern drawl in the gravelly voice of a man who probably smoked too much.

"This is Police Chief Simmons. How can I help you?"

"Chief, this is agent Steve Markham. I am a federal investigator working on the Fresno incident, and I have immediate need of a police sketch artist. I assume you have a talented artist on board?"

"You betcha, Mr. Markham! Where do you need her?"

"We need her at the Exxon station on Eagle Drive. How soon can you get her over here?"

"I'll have her there in about ten minutes, Mr. Markham, and I'm sending some muscle and firepower with her, just to make sure she's safe."

Steve raised his eyebrows and responded, "I *said* I'm a federal investigator, Chief, not Mafia or Colombian drug cartel!"

"OK! OK! Just trying to protect my people, especially her. She's petite. I'm not questioning your honesty Mr. Markham. Sorry. Her name's Sylvia Amoretti."

"Thanks, Chief. This could be very important."

"No problem at all, Mr. Markham. Glad I could be of some help! You need anything else, please don't hesitate to call me, ya hear?"

"Yes, Chief. Thanks again."

Steve reentered the building and strode into the small office. "There's a Mobile police department sketch artist on her way. Name's Sylvia Amoretti. Be here in about ten minutes."

The Bishop trained his piercing eyes on Roger's and continued in a deadly serious tone. "Tell me *everything* you know about the driver and the truck."

"Well, the guy who drove that truck came into my store and bought some No-Doz, a bottle of water and a Snickers candy bar when he paid in cash for the gas. Had a *wad* of cash! He was obviously not originally from this country, I would say, because he had a slight accent, maybe Indian, Pakistani, Iranian or something like that, but he spoke pretty good English anyway. I remember another truck, almost exactly like the one he drove. Same size, only it looked older, parked across the street, had no markings on it. Just a plain box truck. Anyway, after the first guy left my store, he looked like he was talking for just a few moments with the guy who drove the other truck. Then the other guy got in his truck and turned into my station, and the first guy started his truck and followed the other guy out of the station going south on Michigan Avenue. That's the last I saw of either of 'em."

"Can you describe the other driver?"

"Didn't really get a good look at him, and he never came into the store, but I'd say he was about the same size as the first guy, slightly darker complexion, dark hair, not short but not really long, either, wore dark tan pants, blue short-sleeved shirt not tucked in, white sneakers. That's about all I can give you on him. I never really got a good look at his face."

A few minutes later, a Mobile Police patrol car eased into the gas station and parked head on next to the store building. The petite red-haired Sylvia Amoretti gracefully exited the car from the passenger seat in the front while her oversized, baby-faced 'escort' got out from the driver's side, allowing the car's suspension to recover from his considerable weight as it returned to its usual slightly lopsided posture. He lumbered along behind her into the convenience store building. Sylvia introduced herself politely to Lou and Roger. Lou clarified that he was a federal investigator, and indicated that Roger Benson would be the man she would be working with. The office was quite crowded with Roger, the Bishop, Sylvia, and her sidekick, so the Bishop illuminated the obvious, suggesting that 'muscle cop' and he would wait outside, leaving Sylvia and Roger alone in the office to get the needed sketch done as soon as possible without wasting what little air was available in the small, almost suffocating office. The cop was not much of a conversationalist, so he just stood where he could see into the office, keeping an eye on Sylvia as he was instructed, and the Bishop leaned against the building looking out into nowhere, wondering when a button would explode from the front of 'muscle cop's' light blue uniform shirt.

She sat down at the desk and unzipped her leather utility case, revealing a sketchpad of small poster proportions, but larger than typical letter-sized paper, and started questioning Roger with the patient gentle tact of an experienced third-grade teacher in combination with a thoroughly professional business attitude. He responded with unusually specific details as Sylvia followed with her pencil his explicit directions and descriptions with remarkable precision, intuition and obvious artistic ability. Roger insisted that she make certain final adjustments in facial features to correspond with his incredibly unusual and precise visual memory. After slightly more than a half hour of this process, Roger appeared to be satisfied, because he stopped telling her how to change the drawing. Sylvia exhaled heavily after what had to be the most extensive artistic effort of her police career, and actually admired her own work for several seconds. So did Roger. He stood up and studied her sketch carefully, looking over her shoulder one more time.

After another fifteen seconds, he exclaimed with great satisfaction, "That's your man! That's *exactly* what he looked like! I absolutely *guarantee* it!"

The bishop mused to himself that Roger probably also guaranteed automobile service, but discarded the thought because he wanted to stay positive and constructive. He needed every scrap of information and evidence he could get. He also admired the sketch as a sign of progress and was eager to start connecting the next dots. The two agents thanked Sylvia respectfully for her excellent assistance, took the drawing and then left the building. They entered their vehicle and compared notes, satisfying themselves that they were indeed on the right track. Sylvia got back in the Mobile Police patrol car and 'muscle cop' got in on the driver's side, again weighing down the tired, overworked suspension, and drove the lopsided cruiser back to the police headquarters building.

The bishop said, "Let's get this sketch into the computer system as soon as possible."

The two men rushed to the Mobile Municipal Airport and boarded a small CIA plane for the flight back to Washington, retrieved their car, and then drove to General Murray's headquarters with the sketch. They did not want to fax the sketch from where they were, because their headquarters equipment was far superior to most fax machines, which would have sacrificed the resolution and clarity they wanted in the transmission process. The CIA had several computer programs designed to enhance and modify any image input that would effectively create almost a photographic-quality representation of the subject of Sylvia's sketch. They then ran another image program which essentially raced through a large image database of known or suspected 'persons of interest,' looking for a match.

After twenty-one minutes of running this program, they discovered that they had a completely new 'person of interest.' Rasheed's image was not on file. This was not a welcome discovery. It meant that the field of associated persons was vacant. If the mastermind of this deadly plot was unknown to the FBI and CIA, then quite possibly he might also be unknown to the other major clandestine investigative organizations around the world, and would represent one of the most dangerous threats to western civilization to date. They would still have no idea who this man communicated with or associated with, who funded him, or with what organization he may have been associated. They would be working from scratch, if it were not for the very useful sketch. They did not fully appreciate the combined talents of Roger and Sylvia. The latest computer-enhanced image was for all practical purposes a *realistic black and white photograph* of Rasheed Shirani, heretofore an unknown Pakistani citizen.

CHAPTER 46

Friday, September 14, 2007
Reading, Pennsylvania

Jake visited The Lutz Funeral Home on Perkiomen Avenue to arrange for his mother's funeral. He would keep it simple, honoring her wishes. A little more than two hours later, he contacted the Diefenderfer Auction Company in Laureldale on the western side of the metropolitan area to arrange for the sale of her house and household goods that he did not have room for in Denver.

After finishing these arrangements, he drove back to the Philadelphia International Airport, and boarded a USAir flight at eight forty-five that evening to return to Denver. The plane landed around eleven that night and Jake did not get back to his condominium until almost twelve-thirty in the morning. He was exhausted physically, mentally, and emotionally, and decided to spend the next day at home doing very little, and possibly nothing at all.

CHAPTER 47

Monday, September 17, 2007
Seattle, Washington

FBI Agent Harrington was back in his office in Seattle. He was not officially assigned to the Fresno case, but *everyone* who worked for the FBI was at least unofficially on it, at least to some extent. He sat at his relatively tidy desk, staring at a map of the western United States on the wall across from his desk with little colored pushpins stuck in it from various prior investigations. He did not have any yellow pins on the map, so he retrieved a new plastic case of yellow pins from his center desk drawer, and stuck one into 'Fresno' on the map. He then took a string from his desk drawer and measured out twelve hours of driving distance, more or less, as an estimate of the maximum distance he thought one person would be able to drive with a large load of dangerous explosives. He was thinking in terms of psychologically how far someone could drive, not just how far in terms of physical or mechanical capability, but also in terms of knowing that he could be detained by the police or could be forced to abort his mission, probably by detonating the device under threat of discovery at almost any time.

He then put the point of a pencil in the loop of string he tied together to estimate that driving distance, and anchored the other end on the pin stuck on 'Fresno' on the map, and then drew a large circle on the map with the string acting as the radius. It was far more likely in his opinion, that few, rather than many people would execute an apparent terrorist attack in order to keep information flow to a minimum, and would use commonly available transportation methods and freedom of movement, which of course, is one of the main freedoms in the United States. That would mean a truck or a car, but most likely a truck, because of the size of the explosion and implied weight of the explosive material. FBI and police evidence of remnants of a trailer of some sort at the scene further narrowed down the possibilities to a vehicle with sufficient horsepower to make the trip hauling a certain amount of weight, guessing again about how much the gasoline and C4 would weigh, let alone the weight of a trailer. The federal investigators at the scene had estimated the quantity of C4 necessary to cause the damage they witnessed, and concluded that it was around 8,000 pounds—more than a typical trailer could hold, and more than the largest rental trucks could hold. However, he could not know with certainty that such a trailer was used in the attack. The more vehicles used in the attack, the greater the logistical and communication effort would be required, and the more people would be involved, implying increased probability of discovery or error in execution. There was obviously no effective discovery prior to the incident, so he assumed minimal vehicles and only one or two people involved, possibly three, by the time the device was detonated. Evidence of a trailer might have been from an innocent driver who just happened to be in the wrong place at the wrong time, for all he knew. Maybe there were several vehicles carrying C4, he thought. He was guessing, but guessing with ten years of FBI experience and training. He settled on the idea of a single vehicle and a single driver with a V-8 engine or a strong diesel engine as more likely than a six-cylinder gasoline engine. Most suicide terrorist attacks he knew about other than 9/11 ultimately relied upon a single person, regardless of how many participated in the planning and logistical operations. A four-banger gasoline engine was out of the question. It was all he could do for the time being to satisfy his restless aversion to doing nothing about the Fresno incident, and with so little evidence. His mind was racing, but his 'mental clutch' was not engaged.

He knew that C4 was non-volatile in the sense that it required an electrical charge from a blasting cap to ignite it. Simply dropping it on the floor or pavement, shooting a bullet into it, or even attempting to burn it with a match would not detonate the explosive material. He had nothing else to go on but the probability of the high explosive and an accelerant, probably gasoline. Airplanes were essentially out of the question. He simply did not believe that anyone could ship a load of C4 that large on an airplane undetected. There was enough standard security, including well-trained dogs, and plenty of procedural impediments since 9/11 to keep that possibility extremely remote. He concluded the same for transport by ship. He thought shipping procedures were too thorough to allow one individual or a few individuals to organize a shipment of that much C4 from some foreign port to California undetected, unless, of course, it was hidden within one of those large containers ahead of time. He committed that point to memory. He also had to consider that the final load of C4 might have been manufactured and delivered in several smaller quantities over time, perhaps many weeks or months. A smaller boat, maybe a fishing vessel or a private yacht, however, was another story—one that he had to keep in mind. He went back to staring at his map.

CHAPTER 48

Monday, September 17, 2007
Denver, Colorado

Jake arrived early at Eddie's Place on Monday, a little after five o'clock, so he could make sure he would have the same table where he and Sasha first sat together and got to know each other a little. He was wearing a new tan sport jacket and burgundy silk tie with dark brown casual slacks. He brought with him a single white rose in a beautiful eight-inch high clear glass vase with a light pink hue flowing through it in a spiral design as if the vase had been twisted gently in its molten form around the vertical axis into its final shape. He set it on the table across from him in front of where she would sit. He took the CD out of his jacket pocket, and placed it next to the vase with a note on it, 'For Sasha, with all my love. Jake.'

Fifteen minutes later the room was not yet full, so he did not feel like he was hurting Eddie's business by holding the table without ordering anything other than water. He watched people gather as he nursed his glass of ice water. He took the time to check his phone messages, and noticed a message from Jenny.

'Richie called after you left and said he was very worried about you.'

Two women took a table across the room from Jake, and settled into a busy and animated discussion of their activities during the day, men, clothing, and whatever else struck their fancy. 'Stealth' seemed to 'float' over to their table and offered them menus.

"Can I get you something to drink, ladies?"

"Lemonade, please."

"Make that two, thank you."

"Sure thing! Coming right up!"

The two women leaned closer to each other in conspiratorial postures as they both noticed the handsome gentleman across the room near the stage at the small table for two with the beautiful pink vase containing a single white rose.

The trim dirty-blonde-haired woman whispered to her friend, "Isn't that *something!* I've never seen anything like *that* before!"

"My God! What a *beautiful* flower! He must be completely *smitten!* Why don't I meet guys like that?"

"Well, it's not because you don't button your blouse all the way up!" she teased her better-endowed friend.

The entertainment for the evening was a group from Chicago, including a longhaired 'thirty-something' man on drums, a pudgy average-looking fellow on bass guitar, and two reasonably attractive women in black dresses with guitars. They looked like sisters, each with straight long dark blonde hair to the middle of her back. They started with a nice duet and an engaging beat, smiling naturally, as the growing crowd quieted down a little. They were rather good, but they were not The Autumn Dream. The girls were definitely not the caliber of Sasha—not even close.

Jake listened attentively, trying to make time accelerate by focusing on something other than Sasha. It was not working very well. He looked around the room. It was five forty-five. Sasha was not there. Five minutes later, he pulled his cell phone from his pocket, and dialed her number and waited through four rings.

Her cheerful recorded voice answered after four rings, 'Hi! This is Sasha! I can't take your call right now, so please leave a message after the beep! Thank you!'

He heard the 'beep.'

"Hi, Sasha. It's Jake. It's ten 'til six. I'm at Eddie's, and I'm getting a little worried. I hope you are OK. Please call me as soon as you can. I love you. 'Bye."

If she were in trouble, or knew she could not make their date on time, he thought she surely would have tried to call him at the V.A. hospital earlier in the day. She knew where he worked, and there was only one man named Jake Lewis in the entire hospital! Surely, she could have reached him that way. However, once he left the hospital, she could no longer get in touch with him. They were apparently unable to communicate with each other, and that gave Jake a great deal of anxiety.

In his funk brought on by his mother's tragic death, he had also neglected to read newspapers during the week, or watch the news on TV or the internet. He kept busy at the hospital, maintaining a full schedule of counseling appointments in an effort to make the time until this evening pass more quickly. When he returned to his condominium during the week, he usually made a light or easy supper for himself, and read up on professional journals before retiring for the night instead of paying attention to the outside world.

A middle-aged couple was sitting at a table next to the two women, and the woman followed their gaze across the room.

After about twelve seconds, the woman turned back toward her husband and said, "That man over there on the far side near the stage is in love! It's so *obvious!*"

He turned his head slowly to look where her eyes had focused.

"*That's* for sure," he said, and casually turned back to his wife with a wink and a smile.

The two women heard their exchange and turned around to share their private enjoyment of what must have been a very unusual real life love story played out before them with unabashed openness.

"Isn't that sweet!" the dark-haired young woman said to the married woman behind her, raising her hand to hide her mouth from the side view.

The music continued with another number. Jake looked at his watch. It was five minutes after six. By this time, the dining area was completely full, yet he felt very much alone and extremely disappointed, and felt he was losing the battle against increasing anxiety. Another arrhythmia episode interrupted his thoughts. He quelled it with a few seconds of deep, controlled breathing.

'Stealth' glided over to Jake's table, "Would you like to order, sir?"

'Stealth' glanced down, and could not avoid reading the note, but looked back at Jake quickly before Jake looked up at him.

"I'm expecting my friend shortly. Will you please give me, say, another five minutes? I'm sure she will be here very soon."

'Stealth' said, "No problem, sir. I'll be back in five."

"Thank you!"

The server recognized Jake, and remembered the beautiful singer from that Friday, the week before last. How could he forget! He was absolutely sure Jake was waiting for the woman in the white dress. He thought to himself that most men would wait almost an eternity for her.

The two women on the other side of the room noticed the exchange, but could not hear what the two men had said.

The dark-haired young woman spoke in a hushed voice, "I'm going to the ladies room and then I'm going to come back after going by his table for a closer look. I absolutely *adore* that vase and flower!"

She was gone only five minutes—probably a world speed record in Denver—and took the long route around the room before reporting to the dirty-blonde woman at her table.

"Well?" said the 'dirty blonde' in almost controlled, eager anticipation.

She sat down and leaned closer to her friend hunched over her forearms resting on the table and said, "There's a CD on the table with the name 'Jake Lewis' and '9/11/2007' on it next to the vase and a little love note next to it that says 'For Sasha, with all my love, Jake.'"

"Oh, that's *soooo* nice! She's a lucky gal, whoever she is!"

Eddie came out of his business office upstairs after having finished some accounting work, and quickly took the stairs two steps at a time down to the main floor. He slipped behind a young server near the bar, and walked the length of the bar, until he saw Jake across the room at the table with the white rose and pink vase on it near the stage.

He froze instantly in his tracks, and exclaimed "OOOOOH MMMMYYYYYY GOD! NNNNOOOOOOOOO!"

A patron at the bar near him looked up and slightly to his right at Eddie. Eddie's eyes were full of tears. His mouth hung open, and he was shaking rapidly, sobbing with a mix of fear and anger and hurt in his face. He fell involuntarily toward the bar, and caught himself with both hands on the inside rail of the bar.

"Hey. Hey! Eddie! You OK?"

'Dirty blond' and 'dark hair' at their table less than fifteen feet away heard Eddie and turned around to see that he was sobbing and shaking uncontrollably as his face turned red. They looked at each other, then back at Eddie, and followed his gaze across the room to the table with the pink vase and the white rose, then back at each other with raised eyebrows and serious concern on their faces.

'Dirty Blonde' cupped her hand near her mouth and said to her friend in a conspiratorial voice, "Something's *definitely* not right here!"

Eddie tried to control himself but he continued to sob as quietly as he could, leaning against the inside of the bar, wishing he could stop. Nevertheless, he continued weeping softly. Marie, his head bartender quickly went over to him with her typically maternal concern. She was a widow and mother of two grown children, out on their own. She carried a little extra weight reasonably well, and almost always presented a naturally vivacious, optimistic personality. She had kind brown eyes and an easy and unusually engaging smile that was now missing from her face.

"Eddie. Eddie? Eddie! Listen to me! What's going on? Why are you so upset?"

"H . . . h . . . h . . . he d . . . d . . . doesn't . . . doesn't KNOW!"

"Eddie! Try to get a hold of yourself. Who doesn't know what?" she coaxed as kindly as she could as she looked intently into his eyes.

He swallowed hard and wiped most of the tears from his face with his arm, and just barely pulled himself together for a moment.

"Look . . . Look over there, Marie" he nodded toward Jake.

Marie looked where he indicated, and saw the handsome, well-dressed young man sitting at the small table near the right end of the stage with slumped shoulders, resting his head in his hands with his elbows on the table in front of him. There was a white rose in a pink vase across the table from him with a CD case, and a small note near it. The other chair was empty. It was obvious to her that a young man was being stood up.

It happens all the time, she thought to herself. "Yeah, it's really sad sometimes, but listen to me, Eddie, relationships rise and fall, come and go all the time. You're overreacting!"

He started to pound his right index finger into the front page of a recent copy of the Denver Post that was on the bar next to him. He kept pounding his finger into the paper, staring over at Jake in real pain. Marie picked up the paper and reviewed what she already knew about the horrible explosion in Fresno in bold type and photographs.

"What's this all about, Eddie?"

With some extra effort, he finally stopped sobbing for a moment, inhaled deeply with gradually increasing self-control, and then exhaled slowly as he turned toward her.

"Remember The Autumn Dream, the musical group that played here two weeks ago?"

"Yeah! I remember! I was out Monday and Tuesday, but I heard them on Wednesday, Thursday and Friday. The girl was absolutely *fantastic!*"

"Yeah, well, I stayed late that Friday night cleaning up, if you remember. See that guy sitting over there? The girl from the group—Sasha was her name—sat with him for half an hour or so after you and almost all of the other people left. I saw them talking together and touching hands. She took him to the piano backstage, and he played beautiful music on the piano while she sat next to him. I saw the look in her face. She liked him, Marie. She liked him a *lot!*"

"So . . . that's good! Right?"

"Yeah, but when I signed the contract in Manhattan over a year ago when I first heard her sing, we were chatting about her group, how she got started, and where she had been and where she was going. She told me her next gig was in Fresno the week after the open week in her schedule—the week I booked her for. That would have put her in Fresno this past week!"

He held the paper up in front of Marie's face and said, "I tell you, I know when a guy likes a girl. He likes her, a *lot!* They walked out of here holding hands that Friday night, Marie. I saw that with my own two eyes! They were *not* going to a candy shop in the middle of the night! My bet says he's waiting for her to walk in here tonight and have dinner with him. She would have been on time! I know that from having talked with her. My bet says that Sasha died in that explosion in Fresno. My bet says that he *DOES NOT KNOW THAT SHE IS DEAD!*"

"Ooohhh . . . mmmyyyyy . . . God . . ." she said, as tears suddenly welled up in her eyes.

"Yeah, that's what I said!"

"What are we going to *do*, Eddie?"

"I don't know, Marie. I don't know how to tell a guy who is so head-over-heels-with-a-royal-flush in love that his lover is dead. Do you?"

She ignored his question. "We don't *know* that she's dead, Eddie, and we don't *know* that they were lovers!"

"Jesus H. Christ, Marie! Look at me! I wasn't born yesterday! I'm a businessman! I've run this bar for over twenty-eight years! I know *people!* I hear all kinds of stories about people every day that sound like they came out of a storybook, but they are very, very *real!* I'm a man! I know MEN! I know when a guy has fallen for a girl! I know what it feels like! I see it all the time! I told you I saw the look in her face when he played the piano for her! You don't see my point in that beautiful flower over there? How many times have you seen a guy bring a flower in here, Marie? Usually, the only 'flower' men know about walks on two legs through the front door over there!" he said, pointing a shaking finger toward the front entrance as his face flushed red again.

"OK, Eddie . . . OK. OK. I understand your point. It's . . . It's just so sad—so incredibly *sad.* Why do people have to *suffer* so, Eddie? *Why?*"

Eddie continued with a little more self-control, "I honestly don't know, Marie. I just don't know. It says here that at least 419 people perished in that blast. It was in the night club district on Van Ness Avenue, near Club One Casino for God's sake, right where she said she would be last weekend!"

The first patron at the end of the bar turned to the young man in the Cooperstown sweatshirt to his left, and repeated the gist of what he could not help overhearing from Marie and Eddie. 'Cooperstown' looked toward Jake and elbowed 'Red Tie' to his left, leaned closer and repeated the story in a low whisper.

'Red Tie' whispered "Holy shit!" Then he lightly tapped the willowy blond next to him on her shoulder and motioned with a tilt of his head toward Jake, and told her what he had just heard.

"Ohmigod!"

She passed on the story to the petite young woman in the pretty, green skirt next to her on the other side. The story spread throughout one side of the bar with what seemed to be more references to God than had occurred in all the churches throughout the entire metropolitan Denver area the day before.

On the other side of the room, 'Dirty Blonde' and 'Dark Hair' were leaning toward the table behind them whispering the story they had pieced together from their own earlier observations and overhearing much of the conversation between Marie and Eddie behind the bar. The story was spreading like wildfire throughout the main room of the bar, and the band noticed a growing gentle, but ominous 'breeze' of whispers flowing throughout the room as if the audience were a heard of antelope, suddenly aware of an ill wind or a predator. They kept playing, but glanced back and forth among themselves with uncertain and quizzical looks, and then their music just began to crumble note by note, with a final solo 'twang' from one of the guitars as the group stood still in silent confusion on the stage for several moments. They looked out over the now quiet audience, only partially blinded by the spotlights overhead shining down on the stage. However, they got the general impression from various colored lights and white spotlights in the ceiling illuminating most of the main dining room before them that almost everyone was looking at the handsome young man at the table with the white rose in the beautiful pink vase. He was burying his face in his hands, shaking uncontrollably, but ever so slightly, with muffled sobs.

Gradually, Jake felt the silence around him. He slowly raised his head and looked around the room with wet red eyes, and saw clouded expressions of sorrow and sympathy through his tears. Women's periodic sobbing voices from different locations around the room softly punctuated the silence. 'Stealth' stopped dead still in his tracks, holding a serving tray with two plates of sandwiches, drinks and potato chips, looking over at Jake. Jake looked around the room, overwhelmed with confusion. Another fork dropped on the tile floor in the kitchen, briefly piercing the silence in the main dining room.

Something is not right here. He felt waves of sympathy flowing toward him from the crowd. *I'm being stood up, and 100 strangers feel sympathy?* He wondered to himself. *Something is definitely not right here!*

He felt his arrhythmia once more, stood up and took several deep breaths, then picked up his CD and the note to Sasha, but left the flower in the vase on the table. He took out his handkerchief and wiped his eyes, deliberately folded it and put it back in his pocket just to do something that he felt he had some actual control over, even if it was apparently pointless and lasted only for a few seconds. His heart was pounding so hard that he feared that those nearby would actually hear it. He stood and turned slowly with weak legs toward the door, and walked bravely across the room with the maximum self-control he could muster under the circumstances. He turned briefly from side to side and then made one complete turnaround before heading back to the front door, looking into the sad and self-conscious faces around him, as those who were standing nearby parted to make a respectful and unobstructed path for him to the front exit.

Eddie started after Jake around the bar, but Marie caught him by his arm and said, "No, Eddie, leave him be! He needs to be alone right now!"

"That's precisely what he does *not* need right now, Marie!"

The band members were still standing helplessly on the stage, wondering what was going on. Half the crowd turned toward Eddie and Marie. The other half was still staring at the front door, which was slowly closing against the pneumatic control. Jake was gone.

Eddie started for the door, but Marie moved in front of him and issued a persuasive "NO, Eddie!"

He looked at her carefully and sighed, respecting her intuition, and then backed away with tears welling up in his eyes again. Then he turned away from her, and walked slowly and deliberately over to Jake's table and picked up the two chairs and carried them behind the entertainers to the storage room behind the stage. He vowed to himself that no one would sit at that table as long as the flower lived, and he would see to it that the water in the vase never went below an inch of where it was then. He got a small stepladder from the back storage room, brought it over near Jake's table and climbed up on it unsteadily until he gained security by pressing his left hand on the ceiling. He carefully repositioned one of the intense white spotlights with his right hand to illuminate only the white rose and the pink vase below. Eddie had to do something to try to dissipate his grief and show proper respect for the beautiful and talented young singer in the white dress.

CHAPTER 49

Thursday, September 20, 2007
San Diego, California

After seven days of driving almost 3,761 miles, Hector Johnson found his way with his Garmin GPS to the address on the invoice of his boot order he received seven weeks ago. He was driving at thirty-five miles per hour in a twenty-five-mile per hour zone for a while before he pulled up to the front of the house. A San Diego Police patrol car seemed to appear out of thin air and pulled up right behind him with blue and red LED lights flashing on the roof. Hector's big truck with Alaska plates drew the patrolman's attention in addition to the radar beep telling him the vehicle was traveling over the posted speed limit. Police all over California were on a heightened state of alert because of the Fresno explosion, so Officer Dennison thought it would be better to stop the out-of-state truck than not, even though he simply could have ignored the speeding violation if he had wanted to.

Hector was not in a good mood, and communicated that fact to his truck by slamming his fists into the steering wheel three times before regaining his self-control. The police officer remained in his patrol car behind the truck for a few moments tracing the registration plates on his mobile computer terminal, further aggravating Hector. The search finished within a few moments indicating no criminal record or violation history. Officer James Dennison got out of his patrol car and approached the driver's door of the big grey Chevy truck as Hector opened the driver's side window.

"Good day, sir. Do you know why I stopped you?"

"Officer, you didn't stop me," he said evenly, staring straight ahead. "I decided to stop here by myself because this sonofabitch here in this place has my $180 deposit on a pair of $1,200 boots and he hasn't sent me the damn boots that I ordered over six weeks ago!" Hector then turned to face the officer. "I need those boots so I can work in the cold, and earn a living and stay off the goddamned welfare rolls, dammit! I ordered them special from this middle-eastern guy—Iranian, Pakistani or something—who I heard about as making really good boots. I drove all the way down here from Anchorage to get my money back or my boots!"

Officer Dennison knew he had a hot potato on his hands, and a very large one at that.

"I'm sorry to hear that, sir. You were traveling at thirty-five miles per hour in a twenty-five-mile-per-hour zone. May I please have your driver's license and vehicle registration?"

The tone of his voice clearly implied that there was only one correct answer. Hector twisted in his seat as he reached in his back left pocket for his wallet. He picked out his license and registration cards and handed them to Officer Dennison, who noticed that the big truck rocked a little as Hector squirmed in his seat reaching for his wallet. Hector had a temper, but he also knew enough not to get ornery with a police officer, especially one that far away from home.

"It's not right, you know, taking someone's money and then not producing what he paid for! It's just not *right*, dammit!"

Officer Dennison continued without obvious empathy, "Please stay in your vehicle, sir. I will be back in a few minutes."

Officer Dennison returned to his cruiser and was about to call in to his dispatcher, and then immediately broke the connection. He was curious about the big man's statement about the 'Iranian or Pakistani' man. He looked more closely at the house Hector stopped in front of. It was a relatively small house, usually the kind rented and not occupied by the owner in this area. There was a narrow driveway leading from the street past the side of the house to a garage in the back. The entire place looked deserted. What little grass there was around the house obviously had not been cut recently. All the windows Dennison could see were closed. Usually in San Diego, people open their windows at least some of the time in September. His computer indicated that Johnson had no record. Dennison decided he would overlook the violation and issue a warning.

He returned to the truck and handed Hector his license and registration card and said with a practiced sober expression, "I'm letting you off with a warning this time, Mr. Johnson. You said you had some business here. I am going to stay here and watch you until you leave. When you do leave, sir, please obey the traffic regulations. The next time you get stopped by a police officer in San Diego, you might not be so lucky."

"Yes, sir," Hector replied with effectively adequate, but contrived respect.

The officer walked back to his patrol car and got behind the wheel. He left the flashing LED lights on, and waited. He watched Hector get out of his truck, which rocked slightly as it recovered from his weight when he stepped out onto the street. He lumbered up the uneven concrete front sidewalk to the front door and knocked heavily on it six times with his beefy right fist. Hector stepped back and waited with his hands in his back pockets, looking at the door, then to the right, then to the left, then back at the patrol car, and then back to the house. He pounded on the door ten more times. Officer Dennison could easily hear the noise from his patrol car. Hector waited another minute. Then he walked to the driveway, and continued to the back of the relatively small house, looking into the two side windows along the way. He apparently saw nothing of interest, because he continued toward the garage. He tried to raise the door with the center handle, but it was apparently locked and would not budge. He walked around the garage, stopping to look through a window for a minute or two on the side visible to Officer Dennison. Hector returned to the locked garage door in the front, wound up his right leg and kicked it—hard! Dennison heard the relatively loud 'boom' from the metal garage door and thought of what must have been a loud 'boom' from the explosion in Fresno, even at a distance.

After Hector left, he would examine the property himself. He was already curious, and was becoming increasingly suspicious because of Hector's story. Hector started walking back to his truck, glanced toward the patrol car, and threw his arms up over his head in a gesture of frustration and swore with futility into the clear blue San Diego sky. Within a minute, he was back in his truck, started the big engine with a roar, but gently eased away from the curb and drove down the street with due respect for Officer Dennison's warning. He turned into a nearby driveway and then backed out to face the other direction and drove respectfully slowly by Dennison's patrol car and headed for Fresno to see what he needed to do to take care of his sister's belongings.

Dennison waited for a minute, then got out of his car and walked up to the house. He also knocked on the door, just to make sure no one was there, or if someone was there, was deliberately not answering the door. He waited longer than Hector had waited. Nothing happened. He started walking around the house, peering through the windows. He saw what looked like a normal household, including furniture, rugs, lamps and a kitchen toward the back. There were no children anywhere, and no evidence of children's toys. He went to the garage and tried the main door, just as Hector had, with the same result. It was definitely locked. He walked around to the window on the right side and looked in. He saw all the appearances of a boot-making business, with cartons labeled with one style or another of leather. A rather complete workbench occupied the entire back wall of the garage, with three stools in front of it. Although Dennison was not very familiar with the shoe business, he could determine with reasonable certainty that this was obviously a small boot-making operation.

He thought to himself, *a foreign artisan with a reputation for making very good, expensive boots does not deliver what obviously provides a reasonably good income, and is apparently not busy making boots right now. That is rather odd.*

Dennison walked over to the next house and rang the front doorbell.

An older woman opened the door, and said, "Yes?"

"I am Officer Dennison of the San Diego Police Department, Ma'am. May I please ask you a few questions?"

"Why, yes, Officer! Please, do come in!"

"Thank you, Ma'am."

"Please sit down, Officer."

She had not had a visitor in more than three weeks, so this was a real treat for her. She was apparently retired and lived alone. She was also obviously lonely and eagerly welcomed any attention in her tidy little house. Dennison sat on the green upholstered chair she offered, and she sat across from him in a matching green chair, looking expectantly at him with a kind and innocent smile across her thin, wrinkled face. Her curious calico cat entered the living room to join them, sat down in the middle of the room and stared dutifully at Dennison.

"I would like to know about the people who live next door," he said as he gestured with his thumb over his shoulder in the direction of the house he had just looked into.

"Oh! No one lives there, Officer! It didn't seem like they got along very well most of the time, and then one day he just left and never came back. She came over here shortly after that and told me how worried she was that her husband never came home. She said he was going to Fresno to pick up some special leather for his boot-making business, and he took that bright green motorcycle of his on a trailer behind his van, but she said he never returned with the leather! That seems odd, doesn't it? She's gone, Officer! I don't know where she went, but she's gone!"

Bingo! Police officers seem to be born with extraordinary facility for suspicion and cynicism, or if not, they develop it early in their careers. Dennison was no different. He believed he was discovering something related to the Fresno incident, and he wanted to follow it up. He simply could not and would not let it drop. He stood up to leave, reached into his pocket to retrieve his notepad, and then made notes of what the old woman had just told him.

"Ma'am, I need to know your name and phone number, in case I need to speak with you again."

"My name is Muriel Miller. I'm retired, you know."

She smiled pleasantly.

"Yes Ma'am. Thank you for your cooperation."

"My phone number is 619-668-4459," she said with a smile of anticipation as she carefully watched him write it down, delighted that she would probably be having more visitors soon, and phone calls as well to provide some excitement in her otherwise quiet, orderly and simple life.

"Thank you," he said, and smiled briefly at her.

Officer Dennison left the small house as quickly, yet as politely as possible, and strode briskly to his patrol car. He got in, started the engine, and wheeled around in a 'U' turn without turning off his flashing lights, and accelerated to forty miles per hour down the twenty-five mile-per-hour residential street toward the main road and then on to the police headquarters building near 15th Street and Broadway. Dennison kept his flashing roof lights on during the entire route to the headquarters building, and pulled into the parking lot with a little too much speed and brought the vehicle to a screeching halt in one of the empty diagonal slots behind the building. He turned his lights off, got out of the car, slammed the door behind him and raced up the stairs and through the rear entrance.

He asked the first officer he saw, "Is Chief Thomson in?"

"Yeah, he's in his office, I think," another officer answered.

Dennison rushed to the Chief's office and through the open door.

"What is it, Dennison? I thought you were still on patrol!"

"I am, but I believe I have something useful on the Fresno explosion, Chief. I thought it was important enough to come right in."

Thomson dropped his pen on his desk, looked up at him and said with clear and urgent interest, "OK. Close the door and sit down. Let's have it!"

Officer Dennison sat directly across the desk from the Chief, and said, "I made a routine stop on a big grey Chevy Silverado with Alaska plates and a really big ornery dude at the wheel. As it turns out, this big guy was all bent out of shape because he didn't receive some very expensive custom boots he ordered from a middle-eastern boot maker, either Iranian or Pakistani he said. He said he decided to drive all the way from Anchorage to visit the boot maker here in San Diego to get his deposit back, or get the boots. As it turns out, I stopped him right in front of the place from where he said he ordered the boots. I ran his plates, and he's perfectly clean—nothing on him and nothing on the truck—so I bought the boots story and gave him a break. I waited there until after he left, and checked out the house. It's locked up tighter than a drum, but there's evidence of a boot-making operation in the garage. I looked through a window and saw it. Seems that the boot maker took a trip to Fresno to pick up some special leather the day of the explosion, by my estimate from the next-door neighbor's account of what the boot maker's wife told her. She said he was towing a bright green motorcycle behind his van and never came back. The wife got worried when he didn't come back when she expected him, and skipped town. She's gone, according to the neighbor, a little old retired lady. She seemed very credible to me. Chief, I don't know of any reason why Fresno is a special place to buy or trade leather, especially with a motorcycle in tow. Do you?"

"Good question! *No, I don't!*" he said with growing interest.

"Chief, I think the boot maker delivered the explosives that killed all those people, and killed himself in the process! That's why he never came back home! I'm *sure* of it!"

"That's good work, Dennison. I want a full written report with all the details and your conclusions on my desk ASAP! I'm calling the FBI. They need to know about this!"

Dennison left to write his report. Thompson was already dialing the FBI number on his rolodex for the San Diego field office in the Federal Office Building on Aero Drive.

A woman answered in a curt, business-like tone, "FBI. This is agent Wilson."

"Agent Wilson, this is Police Chief Thomson here in San Diego. One of my officers stumbled upon some information within the last half hour that we think is related to the Fresno incident, and I wanted to pass it on to you guys as soon as possible."

"Chief, I'm going to put you on speaker phone, OK?"

She waved urgently to another agent and her boss to come to her desk mouthing the word 'Fresno' in their direction, pointing to the phone with her free hand. She did not want to be accused of misinterpreting anything the chief might say or might not say. The case was too important for mistakes or possible misinterpretation of who said what to whom, so she wanted others in on the conversation.

"No problem. It may not be much, but my officer has very good police instincts and believes it's important, and I agree with him, so I'm passing it on to you guys as quickly as possible."

Field agent Warner and agent-in-charge Flaherty walked briskly over to Wilson's desk. Warner picked up a copy of the faxed map from Harrington that was on his desk, showing the arc of a day's driving distance from Fresno. He started to think back to when they had absolutely no information whatsoever. Maybe this was their big break.

"Chief? I have agent Warner and agent-in-charge Flaherty here listening in. Go ahead."

"Officer Dennison stopped a man named Hector Johnson from Anchorage Alaska for a minor traffic violation in front of a house where Johnson claimed an Iranian or Pakistani man made expensive custom boots he had ordered, put a deposit on, but did not receive. Johnson was apparently quite upset and in the process of either getting his money back, or getting his boots, but no one was there, and the property was completely locked up. Officer Dennison verified the existence of an apparent boot making shop in a garage on the premises. He interviewed the next-door neighbor and ascertained that the boot maker apparently drove to Fresno, towing a bright green motorcycle behind his van, to buy special leather the same day of the explosion, according to her—the neighbor's—recent conversation with the boot maker's wife. The boot maker never returned, and his wife apparently became concerned, and left the house with no known destination or current location. We believe that Fresno is not a particularly special location for leather merchants, so we became suspicious, particularly because of the timing of the trip to Fresno relative to the explosion, the wife's story from the neighbor that the boot maker never returned to his home, and, of course, the towed motorcycle and the disappearance of the wife. That's basically all we have."

The agents looked at each other with raised eyebrows. San Diego was definitely within Harrington's circle around Fresno!

Flaherty said with growing excitement, "That's very encouraging, Chief Thomson. Thank you very much! Please fax a copy of your officer's report to my office as soon as possible—858-565-1256."

"It'll be coming right up in about fifteen minutes at the most."

"Thank you! We'll work with what you have given us, and get back to you if we need anything further, and of course, please let us know if you discover anything else about this."

"Will do!"

Agent Wilson terminated the telephone connection. Flaherty became animated with a plan to start working on something other than pushpins, string, dead ends, conjecture and theory.

"Wilson, you go and talk to the neighbor again, and get as much detail as you can, including a description of the vehicle the boot maker drove to Fresno, and then find his wife. Also, find out what you can about sources of C4 or other high explosives and any unusual purchases of gasoline and nails around San Diego, or within the entire southern California area, including possible links in Mexico."

"Warner, you find every video recording of all of the most reasonable routes from San Diego to Fresno. I don't care whether it comes from a patrol car, a private citizen, a nine-year-old kid, a building surveillance system, an airplane, or what! Use public notices to get cooperation from people in the area who may have seen or heard something we can use. Set up a website for people to send us information. We need to find anyone who used a camera of any kind, saw or heard something suspicious, or might have taken pictures anywhere within the travel corridor between San Diego and Fresno during the timeframe we must focus upon. Contact Harrington in Seattle and bring him into the loop with what we have learned, and check out that motorcycle to see if you can get the owner's name. I think Harrington said he saw the explosion from an airplane. If you need more people, you will have them. Let me know. I'm going to NASA, CIA and the military to get information from satellites that may have photographic evidence in our area of interest during that timeframe. As soon as we can discover who that boot maker is, we can find out who he associated with, maybe leading us to the source of the explosives or perhaps someone or something else of interest."

The official investigation was getting traction. The hunt was on. They could all feel it. Within the next several days, Agent Wilson would identify the abandoned Toyota van on the northbound side of Route 99 as belonging to Khalid Kayani, after she traced the serial numbers on the engine block. Agent Warner would eventually discover the high-resolution and infrared photographs taken by Air Force Major Thomas Henderson on September 8 on his approach to Monthan Air Force Base at the end of a routine training mission.

Jake took USAir flight 1552 from Denver at one thirty arriving at Philadelphia International Airport at three minutes after seven. He picked up his rental car, and was back in Reading by nine thirty. He had a meeting the following morning with the estate attorney.

CHAPTER 50

Friday, September 21, 2007
Reading, Pennsylvania

After the accounting for his mother's relatively uncomplicated estate, Jake learned he was to receive about $892,000 in cash after the auction sale of her home, furniture, and various other possessions, legal fees and taxes. However, he deliberately kept certain pieces of jewelry and various personal records of the family history. One of the keepsakes was his mother's diamond engagement ring, which Jake had appraised at Diller's Jewelry store in West Reading on the northwest corner of the Penn and 6th Avenue intersection. He was astonished to learn that the stone was the most nearly perfect stone that Diller had ever seen in his forty-nine years in the Jewelry business. He graded it highest for clarity, brilliance and color. The style of cut was 'round brilliant,' and was as nearly perfect as anyone could cut it. The high-grade features of the stone, in addition to its size, which was not small, but not exceptionally large at 2.62 karats made it worth $77,500, according to Diller's appraisal.

Jake knew that this was his father's engagement gift to his mother after an unusually long search for the 'perfect' diamond. Although his father had not paid anywhere near the current value, he obviously spent a considerable portion of what little money he had at the time. His father had told Jake that he spent more than six months shopping on his own in the New York diamond district and researching diamonds at the local library before finding what he wanted. The stone had just that much more meaning to Jake because he could appreciate its quality, and what it had meant to his father. Jake had the ring with him in his pocket when he went to Joe's for dinner that evening.

Jake sat at a relatively small table for two, and looked over the one-page menu. He knew that Joe's was an expensive restaurant, and that the offerings were relatively few, but very good. He chose the all-American roast beef with mashed potatoes and green beans, served with Joe's famous, but secret brown mushroom gravy. A very pleasant young woman took his order with a smile, and asked how he wanted his roast beef cooked.

Jake responded, "Well done, please" as she removed the menu without removing her interested smile, turned and disappeared through the far door of the dining room into the kitchen.

As usual, Joe was there to stop by every table to greet his guests and chat about whatever his brilliant intuition brought before him. It was just another normal day in the restaurant business for Joe, as he walked toward the young man sitting alone at the small table near the east wall, staring at something before him on the white tablecloth. As Joe approached, he squinted slightly to bring into focus the flashing light from a small point on the table, realizing that it was indeed a jewel of unusual brilliance, because there was no sunlight in Joe's restaurant. The light playing from the stone was coming only from the overhead lights in the room. Joe quickly assessed the situation, as usual, and deduced that the young man was in love, and not selling diamonds, or stealing them. That never stopped Joe from inviting himself into other people's lives with remarkably intuitive relevance in the past, and it would not stop his curiosity now, either. Jake sensed Joe's approach, and casually gathered the ring in his right hand as inconspicuously as possible and placed the ring back in his pants pocket.

Joe walked up beside Jake, and said with his easy natural smile, "Hi! I'm Joe, the owner of this establishment. And, what is your name, sir?"

"Jake. Jake Lewis."

"Good evening, Mr. Lewis! I am very glad you chose my restaurant this evening! Did you find the menu selections to your liking?"

"Yes, as a matter of fact, I did!" Jake answered politely, as almost everyone did with Joe's approach. "I ordered the roast beef dinner."

"Excellent choice! Excellent indeed!"

Joe noticed that the young man gave him a longer answer than he would ordinarily expect under the circumstances, and took that as an invitation to further conversation. It was early. Jake was the only guest so far, and he had the time.

"What brings you to my modest little restaurant this evening? I don't ordinarily get young single male guests at this hour of the day!"

Joe laughed with his special infectious invitation to join the laughter, putting Jake at ease with his unique talent for softening up even the most hardened of the human lot who still had the means to afford his cuisine.

"Well, I grew up here in Reading, but moved away quite some time ago. Recently I had to return to settle my mother's estate. She was severely injured in a truck accident last Tuesday evening, and died on Thursday in the Reading Hospital."

"Oh! I'm so sorry, sir! I heard about that accident. It involved a truck going up Route 222 north of the city, I believe, right? The truck driver lost control and died in the accident, as I recall reading in the Reading Times."

Joe paid attention to the news. It was part of his job as well as one of his many natural interests.

Jake said, "Yes, that's the one."

Joe immediately wished he had not gone down that road, as it were, and quickly gathered his intuitive bearings as he started to reduce Jake's bill for the dinner in his head as a courtesy in sympathy for his guest's state of grief. He sat down across from Jake in the empty chair and changed the subject.

"So, tell me please, what do you do for a living, Jake?"

He believed that Jake had a job of some kind, because he ran an expensive restaurant, and people who came into his restaurant usually knew what his food would cost.

"I'm a psychologist."

"Oh, really? I majored in psychology in college, a long time ago, of course!"

"Where did you go to college?"

"Yale, '77."

Jake smiled and relaxed even more.

"Well, *that's* certainly a coincidence! I graduated in 1999, and got my Ph.D. in 2003!"

Joe continued with his perceived invitation to talk, and remembered the brilliant sparkle of what he thought was a diamond that he saw earlier. He used his engaging personality as advertising. He knew that people who had an enjoyable experience in his restaurant would tell that to their friends, and they would in turn tell their friends, and thereby contribute to Joe's business.

"While you're waiting a little longer than usual for your dinner, tell me about that beautiful diamond you had on the table earlier! My chef takes his time, you know. That's what you pay for here—gastronomic TLC," Joe quipped, and laughed at himself.

Joe was so atypically friendly and naturally brazen, and Jake was so impressed with the man's obviously very keen powers of observation that he had no choice other than to answer.

"Oh! Well, that was my mother's engagement ring that I just inherited. I was just admiring it. It's really quite amazing, when you think about how it was formed and how long ago that must have been, and the path it took throughout the years to come into my possession. I'm not an expert, mind you, but I have some minor understanding of the geological formation process, and a little more than two generations of personal history that I think I know about the stone. Still, it's quite amazing! It's a rare statement of Mother Nature's perfection. I guess if humanity had no artistic ability or innate sense of beauty, form and structure, then these little things wouldn't be so expensive!"

"The story my father told me is that this particular diamond came from a shipment of rough diamonds from near the Orange River in South Africa sometime between 1848 and 1851. Apparently, they disappeared for quite a while until a six-year-old orphan boy playing in an abandoned, war-torn building discovered this single stone in a felt pouch in the walls of a Polish farmhouse near Gdansk after the end of World War II. Apparently, the boy kept his secret treasure for years without telling anyone. Even if he had wanted to, he couldn't tell his parents because the Nazis murdered them before the Russians swept across Poland, pushing what remained of the Third Reich toward the advancing Allied forces from the west. It is rather remarkable that a little boy apparently never told anyone his secret during his early years of growing up in various orphanages and foster homes.

Eventually, he emigrated to the United States around 1959, when he was about twenty-one, and settled in the Bronx. His name was Teodor Michalik."

Joe instantly sustained, but effectively masked a significant internal flush of recognition.

"He got his start in this country with proceeds from the sale of that little treasure, which eventually found its way into the hands of a highly skilled diamond cutter from India, and then into a display in the diamond district of Manhattan where my father, Daniel Lewis found it in 1970. My father got that story from the diamond dealer, who apparently got it from the diamond cutter, who in turn got the story from Michalik. I'm not sure the story is really all true, but I never heard of a diamond with such an interesting story attached to it, although I'm sure there must be other stories associated with such gems. My guess is that such stories tend to be altered throughout their transmission to the present. Anyway, it makes the stone that much more interesting and valuable to me."

"That's an absolutely incredible story, Jake! No wonder you were admiring it!"

Joe was doubly interested because he knew exactly who Teodor Michalik was—a full professor of philosophy at Harvard and formerly at Oxford University—who was also a member of The Chancellor Organization. Joe's intuition was that a young and rather handsome man looking that closely at a diamond in his restaurant was more likely thinking of a very special young woman, as much as, if not more than his mother. He was more likely imagining where the ring would go next, than where it had just come from, or what its ultimate origin and subsequent fascinating history was. Most men would not show that stone within sight of another human being, particularly a stranger, other than a very special woman, for fear of attracting unwanted attention, if not violence, unless he was so impossibly in love as to be oblivious to such potential. Even though Joe's restaurant was relatively small and certainly safe, affording a respectable degree of privacy and intimacy, it was still a public place. Joe had an incredible ability to make the transition from 'stranger' to 'friend' in world-record speed, and it did not matter whether he was playing 'at home' in his own restaurant, or 'away' in any other part of the world, so he continued to inquire.

"So, who's the lucky young lady?" Joe pressed on with his innocent, but sincere and friendly fascination with other people's lives in general, and Jake's in particular with at least this one very remarkable coincidence.

Jake became somewhat uncomfortable. He was fighting the internal battle again. Should he bring her back into his life by talking about her, or continue to push her even deeper into his memory? Joe's question was just friendly and genuinely innocent enough to invite Jake's fondest memories of Sasha. He answered carefully, controlling his emotions as best he could with a weak smile and moist eyes.

"Her name is Sasha. She's an incredibly talented singer, and I don't know where she is right now or even whether she is alive or dead."

A tear fell from Jake's right eye while Joe inhaled involuntarily as his emotions surfaced.

HOLY SHIT! OH MY GOD! OOHH MMYY GOD! OHHHHHH MYYYYYYYYY GOD!

Joe knew Duke had a niece named Sasha who was about Jake's age, and that she was a singer. Jake *had* to be describing Duke's niece!

What was this about not knowing whether she was alive or dead?

Joe was never convinced that coincidence was a final explanation for most of what he knew about life on this planet. He guided his relationships with people with an unknown but powerful, intuitive and genuine gift of friendship and respect. Because of that attitude toward life, he was very rarely fooled or blindsided. However, for once in his life, Joe was speechless. There was no way he could not tell Duke about his niece and Jake. Keeping secrets necessary for the operation of The Chancellor Organization was one thing and absolute, but keeping secrets about people's lives he cared about was quite another. He could not and would not do that, particularly within his special friendship with Duke, and *especially* if there was some question about Sasha's health or safety.

The young server strode toward Jake's table with his roast beef dinner as Joe stood up to leave and said with well-disguised and considerable effort, even for him, "Well, enjoy your dinner, Jake! We'll talk a little more later, after you have finished. The meal is on me."

Joe welcomed the coincidence of the arriving dinner as a reason to excuse himself, because he wanted time to think this through, although he was leaning heavily toward the simple truth when it came to personal relationships, as surprising and threatening as that might be from time to time. Joe decided to approach Jake with the whole story about Duke Chancellor, their relationship and the obvious link to Sasha, thereby bringing Jake into his secret world in an unexpected, but possibly very useful manner. He could not live with himself if he severed his relationship with Jake from that point with so many unanswered questions about rather personal ties. He could not live with himself, knowing that there was obviously some uncertainty about the life of Duke's only niece, whom he loved dearly, as if she were family. He could not live with himself harboring all of those unanswered questions. After Jake had finished his dinner, Joe did indeed return to his table to 'talk a little more' as he had promised.

"Well, how did you like the food, Jake?" he said with his naturally infectious smile.

"It was quite good, actually! It would be easy for me to offer an insincere compliment, but you do not strike me as the kind of man who would not see, let alone accept that, so you should know that I am sincere in saying I liked it."

"Thank you! That's pretty close to the mark, Jake. So, while we're being unusually intuitive, suppose you tell me a little bit more about this young lady friend of yours, since I really must confess that I think I know of her in a rather indirect way," he said with the well-disguised caution of veiled truth.

Jake was astounded, and practically shouted, "*YOU DO?*"

"Yes, actually. A very good friend of mine in Maryland happens to have a niece about your age who has a rather unusual singing voice, and she's also quite attractive!"

Jake had no choice. Joe had piqued his curiosity beyond his control and his defenses declined considerably as his hopes advanced once again. All of a sudden, talking about her was the only way he could manage the uncertainty about her failure to show up at Eddie's Place in Denver or to call him.

"Well, the short version of the story is that I met this rather talented singer, who also happens to be rather attractive, like you described this niece of your friend, in an entertainment restaurant in Denver a few weeks ago, Friday, September 7, to be exact. I'm sure you can understand why I remember the date. We talked and got to know each other, and arranged to meet again a week from that following Monday after she returned to Denver from her next singing engagement in Fresno."

FRESNO? Oh God! No! THIS CAN'T BE!

The pieces of a tragic story were falling together rapidly in Joe's mind, without his assistance. He felt thoroughly compelled to know with certainty whether the Sasha he knew as Duke's niece was really the young woman they were both talking about and whether she was injured or killed in the Fresno incident. Joe quickly concluded that Jake actually did not know about the Fresno explosion, or he would specifically have mentioned it by now. It was possible from Joe's perspective that Jake actually was so emotionally involved with Sasha and his mother's death that he had been completely oblivious to the rest of the world recently. Normally, Joe was a master of social diplomacy and tact, but his realization of the reality implicit in the series of facts he was sure of and the probabilities implicit in Jake's story and behavior drove him to want to learn the whole truth as soon as possible.

Joe steadied himself physically and emotionally, and managed to utter a simple "Oh?" as a limp response to keep the conversation going while his brain was desperately searching for a way to leave Jake politely and get to his computer to find out as much as he could about Sasha. He needed to get the facts straight before he went any further with Jake and possibly needlessly upsetting him, or Duke.

"Yeah. The problem is that she never showed up for our date in Denver on Monday the seventeenth, so I thought she stood me up."

Joe knew from his interaction with Duke and what he knew about the Chancellor family history and values, that Duke's niece would not stand *anyone* up, especially a young man with Jake's credentials. Her mother raised her with respect and taught her to show respect. Sasha would speak her mind honestly and tactfully or bluntly as a last resort if necessary, but she would never just ignore a commitment of any kind, and most certainly would never deliberately leave any man in the lurch like that. If a man did not hold her interest, then she would politely make him completely aware of that fact in clear, convincing, plain, but tactful English.

"Well, I'm sure there must be some kind of reasonable explanation, Jake. I actually suspect that we are taking about the same young woman, so I would like to do a little investigating myself to find out what happened. I have a rather extensive network of business associates around the country, believe it or not, so I think I can find out what's going on here, *if you don't mind*, of course! I'll be sure to let you know what I find out as soon as possible. What is your phone number where I can reach you easily?"

Jake was just curious enough and hopelessly devoid of any idea of how to find out about Sasha by himself that he agreed to let his new friend do some investigating on his own. He wanted all the help he could get.

He said graciously, "That would be absolutely *wonderful*, Joe! Thank you very much for your kind offer! My cell phone number is 303-525-6101."

"By the way, Jake, the meal is on me!" Joe said in his uniquely final manner, prohibiting any further discussion.

Jake did not argue, but did leave something greater than the average for the server as he rose from his seat.

"Thank you for your generosity, Joe. Obviously you can expect me to come back, and I promise you I will pay for the next meal, and there will be no negotiation!"

Jake left the restaurant to return to his motel to get a good night's rest before flying back to Denver on Saturday.

Joe contacted one of his friends at FEMA, the Federal Emergency Management Agency, in California to try to get a list of people injured or killed in the Fresno explosion in an effort to learn whether Sasha's name was on such a list. Joe's network of contacts produced a list within two hours that he could access through Duke's System 12 on his computer. He discovered that Sasha's name was not on the official list of 419 deaths or the 1,647 injured. He knew, however, that the absence of her name did not absolutely assure her safety or that she had escaped death. It just meant that her name was not on the list, period. If her name had been on the list, then obviously he would know the painful and devastating truth. As it was, he had only confirmed the bare hope that he started with. Then he remembered what many New Yorkers did after 9/11. They made simple posters with photographs of missing people and loved ones, including phone numbers to call with information, and posted them on fences, walls, sidewalk trash baskets, streetlight posts and other available public surfaces in lower Manhattan in efforts to elicit information to help discover their fate. With his resources, however, Joe could do the same, only on a larger and more effective scale.

Joe secured copies of two of Sasha's most recent promotional photographs from her agent in Manhattan, whom he discovered after some relatively minor detective work, and built a poster template around them, two images per poster, with a brief explanation underneath that she was missing in the Fresno area after the explosion. One image was a full-height side view at a night club with a dark-colored background and an overhead spotlight on her wearing her trademark white sequined dress, standing before a microphone looking out into the audience. The other was a more professional simple facial portrait, with her looking straight into the eyes of the viewer with her almost seductive dimpled smile and her auburn highlighted brown hair flowing only slightly across her left eye down to her shoulders like she was in a high-end hair shampoo advertisement. He sent the file to his contacts in California with instructions to get them in front of the public. He also had them create 'audio posters' for the internet with a sample of her singing voice from one of her performances in Manhattan. He included a recorded voice message as well as a printed message asking people to respond to an '800' toll-free number with any information, which would be channeled immediately and confidentially to him. He made sure these messages also aired on radio and television stations covering the greater Fresno and surrounding areas. He also set up a web page with the same message along with the photos and a special e-mail address exclusively under his direct control for responses. He could monitor the entire process through System 14, which Duke cleared for that purpose only. He also included an effective financial incentive of $10,000 for any verifiable information that would lead to confirmed discovery of her fate.

CHAPTER 51

Sunday, September 23, 2007
Denver, Colorado

Jake arose early to make his favorite meal of the day. While he was preparing scrambled eggs, link sausage, orange juice and two slices of toast, he casually turned on his laptop computer on his kitchen table, which also served as his desk, to get ready for a day of preparation for his presentation at New York University on October 3. After taking his toast out of the toaster, he logged on to his computer, and clicked on the internet icon and returned to tending to his sausage in a frying pan on the stove. After he browned the sausage links to his satisfaction and placed them on a paper towel on the counter to absorb the excess grease, he wiped most of the remaining grease out of the pan, and then cracked two eggs and dropped them into the hot skillet and scrambled them. With the eggs cooked to his satisfaction, he put all the food on one large plate and set it on his breakfast table with a large glass of orange juice with ice cubes in it, and then went to the stove again to make sure the gas was completely off. He returned to his seat at the table, and started to eat.

After swallowing the first fork full of eggs and sausage, he glanced at his computer monitor and immediately choked for a few seconds on the next fork full of food. He finally understood why Sasha did not show up at Eddie's last Monday evening. Joe's 'poster' project had filled the internet with such thorough and intense saturation that Jake simply could not avoid the message. His heart raced as he read the poster and then stared at the picture of Sasha, now in full realization that either she had died in the explosion, or was seriously hurt because of it. Otherwise, he most certainly would have heard from her by now. His emotions were 'red-lining' his capacity to sit still. On the one hand, he was overjoyed that she did not 'stand him up' at Eddie's Place last Monday. He felt completely reassured of her love once again. However, the simultaneous anxiety about her welfare, even her life, dominated his consciousness and ripped at his emotions. He simply had to know whether she was alive or dead, and until he actually heard her voice or saw her within reach, he would have to maintain even the most improbable hope of her survival. To assume that she was dead was impossible. She would remain alive in his heart and mind until he had incontrovertible proof that she was dead. That meant he would have to see her lifeless body with his own eyes. His intelligence, his psychological training, his education and his professional experience in life were no match for his simple basic human emotional demand for her survival. Under the circumstances, he translated that into concern about whether she had been mercilessly murdered or maimed along with hundreds of other innocent people, whether she had suffered, or was still suffering.

The death of his mother was a major shock. He had lost that most unique, natural and precious life-long relationship at the hands of a selfish, foolish and ignorant truck driver. He could almost accept his father's premature death due to leukemia more easily than the death of his mother. The disease was not man-made. It was neither accidental nor the deliberate fault of a deranged human being. He died because of the mysterious forces of nature, so far beyond current human understanding as to eliminate blame or guilt altogether.

Sasha, on the other hand, was either dead or injured precisely *because* of the deliberate and evil thoughts and behavior of at least one human being. Someone had planned and executed that explosion with only one hellish objective, and obviously maintained that purpose and plan throughout a considerable period. The deliberation was well beyond human accident, coincidence or uncontrollable forces of nature. It was completely intolerable and unforgiveable. It was sheer evil at any level of understanding and enraged him to the point of almost losing his sanity, if not his humanity. She had both encouraged and accepted his love and held that part of him within her. Whoever had hurt or possibly murdered her had also injured a part of him, a part he felt he could not live without.

He would have to live from this point forward with considerable effort beyond his experience, to balance the bedrock uncertainty about Sasha's fate with his innate identity and what he feared would be an enormous effort to go on with his life without her. For the rest of the weekend Jake wrestled for the first time in his life with the most basic male animal instinct he never knew he had—the desire to kill another human being, whoever had hurt Sasha. Yet, he knew that person was almost certainly already dead. Therefore, his rage would be both fueled and denied satisfaction forever. With great effort, he tried to concentrate on his presentation, but inevitably succumbed to the torment of terrorism. He did not know anyone personally who had suffered through the 9/11 attacks, but he still felt the national, sociological, intellectual, as well as the basic human anger at the time. Now that they had hurt Sasha, his understanding of terrorism pushed well beyond all conceivable emotional or intellectual comprehension into a realm for which he had no words. He now had the ultimate understanding of the law of the jungle—me against you and us against them—no rules, no laws, no warnings, no boundaries, and no civil or cultural procedure, protocol, sense or custom, at a basic animalistic level of completely selfish, vicious mauling of one by another until death defines the next course of behavior for the survivor.

I can't live like this! This is not life! What is happening to me?

He would spend the bulk of Monday and Tuesday counseling others with much greater than his usual effort and concentration while simultaneously trying to suspend this very private and intense internal turmoil. On the one hand, it was obviously extremely difficult, but on the other hand, he developed a renewed and much fuller appreciation of the internal pain of so many of his clients.

CHAPTER 52

Tuesday, September 25, 2007
State Highway 72, Coal Creek Canyon Road, West of Denver, Colorado

The Acura speedometer registered forty, forty-five, fifty, fifty-five, sixty, sixty-five . . .

After having left his office a little early for the day, Jake was driving up to his temple, toward his refuge from the pressures of everyday life, the beautiful Colorado Rocky Mountains just west of Denver. They offered him peace and quiet with vistas that fostered perspective and invited private thoughtful reflection.

Tears were welling up in his eyes. He was balancing his future between keeping his right foot on the accelerator pressed to the floor on the one hand, and yielding to the basic natural urge to live inherent in the human reflex system on the other. The forces demanding survival were entangled with the beginnings of disintegration of his all-too-human psyche since Sunday. He could not see clearly through his tears, and suddenly realized he could cause an accident involving another human being, and he could not bear that on top of everything else.

He finally eased off the accelerator and braked hard into a pullout facing northeast, skidding over the loose gravel before coming to a complete stop precariously near a low and obviously inadequate stone retaining wall. He jammed on the parking brake, turned the engine off and slumped against the steering wheel, sobbing uncontrollably until he was exhausted. Then he sat up and wiped his face with his sleeve. He opened the driver's door and stepped out of his car. He slowly closed the door, leaned against the car with his arms over the roof for support, facing to the East, looking down to the distant city of Denver and the vast plains beyond to the east through a large 'V' in the mountain range. The sacred vista before him was fading into the ending dusk of another day as the earth continued its mindless, relentless spin on its axis, speeding on its way around the sun as if nothing unusual had happened.

Jake summoned all of his rage and anger, and let the raw animal in him bellow out at the top of his lungs the mad shriek of a soul in the agony of astronomical proportions. They had taken his beautiful and beloved Sasha from him. They had deprived thousands of people of the joyful peace of hearing her sing. They had taken from him that part of his soul that was hers. He had never known such anger, and started to feel his body's inability to express it. He wrestled with the belief that he could actually try to kill another human being, whoever was responsible for taking Sasha from him, with his own bare hands, the same delicate and artistic hands he would not risk injuring by playing football in high school. He could not rid himself of the basic animal in him that he had never known before. No recollection of his modest Christian upbringing could rescue him from this torment nor quell his newly realized belief that he could actually *kill* another human being. Tears started to roll down his face again. His body started to flush his entire being with a tremendous torrent of tears, once again clouding his vision of the vast natural beauty before him. Mucus flowed from his nose, and saliva spilled from his contorted mouth as he began shaking uncontrollably, heaving in desperation for breath, gradually losing control of his body, as he slumped to the gravel pavement next to his car, and with fading consciousness rolled onto his back before everything went black.

Within thirty seconds, a state police patrol car pulled up just behind the Acura with bright flashing red and blue LED lights and a glaring white spotlight trained on the Acura. Patrol Officer David Fleming had the Acura clocked at more than sixty-five miles per hour in a fifty mile per hour zone, and he was going to nail the driver, *hard!*

Fleming was a sixteen-year veteran of the Colorado State Patrol. He had seen much more of life and death than most people had during that period. However, he always tried to go the extra mile in circumstances that in his judgment would allow for reasonable results. Those who crossed the line he offered, either implicitly or explicitly, however, were doomed to the full extent of the law. He was all of six feet, five inches tall, with a solid, 244-pound trim body that he kept in shape, with almost daily visits to the YMCA in downtown Denver. He was the quintessential no-nonsense enforcer of the law and protector of the public. He was not known to have smiled while on duty.

Fleming looked ahead through his windshield at the Acura and did not see anyone in the car, or anywhere else near it. He got out of his patrol car, and moved cautiously around the rear of the Acura looking quickly in all directions, making maximum use of his peripheral vision before he saw a man lying motionless and face up on the ground near the driver's door. The man's clothes were tasteful, and obviously not from the bargain rack and his shoes were polished. He quickly realized that the man lying before him on the road was not a threat to him or anyone else.

"Hey, Mister! You OK? Can you hear me?"

Jake did not answer and he did not move. He did not appear to be breathing.

Patrol Officer Fleming suddenly launched into hyper-police mode from his instinct and training. He knelt down at Jake's side, and saw his chest rise, but ever so slightly and then fall, so the airway was probably clear, at least for the moment. He felt for a pulse at the carotid artery near the surface of his sopping wet neck. He had obviously been crying. He felt no pulse, then put his ear on Jake's chest near his heart but could not hear a heartbeat. Instinctively he raced to the trunk of his patrol car, opened it and removed his portable defibrillator. Fleming could have been an Olympian, for all anyone watching might know, as he gracefully ran back to the fallen man, opened his shirt and applied the electrical pads on each side of his chest. The defibrillator triggered a shock shortly after failing to detect a heartbeat. However, no one was watching. There would be no medal or applause for his efforts. Within a few moments, Jake coughed, and then inhaled deeply, then exhaled. He coughed again repeatedly, then opened his eyes, and looked around as his brow wrinkled in evidence of obvious disorientation. Officer Fleming breathed a sigh of relief as Jake looked up at him, still somewhat confused. From Jake's perspective, a state patrol officer was still kneeling next to him, slightly out of focus for what seemed to be a period of minutes as time appeared to have a different pace.

"Stay still, buddy. Don't move. I'm going to call for an ambulance."

He spoke firmly into the microphone at his shoulder, "Ten, fifty-two, just past mile marker twenty-two north on the Coal Creek Canyon Road—*NOW!*"

He turned his head back to Jake.

"What's your name, Mister?"

"Jake. Jake Lewis."

"Tell me what happened, Mr. Lewis."

He made a point of not asking why Jake was speeding. Traffic violations were of secondary importance at this point.

"I had a date with my fiancé last Monday evening at Eddie's Place at six o'clock for dinner. She never showed up. She is a singer with a group that had a show in Fresno the prior weekend."

Jake stopped talking for a few moments, as he tried to regain control of his emotions. Fleming waited patiently for him to continue.

"I just learned about the explosion in Fresno on Sunday on the internet, because I have been dealing with my mother's death almost two weeks ago as a result of an automobile collision with a truck in Pennsylvania, on top of everything else with my work at the V.A. hospital in Denver. I have been out of touch with the rest of the world for a while. My fiancé was going to return to Denver last Monday after her performance in Fresno. I was extremely angry, anxious, restless and fearful after I put two and two together and figured out why she did not show up. She did *not* stand me up. She *loved* me! I *know* it! The only reason she would not have shown up for our dinner is that she was either badly hurt, or dead! I started to drive up into the mountains to vent my rage in private, where no one else would hear me. I needed to get out of my condominium. That's all I can remember right now. I realize now that I should have stayed home, but I just lost it and had to do something to rid myself of the rage and cool off before I upset the neighbors or before it killed me."

Officer David Fleming, sworn protector of the public and enforcer of the law, felt rare genuine compassion for the man whose life he just may have saved. He wondered about what kind of woman could have such an intense effect upon a man like what he had just seen. He may have been a conscientious officer of the law, but he was not the kind of man who would revive another person only to give him a speeding ticket. There would be no traffic violation on Coal Creek Canyon Road that night. This story was simply too fantastic to have been a typical fabrication just to avoid a ticket.

"It almost did, he said."

Within minutes, another distant wailing siren from an ambulance grew louder and louder as a periodic red glow pierced the advancing quiet darkness toward mile marker twenty-two north, high in the otherwise peaceful Rocky Mountains west of Denver.

In the city far below them, Eddie sadly picked up the pink vase with the wilting white rose from the small table near the stage, walked over to the bar and carefully dropped the dying flower in a trash basket under the bar and placed the vase on the bar as he tried to hold back tears. The band that evening was offstage on a break. No one paid much attention as Eddie went backstage to retrieve the two chairs he had removed from the table closest to the stage. He placed them at the empty table and fought the lump in his throat as he walked quietly back behind the bar, picked up the vase and then slowly walked up the stairs to his office. He sat alone for several minutes, looking at the empty vase as he placed it on his desk, listening to the muffled rush of noise from the bar downstairs, trying to gain control of his emotions until he felt he could return to the bar with a smile.

Jake's doctor released him from the hospital after a day of observation since his vital signs remained steadily within normal ranges. He spent the remainder of the day trying to rest and work on his NYU presentation in spite of persistent anxiety about Sasha's fate. He came closer to praying for her safety than he had ever come to praying about anything in his entire life.

CHAPTER 53

Tuesday, September 25, 2007
Fresno, California

Meanwhile, about 830 miles to the west, a beautiful young woman with long dark brown hair and auburn highlights opened her eyes for the first time in fifteen days at Saint Agnes Medical Center in Fresno, California. Regina Rogers, a nurse's aide happened to be in her room when Sasha opened her eyes, and recognized a vague but haunting resemblance between the missing person image she saw all over the internet and the young woman who had just regained consciousness in that room. Regina watched Sasha carefully as she moved her eyes, looking around the room, obviously confused and disoriented. She moved closer to Sasha's bed with increasing confidence and anticipation now that she could see her beautiful eyes for the first time. Regina focused more closely upon Sasha's long flowing hair with auburn highlights, and recognized that she was indeed the woman identified in the internet notices as missing after the Fresno explosion.

She leaned toward the woman and asked softly, "Is your name Sasha?"

Sasha tried to focus on the other woman as she said, "Yes, my name is Sasha. Where . . . where am I?"

"You are in Saint Agnes Medical Center in Fresno, California. You have been in a coma for more than two weeks. I am going to call your doctor right away," she said with measured professional urgency.

Right after she called Doctor Caldwell, she called the phone number on the internet notice to report that Sasha was definitely alive. Joe finally had the information he wanted from a very credible source, including realistic details of her location and condition, and drew the correct conclusion that she did not have any identification or her purse with her. If she had, someone surely would have known who she was well before now, and he would have discovered that. He immediately informed Duke on System 7.

Doctor Caldwell hurried up to Sasha's room and greeted her with a warm smile.

"I am Doctor Caldwell. I have been taking care of you for the last two weeks or so. I'm glad to see that you are awake!" he said with a smile and genuine personal and professional relief.

"I've been sleeping?" she asked as she struggled to sit up in her bed, and obviously not yet completely aware of her condition.

"In a manner of speaking, yes. You have been in a coma for more than two weeks."

"Why am I in Fresno?"

"I was hoping *you* could tell *me* that, Sasha."

"I don't have any idea why, but I want to go home."

"And where is home?"

"Union City, New Jersey," she said without hesitation.

"And how are you going to get there?" he asked kindly, further trying to assess her mental functioning as long as she was still awake and inclined to talk.

"On an airplane, of course!" she responded confidently.

"Well, I can't let you leave the hospital for a day or two without first examining you to make sure you are able to do that. You have survived an apparently life-threatening injury that you sustained fifteen days ago when you were relatively close to a terrorist bomb explosion in Fresno.

"Oh. *Oh, my!*"

"We will start by giving you a thorough examination, and then see how you progress from that point."

Sasha waited for just a moment, apparently trying to think through what he was saying.

"OK," she finally said in cautious resignation.

By this time, Joe and Sammy had verified the integrity of all of her bank and credit accounts, and discovered that no one had attempted to access them. Joe immediately forwarded $2,000 in cash to her at the hospital to cover whatever her immediate needs were, and separately arranged for an equally untraceable direct payment of her hospital costs.

After verifying the identity of Regina Rogers and her checking account, Joe transferred anonymously two separate $5,000 deposits from The Chancellor Organization in a circuitous, completely anonymous and undiscoverable manner—one into her checking account, and a few days later, one into her savings account. His method was a precautionary measure to minimize attention from bank regulators.

CHAPTER 54

Thursday, September 27, 2007
Denver, Colorado

"Doctor Lewis, you have a call from a Mr. James Leventhal, an attorney in Philadelphia?"

"Thank you, Jenny, I'll take it in just a few moments."

He was finishing a progress report on a twenty-two year old suicidal soldier who had just returned from Afghanistan, and then lifted the telephone receiver.

"This is Doctor Lewis. How may I help you?"

"Hello, Doctor Lewis. My name is James Leventhal. I am an attorney in Philadelphia, representing the Sargent Trucking Company, owner of the rig that collided with your mother's vehicle. First, let me offer my sincerest condolences regarding the loss of your mother. I realize that this must be an especially trying time in your life, and I do not wish to make it any more difficult than it already is."

"Thank you, Mr. Leventhal, I appreciate that." *You have NO IDEA how trying my life is right now!*

"Doctor Lewis, we all know that this is not always the best of all possible worlds, and sometimes things happen that we all regret, but have no control over."

"Yes, Mr. Leventhal, I know." *Believe me, I KNOW!* "Please get to your point."

"Doctor Lewis, I am prepared to offer your mother's estate a $3.5 million settlement out of court to avoid potential litigation costs. The Sargent Trucking Company's insurance provides for this settlement, and I strongly suggest that you take it, but, of course you are entitled to your own legal counsel."

"Thank you, Mr. Leventhal. I'm sure you will understand if I ask for your number and call you back after I have had an opportunity to consult with my attorney."

"Very well, Doctor Lewis. My number is 215-788-7838."

"Thank you. Is there anything else you need to tell me?"

"No, Doctor Lewis. I will await your call."

"Thank you Mr. Leventhal. Goodbye."

Jake did not have an attorney, but he would find one today. After a brief search, he found it curious that there were obviously far more lawyers than psychologists listed in the greater Denver Yellow Pages.

What is that saying about the nature of man, he thought to himself.

He decided instead to ask who his associates at the hospital used for legal services, and settled on Jeremy Hartman, whose office happened to be nearby. He called Hartman and explained his situation and the details of the accident, as he understood them.

"It appears that the truck driver, from what you have told me, was negligent, and a jury could award sizeable punitive damages to your mother's estate. However, I'm not saying that is what will happen, but unless you are prepared for lengthy and probably expensive litigation, I would suggest that you take their offer, Jake. Otherwise you might even come out of this with less than the offer you have now and a lot more drawn out headaches than you need."

Jake saw his point, and was in no mood to launch a major legal battle. He had quite enough on his mind as it was.

"Thank you, Mr. Hartman."

Jake broke the connection, and then called James Leventhal back and told him he would accept the settlement for the estate.

He spent the rest of the day assembling his notes and preparing for the conference at NYU in Manhattan. His flight left Denver the following morning at nine minutes after eleven, and would arrive at LaGuardia at four fifty-six that afternoon. Completely unknown to him, Sasha was returning from Fresno via a stop in Los Angeles, and arrived at LaGuardia at five fifty-nine that evening. The two would not see each other that night. Sasha took a taxi from the airport and arrived back at her condominium safely. Since she did not have her key, she buzzed her next-door neighbor to let her in the building and into her apartment with her neighbor's key to her condominium. That night she dreamt that she was near an unknown lover.

CHAPTER 55

Friday, September 28, 2007
Manhattan, New York

After a restful night, Sasha awoke with the sudden and fearful realization that she did not have a job. She picked up her spare key from her neighbor, and then immediately prepared to go into Manhattan to look for work and get another key made. She had no memory of her backup musicians. As far as she knew, she was out of work and needed to find a group of instrumental musicians to sing with, so she went to the Fat Black Pussy Cat in the hopes of meeting people who knew musicians or had other connections to help her get established, or at least get some traction toward forming a band. That is where she met Rob Reynolds, who later assembled a group of his friends who played the instruments she wanted for her backup. They rather quickly formalized their identity as 'The Autumn Dream' and secured an engagement at Club 46 in Manhattan, primarily because of the superior quality of her voice, persuasive personality and Reynolds' unusual 'connections' in the greater New York entertainment world. Rob marveled at how efficiently she orchestrated everything, as if she had done it all before.

CHAPTER 56

Tuesday, October 2, 2007
Manhattan, New York

Joe decided to put Chris Morrow in charge of watching over Jake, both to ensure his safety and to learn as much as possible about Jake as a prospect for joining The Chancellor Organization, and about Sasha out of respect for Duke's profound fondness of his only niece. Joe himself was genuinely beginning to care about both of them more and more, both individually and as a couple.

Chris was no stranger to the internet. He learned as much about Jake Lewis, Ph.D. as he could from public sources, and found his association with the Veteran's Administration Hospital in Denver, his other professional associations, his educational history, and with some minor extra effort, his home address and phone numbers, both his office and his cell phone. Because the NYU conference had been in the planning stages for many months, he easily found various links to the event, including Jake's name on a list of presenting researchers.

Chris was in Manhattan because he knew that Jake had committed to giving a speech at NYU about various structured methods of promoting and measuring progress toward adjustment to civilian life for psychologically impaired veterans. He arrived in Manhattan several days before the conference with Jim Harley, another of Joe's 'helpers,' to make learning about Jake a little easier. He and Jim treated themselves to a Broadway show since they had the time. Once they started to follow Jake, however, they knew that they would not have the luxury of entertainment, convenient meals or normal sleeping patterns until the job was finished.

The law of the jungle governed events every day in the streets of every large city on the planet. Low-grade, but clever street criminals took advantage of human nature every day to steal from or otherwise prey upon others with impunity, knowing that their techniques would not be challenged, and that if push came to shove in the court system, the situation would dissolve into 'your word against mine.' These low-grade crimes almost never resulted in a conviction, and apparently, most of the time never made it into a court of law in the first place. The perpetrators took advantage of the common probability that most people, particularly apparent visitors or tourists, will not stand up to a threat, and will easily give up property or money at the slightest provocation under sudden implied or perceived risk to their health or life if they do not cooperate. The proceeds from their activities generally were below the amounts that financially justified prosecution, which included legal and investigative fees that far surpassed the value of the stolen property in most cases, as well as general aggravation and often-inconvenient court demands upon their time, so incentives to prosecute remained minimal or non-existent, and therefore encouraged further similar theft. Such theft was in effect a 'criminal specialty' that apparently often stayed essentially under the police radar. It was as much a criminal specialty as real estate law in the legal profession, teaching history in education, or pediatrics in the medical field in the 'civilized' world.

Chris and Jim were in Manhattan in the theater district moving slowly with the after-performance crowd east on 42nd Street toward Broadway. Then a young woman in black slacks and a red jacket strode past Chris on his right, walking much faster than the rest of the crowd, elbowing rudely past people, and caught his attention. He saw the woman grab a purse from a middle-aged woman walking several yards in front of him and Harley.

Chris took off after 'Black Slacks' and yelled over his shoulder, "Stay with her!" meaning that Harley should stay with the middle-aged woman.

He kept pace with the younger woman with his long loping strides as he dodged and slipped between pedestrians in the crowd like it was an Olympic sport. Then he noticed her subtle hand-off of the purse to another woman walking in the opposite direction, dressed in a smart red and black polka-dot outfit. She did not look at all like a street thief any more than 'Black Slacks' did. 'Black Slacks' sensed that a rare person with respectable athletic ability and a conscience, and probably some other unwelcome or inconvenient characteristics was pursuing her. Chris knew this was a planned, sophisticated and deliberate theft operation, and he was not going to let it succeed. He knew that if *he* did not do something, the theft would succeed. The victim would never recover what was rightfully hers, and the 'black and red' theft team would feel empowered to repeat their scheme with impunity. No one else was paying attention or apparently did not care about what was happening, and it was obvious no one else was going to come to the aid of 'theater woman.'

Chris would have none of this cowardice. It was in his nature. It really pissed him off. The last time he stood up for an unknown woman in distress was while he was a junior at the University of Pennsylvania in Philadelphia. It cost him the scar on the right side of his face from a switchblade knife to save a young nursing student from possible abduction, and possibly even rape, or who knows what, late on a Friday evening if he had not stumbled into the situation. That incident motivated him to learn the martial arts to a very accomplished degree, so he would have little or no fear of such confrontation again. The relatively few times he stepped up to the call of conscience between college and today left would-be thugs and bullies in severe physical distress. He never had the somewhat intimidating scar surgically removed because he wanted it to serve as a reminder to himself and as a suggestion to others that he would go the extra mile, or more if necessary, and that he would never back down from a confrontation against what he knew to be the right thing to do.

He 'clothes-lined' the oncoming woman with his rock hard right forearm with shocking speed at neck level, hitting her windpipe and simultaneously applied a vice-like grip to her hand clutching the stolen purse with his left hand. He physically lifted the stunned woman off her feet with his right arm hooked around her neck and swiftly bulled his way to the building next to the sidewalk and pinned her against it, letting her breathe, but he kept her feet off the pavement.

She was kicking and shouting at the top of her lungs "HELP! POLICE! HELP! POLICE!"

Chris tightened his grip and kept her pinned against the wall, in total disregard for her obviously well rehearsed 'damsel in distress' act. Her friends had abandoned her.

"Sorry, lady, but this is your last heist for the day!" he announced with conviction.

Sure enough, the scuffle and gathering crowd drew the attention of two police officers in their patrol car on Broadway, who stopped, got out of their car and immediately approached the scene as the crowd scattered to a distance from which they could eagerly observe in typical big city fashion what promised to resemble some kind of TV reality show.

Chris thought to himself, *the only things missing are the camera and the popcorn!*

The older of the two cops, Officer R. O'Reilly approached Chris and the pinned woman, noticed that no firearms were obviously present and all hands were visible and called out as he approached.

"OK, mister, let the woman down, NOW!"

Chris announced in his best resonant Navy SEAL command voice, "I am making a citizen's arrest, Officer. If you take a close look at my left hand, you will see that I am firmly grasping this woman's hand, which is in turn holding the straps of a purse, which I personally witnessed her take in a hand-off from another woman who got away. If I wanted to steal this woman's purse, I most certainly would not still be standing here holding her up in the air against this wall, now would I. I would be long gone by now, and you know it!"

"He's lying! He's lying!" shrieked 'Polka-Dot.'

Officer R. O'Reilly had been on the police force for over twenty years, and had never seen a citizen's arrest, so he was caught off guard somewhat. He figured no reasonably well dressed man in his right mind would have a woman pinned against the wall like that in front of a police officer unless he was particularly fit, confident, and had a good reason. He did not look like a street thug, and the woman protested too much for his intuition, so he let Chris continue.

"I have a cell phone in my left hip pocket. I want you to take it out and dial the number I will give you. My friend, who is about half a block away with the woman who is the rightful owner of this purse, will answer that call. You will be able to talk to the woman, identify her and ask her for identifying information about the contents of her purse, which I will bet you $1,000 right now is the one in this woman's hand."

Officer R. O'Reilly had never seen anything like this, but took Chris at his word. He approached Chris with his left hand on his baton and maintained cautious eye contact as he reached inside Chris's left hip pocket with his right hand and indeed found the cell phone under the watchful eye of his partner. He removed it and opened it to its operating position, still watching Chris warily.

"OK. Now dial 1-703-399-4515."

Officer R. O'Reilly noticed that 'Polka-Dot' was not protesting any more, and started to believe Chris's story. The evidence was making sense, and the man was calling the shots confidently in a way that could be supported only by the truth. He dialed the number, and a voice came on the line after two rings.

"Hello?"

Chris yelled toward the phone, "It's OK, Jim! A policeman has my phone, and he's calling you to get information from the woman you're with!"

He learned from experience that addressing the local authorities as 'police' would yield more cooperation than 'cop.'

Officer R. O'Reilly spoke into the phone, "This is Officer O'Reilly, NYPD. Put the woman on the phone, please."

After a few seconds of scratchy sounds and muffled voices, a woman's gentle cultured voice answered.

"This is Dorothy Jefferson. To whom am I speaking?"

"Ms. Jefferson, this is Officer O'Reilly of the NYPD. Did someone steal your purse this evening?"

"Yes indeed, Officer!"

"I have reason to believe we may have recovered your purse, Ma'am, but I need you to identify the purse for me, including specific information about the contents of the purse, your full name and address, and any other information that only you would know. I understand you are not far from here, so I want you to come to the southwest corner of Broadway and 42nd Street as soon as possible."

"OK, Officer. I will be there shortly."

'Polka-Dot' was fading in Chris's grip. Officer O'Reilly terminated the connection.

He said to his beefy partner, "Get the woman and then give me the purse."

He closed the phone and handed it back to Chris, took the purse, and held it behind his back so Dorothy Jefferson could not see it. Chris was relieved to let the woman go. He was getting tired of holding her up against the wall. The other officer made sure he had a firm grip on her arm. In about three minutes, Jim and Dorothy arrived at what was obviously a police scene with officers exiting two more cruisers lined up behind O'Reilly's at the corner of Broadway and 42nd Street. Jim walked up to Chris with Dorothy in tow.

Chris cocked his head toward Officer O'Reilly and said, "He's the one you need to talk to."

O'Reilly was all business as he said, "Good evening, Ma'am."

He repeated his earlier question to make sure he was talking to the same woman.

"Was your purse taken from you this evening?"

"Yes, it was!"

"Please describe it to me."

"Well, the purse is made of beige-colored leather, and it has a brass-colored metal zipper all the way across the top with a double stranded leather shoulder strap."

"Like this one?"

He brought the purse out from behind his back and showed it to her.

"Why, yes! That's my purse!"

"Yes Ma'am. Now, just to make sure I am absolutely convinced, please describe to me what is inside this purse, including some form of identification."

"There's a lady's wallet, tan in color, which has my driver's license, credit cards, less than $100 in cash and other identifying information, including my address. My name is Dorothy Evelyn Jefferson, and I live at 8 Jockey Terrace, Richmond, Virginia. There is also a black electronic key fob with a Lexus logo on it. There should also be a theater program, a packet of tissues and a small pink and white makeup bag."

"May I open your purse, Ma'am, to verify what you just told me?"

"Yes, you may," she responded in typical genteel visitor's respect for the local police.

He opened the purse, and found everything the woman described, exactly as she described it, including the Virginia driver's license with her name, photograph and address on it. The credit cards had her name on them exactly as she said. Street justice had just taken a new turn.

The officer handed Dorothy her purse and said to his partner while staring menacingly at 'Polka-Dot,' "Read her her rights, cuff her, and take her to the car."

He turned back toward Dorothy and said, "Thank you, Ma'am. I'm sorry this happened to you this evening."

O'Reilly turned again and walked up to Chris and said, "The next time a police officer gives you an order you do what he tells you to do. Got it?"

"Yes sir!"

Then O'Reilly leaned a little closer toward Chris and said quietly, "Nice work, mister! However, I'm going to need your name, address and phone number for the record. You understand, of course."

What Chris understood was that it really did not matter what information he gave to the police, because he knew Duke could arrange to make it disappear. His job was to take care of and learn about Jake and Sasha, and not to be available to the police. It was precisely for these qualities of strength, decisiveness and sense of right and wrong in Chris, in addition to his loyalty to Joe, that Joe entrusted him with the special task of looking after Jake's safety and learning more about Jake and Sasha.

CHAPTER 57

Wednesday, October 3, 2007
Manhattan, New York

It was a little over three weeks since the Fresno incident, and Jake had been working very hard to put his emotional life back into some kind of equilibrium. He had approached emotional gridlock many times, when he had to decide whether to work harder to put Sasha out of his mind and continue his life the best way he could without her, or invent some kind of special separate place in his memory just for her, to which he could retreat and try to enjoy at least his memories of her. He could never make the decision to forget her. She was simply a fixture in his heart and soul. He had failed miserably at every challenge of his mind to overcome his heart. Intellectually, he knew that if he concentrated hard enough and worked hard enough to keep himself busy, he would have less and less time to entertain thoughts about Sasha and the lovely memories she left with him. He believed that if he moved to another location, he would be so involved with assimilating a new environment, both physical and social, that his life in Denver, with all of its reminders of her, would slowly but surely fade into the deepest recesses of his mind, and he could in essence start a new life. He could let the inevitable social forces of new circumstances absorb old memories and neutralize their emotional overtones and associations. A life of new experiences would help camouflage or otherwise paint over his most precious memories of her in a way that protected him from dwelling upon the past to the point that it would injure his mental health and chances for building a new life. He had to learn to manage his memories.

But what is life without precious memories? he thought to himself.

He simply could not let her go, regardless of what he decided or tried to do. Cutting her out of his life would be the same as cutting out a part of his own psyche, or even his own body. He could no more remove Sasha from his life than he could cut out his own heart and expect to live. His dilemma appeared to be insurmountable. He would simply have to invent a crutch to help him walk through the remainder of his life without her by his side. She was in effect a permanent part of his mind and soul. He wondered why he had to bear such an enormously difficult and painfully impossible burden.

Life is not fair, he reminded himself.

Jake had committed to making a presentation at the NYU Psychology Conference nine months ago, so following through at this time with his presentation was a convenient 'task' in which to immerse himself, to occupy his mind in a reasonably constructive manner, and deflect his thoughts away from his heartaches for at least several days.

He was entering a peculiarly unsettled period in his life. He had pretty much come to terms with the loss of his mother, but the uncertainty about Sasha was like a smoldering fire in his heart that interfered with almost everything he did or thought. He had just inherited a significant amount of money, including the insurance settlement from the accident, and had income coming from the investment of that tidy sum, so he did not really have to work in a traditional employment situation in order to feed and house himself and have reasonable discretionary income. However, the money did absolutely *nothing* to ease his torment. He wanted to take some time off to try to decide what he wanted to do with the rest of his life after the conference. He still had a few commitments at the V.A. hospital in Denver, but he could wrap them up within several weeks, and then be free to try to clear up his life at his own pace.

CHAPTER 58

Thursday, October 4, 2007
Manhattan, New York

After the second day of the conference on Thursday evening, Jake saw an old graduate school classmate in the audience and made a point of meeting him after the final presentation for the afternoon.

"Jake! Jake Lewis! How the hell are you?"

"I'm just great!" he lied in the expected socially graceful manner.

Henry Winslow was a very talented and insightful therapist, and casually accepted Jake's response with only the slightest intuitive doubt out of respect for an old friendship not too old to rekindle. Henry and his wife Julie, who was also a practicing psychologist, ran a private psychological counseling service in an office building on Route 10 in Cheshire, Connecticut. They decided to combine work and pleasure by attending the conference together and see a few Broadway shows while they were in Manhattan during the conference. They had not yet started a family, so they could still exercise their 'dating' freedom as a married couple, taking advantage of opportunities and adventures usually available when they traveled.

"I see you are going to bring us up to speed with Goal Attainment Scaling as applied to recovery from military life, or should I say re-entry into the real world?" Henry said.

"Actually, I work it both ways, Henry, depending upon how my client sees the process, but then you will have to wait until tomorrow afternoon for the details. In the meantime, I hope you will introduce me to this lovely young lady by your side!"

She was lovely indeed, with long flowing golden hair, and captivating emerald green eyes, and with heels stood six inches shorter than her six-foot one-inch tall husband.

"OH! Please forgive me! Jake Lewis, this is my wife Julie. Julie, this man is one of the more gifted psychology researchers I met in graduate school. He came all the way from Denver to enlighten us about some of his work with returning servicemen!"

The genuine warmth of Julie's smile seemed to flow all the way through her right hand as well, as she gracefully shook Jake's hand with evident class and poise. Jake was somewhat comforted by the friendly female contact, simple and innocent as it was, after such a long period without Sasha.

"Let's all go out tomorrow evening for dinner and a show or something after the day's conference schedule ends!" Henry said.

He studied Julie's face as he tried to read her reaction and approval as he continued, "We'll bring along Julie's sister Jayne Astor, who happens to be a movie star here in Manhattan, just to even out the occupancy of a table for four," he joked smoothly.

"Henry! Isn't that a little premature? We don't know whether Jake is even . . ."

Jake interrupted, rescuing both Henry and Julie from any potentially unnecessary embarrassment or discomfort, "I would love to!"

She continued with a slightly apologetic tone, "Really, Jake, she is *not* a movie star! She is an actress who happens to get work from time to time in that crazy business, but I believe you would at least enjoy her company for the evening. I realize that I do not know you well enough to say that for certain, but I do know her well enough to believe that she would make you comfortable with her, and since we have somewhat similar taste in men, I'm sure she will find you attractive! She is two years younger than I am, and has long blonde hair—naturally blonde—and she can hold a conversation with *anyone* about *anything,* and I do mean *anything*, in spite of her hair color! When she chooses to dress up, she can be very easy on the eyes, if you get my drift! Even if she doesn't love you, she's a good enough actress to make you feel special!"

"Jesus, Julie! Did you have to go that far?" Henry interjected in an urgent audible whisper.

Jake and Henry looked at each other with some kind of special 'male understanding' unique to their gender that was lost on Julie.

She turned to her husband with the completely innocent look of an experienced matchmaker and whispered in his ear with conviction, "I have a 'read' on your friend here, smarty pants, and I *know* my sister! Trust me on this! They're *ripe* for each other!"

As true as that may have been to Julie, she did not really know her sister as well as she thought she did.

Jake was intrigued just enough by her rather confident and audacious description to say, "Why not?"

He had absolutely nothing else to lose and at least something to gain. He was putting significant effort into trying to push his life in a new direction and out of the painful and emotionally uncertain dark valley of the last several weeks. He detected a little momentum developing in the right direction with this invitation. He was ready for some carefree, even exciting time with some friendly people, even if it was just to clear his mind for a few hours. It had to be therapeutic, he reasoned to himself.

Psychologist, heal thyself raced briefly through his mind as if it were a subliminal television advertisement.

She continued, "I know the perfect place. I'll make reservations for six o'clock tomorrow evening at Swing 46 Jazz and Supper Club. It's between 8th and 9th Avenues on 46th Street. You can't miss it! You guys can even get in without a tie! We'll bring Jayne and meet you there at the door, Jake. That way we'll make sure you two have a non-threatening experience, and we can all get to know each other a little better. OK?"

"Sounds great to me! I'll be there!" Jake said with growing excitement.

At this point, Jake would also have bought the Brooklyn Bridge.

CHAPTER 59

Friday, October 5, 2007
Manhattan, New York

Jake strolled west on 46th Street and got a distant glimpse of two women and a man standing in front of Swing 46. As he approached another thirty feet, he recognized Henry and Julie standing with another striking blonde-haired woman almost as tall as Julie. She was wearing a dark blue dress, which contrasted nicely against her light blonde hair and hung provocatively from all of the male points of interest on her well-defined female form. Jake was already visually impressed, but had to know what was between her ears before truly relaxing for the evening. So far, Julie was batting a thousand!

Julie saw Jake approaching, elbowed her sister gently and nodded in Jake's direction. Jayne smiled easily, as she knew immediately that the evening was not going to be one of those proverbial 'double-date disasters' that everyone jokes about. Julie handled the introduction smoothly like a professional match-maker, almost obligating Jayne and Jake to shake hands, which they did. It generated an invitingly warm and pleasant sensation in Jake, since he had not touched another available woman in any meaningful way at all before this weekend since he last touched Sasha. They entered the club and quickly identified their reservation, as Jayne turned on the charm apparently with very little effort. She decided she was going to enjoy herself this evening. Jake was losing his defenses little by little. It was a good start—good enough for all of them to enjoy each other socially for the evening, which was really all Jake wanted at this point. After all, he had his friend Henry to run interference for him if necessary, or to help guide the evening in a helpful manner. Julie thought she knew her sister well enough and could help make Jake comfortable when necessary. With that relatively minor but adequate comfort, Jake was ready to relax and enjoy a carefree evening.

Chris and Jim, the two men who had been watching them from across the street and halfway down the block quickly approached the entrance to the club and innocently walked in after them.

A hostess took Henry, Julie, Jayne and Jake to their table. Jake was the only one at the table facing away from the stage. Henry had the only direct view of the stage from their table, and Jayne had merely to look to her left and Julie to her right to see the stage easily. They all settled into intertwining discussions about their lives, where they grew up, schools they attended, where they lived, what kinds of food they liked and where they traveled. Jake kept his recent personal life under wraps, however, because he did not want to depart from the basic 'what you see is what you get' relationship level. Getting too far into personal circumstances was too much of a threat to him at this point, and would possibly send the wrong message. Jayne smoothly delivered a few 'dumb blonde' jokes in a way that only a *smart* blonde could, and Jake noticed with excited mental approval. Her vocabulary was broad, and her manner was sophisticated and confident. Julie deliberately flashed periodic *'I told you so'* glances at both her husband and Jake from time to time as she mentally filled out her sister's report card for the evening so far with 'A+.' Jake was slowly letting his defenses down. He actually liked Jayne.

There was a very good reason for why Jayne scored high social marks on anyone's 'report card.' She was an experienced 'professional entertainer' to supplement her meager acting wages, and was arguably the highest-paid 'professional' at the table, and possibly throughout the entire dining area by far on an hourly basis. However, this evening she was simply doing her sister a favor, only Julie had no idea whatsoever of her sister's secret life, and the men were ignorant as well. It did not really matter to anyone else from Jayne's perspective, so she played her part at the most sincere level—just helping her sister and brother-in-law out in a pinch and enjoying herself in the process, and for once enjoying an evening out on a personal instead of a 'professional' level.

Their server finally came around to their table and took orders for drinks. Henry and Julie ordered wine, and Jayne and Jake looked at each other in pleasant carefree approval and ordered the same. A basket of fresh bread followed shortly thereafter. Jake eagerly started with the bread, since he was already unusually hungry, and discovered that it was warm, fresh and actually quite tasty after he dipped it into a small bowl of olive oil and mysterious herbs.

The entertainment for the evening was preparing on the stage at the far end of the dining area from their table. An electronic double-keyboard instrument stood on the left, a grouping of blue and silver drums was centered toward the rear, and three stools—one set center forward, and the other two slightly to the right and toward the back of the stage. The lighting remained focused on the stage and increased slightly in intensity as it diminished slightly everywhere else in the dining area, but remained bright enough for eating. Conversations buzzed and hummed at a rather low level throughout the room with typical dining noises of occasional silverware-to-plate and glass-to-glass tinkling sounds.

Then a handsome young man stepped out onto the stage with a soprano saxophone. He was dressed in dark blue trousers, black shoes, and a dark blue shirt open at the collar and had relatively long slicked-back hair. The rather stocky drummer appeared next and wiggled his way into the somewhat cramped drummer's position toward the rear. He also wore dark blue clothing with an open collar. His hair was apparently naturally blonde in a somewhat disheveled style, and along with his relatively broad facial features suggested Scandinavian heritage. The keyboard player appeared in similar dark attire, with one earring and a completely shaved head, and sat on a black cushioned bench behind the sophisticated electronic keyboard instrument. The last musician appeared from between the two rear curtains with a guitar, also dressed in what was apparently the group's signature style, and sat on one of the two remaining unoccupied stools and looped the instrument support strap over his shoulder. Jake continued to chew on his bread without turning around, but felt a small heart murmur, inhaled deeply a few times, and recovered quickly.

An official professional voice announced through the public address system, "And now, ladies and gentlemen, please welcome New York's own *Autumn Dream!*"

Polite applause started to build throughout the dining area, as Jake immediately choked on his bread as his heart rate accelerated and his palms became clammy. He coughed several more times, as his heart continued to race while he looked around the table at Jayne, Henry and Julie, simultaneously feeling the color drain from his face. They were looking toward the stage with anticipation, clapping politely. Jake quickly came to his senses with concentrated effort, took a deep breath and clapped as well, breathing heavily, but trying to suppress evidence of it as his heart pounded so hard he feared they would actually hear it. Julie glanced ever so briefly at Jake, and then at Henry, then back to Jake and back to her husband again, who caught her eye with concern, and stole a glance at Jake, but quickly looked back toward the stage and joined the general polite applause as it started to simmer down to quiet. Jayne was intuitively very alert, watching Jake with a practiced inscrutable expression that melted into a perfect smile at will.

She gently put her warm left hand on his right thigh, leaned over to him and whispered with genuine concern close to his ear, "Are you OK?"

Jake summoned all the self-control he could manage under the circumstances, took a deep breath and spoke just above a whisper with a polite smile, "Yeah. I'm . . . I'm OK, thank you."

She removed her hand and looked back toward the stage without conviction, glanced one more time at Jake, and then looked back toward the stage and rejoined the diminishing applause but stopped shortly thereafter with everyone else.

The musicians on the stage began to play. The harmony started with a simple middle C tone from the soprano sax, and then slowly, invitingly ascended to F, then G, then A, and then rewarded the listeners with a full C-major harmonic resolution from the keyboard and guitar as the drummer melded the pace of the music into his drumbeat. Jake knew what the notes were because he had perfect pitch. His heart was racing. His breathing accelerated. He was listening to the beginning of the improvisation he played for Sasha that first night on Eddie's piano backstage in Denver! He became pale again. He just could not turn around and face the stage. He froze in emotional gridlock.

This can't be! Jesus! What the hell is happening here?

Jayne carefully glanced over at him, with deep concern in her eyes, then at Henry, then at Julie with a worried expression on her face, almost panicking but keeping a lid on her emotions with extraordinary effort, in spite of her respectable acting ability and considerable formal and informal social skills.

Jake concentrated with some difficulty and said, "Excuse me, please. I'll be right back."

He stood up and almost lost his balance, feeling a little light-headed, but recovered quickly, and made his way from the table toward where he thought the men's room might be. One of the servers was watching him by that time, and graciously pointed him in the right direction with a smile and a nod of his head. Jake entered the men's room and went to one of the five urinals, even though he felt no urgency and there was not much to relieve. He had to go through the motions anyway, just to try to do something other than let his body betray his mind and heart so readily in public—to kill some time and try to feel normal. He needed a little time to recover, to get a grip on reality—or what he thought was reality.

Back at the table, Jayne whispered to Julie and Henry "What's going on? Is Jake OK?"

Henry and Julie whispered back in unison, "I don't have any idea what's going on!"

"He didn't look very good there for a moment."

Julie turned to Henry and said, "You go to him and see if he needs help—*now*, Henry!"

The same server saw Henry get up and walk deliberately in the same direction Jake had gone, and quietly gave him the same general intuitive guidance, "That way, on your left."

Henry whispered "Thanks," and quickly found the door marked 'MEN' in spite of the relatively low light.

He walked into the relatively small well-lighted room with evident surprise as he saw Jake leaning over one of the four sinks, splashing water over his face.

"Hey, Jake! Are you OK?"

"I'm just a little queasy."

"Do you need medical help? Are you ill? *Talk to me, Jake!*"

Jake splashed more cold water on his face and said with obvious effort, "I'll be OK. I'll be OK, Henry, thank you. I'll be OK."

Henry noticed that he repeated himself twice, almost with the appearance of trying to convince himself at the same time. The cold water really felt good! Jake absolutely could not tell the story now. It would ruin the evening for everyone, he thought, particularly for Jayne. He turned to Henry and smiled weakly, as he grabbed several tan paper towels from the dispenser on the wall and wiped his face and hair, as well as the errant drops of water on the front of his jacket that had yet to soak into the fabric. He took several very deep breaths and stretched his arms over his head and then bent down to touch his shoes several times in a somewhat civilized but odd effort to get blood moving a little faster throughout his body and to distract his attention somewhat from his emotions. He turned to the mirror and tried to make himself look reasonably presentable again, as Henry watched him carefully, feeling rather helpless.

Jake took another deep breath and turned to Henry with a carefully manufactured polite smile, and said, "Let's go back to the table."

The two men rejoined the women at the table. Both women looked intently from Jake to Henry in anticipation of an explanation, or at least some indication that everything was OK, just as the musical introduction sounded like it was winding down.

Jake took the implied responsibility, and said, "I'm sorry, but I just got a little light-headed for a minute there, and thought it would be a good idea to leave the table. I feel OK now."

He smiled convincingly enough to see Julie relax somewhat as he sat down in his chair, but Jayne was not convinced. She had heard and seen significantly more of the human male animal under a much broader spectrum of situations than Julie had, or Henry for that matter, regardless of their formal psychological training and experience. She was unsettled. Her intuition was firing alarms, but she felt no conviction. She masked her feelings well, like the professional woman and actress she was, and flashed a perfect soothing smile at Jake in a genuine effort to neutralize whatever had triggered his discomfort. She was slowly letting the 'maternal woman' in her take over from the 'professional woman.'

Then the black curtain at the rear of the stage parted, and the beautiful Sasha Chancellor stepped out as gracefully as ever onto the stage in her trademark sequined white form-fitting dress. She seemed to glide with only four graceful steps to the empty stool at the front and center of the stage, already soaking the audience with her powerful smooth mezzo voice in duet with the soprano sax. Julie looked briefly at Henry, and saw complete raw male appreciation of the opposite sex in his facial expression. Jayne looked at Jake, and saw a man in silent tears, yet smiling.

There is something about that woman on the stage, she thought.

She glanced quickly around to the tables nearby, and saw every man with just about the same look of appreciation as Henry's. She was a professional expert at getting a man's attention, and yet she was dumbfounded by what she saw happening around her. The woman on the stage was getting the reaction from men all around the room at a distance of fifty feet or more that she could get usually only within arm's reach! Jake still had not turned around. He was the only male in the place *not* looking at arguably the most attractive female in the entire dining area. What was so different about Jake from every other man in the room? What was so different about this woman? It had to be *her voice!*

Moments later, Jake still had not turned around to face the stage. He did not have to. He recognized the voice so pleasantly and permanently engraved into his mind and heart from that first night at Eddie's Place in Denver. He was overjoyed to the point of really losing his composure. He knew it was coming. He had to explain himself to his friends, even as he was beginning to like Jayne. He felt as though his central nervous system was about to sustain a major short-circuit as he visualized his graduate school physiology texts with pictures and illustrations of the body's complete nervous system, only with brilliant glowing red hot shimmering images for the brain and the heart.

Keep it together, Jake—you can do this, he said to himself. *You can do this!*

He steeled himself for just a few seconds, inhaled and then lowly turned around and saw his beautiful Sasha for the first time in almost a month. He just lost it. He immediately burst into tears of joy and sobbed openly as Henry quickly arose from his seat, went to his side and grabbed him under his arms as he felt Jake go limp. Another man at a nearby table immediately got up and came to Henry's aid as inconspicuously as possible. The two men quickly gathered Jake between them. Henry put his left arm around Jake's waist and held Jake's right wrist over his right shoulder, as the other man assisted Jake similarly from his left side. They quickly half dragged, half carried him from the dining area, as Jake attempted to move his legs like he could walk, but they would not cooperate. He did not protest or resist the two men. He knew he was making a fool of himself, but he absolutely could not help himself, either. This was just another episode of real life in real time. It was inconvenient. It was embarrassing. It was unplanned. Jake was almost literally *lovesick.* His body had never betrayed him like this before. He had just seen what most people would have called a ghost, and most people would not have blamed him for his reaction, and probably would have considered his response rather mild under the circumstances if they knew the whole story.

Sasha and her backup band never missed a beat. The incident was too far away from them to notice with any obvious degree of attention, and was handled as quickly and as efficiently as spilled coffee from the perspective of almost everyone close enough even to have noticed the young man in some kind of distress being removed quickly and quietly from the audience. Henry and the other man took Jake out the front door onto the sidewalk, hoping that the fresh, cool early October evening air would help him recover.

Henry said, "Jake, you're going to be OK. Just take some deep breaths."

He steadied Jake in an almost vertical, almost standing position, but leaning against the front of the building with the other man's help. Jayne and Julie came out of the building very shortly thereafter. Jayne brought a glass of water with her.

"I think we can handle him now," Julie said confidently to the attentive stranger. "Thank you very much for your help."

"You sure, Ma'am? I mean, I'd be glad to stick around if you need me."

"No, really, thank you. That's very kind and thoughtful of you, but we'll handle it from here." She flashed him her best classy 'thank you' smile as she continued, "You should go back and enjoy the show and your dinner. Thank you very much!"

Jayne was now in full 'maternal mode,' and handed Jake the glass of water and placed her hand on his arm as if to make sure he remained standing.

"Here, Jake, drink some water."

He was gradually gaining control of his body, absorbing the shock as well as he could. He took the glass and drank all of the cold water in continuous gulps. The other three were studying him carefully, watching urgently for any sign of further trouble. Jake inhaled deeply, then let the air out of his lungs slowly, and then inhaled again, letting it out slowly, and then again.

After a few settling moments he said, "I'm really terribly embarrassed by my behavior, and I sincerely apologize to all of you. I owe you an explanation, but like a lot of the truth these days, you may find what I have to say very hard to swallow. I am obviously emotionally distraught, but I'm pulling myself back together little by little. I need to go back inside to the table. I'll be OK. I really *need* to hear her sing. I will explain everything to you all later. *I promise!*"

He looked deep into Jayne's eyes, practically begging for understanding, and she answered him visually with her complete and genuine understanding and forgiveness.

"But Jake, are you sure you're OK?" Henry asked with sincere personal as well as professional concern.

Jayne's intuition was in 'free-fire' mode. She interrupted with her special female confidence, trumping Henry's concern.

"OK, Jake. Take my hand and let's go back inside to our table."

Henry and Julie looked at each other for several seconds with raised eyebrows, resignation, and total lack of comprehension, if not palpable relief because Jayne took such effective control of the situation. They walked back into the dining room behind Jake and Jayne, and took their same seats as Sasha was just getting to the refrain of her song.

"I want to feel you near me.
I need to feel your soul inside me.
I gave you all that I am—
My soul, my heart, my tears of joy,
I want to hold you near me
And touch as one with you.
I want to see again as one with you,
The sunrise of a new day.
I yearn for the part of me in you
To make me whole again,

As I hold dear that part of you in me.
I hear your song every day,
The part of you that's in my soul.
I need to give my love to you again.
No other will share my soul,
Nor will I ever leave your heart.
I need to be whole again with
The part of me I left in you."

Jake was completely overwhelmed. Tears streamed down his cheeks, just as they did that first night at Eddie's Place. He sat transfixed, listening to her unique voice with what he thought had to be *her* words put to his music, because he never wrote any words to his music. He felt whole again for the first time in several weeks, believing that she was really singing to *him.* She was speaking *to him alone*, separate from all the others in the room. For just a moment, Jake was alone, oblivious to the people around him, focused completely upon the woman of his dreams, comforted by her unique and beautiful voice that excited his musical soul so profoundly.

He was so isolated in his thoughts, that he did not notice that Jayne was watching him *very* carefully. She knew. She did not know all of the details, but she had essentially figured it all out. Jake—*all of him*—belonged completely to the woman in the white dress. She worked in the competitive world of entertainment as an actress. She had seen her share of competition among women for a man. After seeing Jake's response to the woman on the stage, Jayne imagined that if someone wanted to hire her to get involved with Jake to make that other woman jealous, she would have laughed at the utter foolish absurdity of it. There was no way she, or any other woman could have torn Jake from that singer for any price, even with her considerable professional amorous talents and skills. She genuinely liked Jake.

Although she had been close to *many* men, she smiled to herself as she thought, *I have never been this close to a really sensitive man before. Well, maybe the next time will be my time!*

After the end of the show as the entertainers left the stage with the final applause, Jayne turned to Jake, and Henry and Julie deliberately repositioned themselves in their chairs as they all looked at Jake in simultaneous kind anticipation of 'the promised explanation.' Jake looked around the table and got their unspoken message quite clearly. He looked into their eyes one by one, took a deep breath and exhaled freely.

"OK, here's the story. On Friday, September 7, I was in Eddie's Place in Denver, which is an entertainment restaurant and bar much like this one. The entertainment group for the evening was 'The Autumn Dream' from New York, but it was not the same group we just heard here this evening. The same female lead singer was there at Eddie's, however, and the instruments were the same, but a different group of male musicians was there. Her name is Sasha."

"From the first note I heard her sing that evening, even *before* I saw her come out onto the stage, I fell in love with her. I know that sounds really naïve, adolescent and preposterous, but it's true. I actually cried with joy through her whole performance, and it certainly didn't hurt that she was just plain 'both barrels' beautiful. I stayed for a while after the show because I had neglected to eat my meal during her performance, and I was still very hungry. I knew I absolutely had to talk with her before she left, because I had heard that was her last night in Denver."

"After the show, and after almost everyone had gone, she actually came down to my table of her own volition, sat down, and struck up a conversation. I got the impression that she was interested in me, so we talked a little. She said she wanted to know 'everything about me' and I eventually told her that I play the piano. She insisted that I play Eddie's Yamaha grand piano hidden backstage right then and there, so we went to the piano and I played for her. Believe it or not, what I played for her that night is very much what you just heard here tonight, but I did not put any words to it. I just made it up as I played. She must have remembered the music and made up the words for it later."

In recognition of what she perceived to be Jake's continuing elevated stress level, Jayne spoke up to help him relax, "That's really amazing that she obviously remembered what you played *and* put words to it!"

"Yeah. Well again, believe it or not it started to get really complicated! I learned a little later that night that we had fallen for each other all the way, and I mean *completely*, and that we had to keep seeing each other. It was honest, straight up, in-your-face natural mutual attraction at an incredibly compelling, yet almost fairly-tale level. For lack of a better phrase, it was 'love at first music.' I had never experienced anything like it before—with anyone—and would not even have believed it was possible if had I not personally experienced it!"

"Now, here's the hard part. You all have heard about the Fresno incident, I'm sure. Well, after Denver, she and her backup were going to Fresno for a week that, as it turned out, overlapped the time of the explosion. We had agreed that first night to a date back at Eddie's after her Fresno engagement on the 17th, but she never showed up. I was absolutely devastated, because I thought she 'stood me up' and I absolutely could *not* believe it after what we had shared together. I had not been reading the papers, watching TV or getting much news at all, even on my computer. I just immersed myself in my work to help pass the time until I would see her again, so I didn't even know about the Fresno incident, incredible as that may seem, until the Saturday *after* that planned second evening at Eddie's Place. After I eventually learned on the internet about the Fresno explosion and her disappearance, I was worried sick that she had died in the explosion, but I had no good information one way or the other. I was really devastated."

"I became depressed, and on top of that, I was still dealing with my mother's death after a truck accident a day after the Fresno incident back home in Reading, Pennsylvania, so I was really, really in bad shape emotionally. I went back to Reading to take care of my mother's affairs on Wednesday. I inherited a very special beautiful diamond, and I was going to have it reset and then give it to Sasha as an engagement ring. Until tonight, I really didn't know whether Sasha was alive or dead, but I was all but convinced she was dead. So, you can appreciate why I reacted the way I did, first when I heard the beginning of that song, and second when I heard her rather distinctive voice, and third when I actually turned around and saw her for the first time since that Saturday morning after we first met."

Jake stopped talking, and took a very deep breath and let it out slowly, raising his gaze to the ceiling, trying to discourage more tears from falling. None of them made a sound for the next fifteen seconds.

"OOOOOOHHHHHH MMMMMMYYYYYY GOD!" the others all finally said in unison, staring helplessly at Jake.

Another brief period of raw, paralyzing silence hung over all of them. Then Henry spoke up in an honest effort to support him.

"Jesus! I don't know that I would have held up anywhere near as well as you did this evening, Jake."

Julie added, "Jake, you're only human. You're not *superman*. You've sustained a tremendous, unbelievable emotional shock! You have absolutely nothing to be ashamed of or to apologize for!"

Jayne offered her support as well in obvious sincerity, "Jake, I really like you a lot. After that story, I admire you even more, and I *love* that song! I've been around the entertainment industry for a while. I've heard good voices and good music before, and I understand how you have been taken by her voice, let alone her obvious beauty. You deserve her, and she certainly deserves you!"

Then Julie said in a moment of inspiration, "Hey! Let's all go backstage, and introduce ourselves, and make sure Jake and Sasha are reunited for good!"

Jayne looked at him with a genuine smile and added, "That's a *great* idea!"

Henry piped up, "Are you ready for this, Jake? I'd kind of like to meet her up close and personal as well!"

Julie glanced at Henry with a look that said, '*don't push it, buster!*'

Jake assessed for a moment the considerable support he was getting and slowly looked each one of them in the eye one by one for a few seconds, and finally said, "Yes, actually, I am!"

He took another very deep breath and let it out as if he were preparing for some ultimate and inevitable vital test. They all stood, left the table and walked toward the stage looking for a way to enter the backstage area. Just as they approached the front of the stage, the sax player came back out to start collecting some of their equipment.

He noticed them approaching the stage and said in a practiced, but still genuinely friendly manner, "Hi folks! Did you enjoy our show?"

"More than you can imagine," Jake said without thinking.

Jayne added, "We would all really like to meet Sasha. May we go backstage to see her?"

"How about I go backstage and ask her to come out here to meet you, because it's rather cramped back there," he said cheerfully with a professional entertainer's easy smile, as he suddenly realized that they had asked for her by name. *How did they know her name?*

"That would be absolutely wonderful!" Henry and Julie said simultaneously and then laughed at each other, taking some of the tension out of the group.

Jayne was looking very carefully at Jake after having heard that almost unbelievable story, anticipating something, but she could not focus on anything in particular. Her woman's intuition was starting to buzz, but without clear definition. She said nothing. Jake said nothing. He was looking at his shoes.

'Sax guy' disappeared backstage, and they could hear him talking to someone, but could not hear the conversation clearly enough to understand everything, but the phrase " . . . asked for you by name . . ." escaped the otherwise muffled sound of voices behind the stage. After about twenty seconds, Sasha walked out from behind the stage curtain, and stepped forward as gracefully as ever down the two steps to the main floor level, still wearing her white dress, and flashing her natural captivating smile at the four of them.

"Hi! I hope you all enjoyed the show!" she said cheerfully with no special recognition of any of them.

"We did indeed! You have a *very beautiful* voice!" said Jayne.

"Thank you very much!" she responded with poised genuine personal and professional appreciation.

Jake looked up from the floor into Sasha's eyes, as his heart continued to race.

She met his gaze, smiled at him and said innocently, "Hi!"

Jayne's intuitive fire alarm went off immediately. It was a 'ten-alarmer!' This scene was not looking, feeling or sounding like the reunion of two long-lost lovers!

Just before Jayne could rescue Jake, he said cautiously, "I've really missed you!"

Jayne's mind raced instinctively to protect Jake as she immediately looked carefully into Sasha's eyes and did not see the look of a woman just reunited with her lover.

"Oh, my! I'm . . . I'm very sorry, but . . . have we met?" Sasha asked agreeably, but very carefully and as politely, and as professionally respectfully as possible under the increasingly awkward circumstances.

Seconds passed silently as she looked around at each of them searching for a connection, still smiling graciously with mild disguised effort.

Jayne was reading the exchange, or lack of it, with all of the intense concentration and alertness of a demolitions expert trying to defuse a live bomb with the timer at single digits and counting to zero. Henry's mouth went dry as he looked from Sasha to Jake and saw the absolutely devastating and crushing hurt of a lifetime in his eyes.

Immediately, Julie's heart skipped a beat as she thought to herself, *Oh my God! Something is definitely tragically wrong here!*

Jayne alertly spoke up in 'full-power maternal intuition mode' reinforced by her acting experience, "Well, we just wanted to meet you and thank you in person for such a *lovely* performance. All of us really enjoyed it immensely! We know it's getting late, and we understand very well that you must be tired and need to relax for a while. Thank you again for such a perfectly *wonderful* performance! We will have to hear you again sometime!"

She grabbed Jake's elbow with determination and surprising strength and steered him firmly in the opposite direction toward the front door as Henry and Julie thanked Sasha graciously once more for coming back out to meet them. Jake was still too stunned to resist. Sasha smiled her most pleasant 'meet the audience' smile, and thanked them again for coming to hear her group, then turned to go backstage with an uncertain quizzical expression on her face. Henry and Julie turned to follow Jake and Jayne across the room to the front exit and out onto the sidewalk into the fresh October evening air. Jake was silent. He felt like a pin-ball in a pin-ball machine, ricocheting from prize bumpers to penalty holes, being slapped around the table of life only to fall helplessly between the lowest flippers into the final 'black hole' ending the game of love with very little hope of being 'spring loaded' back into the game again.

Chris and Jim had been sitting in the corner farthest from the stage, watching the exchange with effective anonymity, making their coffee last beyond its tolerable but deteriorating taste. Chris had been listening to the entire exchange with a miniature directional microphone, amplifying their voices through a very thin wire to an earplug in his right ear.

After walking out of the club, the four of them continued to a nearby coffee shop with Jayne still holding on to Jake's left arm, now with two hands. They walked in and found only one table for four in the back corner. Henry secured the table and ordered four cups of coffee, merely to justify holding the table. They needed to talk as soon as possible, and this was the best they could do quickly for a place to talk at this hour in Manhattan. Staying in the club would not work at all, and the street was absolutely out of the question. Jim Harley strolled innocently into the same coffee shop after them with his own miniature directional microphone, and took a seat at the counter, ordered a cup of coffee, and paid for it immediately. However, he never touched it because he did not want to have to choose later between keeping tabs on Jake and Sasha, and trying to find a men's room somewhere at an inconvenient time or place.

Henry said, "We have to talk about this, Jake. I've known you for a few years—not as well as some, perhaps—but well enough to know that you are certainly not a liar. The story you told us back at the club was a little too complex and unique to be a fabrication, and your body language has spoken quite eloquently of your sincere passion for Sasha. I'm telling you as a friend and as a professional psychologist, that I believe Sasha is suffering from some form of retrograde amnesia. I believe you created that music that she sang, so there was obviously a relationship between the two of you at some point that I believe is beyond both doubt and camouflage, and music may actually be the key to reuniting the two of you. I also believe she is no more capable of masking her feelings for you than you are of hiding your feelings for her. As the old saying goes, 'When you're in love, it shows!' Therefore, I am inclined to believe that the tragedy in Fresno has something to do with her behavior toward you this evening. I actually believe her memories of you, and probably of much of her life during the period surrounding the Fresno incident, have been impaired to some extent by some kind of critical experience, perhaps life-threatening, and my guess is that it is whatever happened to her in Fresno. I've done some work with amnesia over the last several years, Jake, and I actually honestly do believe we can restore her memory and your relationship with her."

Jake looked up at Henry after having just stared at the table for the last three minutes. He was slowly emerging from the emotional fog that had been distorting his understanding of Sasha's behavior since that night at Eddie's when he thought she had stood him up. He wanted to believe in anything that would bring Sasha back to him. This time, however, it had the ring of credibility. Although Jake was also a psychologist, he was in no position to 'heal himself.' He knew that task would require another professional outside the emotional context of his relationship with Sasha. Jake knew it, Henry knew it and Julie knew it. Jayne was not a psychologist in the academic or professional sense, but she was one hell of an 'armchair psychologist' with her wealth of understanding men on a very basic, common and personal level. She knew it, too.

Shortly after midnight that night, Joe had all of the details of Sasha's condition, as well as an appreciation of the history of her relationship with the young psychology researcher, Jake Lewis, Ph.D., and immediately relayed that information to Duke on System 15. Duke was determined that he would stop at nothing and spare no expense before he had complete proof of his lovely niece's full recovery from her tragic life-threatening ordeal in Fresno.

CHAPTER 60

Tuesday, October 9, 2007
Ashton, Maryland

Duke examined the RSI indicator on his S&P futures chart and decided that the price had to come down a few points. He entered an order to short 1,000 contracts for December delivery at $4.05. The market was $4.03. He waited.

CHAPTER 61

Wednesday, October 10, 2007
Reading, Pennsylvania

The UPS driver was making his way east on Franklin Street toward Joe's. He slipped into a vacant space marked "NO PARKING AT ANY TIME" stretching out about twenty feet on both sides away from a fire hydrant, left the engine running, and dashed into Joe's through the open front door.

"Hey Joe! Package for you!"

Joe came out of the kitchen on the far side of the dining room and wiped his hands on a large food-soiled heavy white apron tied around his waist. There were no customers yet. He did not open until four o'clock.

"Yeah Billy, what is it?"

"Sign here, Joe. I'm illegal out there and behind schedule."

Joe drew some lines on the electronic clipboard Billy held for him. No one could decipher what he wrote—just like his dentist's signature—and no one would care. His signature was just 'business as usual.'

Billy handed him the manila envelope and turned to dash out the door to his truck, yelling over his shoulder "See ya, Joe!"

"Yeah, Billy. Thanks! Drive carefully, now. You're important!"

Joe sat down at one of his dining tables and opened the envelope only to find another envelope inside addressed to Paul and Sarah

Jepson at a rural post office box in Iowa. A note was attached on Duke Chancellor's secretary's stationery at the Plymouth Building, one of Duke's several office buildings just north of Washington, D.C.

'See that this gets to the Jepsons. DC.'

Joe knew that DC did not mean 'District of Columbia.' it meant Duke Chancellor. He also knew that when Duke said, 'see that this gets' somewhere, Joe was to use special delivery, which meant private personal means on the payroll, return receipt guaranteed, without fail!

Joe called Wesley Simpson. Wesley did odd jobs for Joe, and was pure as could be. He owed his good fortune to Duke Chancellor.

"How'd you like to go to De Moines, Iowa, Wes?"

"Sure Joe, when?"

"As soon as possible. Stop by the restaurant on your way to the airport."

Within a half hour, Wes was at the back door of the restaurant, where Joe met him with the envelope, which was thicker than Wes would have expected for a single letter.

"Please see that this gets to the Jepsons—standard confirmation and receipt. You will find the address and other helpful background information inside in a separate packet as well."

"Got it, Joe! Be back in about thirty-six."

Joe smiled as Wes turned and walked back to his old tan 1980 Cadillac Seville in the back lot. The car belied his true wealth. Wesley Simpson was a retired junk dealer. He bought and sold scrap metal and old cars like the one he was driving, machinery, and whatever else had metal in it back in the seventies, eighties and nineties. Of course, it did not hurt that the Carpenter Steel Company was located in Reading as well, giving him a certain regular pace of business. Duke Chancellor directed business to Wes when he was injured, and could no longer operate his cranes. Customers eventually drifted away because of slow deliveries and late payments. Joe interceded for his friend, knowing Duke would welcome another loyal employee.

Wes recovered from his back injuries, stayed in the main office and hired a crew to handle the heavy lifting part of the business. There was plenty of business, as Wes took orders from all over Pennsylvania, Delaware and New Jersey arranged by Duke Chancellor. Duke told him through a shell 'business advisory' company how to charge for his services, and subsidized the difference between his metal prices and the competition until Wes gained the loyalty of enough customers to keep the business legitimately profitable on his own and Duke diminished his subsidies to zero. After accumulating a tidy $6 million nest egg Wes called it quits, sold his scrap metal business for another $15 million and did odd jobs for Joe. Duke had been hedging his 'help' in the futures markets, so he really did not suffer meaningful financial losses.

Wes drove out to the municipal airport north of the city, and found his private jet on the tarmac, ready to go. His friend and co-pilot Chester Chzyrzynski was already there after getting Wes's call asking him whether he wanted to fly today. He lived much closer to the north end of town than Wes did. Of course, he knew the answer would be a resounding 'Yes!' He filed his flight plan and then walked to his favorite toy on the tarmac. Wes followed Chester up the stairs, pulled them up after himself and locked the door with religious regard for the instructions. Wes knew airplanes. He did everything by the book. After settling into the cockpit next to his flight companion, a retired school teacher, who obviously could not afford his own jet, but could afford to fly with Wes for free to enjoy the friendly companionship and his favorite hobby. It was a victory for 'win-win' once again.

Chester taught algebra at the high school level, and loved every minute of his career. He was born in Saint Petersburg, Russia, but emigrated to the United States at the tender age of eight. He taught at 'The Castle On The Hill,' as the Reading Senior High School was known, after graduating from the University of Pennsylvania in Philadelphia with a major in mathematics. Indeed, the original main building did look somewhat like a massive castle, accommodating over 4,700 students on three solid floors of more than century-old cement and stone construction as well as the newer building. It was located on a carved-out plateau near the base of Mount Penn, bordering the eastern side of the city. One could see almost the entire city from the high school main entrance, including several of the outlying suburbs to the north, west, and south.

Wes looked over at the control tower and pointed thumbs up, basking in the bright morning sunlight.

The intercom hissed and clicked before the air traffic controller's voice came through, *'Clear to go. Take runway 13/31 north.'*

Wes taxied briefly to the end of longest runway, turned into it and pushed the throttle fully forward. He smiled from deep within himself as the plane left the ground within fifteen seconds, cutting smoothly through the air and beginning a gradual, ascending arc to the west. He looked briefly at his copilot, who was all smiles as well.

CHAPTER 62

Wednesday, October 10, 2007
Ashton, Maryland

'*Order filled,*' said a voice from his computer.

Duke was short 1,000 S&P contracts. The market lifted a few pennies. He watched dispassionately and took a sip of his coffee as the position started losing money, then turned back to his computer price charts. He was watching a fifteen-minute price chart, but then changed it to a one-minute chart with a fifteen-tick window in the corner. Duke stared closely at the fifteen-tick chart. The price crept sideways, then higher—another $100,000 in the hole. Then it started to drift lower. A minor rebound developed, and then another slow descent to another new low for the fifteen-minute period. Like life itself, the price appeared to bob around randomly to those without an education from the financial 'School of Hard Knocks,' but there was order behind it, and Duke knew that order. Then the fifteen-minute price plot turned to the downside and the RSI indicator fell sharply. Duke was right again. His lost $100,000-plus came back, and expanded to $50,000 profit, then $60,000, then $80,000 as the contract price abruptly dropped again. It kept falling when Duke placed a buy stop just above the market, assuring himself of a tidy profit. The market fell again. Duke cancelled and replaced the stop price with a new, lower 'stop limit buy to cover' price well within the market's capacity to absorb his eventual purchase to cover. He kept canceling and replacing, pushing his buy stops down as the market moved lower.

Several minutes later his computer announced *'Order filled.'*

Duke Chancellor had just pocketed another $243,000, give or take, for a morning's work.

CHAPTER 63

Wednesday, October 10, 2007
De Moines, Iowa

Wes set the jet down almost perfectly with only three simultaneous screeching tire impacts on the runway and no bounce of any consequence as the well-tuned shock absorbers did their job. His flight instructors would have been proud of him. He applied the brakes and followed the instructions coming through his headset. He rolled his plane to the auxiliary hangar for rentals and private planes, following the young man with the two red flashlights as he crossed them above his head, indicating that Wes was 'on the mark' or close enough to it. He cut the power to the twin engines and flipped several switches in front of and above him, removed his headset and hung it on a hook in the ceiling above his left ear. After a few moments of registering flight details in his log as the high pitch of the whining engines continued to fall, he twisted his aging body out of the pilot's seat and simultaneously ducked his head and stepped through the narrow path out of the cockpit area with his packet of papers and a large manila envelope. Chester was already at the door releasing the latch. Wes opened the door, and he and his copilot exited the sleek white jet and raised the folding stairs back up to their automatic latch. The young man who guided him in to the parking slot came up and asked what he needed and how long he would have his plane on the ground, as he noted the registration number on the plane.

Wes said, "Check my wheels and brakes in particular, and give me a full load of fuel. Put it on my tab and bill it back to me through my registration information. I'll be taking off again in less than twenty-four hours."

He signed his name on the pad the young man handed him.

"Yes sir. Good as done!"

Wes and Chester arrived at the small local Hertz car rental office, picked up the keys to a late model Ford Fusion, and walked out into the lot to find their car. Chester entered the address information into his portable Garmin GPS and the little lady's voice inside chirped instructions. After an hour of driving through mostly flat farmland, they arrived at the coordinates of the Jepson residence. A perimeter white picket fence handsomely outlined the property, which included several large oak trees and a barn in the back. Huge twin deep purple silos towered into the blue Iowa sky behind the large nearby barn. It was the perfect image of rural tranquility in the heartland of the United States of America.

"This won't take long, Chester, but I do need to do this privately."

"Take your time, Wes. I understand."

With that, Wes left the car, and Chester released his seatbelt, opened the window a crack to allow some of that fresh, cool Iowa air to flow through the car and pulled the lever under the seat to let the seatback down as far as it would go. He reclined and fell asleep within just a few minutes. Wes quickly traversed the 100 yards or so to the front of the house, went up to the front door and pushed the doorbell button at the left side of the doorframe. He held the resealed manila envelope under his arm, and waited. He stepped back just as the door swung open, and Sarah Jepson stepped into view with a quizzical expression on her face.

"Yes? Can I help you?

Wes cleared his throat, "Sarah Jepson?"

"Yes, I'm Sarah Jepson," she responded cautiously.

"I need so speak with you and your husband, Ma'am, about your farm."

"We just sold the farm six months ago! What's this all about?"

"Please excuse me, Mrs. Jepson. My name is Wesley Simpson. I represent the buyer of your farm."

"Oh? Why are you here? I thought that was settled long ago!"

"Ma'am, please let me explain. This is not . . ."

Paul Jepson entered the room and stood behind Sarah. "What did you say your name was?"

"Wesley Simpson."

"Oh, yes. Yes, of course! Please come in, Mr. Simpson. I had a phone call about an hour ago from a gentleman named Joe in Pennsylvania saying you would be stopping by with a subject of interest."

Sarah turned around and looked at Paul with an open mouth and questioning pale blue eyes and said, "You did? Why didn't you tell me?"

"You were not here when he called, and you just got back from the store ten minutes ago, Sarah, and I was not thinking of that at the time. Please, Mr. Simpson, do come in . . . Come right in!"

Paul motioned Wesley to the couch near the front window with sheer white curtains and an antique coffee table in front of it. The living room was of moderate size, but filled with the unique warm comfort of an old farmhouse emphasized with a large fireplace. Paul pulled up a chair across from the table, and Sarah sat next to the couch in her favorite burgundy upholstered reading chair.

"Thank you for seeing me. As I mentioned earlier, Mr. Jepson . . ."

"People around here call me Paul . . ."

"Yes. Well . . . Paul, as I mentioned to Mrs. Jepson earlier . . ."

"My name is Sarah, Mr. Simpson," taking a cue from her husband.

Wes could tell that it was going to get a little less complicated with the 'first-name' approach.

"Please, call me Wes. Everyone else does! My principal must sell the farm he bought from you last year, so he is offering you the right of first refusal."

Duke Chancellor was not *obligated* to sell *anything* to *anyone,* but Wes believed that little white lie was forgivable.

"Oh, I see. Well, Wes, our circumstances have changed somewhat, and we do not want to buy the farm back. We have decided to retire, and have no interest in farming again, thank you."

"Please hear me out, Paul." He glanced to his left at Sarah, who was simply fixing him in her kind, innocent stare.

"Well?" She said evenly, with no particular hint.

Wes took a deep breath and prepared himself for the inevitable incredulous response. The Jepsons were obviously not interested in buying a farm, even if it used to be their farm, simply because it would cost a lot of money. Wes knew that often enough in this world, people made decisions based upon their own unique experiences, as well as general common perceptions and assumptions that were expectable, but not necessarily true. Things were not always as they appeared to be, particularly in his association with Joe and Duke. He took one more deep breath before taking the plunge into inevitable incredulity.

"I am authorized to sell the farm back to you for $100."

Silence filled the room for longer than Wes had expected. Wes looked down at the envelope briefly and then back up at Paul with a furrowed brow and a slight squint in his eyes. Paul was staring back at him, motionless, with his mouth open. More silence. Wes turned to Sarah, about to continue, when he saw that she, too, was just sitting there with her mouth open, staring back at him. More silence lingered.

It was getting back to 'difficult' again, as Paul finally said, "Is this some kind of joke, Mr. Simpson?"

"I can assure you, Paul, that this is a legitimate offer, and not a joke of any kind, whatsoever! I have all the legal paperwork right here in this envelope. Look at me, Paul. Do I look like a shyster? Do you think I don't have better things to do with my time than barge into other people's personal lives 1,000 miles away from my home at significant expense and tease them with false hopes and snake oil? Listen to me, Paul. I flew my own jet airplane from Pennsylvania to deliver this offer in person. My employer wants it that way. He is a businessman. I imagine he does not make very many mistakes—certainly none that I am personally aware of. I learned long ago, when I was in the scrap metal business that the world can be a hard, cruel place, and without help sometimes, people suffer and some of them die without help. I cannot thank the man who rescued my business, because I do not actually know who he is, or where he is. To me, he might as well have been an angel, although I am not really a religious person. I can only give to others as he gave to me. My business was failing, Paul. My dozen employees would have been out on the street without his help. Now I am retired, with my own jet airplane. Think about that for just a minute."

Paul sat still for a few seconds, as Wes's words made the rounds in his memory of how people really behave in this world. Not very long ago, he could not afford to send Michael to Harvard, but that is where Michael was right now.

Now, exactly how did all that happen?

Wes looked over at Sarah, locked in confusion without moving her eyes from his. The only sound in the room was the faint hum coming from the refrigerator in the kitchen. Wes pulled out his pilot's license from his wallet, and a picture of his jet. He withdrew a ballpoint pen from his left shirt pocket along with a small spiral bound notebook, and ripped a page out of it. He leaned over and placed the paper on the envelope on the coffee table, and wrote down a phone number, and the registration number of his airplane, 77WR85.

"This is the phone number at the private plane hangar at the De Moines Airport, Paul. Call this number and ask whether a small jet aircraft with this registration number is parked on the tarmac outside the private hangar."

Paul looked at the picture and Wes's license, and slowly arranged his thoughts in the direction Wes was nudging him, but he was still not quite convinced of Wes's story. He slowly picked up the paper, and rose from his chair and went into the kitchen to the phone on the wall in full view of the front living room where they were sitting. He dialed the number on the notebook page and waited through twelve rings at the other end of the connection.

"Municipal Airport, Barry Abrams. How can I help you?"

"My name is Paul Jepson. I'm sorry to disturb you, but I have been asked to verify the existence of a jet airplane at your private hangar."

"I'm sorry sir, but I can't do that. Security, you know."

"Just a minute please . . . Give me just a minute . . ."

Paul covered the mouthpiece against his stomach and waved Wes toward him with his other hand. Wes instantly knew what the problem was, and virtually ran to the phone as Paul handed it to him.

"Hello. This is Wesley Simpson. I flew that jet plane in just this morning and parked it outside door number two on the left. It's a twin engine white Cessna Citation Mustang. That should verify that I am the pilot. It would be a big favor to me if you would please verify the registration number to the man who just called you. He is a friend of mine, and we have been having a friendly little side bet about whether I have been telling him the truth about whether I actually flew that plane here from Pennsylvania. Surely, you understand. It's not a big deal, so please tell him what the registration number is. It's the only way he will believe me. A fresh home-made apple pie is at stake here!"

Another little white lie. Wes used little white lies like he used lubricating oil on his cranes. It made them work better.

"Oh! Hi, Wes! Sure, if you say so. Put him back on. I'll give him the number!"

Wes handed the receiver back to Paul and saw the look of a man about to be convinced of something he had not expected, and returned to the couch in the living room. He glanced at Sarah again in hopes of softening her facial expression of suspicion, but it was not to be.

"This is Paul Jepson again . . ."

"Sorry about that, Mr. Jepson, but I have regulations to follow, as I'm sure you understand. Here's the number, 77WR85. Is that all?"

"Yes, sir. Thank you! Goodbye."

Paul replaced the receiver on the wall-mounted phone base. He turned toward the living room with a slight bow to his head and a furrowed brow as he looked over his glasses at Sarah, then Wes, and then back to Sarah.

He was in front of her when she raised her eyebrows in a silent expression, *'Well?'*

Paul kept a straight face but shut his eyes for a moment and simultaneously gave her a quick reassuring nod of his head. That made it OK for Sarah. She exhaled as if she had forgotten to breathe during the last five minutes.

"So now we know that you flew to De Moines in your own private jet, but that does not mean that you legitimately want to sell this farm to us for $100!"

Paul needed more persuasion.

"I happen to know that your son, Michael, will be studying biology next semester at Harvard. I also know that before you sold the farm, you would not have been able to afford a Harvard education for him. Was it luck Paul, when Michael got into Harvard, which was his dream? Do dreams come true, Paul? Or is this world simply a random, senseless jumble of colliding lives and circumstances beyond our control?"

Sarah's eyes widened, as she looked right into Paul's eyes to his very soul. Strangers could not know that their only son was at Harvard!

Furthermore, not many people could have known that Michael was going to study biology, and certainly not Wesley Simpson!

"Paul . . . PAUL! I need to talk to you! *Now*, Paul!" she said as she gave him her best laser imitation from her eyes through his.

Paul looked at her and knew immediately that this was serious. He turned to Wes and in spite of just having his eyes 'lasered' and calmly said, "Please excuse us for a moment. We need to talk. Can I get you a cup of coffee?" he asked in a genuine mid-western civil gesture of maintaining comfort and keeping his options open.

"No . . . Thank you very much, Paul. I'm fine."

Wes looked at his watch.

"We'll be back in just a few minutes. Please excuse us."

"No problem. Take your time!" It was back to 'difficult' again.

Sarah marched with a deliberate pace through the house into the kitchen and out the back door and kept going another fifty feet into the back yard. Paul followed behind her with his lanky long stride, and caught up with her next to one of the clusters of old oak trees still standing relatively close to their house in the vast farmland around them.

"Paul! Listen to me! We need to know who this man really is! He just said Michael is going to study biology next semester. Now, exactly how did *he* know that, Paul, when Michael just told *me* that last week on the phone?"

While they were outside talking, Wes took out his cell phone, and dialed the offices of Maynard & Maynard, LLC, Attorneys at Law, Perry, Iowa.

"Maynard & Maynard. This is Sandy. How may I help you?" flowed through the phone with a sweet mid-western accent.

"This is Wesley Simpson, Sandy. Is Al in?"

"Oh! Hi, Mr. Simpson. Yes he is. Just a moment and I'll get him for you."

Wes waited thirty seconds, which had to be a world speed record at a law firm.

"Yeah, Wes, what's up?"

"I'd like you to come out to the Jepson residence and help me do some good. Will you do that, Al?"

Al Maynard knew exactly who Wesley Simpson was.

"Be there in fifteen minutes."

"Thanks, Al. I really appreciate it!"

"Sandy, reschedule Mr. Talman's appointment for tomorrow, please. I'm going over to Paul Jepson's place for a while, and then I'm going to my daughter's birthday party, so I won't be back in the office today at all."

"OK, Mr. Maynard. I'll call Mr. Talman right away."

Sammy had been following Michael's progress at Harvard as he had been instructed through System 8, which was another one of Duke's custom channels of communication. Duke was merely interested in seeing that Michael would continue at Harvard, and graduate. His course load was simply a normal report from Sammy, who was remarkably good at following Michael's course registration process over the internal Harvard communication network in spite of their 'safeguards.' Joe checked with Duke just before he assembled the package for Wes, and included that last-minute piece of information, Michael's course schedule for the next term.

The Jepsons returned to their living room. Wes sensed a storm coming. Sarah sat upright in her reading chair as Paul sat down in his chair across from Wes. Sara looked at Paul with her lips pressed together and slightly raised eyebrows, effectively confirming Paul's agreement that she should start talking first. Paul closed his eyes briefly, and nodded affirmatively. Then he crossed one leg over the other and turned toward Wes, who noticed the shift to defensive body posture. He sensed that he and Sarah were about to 'have a talk,' like he remembered having with his mother from time to time as a teenager so many years ago after he crossed one line or another in her well-ordered sense of how the world should be. Paul would not be available to assist Wes. This was going to be one of those 'maternal prosecutor-judge-and-jury' experiences. Sarah proceeded with what could have been the look of a small-town judge ordering the witness to 'take the witness stand.'

"You just informed me that Michael was going to study biology next semester. I spoke with my son on the telephone a little more than a week ago, when he told me *for the first time* that he would be taking biology next semester. *Exactly how* did *you* know that he would be taking biology next semester, Mr. Simpson?"

Sarah (the prosecutor) feared that a stranger had a closer relationship with her only son than she had, and could not abide that in any way, shape or form whatsoever. Not only that, but she had never met a man like Wesley Simpson before in her entire life. Everyone she knew was straight forward, and had no special insights into anything more profound than a field of corn or soybeans, and most certainly did not fly jet airplanes! And here he was in her house, a stranger with knowledge of sacred information about her only son, and a preposterous offer to sell them the farm that she and her husband had sold more than a year before, *for a mere $100*, no less!

Wes 'took the witness stand.'

"As I believe I implied to you earlier, Sarah, I am motivated by doing good deeds for others. I pursue that goal only with the consent of my gut and my heart. I have been exceedingly fortunate to have employment that satisfies my soul in a manner I had not known nor even imagined was possible."

"As strange as it seems, Sarah, I do not know the whole story. I work directly for a man I know and trust. Trust is akin to love, and is the foundation of all civilized humanity. I understand that he in turn works for someone with extraordinary wealth, information and influence. These three attributes are obviously intertwined in our complex modern world. He is the person who bought your farm. He bought it because he knew you needed the money for your son's education, and for no other reason whatsoever."

"I realize that may be hard to believe, but then, the world was once believed to be flat, and no one would believe that it was not flat, but we know now that it is spherical. My point is that what we see, hear and believe may not always represent the real and ultimate truth. I simply do not know how he knew about your son, or how he knew about your finances. He knows many people, who know other people, who know still others, Sarah, and he uses information like an artist uses a brush and pallet. He listens to the people he trusts. He trusts the people who demonstrate sincere honesty and good will toward others, and feeds their need to continue to do so. He also 'marginalizes' those who abuse power. The world has more than enough suffering to keep him in business beyond his lifetime, unfortunately. We should all pray that he lives forever. The difference between him and everyone else I have ever known about in my long life is that he has the will, discipline and determination to use his considerable resources and talents in a manner to promote what I believe to be the good side of life and to minimize the dark side. I am not by any means aware of all of his dealings, but the ones I have personally participated in are just, fair and noble by any standard I have ever known, and I have yet to encounter a human being involved with any of these circumstances who could sincerely doubt my employer's altruistic motives."

"Maybe I'm biased, and maybe I'm not. It is simply your good fortune that he bought your farm, just as it would have been your good fortune if you had won the lottery. The extent of this man's dealings is beyond your imagination, Sarah. He could not be effective with publicity of any kind, I can assure you, and that means he could not just write you a check, because doing so would create a direct link to his identity, exposing him, and compromising his considerable network and influence for good."

"My understanding of human nature and the real world is that if one wins the lottery, one does not launch a federal investigation into exactly how that happened. When the man of her dreams proposes marriage to her, a woman does not put him on hold, while she investigates his motives. Sometimes life deals a joker, and sometimes it deals the ace of spades, Sarah. Part of the art of life is in learning how to play either card if, and when it is dealt to you. We are all visitors in the casino of life. We do not own the casino, and we do not write the rules."

"My employer has enabled me to learn many things, for which I will be eternally grateful. Among them, when I find beauty, I try to share it. When I encounter suffering, I try to heal it. When I see human beings treating their neighbors with selfishness and cruelty, I try to even the playing field. When I see the cruel or unfair exercise of power against the innocently unfortunate or the weak, I try to sap the power and help the weak. So long as I have good health and the ability to right what I believe in my heart to be wrong, I will strive to do so. I cannot do these things without the help of his organization. No one, two, three or more people can do the things he does any more than I and a few tough friends could walk into a street riot in Detroit or L.A. and single-handedly put it to rest. It takes coordinated organization, communication, dedication, influence, loyalty and trust to accomplish the good things he does. I may die tomorrow, Sarah. Life is uncertain, and, as we all know, it is sometimes too short, as the folks in Fresno recently had hammered home to them."

"I do not know the future any more than you do, Sarah. I apply my experience and knowledge the best way I can, to guide my life the best way I can, and roll with the punches the rest of the time. As good a pilot as I believe I am, I could encounter an unexpected wind shear on my flight back to Pennsylvania today, lose control of my plane and be killed in a crash, but I would die knowing that I had something to do with helping a talented young man achieve his dream by being admitted to Harvard. I believe our world needs young dreamers and fulfillment of their dreams, lest we all become discouraged and fall short of our potential as individuals, as a society, and as a species. Your son has more future before him than I have before me."

"I know this all sounds like a fairy tale, Sarah, but I can assure you that it is very, very real! Not only am I not at liberty to discuss further details, but I am simply not *aware* of the details, Sarah. I do not know how the system works, nor do I have the need, the incentive or the time to spend trying to find out. The person I described to you actually *does* exist. However, I have never met him. I have never met God, either, but I believe He exists. I know enough to trust this man. Trust is precious and fragile in this world, Sarah. It is not easily gained, and should not be squandered when it is honestly discovered and sincerely embraced. I had a choice. I could have refused this opportunity to offer you what is essentially a gift. I decided to take it because I believed in my heart that it was the right thing for me to do. You have won the lottery, Sarah. Take your ticket to the nearest agent and claim your prize."

The doorbell rang. Sarah and Paul jolted upright. Sarah gracefully rose from her chair, and then paused slightly as she felt pain in her right leg, but recovered and strode toward the front door and opened it.

"Yes? Just a minute!" Sarah sang out as she approached the front door.

She reached for the antique brass doorknob and opened the door as Paul turned in his seat to see who was there.

"Yes?"

"Mrs. Jepson?"

"Yes. What can I do for you?"

"My name is Albert Maynard. I'm a real estate attorney in Perry, just down the road. I handled the legal end of the sale of your farm?" he said in his deep baritone voice with slight questioning inflection, inviting her recognition.

"Oh! Of course! Of course! I remember you very well! Come in Mr. Maynard. Come right in!"

She stepped behind him and closed the door. Paul stood up and turned toward them as they walked into the living room.

"What a coincidence, Mr. Maynard!"

Paul thought for a moment, *coincidence, indeed!*

He glanced back at Wesley Simpson, who was just rising from the couch, but deliberately slowly enough to avoid any eye contact until he was ready. He rose to his full height, and smiled at Al Maynard.

"Mr. Maynard, it was good of you to come over. Thank you very much! Paul? Sarah? I owe you an explanation. I called this man to come here for a very specific reason. I anticipated that you might have some questions or doubts about the transaction I am offering, so I took the liberty of inviting Mr. Maynard to come here for the express purpose of examining the legal documents I brought with me, and to answer any questions from a legal perspective that you may have. I took that liberty because I had specific instructions to give you every conceivable opportunity to make an informed decision within the limits of my obligations and ability in the event of your need for legal consultation. I concluded that your lack of immediate acceptance of my offer required such consultation, so I called Mr. Maynard. I could think of no other person more qualified to answer your questions and satisfy your concerns."

Sarah looked at Wes with renewed respect and thought to herself, *You don't miss a beat, do you?*

Wes leaned over to the coffee table, and picked up the manila folder and presented it to Al Maynard.

Paul said, "Please sit down, Mr. Maynard. Wes? Sarah?"

He gestured to their seats with his open right hand. Sarah sat back down on her favorite reading chair, and folded her hands on her lap, which was her preferred posture for waiting impatiently. Paul sat on the wooden chair, and leaned forward with his elbows on his knees and clasped his hands together in front of him. He looked expectantly at Al Maynard sitting on the far side of the comfortable dark leather couch with the papers on top of the manila envelope on his lap, and then at Wes on the near side. Al reached in his inside jacket pocket and took out a pair of reading glasses, put them on and then picked up the papers and began to read. Only his deep baritone voice punctuated the next eight minutes in the peaceful old Iowa farmhouse.

"Hmmm . . . OK . . . OK . . . Mmhmmm . . . Yeah . . ."

Silence filled the room for a few minutes.

He flipped a page.

"OK . . . OK . . ."

He turned another page.

"Uh huh . . . OK . . . OK . . ."

He turned another page as silence lingered. Then Al removed his glasses and put the papers down on the coffee table, as Paul sat up and Sarah unclasped her hands, and Wes sat up straighter on the couch.

"Well! This is indeed an unusual document and an unusual transaction, but it is quite clearly legal in every respect. In simple terms, Paul and Sarah, if you accept this offer and pay this man $100, you will own your former farm in its entirety, in every respect as you did before you sold it, except that it will not have a loan against it. It will be entirely yours, free and clear to do with as you please. You will release forever any other party involved in this transaction from any obligation or liability whatsoever and without recourse forever, and the seller will have absolutely no recourse or action against you, ever. You will have the deed and full title. It will be your farm to do with as you please, period. It's that simple."

Wes looked at Sarah, and then at Paul. Paul and Sarah looked at each other. Sarah thought about Wes's earlier 'lecture from the witness stand.' She looked at Al and repeated in her mind *'free and clear.'* She was on the verge of temptation, and thought about all the Sundays she spent in church being admonished from the pulpit about temptation. She looked again at Paul.

We can cash rent the farm and receive a generous income for the rest of our lives, and leave something substantial to Michael and whoever he marries and his children after we die. It's only $100!

"Paul! Get your checkbook!"

CHAPTER 64

Wednesday, October 10, 2007
Cheshire, Connecticut

Henry Winslow parked outside the moderate office building where he and Julie maintained their counseling offices on Route 10 just south of the town center of Cheshire, Connecticut. He admired the sleek black Corvette parked conspicuously away from all the other cars in the lot next to the far curb as he entered the building.

Katie Lowery managed the office, made appointments, and carefully kept Henry and Julie's counseling business matters on an even keel. She was a single, bespectacled, moderately pretty but slightly pudgy woman in her early twenties, but had a gift of friendly and effective people skills and business sense that Henry and Julie valued greatly.

"Doctor Winslow, there's a gentleman named Joe here to see you. He did not tell me his last name. He does not have an appointment, but he said you would be very interested in what he has to say," she said as Henry walked through the outer reception area in the building where he and Julie maintained their counseling offices. "I told him that he could wait, because you don't have an appointment until eleven o'clock this morning. He's sitting right over there."

She indicated his presence with a sideways glance and tilt of her head in Joe's direction. Joe immediately looked up, rose from his seat and walked briskly up to Henry, and extended his hand.

"Doctor Winslow, my name is Joe. I won't take up much of your time, but I must talk to you about one of your clients as soon as possible!"

Henry shook his hand and glanced back at Katie, who raised her eyebrows and shrugged in resignation at Joe's direct and forward approach.

"All right . . . Joe. Please come into my office."

He looked back over his shoulder again at Katie, with a look that said, *be ready to rescue me if I call you!*

Joe wasted no time after he sat in the chair across from Henry's desk, and said, "I work for Sasha Chancellor's uncle, who has asked me to secure any and all assistance for the proper treatment and therapy necessary for Sasha's full recovery."

"Joe . . . What did you say you last name was?"

"I didn't. You can't pronounce it, won't remember it, and it isn't necessary. Besides, I work better without it. Everyone calls me Joe."

"How do I know you are who you say you are, if you don't mind my asking . . . Joe?"

"I know that you and your wife Julie, also a practicing psychologist in this office, were out on the town in Manhattan with Doctor Jake Lewis, one of your graduate school friends, and your wife's sister, Jayne Astor. Doctor Lewis gave a presentation at the psychology conference at NYU about goal attainment scaling applied to the reintegration of returning service men into civilian life. Last Friday, October 5, after the conference ended, you all went to Club 46 that evening, where Sasha Chancellor was performing with her four-man backup—one on drums, one on soprano sax, one on guitar, and one on electronic keyboard, all dressed in dark clothing during the performance. Sasha was wearing her usual white-sequined dress. After the four of you visited with Sasha at the stage after the end of her performance, you concluded that she suffers from amnesia. How am I doing so far, Doctor Winslow?"

"Very impressive . . . *Joe!*"

"I also know that you have an interest in some unusual therapy for amnesia patients that you are eager to put into practice with your new patient, Sasha Chancellor. Is that not correct, Doctor Winslow?"

"You are unusually well-informed, *Joe,* but she is not a patient of mine."

"She will be, Doctor Winslow."

"What makes you so sure of that, *Joe?*"

"It is my business to be both well-informed and *persuasive*, Doctor Winslow."

"Well, since you seem to have more answers than I do, perhaps you will explain to me how she is going to be my patient, how I will work her into my very busy schedule and how she will be able to pay for this therapy."

"I have a very good friend who does wonders with computers, Doctor Winslow. Please check your professional business checking account. You will find a sum that is exactly $100,000 greater than it was yesterday. That is a retainer. It will remain there if you agree to undertake the therapy. All you have to do is give me your word. If you decline, then that credit will disappear as quickly as it appeared. I have chosen you for this task because I believe you are the most qualified, and you already have important knowledge of and insights into the problem, as well as a professional and personal interest in the success of the endeavor. If you refuse, then I will simply find the next best therapist I can find anywhere in the country or in the world if I have to, and you will miss a golden opportunity for significant professional acknowledgement and recognition, as well as possibly equally significant and rare personal fulfillment and satisfaction."

"Well, Joe, you don't leave me much choice, do you?"

"I try, Doctor Winslow . . . I try."

"Do you mind if I take a few moments to check that account?"

"No, not at all. Take your time!" Joe said pleasantly.

Henry Winslow logged in to his business account from a computer keyboard on his desk within thirty seconds, and indeed, found an 'extra' credit of $100,000.

"Well, *Joe,* you are indeed a very persuasive man."

Henry paused for several moments as he mentally tallied up all of the pros and cons, and the extremely knowledgeable and effective persuasiveness of the short, stocky, balding man sitting in his office. He had never met *anyone* like Joe before.

Finally, he said, "OK. I'll do it, but it's going to cost a lot more than $100,000."

"Let me worry about that, Doctor Winslow. You just do the very best you can do for Sasha."

"I will, Joe. I most certainly will. Where do we go from here?"

"You start immediately, and you give me progress reports at least once every two weeks, for as long as it takes. I have all the proper contact information and instructions you will need here in this envelope."

He handed Henry the business-sized, sealed white envelope he was holding.

"There's one major problem here, Joe. The patient apparently does not know she needs help. I *absolutely cannot* help her until she is aware of her condition and genuinely agrees to counseling and treatment."

"I will see that she acquires that understanding," Joe responded matter-of-factly. "What else do you need?"

Henry wondered to himself, *How in the hell is he going to do that?*

"To my knowledge, this technique has never been used before, and I don't really know with *certainty* that it will work, but I have every reason to *believe* that it should be successful. Results could develop very quickly, or it could take weeks or months, maybe longer. I simply don't know at this point. I will be able to understand more about that over time. That is the nature of the problem, and the nature of the theoretical cure."

"What I will need is every person known to have had meaningful personal contact or some relationship with Sasha, from just a few days before the first performance at Eddie's Place in Denver to the present. That includes her backup musicians and anyone she may have met or interacted with in Fresno or elsewhere in Denver, or along the way. I will need to present to her in persuasive, historically accurate time-ordered fashion exactly what happened to her during the period of amnesia, and the best way to do that is with the actual people who interacted with her in a reasonably meaningful way during that period of her life. Critical among those people, of course, is Jake Lewis. I will want all of these people in the same room at the same time for every session for the duration of the therapy, so maximum interaction and feedback can occur in order to facilitate optimal historical linkage and as much cause-and-effect reasoning as possible on her part. It would be helpful also to have any photographs or video recordings taken of events or people during this period. She must have every opportunity to reason as well as to recognize people and emotions associated with her experiences during the period in question. If necessary, we will actually have to take her and any associated people to important locations during this unknown period in her life."

"OK, Doctor Winslow. I will find the people you need to have for this project and inform you as soon as possible after I get everyone organized. Just let me know where you would like to conduct the therapy sessions, and I will see that everything comes together at the right time and in the right place."

"I believe that the entire therapy process should be based in Denver, probably at the same hotel where she stayed during her singing engagement at Eddie's Place. It is most likely the optimally convenient location for all the people involved, has the added convenience of accommodations for extended therapy and the personal comfort of the people necessary for the therapy experience, and is closely associated with the most important physical and personal psychological relationships within the most likely period of amnesia."

Henry was gaining confidence that his therapy concept would succeed because money seemed to be an irrelevant factor. Most therapy sessions for amnesia he had experienced or read about were complex, sometimes included electroshock therapy and required time, and time is money. What they did not incorporate, however, was the admittedly thorough re-immersion of the patient into the period of amnesia, including the relevant people, locations and other critical circumstances and events during that period, which he believed would have a 'superconductor' effect of reestablishing neural pathways blocked, disturbed or otherwise circumvented or disguised since the period surrounding the initial precipitating event.

Henry had just presented a wish list to beat all wish lists. He might as well have asked Joe to push a wheelbarrow full of smoke from Philadelphia to Manhattan, and find along the way a document certified by God explaining the meaning of life. What he did not understand was how Joe could say, essentially, 'no problem' as if he were arranging a backyard picnic for a few friends and neighbors. Henry did not know Duke Chancellor.

Joe contacted Duke on System 18, which he had never used before, since it was one of Duke's newest channels. He needed a personal meeting to explain what was necessary and make sure Duke understood everything that was involved, especially the requirement of Sasha's recognition of her problem and consent to therapy. Joe was beginning to realize that this was going to be the most expensive venture he had ever participated in during his association with Duke. He knew Duke had substantial wealth, but even he had no idea of just how substantial, nor had he ever really experienced the ultimate full force of Duke's determination when the task was very personal.

Since Sasha was right up there with priority number one right now on Duke's agenda along with the terrorist pursuit, Duke wanted the meeting as soon as possible at his newest office complex just off Interstate 95, north of Baltimore, Maryland where he had just recently moved his headquarters operations. He gave Joe the GPS coordinates via System 18, and described the building location because the building was so new that it was not yet included in the various GPS mapping databases, nor did it have a name yet. It was an attractive five-story square building with a center courtyard, blue-tinted glass and steel frame and support construction, hidden in the woods much like the Plymouth building. Duke had already arranged to bring in Kenny Armstrong from San Francisco. Kenny was Joe's counterpart operating primarily in the western part of the continental United States.

CHAPTER 65

Friday, October 12, 2007
Maryland

Kenny and Joe had worked together before on various projects and were acquainted primarily by virtue of communications through Duke about various interesting projects during the last several years, but had never actually met face to face. They happened to be on the same elevator going up to Duke's office on the top floor and drew the obvious conclusion that they both worked for the same man. Very few others even knew of the existence of this building, so they both concluded they had to be there for the same reason, and introduced themselves. They exited on the fifth floor where Duke's personal assistant at that building greeted them cordially.

Gwen Tully was the mother of a pair of cute eight-year-old twin girls, working for Duke after her husband died several years ago from an unusually vicious bout with bone cancer. Her husband's health insurance coverage had been exhausted and she had a mortgage, car payments and a future to plan for her two girls. She was artistically gifted, but unknown, and could not earn enough from her painting to make ends meet, until Duke saw her work at a local country fair about a year ago.

He looked at one painting of a beautiful sunset landscape. In the foreground was a woman holding the hands of two small girls, one on each side of her, with a look of obvious concern on her face. Another was an abstract close-up image of an eagle, soaring in the brilliant blue background of the sky staring intently at something below. Another one showed a woman with a soiled face and apron with a strained and sad look on her face and both hands raised up in front of her, apparently after releasing two brilliant white doves. In the background slightly to the left were the remains of a farmhouse and scattered broken tree branches and shattered household contents, and to the right of center was an angry dark grey sky with various colored household items floating in its wake after having obviously destroyed the house. Duke looked carefully at all the paintings, all somewhat similar, mostly expressing tragedy and hope. He looked carefully at the simply dressed young woman sitting behind the collection of paintings. She wore little if any makeup, but had a kind face and most likely had not been to a hairdresser recently. He noticed the signature on the lower right of each painting.

He asked the woman behind the display "Are you Gwen Tully?"

"Yes, I am."

"These are indeed lovely works of art!"

"Thank you!"

He noticed her wedding ring and started to form an image of a mother in pain, judging from the images in the pictures and asked as delicately as he could, "What does your husband do?"

She lowered her head slightly and said softly, "My husband died eight weeks ago of bone cancer. He was a high school English teacher."

He liked what he saw, both the talent of the woman, and her grit and attitude evident in sharing her creativity in an effort to earn a living under what had to be difficult circumstances.

"How much do you want for these paintings?" He asked gently.

"They're all $100 apiece," she said honestly, hopefully and as sincerely as she could, trying to mask her utter shock at the specified plural of his question.

"I'll take all fifteen," Duke said, pointing from the left-most painting all the way across to the far right painting she had on display.

He took out his billfold, and counted out nine $500 bills and handed them to her on the spot. He wanted her to remember him.

She started taking the money, but then very quickly realized that he was counting out much more than the total amount she implied and blurted out as politely as she could, "I'm sorry, sir, but I said they are $100 apiece. You gave me too much!"

She immediately tried to hand back most of the money.

Duke politely refused to accept the money and said kindly, "I am paying what I believe to be a fair price, young lady. I would appreciate your sending these paintings to this address via UPS if possible. I will pay the shipping costs upon arrival."

He handed her a plain piece of paper upon which he had just written the new building address for The Chancellor Organization.

"That is my office phone number at the bottom. If you would like an interesting humanitarian job, please do give me a call."

"Of course! Thank you very much!" she said somewhat confused and unsure of herself, but with a renewed sense of hope.

She called Duke three days later, and has worked for him ever since, and still paints.

Inside Duke's private office, Joe brought Duke and Kenny up to speed on the plan to treat Sasha's amnesia. They were sitting in comfortable dark red cushioned chairs around a teak conference table about twelve feet in diameter. Gwen's paintings were on the off-white walls throughout the top floor of the building. Joe began to explain to them what he had learned so far.

"The general idea is to recreate Sasha's life and experiences during the period we believe includes the loss of her memory in a manner as close to the actual sequence of events and locations as possible, and specifically with the same people she interacted with in some way, who must be tracked down and motivated to participate. It's a 'total immersion' solution designed to coax her brain to make the same kinds of associations among various events, thoughts and people during the therapy sessions that she most likely made during the actual period of amnesia. This is a kind of 'buckshot' approach, since we don't really know exactly when her memory became impaired, or exactly how severely."

"However, we do know for a fact that she has some kind of memory of this period, because she sang a song in Manhattan on October 5 using the same melody Jake played for her the first night they met, but with words to it that Jake did not write. Since Jake created the music and no one else has sung it, then she must have made up the words for it. We know from these circumstances, therefore, that she must have at least one hidden link to Jake in her brain somewhere, and we want to reconnect or restore that link."

"We have been thinking theoretically about a separate 'musical memory' that somehow has Jake and his music in it. This all sounds like a lot of ivory tower poppycock, I know. However, we also know that traditional methods of focusing upon just the individual involved many times with hypnosis, electroshock, and medication without the stimuli of actual human interactions with people during the period of memory loss, is not always successful, and sometimes creates some unforeseen damage that takes longer to repair, assuming it can be recognized or repaired at all."

"We have a choice. We can let her go on in her life without trying to help her, maybe without ever reconnecting with Jake and that particular period of her life, possibly with other unknowable and possibly unfortunate consequences, or possibly with no adverse consequences at all beyond simply having a blank spot in her memory. Alternatively, we can gamble with rather persuasive psychological theory from Henry Winslow, who believes that this technique will work. He said that it has never been done before, to his knowledge, primarily because of the enormous logistical and financial efforts necessary to make the complete effort properly, but that does not mean it won't work. Going to the moon was once considered preposterous and too expensive, until technology, determination, and the will to accomplish the goal came together and made the prospect not only believable, but possible, and eventually an accomplished fact."

"If we chose to let her go on living untreated, then we will also probably be leaving a young man locked in emotional pain for some unknown period, perhaps forever, detracting from whatever good he might otherwise do for other people in the future. We can say, essentially 'tough shit' and go on with our work somewhere else, or we can push forward with daring, yet inviting implications of success. Maybe he will still be a functional human being, a professional psychologist, or maybe he will turn inward and have less of a life than Sasha obviously inspires in him. He is quite clearly a talented musician, and he derives energy and inspiration, if not a very special intensity of life from Sasha."

"Speaking entirely for myself, I believe the world would be a better place if I tried to clear the way for these two people to be together the way it seems obvious to me they should be. We will definitely need to rely heavily upon Jake because he is the most knowledgeable, intimate and central character of this period in her life, and knows at least something about most of the important people and events better than anyone else does. The parts he has no direct knowledge of we will have to ferret out, using our best guesses and as many facts, deductions and real historical information as we can get our hands on. That is going to be the big 'detective' aspect of this effort."

"We will also need Sasha's permission to proceed. She must become aware that she has a problem if she does not already know it—that she is suffering from something more complex than just a simple minor lapse of memory. I believe that she can be persuaded to participate willingly once we demonstrate to her that there is a very peculiar relationship between Jake and her knowing that music, and putting words to it, let alone singing it herself in Manhattan. Once she recognizes and understands that, I will bet that her apparently undamaged intellectual side will demand an explanation, and when that happens, she should be motivated to understand and be receptive to therapy designed to reveal the emotional connections to Jake hidden in her psyche."

"I'm an optimist. I am also biased, and I admit it. I have grown to know more and more about Sasha and Jake, and I love them both dearly. I have struggled with personal feelings from time to time in most of the work we have undertaken over the years, but it is precisely the desire to accomplish something good that drives me in spite of the risk of failure. I keep asking myself, am I just going to cook mushrooms for the rest of my life? Is that all there is? *Mushrooms?* I'm going all out for this because I believe Henry Winslow, and because I believe it is important for Sasha and Jake to be together. I also believe it is important to demonstrate successful therapy for the good of others who may benefit from it in the future."

Kenny listened to Joe intently, and was overwhelmed with his passion, enthusiasm, eloquence and optimism. He was cut from much the same cloth. He was an eligible bachelor at the tender age of forty-four and working hard to stay that way. He was a graduate of Stanford University with a major in electrical engineering. He was also one of the current guardians of 'old San Francisco money' originally from merchants who were smart enough to supply the population growth of the early gold rush years with all kinds of clothing, tools, food and general merchandise instead of prospecting for gold themselves. He did not have to work from a purely financial perspective, but like Joe, he had to work in order to stay sane and feel like a real human being. He loved a challenge, and this was developing into one of the most unusual challenges he had ever heard of, and for the most basic and personal reason—*pure love!*

"I'm really fired up! I'm going to help put this young woman's life back together or die trying! I buy it, Joe! I'm all in!"

He virtually shouted across the solid elegant teak table at Duke while pounding his fist on the table. Duke was equally impressed and genuinely pleased by both Joe's eloquence and Kenny's enthusiasm, as he finally spoke.

"OK, gentlemen. Thank you both for your thoughts! This is what I think we can do. We'll get Jake together with the two of you to supply the details and a complete, detailed timeline. We'll get the hotel records of all the guests during the period that Sasha stayed there in Denver and interview all of them until we come up with the ones that had some significant interaction with her or Jake. We'll use a photograph of her from her promotional material to help people recognize her. We'll check Sasha's credit card history to see exactly where she was on the road, buying gas, or whatever, confirming her location and the timeline, and contact those people she may have interacted with along the way to see who remembers seeing her. We'll get the people at that bar where she sang in Denver, as well as whomever she interacted with in Fresno and nail down who knows what about her. We will check her telephone records to see who she called or who called her. We will follow all of the personal contacts and official and business records all the way through the following period until Jake saw her in Manhattan at Club 46, where we know Henry and Julie met her as well. We will motivate all these people to participate with an honest, clear explanation of the humanitarian value of what we are trying to accomplish."

"Most people should understand the romantic aspect of this story and be willing to help restore love, in my opinion. Those who have a problem with that interfere with Henry's idea of getting everyone together at the same time in the same room for the entire process. Therefore, we will 'rearrange' their schedules as necessary, and motivate the people with scheduling conflicts in the same manner—the love story, or sheer greed, or simple business or political muscle as necessary—until we have commitments from everyone we need."

"*Push whatever buttons are necessary to make this happen!* I will pay whatever it takes to restore Sasha's life! As you must know by now, she is my only niece, and I have felt a parental kind of responsibility for her ever since her father died. I agree with Henry that it would be best to conduct this therapy session in the same hotel where she stayed in Denver. It appears to be the most centrally located relative to most of the activities. It is loaded with relevant personal, visual and physical connections, and will provide accommodations for our guests as well as a room large enough for the meetings. Use the same motivation to get the accommodations we will need at the hotel—the love story, or greed, or simple, basic business muscle—whatever it takes. If you require political influence, let me know. I have more than enough chits around the world to call in for this. All contacts and communication will go through System 16, which will be completely dedicated to this particular project and no other. If these techniques fail, then I'll buy the damn hotel!"

Within the following two weeks, Joe and Kenny would unleash the most completely concentrated power of their immediate organizations as well as the greater Chancellor Organization through scores of personal contacts and the internet, interviewing personally, over the phone, or in e-mails hundreds of people connected to the time period and physical locations in Denver and Fresno, and everywhere in between. They developed a huge, color-coded spreadsheet table listing people, interactions, locations, conversations, associations, descriptions and quotes from early September through the last engagement at Club 46. Everyone in The Chancellor Organization working on this project could access the entire schematic outline of events through System 16 and make descriptive, analytical and interpretive notes, suggestions, and additions or corrections until they laced the whole story together, and crosschecked and verified it as completely as possible.

Joe's people and Kenny's people eventually tracked down, located and received enthusiastic commitments from Eddie, Marie, 'Stealth,' 'Red-tie,' 'Green-skirt,' and 'Cooperstown' from Eddie's Place. Both Rocky and Tommy from the recording studio agreed to be there. The Colorado State Police Officer on the Coal Creek Road agreed to participate only after his superior officer changed his mind about not allowing him to take that time off. As it turned out, he was having some difficulty paying the college tuition for his son at Colgate, but 'the college business office' called and indicated that his account would be paid in full if he allowed Officer Fleming to take the requested time off. 'The college business office' was actually Sammy.

The 'odd couple' from the elevator, and the night clerk at the hotel also readily committed their time. Sasha's former college roommate and her husband in Fresno, Ramon, the Emergency Medical Technician and the hotel desk clerk in Las Vegas were quite agreeable to the project. Jake's physician, the doctor who watched over Sasha in Fresno, and the new 'Autumn Dream' ensemble leader, also gladly consented to participate. The Chancellor Organization succeeded in securing all of these commitments without using any 'muscle,' greed, or 'political' motivational techniques. The Denver hotel manager also was eager to help. He quite willingly gave The Chancellor Organization whatever they asked for. It had to be a 'win-win' situation for the hotel from a business angle, as well as from a public relations perspective. Even the city of Denver was interested in being associated with the effort to restore love.

The only other wrinkle was from Randy Theisman's boss, who objected initially to his taking such undefined time away from his law firm. The transfer of certain legal services required by The Chancellor Organization from another firm in Chicago smoothed over that potential problem. That little sleight of hand was unnoticeable from the perspective of those who worked with The Chancellor Organization because it was widely known that such legal services often moved from one firm to another as a kind of 'currency' that Duke used to accomplish various tasks, usually complex real estate transactions. Since he operated various real estate interests around the country and in several foreign countries, such a change in legal services was routine. Randy's employer was suddenly very receptive to his requested unspecified absence.

Duke was planning to visit his niece. He had to know first-hand whether she remembered him in spite of her amnesia, and he needed to assess the best way he could, from his own senses and intuition exactly what her condition was, and persuade her to accept the therapy effort. He easily found where Sasha lived in an old condominium building in Union City, New Jersey, across the Hudson River from Manhattan. He called her on his cell phone to arrange a meeting as soon as possible.

"Sasha?"

"Yes, this is Sasha."

"This is your uncle Duke!" he announced cheerfully, waiting carefully to assess the tone and character of her response.

"Oh, Hi! It's been a while since we've talked! Where are you?"

She remembers me!

"I'm in my new office in Maryland, but I would like to come up to talk with you in person about a very urgent and important matter."

"OK. What is it?"

"I don't want to discuss this over the phone, and I'm sure you will agree when we meet, so I can explain everything to you in person."

"I have performances every evening through the weekend, but you can come up and visit during the morning or early afternoon. I have to be in the city by five every afternoon."

"That's no problem. I would really like to hear you sing anyway! Where are you performing this week?"

"I'm still at Club 46."

"OK. That's great! How would it be if I drive up there tomorrow afternoon and visit with you at your place for about an hour or two, and then I can take you out for dinner if you would like, and then get you to Club 46 in time for your performance?"

"That's great! I'd love to see you!"

"That will be wonderful!" he responded, eagerly anticipating the opportunity both to see her and to hear her sing in general, but also to hear her sing the special song he had heard so much about.

"I expect to be there around one o'clock or so tomorrow afternoon. Is that OK?"

"That's fine! I'll see you then!"

"I'll be there, Sasha, and I'm looking forward to seeing you again! I wouldn't miss this for the world! Bye!"

Duke was satisfied that Sasha was not in any obviously serious immediate difficulty, since she clearly remembered him and expressed an interest in seeing him, and her manner was logical and as normal as it could be from his perspective.

So far so good, he said to himself.

CHAPTER 66

Saturday, October 13, 2007
Union City, New Jersey

The next morning, Duke was up early to attend to some trading positions for the day, enter some stop orders and make a few phone calls. Around nine o'clock, he left his office in his Lincoln SUV for Union City, and eventually arrived at Sasha's condominium shortly before one o'clock. He rang her doorbell, and she answered and unlocked the main entrance with the typical electronic security 'buzz of welcome' at such buildings. Duke took the elevator to the third floor, and found her apartment number just as she opened the door and greeted him with a warm hug. She remembered him as a younger man and noted the physical evidence of his growing older. He remembered her as a younger woman, and was pleasantly surprised to see that she had only grown more beautiful, a refreshing sight under any circumstances.

"It's great to see you again! Was the traffic bad?" she said with a welcoming tone.

"To tell you the truth, I didn't even notice. I was too busy thinking about you!"

"Oh?"

She was beginning to sense something a little unusual in her uncle's visit with that odd statement about not noticing the traffic, which *everyone* notices in the BOSNYWASH corridor, the unusually densely populated area between Washington D.C. and Boston, Massachusetts.

"Would you like something to drink?" She asked pleasantly.

"No thank you, Sasha. I'm fine right now. I'd like to get caught up on your life recently, and make sure you understand your situation in the family. I have updated my will because of changing personal and business conditions, and I want you to be aware of what's going on. I really don't know exactly what your mother has arranged for you in her will, but I have made provisions for you, regardless of what she has done, and you should be aware of that. I know that I will not be able to work forever, but I expect to continue for quite a while as long as my health holds up. I have no indication that it is not going to, but we all move on, sooner or later, and preparation while preparation is possible is always wise."

"Well . . . thank you, Uncle Duke, but I have not been thinking much about that at all."

Sasha concentrated for a moment upon her uncle's statement that he did not know exactly what her mother had arranged for her in her will. The truth about her uncle was that he knew *everything!* She sensed an ulterior motive in his visit.

"I realize that, Sasha, but I can't take it with me, and I don't want to give it to the government! I did not want to get into the details of that very much right now, but I want you to learn the names of the people I have selected to facilitate the conduct of my business if I become incapacitated and after I die. I want you to be able to make informed decisions about what you want to do with the rest of your life. In particular, I would like to know whether you want to be a part of the business, or whether you would like to continue singing, or whether you want to get married and raise a family, or whatever else you might have in mind."

He waited hopefully for some kind of response related to the words 'married and raise a family.'

"That's a lot to swallow all at once," she said without revealing any internal feelings.

Duke tried a more direct approach.

"Sasha. Listen to me. You are a beautiful young woman. I find it hard to believe that you have not met a man who is of some, shall we say, extraordinary importance to you. So, tell me, are you at least dating someone these days, someone I might like to meet?"

"No, Uncle Duke, I'm not. I go out, of course, from time to time with one guy or another, but no one really special. It's a little hard to have a heavy dating life when you're singing almost every evening, and then traveling to some other part of the country half the time."

"So . . . are you telling me also that no one has fallen for you in a big way?"

"Not that I'm aware of," she said offhandedly.

"Sasha, do you actually expect me to believe that men don't notice you?"

"No, I don't expect you to believe that! It's just that I have no one special in my life right now . . . but I dream about it from time to time."

"Dream about what?" Duke asked almost too eagerly.

He wanted to believe that even a dream would be a symbol or a pathway from her hidden memory to one end or the other of the gap in her memory, but he was out of his league. He did not have the psychological or psychiatric training or experience to go beyond his personal beliefs, theories and hopes, in spite of his considerable intelligence.

"Oh, I often dream that I fell in love with someone, but I don't know where he is right now, and I never see his face."

Duke felt like he was dancing at the edge of a cliff, and he could not afford to make a misstep. He was dealing with a fire he might not be able to control if he kept pressing this subject. He needed Henry and Julie right there with him immediately! However, they were *not* there, and Duke was uncharacteristically helpless in this case without them. He had to redirect this conversation quickly, and was angry at himself for skating out on this lake without knowing how thin the ice was or how deep and cold the water beneath it might be. However, he was now convinced more than ever that Henry was going to be able to help Sasha, and all possible remaining doubt about going forward with therapy completely disappeared from his thoughts. As smart as Duke was, he was not willing to tamper with Sasha's mind and emotional health all by himself.

"Well, I'm sure you will know who the right man is when you meet him, Sasha, whether he is in your dreams or not," he said, trying to steer their conversation away from obviously critical thoughts.

"I'm sure I will, Uncle Duke," she responded with her special confidence.

Duke was silent for a few moments, which usually meant that his brain was in high gear, and Sasha knew that. She looked at her uncle with all of the deliberate concentration of a lioness about to pounce on her meal for the day.

"What's really on your mind, Uncle Duke? You didn't come all the way up here just to tell me about your will."

Duke knew he had no good way to escape from or go around this question. Sasha was by far too smart and perceptive for that, and apparently knew him well enough to know when he was cooking horse manure.

"OK, Sasha. You're right to a certain extent. I did not come all the way up here just to tell you about my will, but I certainly *did* want to see you and hear you sing. That is a pleasure *no man* can deny. However, I must also admit that I have come across some information recently that has given me some cause for concern. As you already know, I run a rather extensive information network, and I learn about things often enough that I have to verify personally, and when they concern people I care about, I take particular interest in researching and understanding the information as thoroughly and as truthfully as possible."

"It has come to my attention recently from sources I trust completely, that you have had an unusual experience related to your recent tour visit in Fresno that has left a blank period in your memory that is important for your future happiness. There are certain undeniable, independently verifiable facts that clearly point to this conclusion. I feel strongly compelled to make you aware of them and to urge you to participate in experimental therapy to reconstruct that period of your life. It is abundantly clear to me, beyond any doubt whatsoever, that it is definitely worth the effort to try to regain your memory of that part of your life. I am no psychologist or psychiatrist, Sasha, but I have spoken with my top people who have met with professionals in these fields, and they have persuaded me that restoring that part of your memory is not only personally important to you, but it can actually be done. Although the process is experimental—it has never actually been done before—I have become convinced that it has a *very good* chance of succeeding."

"The reason I am telling you all of this is that you must become aware of the problem in order to consent to participate in solving it, and actually proceed along the path to a cure. By the process of elimination, conveying this kind of information to you has become my personal task, because no one else is in a credible position to explain to you just how important it is that you understand that there is indeed a problem. If I had simply called you on the phone to tell you to see a shrink, you would not have believed me. I know you well enough to be sure of that! I also could not very well persuade a psychologist or anyone else to contact you and give you this information."

"There are other people involved in this situation, Sasha, people who care about you very, very much, so I have decided to assume the moral responsibility of seeing that you get the proper care and treatment. Problems do not solve themselves. Hope is not a cure."

"I did not go to your mother with this information, because it would have taken much more time to make her aware of all of the critical details and internalize their implications, and then persuade her of the necessity to explain it to you in a properly effective and timely manner. I did not want to take the chance of anything important being lost in translation. Besides, I just didn't want to risk upsetting her."

"Please forgive me for making this decision about your life, but I honestly believe it is my unique and special duty, obligation and responsibility as a human being, in addition to being your uncle, to take control of this. I could not expect your mother to do this for me. It would be neither fair nor right. I am quite sure that you have become accustomed to making your own life decisions. You are certainly not a little girl any more, but I simply *cannot* just sit by and do nothing when I believe so strongly in my heart that I can do something to enable you to have the fullest life experience that you deserve while you are on this planet."

"If you were completely convinced that someone very dear to you was living his or her life without awareness of a critical truth, could you simply go on with your life without at least presenting your concerns to that person? Wouldn't you rather make the effort to help and fail, rather than never step forward to help at all?"

"Sasha, I have spent much of my life during the last several years trying to help other people. I cannot continue in good conscience in that endeavor, and ignore my only niece. I will pay for the therapy, so don't even *think* about that aspect! If I am this convinced that it is necessary then *of course* I will pay for it! There are times in life when what appears to be a choice is not really a choice at all, but a necessary and inevitable, if not moral decision—an undeniable commitment or essential requirement for the very health of the soul. This is the position I find myself in. I am tempted to characterize it as a personal and necessary demand of fate."

Sasha sat still, obviously deep in thought, and a little overwhelmed by his eloquence, but still looking at him.

My tour visit in Fresno? "And if I refuse treatment, then what?"

"I'm not a therapist or a psychiatrist, Sasha, so I'm not sure I should even venture an answer to that question. I *can* say, however, that as someone who cares *very* much about you, I would be *extremely* disappointed and saddened."

"OK. I think I understand what you are trying to convey. Let me think about this. If this is such a critical issue, then I am sure you will understand if I don't respond immediately. I want to think it over. Right now, I need to get into Manhattan for tonight's performance. Will you come with me?"

"*Of course I will!* I wouldn't miss it for the world!"

He knew it was time to drop this subject for a while. He drove her into the city, found a parking garage near the Swing 46 Jazz and Supper Club, left his valet ignition key with the parking attendant, took his claim check and walked with her to the club. She excused herself to go backstage to get ready for the show, while Duke found a table and made himself as comfortable as possible, but continued to wrestle with the necessity to secure Sasha's understanding and agreement to proceed with therapy. He thought carefully about his discussion at her place, wondering what he could have done differently to get an immediate agreement, but he could think of nothing other than having come across as a little too overbearing.

Too much 'uncle' authority and not enough basic reason, damn it!

Sasha was a rather strong-willed and self-reliant young woman, so her taking orders from other people, even family, was not very likely. He vowed to take another shot at getting her compliance with a more logical approach. However, that was for later. It was time to eat and enjoy the show. During her performance, Duke experienced first-hand the intense feelings she could deliver with her remarkable talent, and the evidence of genuine appreciation in the faces of the audience around him. After her performance, Sasha went back to their table and sat down to relax and have something light to eat.

He smiled broadly with much more than just family pride, and asked casually without revealing his intense curiosity and anticipation, "Sasha, I would like to know who wrote that last song, the one about wanting to be with, I assume, your lover."

"I wrote the words, but I really don't know where the music came from, actually. Why do you ask?"

He knew he now had another opportunity to get her agreement to participate in therapy, hopefully by appealing to her intelligence with some more persuasive logic and unanswered questions, starting with her admission that she did not know where that music came from.

"Suppose I told you *I know* where that music came from. What would you think about that?"

She looked across the table at him with unusually obvious surprise as she responded, "Really? With all due respect, Uncle Duke, how would you know who wrote that music?"

"Sasha, I make a very good living from *information*, remember? I've heard the whole story of the period missing from your memory, much of it indirectly from the one person who probably cares more than anyone else about what happened to you. I employ many bright and enthusiastic, good-hearted, dedicated people, who pieced together much of your life that is missing from your memory, by tracking down and communicating with almost everyone who had any personal interaction with you during this period of your life. You will meet them during the therapy session. They will present independently verifiable evidence of much of your life during the period in question in a manner that will enable you to understand in a non-threatening way much of what happened to you. You will therefore be able to begin to piece together for yourself, as only you can, that part of your life with their help. In that way, you will actually help heal yourself and learn about some very important things, like who wrote that music."

"These are very unusual and caring people, Sasha. I was prepared to do whatever was necessary to *persuade* them to help you, but when they heard the whole story, they all *volunteered* to come together for this experimental therapy without compensation. That should tell you something, Sasha. Something very real and important happened to you during this period, important enough for quite a few people to take the time out of their busy personal lives to come together and help explain it to you. Don't you want to know what these people realized as so important that they so readily consented to do just that? Don't you want to know who is responsible for producing the music that you sang with such passion and feeling this evening? Don't you want to know *why* you sang it with such passion, the music that you evidently thoroughly enjoy singing and that captivates your audiences so completely, the music that draws genuine raw human emotion out of complete strangers in your audiences and solidifies your reputation and increases your popularity?"

Duke felt confident that he had her 'on the ropes.' He knew that her competitive nature and agile mind could not ignore the challenge he had just laid before her. She sat motionless, looking into his eyes for several moments, seeing the wisdom, feeling it reach her heart, feeling his words and questions elevate her heart rate. She knew she could no longer ignore even the small nagging uncertainty and curiosity about that special song. She waited in silence for almost half a minute, still looking into his eyes, obviously in deep thought. She was finally 'hooked.'

"OK, Uncle Duke. I'll do it. I admit that I have had some doubts and questions about my life recently that I have not been able to put to rest, and you have simply highlighted them again. You are exceptionally intuitive and persuasive, as usual."

Duke heaved a huge sigh of relief mentally, and let a real one out much more subtly from his lungs.

"Sasha, I am absolutely delighted by your decision! Here is the name, website, address and phone number of the therapist you will need to contact. I feel very confident that you will like him—*them* actually. They are a husband and wife team. They have already heard you sing in this very club, so my choice is not some chance expediency from a short trip through the yellow pages. These people actually *care* about you very much. I am *absolutely convinced* of it! I wouldn't entrust your welfare in this regard to anyone else!"

He took an envelope from his inside jacket pocket and handed it to her. She already knew that her uncle's arrival at 'conviction' occurred only after considerable research, verification, thought and effort.

The day was ending, and Sasha was eager to go home. Duke drove her back to her condominium safely in relatively light traffic without any further 'heavy' conversation. He dropped her off at the main entrance and watched her go into the building, and then continued back to Maryland, in spite of the late hour, completely refreshed and invigorated with hope for the future for his beautiful and only niece.

CHAPTER 67

Thursday, October 18, 2007
Cambridge, Massachusetts

"I have decided to interrupt this course with a message from our sponsor, The Truth."

This was Professor Michalik's greeting to his class as he had decided to introduce the Fresno Incident to the subject matter of his course because it was a real-life example of the essence of his discussion about the individual and the nature of humanity and how the individual interacts with social forces, as well as the 'law of the jungle.'

"As I am sure you all know by now, there was a terrible explosion in Fresno, California a little over a month ago, in which hundreds of innocent people perished. The information I have gleaned from the media and my own sources since that time indicates that a single individual or a very small group of people managed to transport a significant amount of a very dangerous explosive material all the way across the continental United States from Miami to California. This person or these people were obviously not detected or deterred, and detonated that explosive device in the heart of a rather large city killing several hundred innocent people, and injuring over 1,600 others. Today we will discuss that individual's behavior in terms of his status as an individual human being, as a member of a social group and as a member of the larger community of human beings. We will consider his 'right' to act as he did, the 'rights' of those injured because of what he did, and the effects upon the rest of us not immediately physically involved with those events. Furthermore, we will consider the implications of this tragedy for all of us as citizens of a free country and as members of the common human species on this planet and beyond, if there is a 'beyond.' I do not want to hear any 'politically correct' discussion here! This is an open academic community in which we develop an intimate and sometimes antagonistic relationship with the truth."

"Now, Mr. Delaney, please tell us your thoughts about why this terrorist acted as he did."

Max fought the visceral shock of being the first one called upon to voice his personal thoughts in front of the class about something for which he had had no time to prepare.

"Well . . . I guess he did what he did because he was really convinced that he was right, and that he believed that he had some kind of special responsibility to act as he did. The only analogy I can think of right now is that he must have been thinking like a street gang member. The gang is everything to each member, and if the gang decides that action is necessary, the members assign the task to someone, who then is required to carry it out. The gang membership identity is stronger than any other identity. The motivation to carry out the assignment is so strong because the risk of refusing is the risk of alienation from the gang, which would be the equivalent of excommunication, banishment or virtual living death. The moral code of the gang supersedes all other moral codes."

"Do you mean to tell us that the gang is stronger than the family?"

"Well, yes! In many cases, gang members do not even have a family in the normal sense, because of divorce, abandonment, death, or incarceration of parents, so I think they 'invent' a family in the form of gang membership."

"Thank you, Mr. Delaney. That is a very good start. Miss Wong, what are your thoughts, please?"

Suzy had the minor advantage of seeing that Max survived his initial presentation without apparent adverse consequences, and felt encouraged to share her thoughts.

"I think that Max's analogy to gang membership is good, but I see a difference between what a gang member might be required to do and what this man did. A gang member might be required to hurt someone or destroy property, or perhaps even kill someone, but this man killed *hundreds* of other people he could not possibly know and did not have any personal association with. In addition to that, he didn't just destroy personal property. He also destroyed *public* property indiscriminately! At least in a gang setting, I would guess that a killer might have some understanding of who his victim is and why he was singled out as a victim. The Fresno terrorist apparently had no requirement to know his victims other than to identify them only broadly as Americans."

"So you believe that this terrorist attack was a matter of cultural or national animosity?"

"Yes, I do."

"Thank you, Miss Wong. You brought up a very good point. We should bear in mind that cultural animosity is not a new concept. History is full of examples of one group or culture's unwillingness to get along with another."

"Mr. Shen! Please contribute to the discussion."

Sam was getting a feel for how the discussion was progressing, and felt his thoughts would be just as good as the others.

"Following up on what you just said, Professor, maybe we should understand that this person or group was targeting anyone *not* a member of whatever group he or they represented, rather like 'if you're not with me, you're against me.' This terrorist was specifically targeting Americans, and apparently felt no personal connection to any one individual person, so the personal tragedy of any particular death was not the least bit important to him. However, I suspect that if he were a witness to his own mother's murder, he would react much like any other person anywhere in the world under the same circumstances. His important point was a statement about Americans or America, and had nothing to do with individual personalities. This act was an attempt to change a culture, a way of life—or an effort to eliminate it. It reminds me of what Hitler tried to do in terms of promoting Aryan supremacy. This terrorist was attempting to promote his own version of Islamic supremacy. To the best of my understanding of history, such attempts have never succeeded, and my guess is that they are not likely to succeed in the future, unless we all fall asleep at the switch."

Sam and the rest of the class had no idea how intimately his reference to Hitler resonated within Professor Michalik.

"Excellent, Mr. Shen! I believe your understanding of history in that regard is correct! I might add that cultural values and associated lessons from our parents tend to have the effect of keeping us awake at the switch. If any of you would like to tackle that belief in a paper, then by all means, do so for our next meeting. It will count as extra credit in your grade. Now, Ms. Brentworth, please tell us your thoughts."

"I want to expand a little upon Sam's point about how someone could murder hundreds, and yet have what we all would believe to be a normal reaction to witnessing his own mother's murder. Two important points come to mind. First, Islamic terrorists see death in a very different manner from how most of us would see it, and second, they live under a social order that is essentially religious in character, as opposed to secular, so they are governed more by religious beliefs than by secular law. They have no separation of religion and the state as it exists in most western countries, particularly in the United States. These two points describe cultural differences that tend to prevent the understanding of one culture from the other's perspective. In our culture, killing another human being is simply wrong and illegal. In their culture, killing another human being is apparently accepted if not encouraged if it serves a higher purpose, usually religious. If there is no understanding, then there is constant potential for conflict, hence continued potential for more terrorist attacks."

"Very good, Ms. Brentworth. I realize that you all have an interest in discussing this subject further, but I would like to focus a little more upon some of the individual or personal aspects of this disaster. I ask all of you to humor me for a while, as I try to present what I believe to be a very important point."

"Let us assume for the purposes of argument and education, that Ms. Wong and Ms. Getman both have a strong natural personal attraction to Mr. Jepson. Let us further assume that this attraction is exclusive, meaning that neither will abide the competition of the other for Mr. Jepson's personal attention and devotion."

The class collectively burst out laughing, but the facial colors of Suzy, Gaye and Michael were distinctly rosier than the rest of the faces in the class. Michael put his head face down on his hands on the table, while Suzy and Gaye both slumped down in their seats in apparent efforts to slide under the table, and covered their faces with their hands, trying to hide the very real biophysical facial evidence of their most secret desires. Professor Michalik continued evenly, as if he were essentially innocent and devoid of superior powers of observation, wisdom and intuition from their first class meeting.

"Now, Ms. Wong and Ms. Getman, you both know that each of you has an insatiable personal interest in Mr. Jepson, and each of you wants exclusive possession of him. Now, *exactly how* are you going to resolve this dilemma?"

Suzy was completely flustered and still red in the face as she bravely took a deep breath and admitted, "I don't know! I've never had this kind of problem before!"

Gaye was equally uncomfortable and just as flushed, as she admitted, "I don't know either, really. I suppose I would just approach him, and keep trying to get his attention, regardless of what Suzy does."

Michael was still hiding his face in his hands on the table, but still smiling to himself.

"OK, ladies, please bear with me as we pursue this scenario so I can make my point. You both continue to pursue Mr. Jepson because of very strong natural personal emotions that you can neither deny nor suppress, and neither of you has gained an advantage, but your determination is so strong that neither of you is willing to give up. What do you do?"

After about twenty seconds of absolute silence in the room, CJ spoke up.

"They duke it out! High noon at the OK Corral! How does it feel to have two beautiful women fighting over you, Mike?"

The class just lost whatever composure was barely supported by traditional academic discipline and decorum, as they all broke out in total raucous laughter at CJ's suggestion. Professor Michalik succumbed just as readily to the laughter that filled the room for the next several minutes.

"Thank you for making my point, Mr. Jackson! You all see where this is going, right? *There is no law or custom to consult in this case!* At least in western civilization, there is no cultural prescription for resolving the issue, and there is no credible natural behavior pattern available to solve this dilemma. There is only the law of the jungle—the law that governs basic animal survival and selfish satisfaction of desire! We have two different sources of identical and very strong natural desires aimed at mutually exclusive solutions. There will be no solution until one of them dominates to the point of completely discouraging the other—physically, psychologically, emotionally, or whatever combination is necessary to accomplish the desired end-result!"

"Do you see the analogy to the presentation of 'Battle at Kruger' during our initial meeting? It was a battle for survival and dominance. What the Fresno incident represents is another example of the law of the jungle. There is no natural resolution to the conflict between two distinctly different views of how the world should be, of what kind of lifestyle or religious foundation should apply to all people other than warfare. The very thought of insisting that only one social or religious structure should apply to all people is extreme in itself. Such conflict can be completely resolved only through persistent battle until there are sufficiently fewer adherents of one philosophy than there are of the other to allow for the continued dominance of the one over the other. Otherwise, it would most likely take literally centuries or perhaps millennia to accomplish the desired end with continued constant, deliberate cultural educational efforts. The sheer size of each of the two major philosophical parties to this dilemma almost *assures* a long and difficult conflict."

"I hasten to point out, however, that the demand for exclusive final resolution is apparently present only from the *extreme* adherents of any particular philosophy, and usually not for the greatest majority of people subscribing to that philosophy in general. The very definition of extremist implies a minority, which is usually an unlikely source of dominance. *However*, the major problem today is that such fringe idealists still have access to dangerous weapons of mass destruction and feel entitled if not obligated to use them to attain their goals."

"The real difficulty for all of us arises in terms of the historical progression of what I would call the individual kill ratio afforded by the 'advances' of technology. Today it is possible for a single individual, particularly an extremist, to cause the deaths of hundreds, if not thousands of people, as we saw in the 9/11 attacks, and the Fresno incident."

"Think back for a moment to the beginnings of warfare, when massive armies of foot soldiers assembled to settle their leaders' differences. Men were thrust at one another until the leadership of one side or the other recognized obvious defeat and stopped resisting, or ceased to exist. Early weapons allowed one soldier to kill *one* other soldier, say, with a spear, a club of some sort, a crude knife or an axe, or maybe even two others before he would be taken out of action by someone on the other side. With the advent of bows and arrows, one soldier might survive to kill *several* other soldiers before being taken out of action. With the invention of gunpowder and firearms, one soldier could extend his 'kill ratio' many times more than with a bow and arrow. When automatic rifles appeared, including machine guns, the individual soldier could kill even more, perhaps *dozens* or *scores* of the enemy before he might die or become incapacitated. With the advent of air power and large guns on battleships and tracked vehicles, the kill ratio expanded even more. An aircraft bomber could eliminate hundreds of lives with a typical load of bombs. Then, of course, the development of atomic weapons enabled the kill ratio to expand almost exponentially, as evidenced in Nagasaki and Hiroshima in August of 1945, where combined deaths in the two bombings totaled between 100,000 and 250,000 people directly from the efforts of a handful of men on just two single bombers. Today, a handful of individuals can apparently act completely on their own without governmental or any other official support or sanction and kill hundreds of people, as happened in Fresno. If these people gain control of small, easily portable atomic devices or deadly biological or chemical agents, then they can kill literally thousands instead of hundreds almost instantly."

"Put another way, the history of 'civilization' has 'progressed' from relative stability within which *one* person *could not* have much of a destructive impact upon *many* others, to current conditions within which *one* individual *can* have a meaningful destructive impact upon *many* other people, and without consulting a higher authority beyond his own imagination or personal belief system! This development helps empower the individual extremist to an extent disproportionately greater than the historical norm."

"Have you ever thought of why it is possible for one individual to cause significant *immediate damage* to many others, while it is almost impossible for one individual to effect significant *immediate good* or benefit for many others? Another extra credit assignment for our next meeting will be to write a paper with your thoughts about exactly that question, along with a response and be prepared to defend your views in class."

CHAPTER 68

Friday, October 19, 2007
Washington, D.C.

"The President will see you now, gentlemen," said Molly Stafford, the President's personal secretary and last gatekeeper of the inner sanctum of the White House.

CIA Director Marvin Miles and General Murray entered the Oval Office. The director was merely acting his part, but General Murray strode into the room with the habitual precision of many years of training, discipline and the self-assurance of a rather completely self-made man. The President rose from behind his desk and greeted them.

"Marvin! General Murray! Come on in! Have a seat! Now, tell me what is so important that I had to see you two this evening . . . and not tomorrow morning," he added with something a bit less than a full smile and a subtle admonishing tone to match.

Director Miles began with his version of political correctness.

"Thank you for seeing us under these rather rushed circumstances, Mr. President, but General Murray just advised me several hours ago that we have identified the location of at least one person responsible for the Fresno incident, probably the ringleader. I'll let him continue from here, since he has the best understanding of the essential details."

The President turned expectantly toward General Murray, who wasted no time with preliminaries.

"Sir, I am here to ask for your permission to exercise certain authority not normally under my command. Although plans for apprehending this individual are proceeding as we speak, I would like the authority to negotiate the release of a known terrorist in a British jail as a 'quid pro quo' to get the bastard who made the Fresno job possible. I know it's a tough choice, Mr. President, but I wanted to have as many options available to me as possible. I need an 'ace in the hole.' I really don't want to do it that way, but it may be the only viable option when we get eyeball to eyeball. I say 'we,' because I am personally going to be the 'eyeballs' representing the United States. The location of this effort is potentially dangerous and outside of normal diplomatic channels. It all comes down to just how badly you want the Fresno guy, Mr. President."

The President of the United States sat perfectly still for a few moments, studying General Murray's face, and then glanced at Director Miles for a second.

"And exactly what makes you so sure we will be successful in getting the right man, General?"

General Murray repositioned himself in his chair, and blinked once. He took a subtle deep breath and decided to drop all but the most secret 'bricks' on the President's lap.

"Mr. President, we have persuasive satellite and Air Force reconnaissance photographic evidence identifying a certain U-Haul truck and one person in particular as the driver, who also was identified and described by an eye-witness who happens to have an eidetic memory. A motel clerk in Tucson also identified this suspect where the same truck appeared in the parking lot. Furthermore, a third eye-witness, a Mexican private detective, identified this same person as he boarded a commercial aircraft bound for Pakistan from Mexico City. As it turns out, that detective boarded the same airplane with that suspect and tailed him all the way back to Pakistan. Although he lost his suspect in Rawalpindi Airport in Pakistan because he could not maintain his official status as a detective in Pakistan and was forced to return to Mexico very shortly after he tried to continue following his suspect, he assured us that the suspect is indeed in Pakistan. We intend to apprehend this man with a special technique. The remarkably unique set of circumstances indicated by my people in this case will make the use of psychological techniques never used before extremely effective."

"Now hold it just a damn minute right there, General! I am personally and this office and my administration are officially on record as forbidding torture of any kind, and that includes psychological torture! You're going to have to find another method, General Murray! Do you mean to tell me that you both knew my policy, and yet you came here anyway to try to convince me to go down that road?" he practically shouted.

Miles visually encouraged the general to continue.

"With all due respect, Mr. President, I did *not* use the word 'torture.'"

"Of course you didn't, General Murray. You used a euphemism!"

General Murray started to boil in anger and frustration inside.

"Mr. President, with all due respect, I feel quite strongly obligated to persist in my presentation until I am satisfied that you understand me completely."

Miles glanced at the President and nodded quickly, with a facial expression imploring him to allow General Murray to continue.

After a thoughtful moment, the President said somewhat impatiently, "Very well, General. Continue."

"I am perfectly and completely aware of your policies about interrogation and torture, Mr. President. I have very good people working for me, and I trust their judgment and respect their assessments. I am so sure that we will be successful, sir, that I will personally resign my commission and step down if I do not accomplish what I expect to accomplish within the current policies of the United States. I am placing a great deal of faith in many hard-working, creative, dedicated, patriotic and talented people—citizens of the United States of America. They want to make a statement to the world that we are capable of effective responses to acts of terrorism, and specifically this most recent one. A significant part of the definition of 'effective' is 'rapid' in this case, sir. Until and unless we demonstrate an effective response to the citizens of this country, and people around the world, we will appear to be inept. We will suffer increasing loss of faith and respect within this country and possibly around the world, and continue to sustain injury in one form or another at the hands of extremists who will thereby gain confidence in their techniques and terrorist activities, effectively elevating and prolonging the struggle indefinitely. How many more bombings and how many more innocent lives lost will it take to persuade us that we have to change our responses and tactics, sir? We have to be just as opportunistic, proactive and creative in our responses to attacks and plans for deterrence as they are in committing acts of terror. We must do more than just battle the Taliban and other extremists with traditional forces and try to 'win the hearts and minds' of the nations involved. That is simply not enough. This is as close to the law of the jungle as it gets. We must go after them one by one if necessary. We must answer them effectively, Mr. President, and the sooner the better!"

The President considered what the General had just said, and again glanced at Director Miles. He was well aware of the General's stellar military record, personal reputation and family history. It would be a very serious personal and family crisis indeed, if the General were to fail after he said he would do the job. He was in the prime of his career. He was risking his entire reputation and career, if not his very identity, on the success of this one endeavor. It was not lost on the president that all of this was happening on *his* watch, and politically, he would be the biggest fly on the flypaper, and there would be absolutely no glory for those left sitting on the fence. He had to gamble. He would at least listen to the rest of what General Murray had to say.

The President backed off slightly, looked at his watch and said, "All right, General. You have exactly ten minutes to convince me to grant your request. It's getting late. Continue."

Without revealing anything about The Chancellor Organization, or exactly which psychological techniques he intended to apply, General Murray outlined the scenario that would put him a position to persuade Pakistani military forces to capture Rasheed Shirani. He explained that his people had 'certain information' about a particularly powerful and influential Pakistani Army General, who they intended to influence to cause him to comply with their 'request' for capture and extradition to the United States of the only known living terrorist responsible for the Fresno incident. General Murray made it clear to the president that in order to arrive at the position of making the final persuasion, his counterpart would probably need some traditional internationally accepted show of good faith. The most persuasive show of good faith he had available according to his sources, would be the release of another Pakistani terrorist from a British jail. The persuasion had to be an exchange of a lesser-known terrorist for one that had just grabbed the headlines, at least in the United States. The currency of such negotiations was dirty, but General Murray knew history very well, and knew that many times the way the world works one must give in order to get, and rarely did one complete such an exchange with clean hands, complete self-respect and a pure soul. The shifting sands of national and political priorities, values and alliances had to be rearranged sometimes frequently or quickly in order to satisfy the self-centered or opportunistic demands of governments and political or other special interest groups and even individual proclivities of one sort or another. In effect, he was telling the president that he had to give freedom to one terrorist in order to take it away from the most recent and more notorious terrorist, and he was drawing the British into a situation they might not agree to.

The president glanced at his watch again. Five of the ten minutes had passed.

"General Murray, Mr. Miles, I have certain reservations, but then not much of the job that I have goes without 'certain reservations.' However, here's the deal. General, you will have the authorization you need, but I will accept your resignation if you fail or embarrass me, and the United States of America. Mr. Miles, your neck is on the line as well. That is all, gentlemen."

The man was indeed persuasive. With that simple statement, the president had cast the die. Director Miles and General Murray stood and 'correctly' thanked the president as the General and the President of the United States took just a moment longer than necessary to part ways for the evening, and looked each other in the eye.

The president's eyes were saying, *do not disappoint me, General!*

The General's eyes were saying, *you are going be one damn lucky son of a bitch in spite of yourself!*

CHAPTER 69

Wednesday, October 24, 2007
Attock, Haripur District of Pakistan, 37 Miles West of Islamabad

Raj had studied the Pakistani military organization from top to bottom as directed by Joe during his visit a month ago. Joe could not do it because he was so obviously American, and Americans were not particularly welcome in Pakistan, especially in the remote towns and villages where the bulk of the work was necessary. Raj, however, was familiar enough with the culture to pass rather easily in Pakistani daily life, and could travel almost completely free of unusual scrutiny anywhere in the country. He had spent much of his time visiting various cities in Pakistan and listening to people, carefully making associations and learning what the social power structure was in each province. He read voraciously as many local publications as possible, paying particular attention to references to extremist behavior, politics and ideas, as well as to subjects *not* discussed in the press. He took advantage of everything he had learned from his father growing up about dealing with people and businesses, as well as little tidbits of useful information and tips that his father passed along to him on his cell phone over the last few weeks about important people and techniques to get close enough to them to learn meaningful facts and opinions. However, his natural intuitive 'street smarts' enabled him to know when to listen, and when to ask well-crafted, innocent questions. He gradually pieced together an understanding of who the 'players' were in the hidden and sometimes dangerous world of Pakistani extremism in the remote provinces as well as who the more progressive individuals were. He did not have either the personal presence or the official power to accomplish anything by himself. However, he could tell his story to Joe and Duke, who could apply their version of power and influence within their international world of connections to have what appeared to be a fighting chance to have an effect in the remote provinces of terrorism within Pakistan.

He had internet communication with Duke made possible by Duke's clever and sophisticated use of encryption and coded messages, even though the Pakistani government maintained a strict and rather complete censorship of the internet. Pakistani government censors did not allow much of anything through the internet to be available to the general population that they could interpret as inconsistent with Islamic law and therefore the appearance of the peaceful Islamic integrity of the country of Pakistan. Although it was in effect a closed society in many ways, governmental agencies could not defeat Duke's encryption and cryptographic systems, which still enabled communications between Raj and others in the Chancellor Organization.

General Murray's Pakistani counterpart in this mission was Major General Raza Arshad, commander of the SSG, the Special Services Group, roughly equivalent to the United States Green Berets. His official command was responsible primarily for hunting for terrorists along the Pakistan-Afghanistan border, but the general did not always restrict his activities solely to the border. Raj had done enough homework to respect the shifting sands of political and military alignment and alliances within Pakistan, and discovered that General Arshad was not a completely dedicated Islamic adherent. He could still exercise appropriate independent judgment and behavior sufficient to maintain communication ties with several suspected extremist groups within Pakistan, primarily in the central and northern provinces as well as progressive journalists and politicians throughout the country. He used these contacts for information in order to help balance his double life as a military General and a sympathizer with those who wanted Pakistan to emerge from the age of traditional Sharia law in some places and eventually move the whole country more toward integration with the secular ideas and culture of the western world. He therefore maintained a current working knowledge of the subtle and changing social quicksand within the diverse Pakistani population. He was more likely an opportunistic individual dedicated to the military and his own well-being, but with proper respect for the government political apparatus that sustained his powerful position. He spoke French and Russian fluently in addition to English and Urdu, the two official Pakistani languages.

Raj further learned that General Arshad graduated first in his class from the Command and War College in Quetta, and had a stellar record of military duty. He had the respect of both the forces he commanded and the governmental powers most immediately responsible for maintaining as strong a military organization within Pakistan as they could manage, given the relatively fractured social character of the country and the constant threat of even more religious resurgence. All of Raj's thorough homework could have been expected of the best CIA field operatives.

However, he had also discovered beyond the call of duty, that General Arshad was a widower and had a twelve-year-old son. The boy had never seen the majestic snow-covered beauty of Pakistan's generous share of some of the world's tallest mountains, had never played soccer, never rode a bicycle, never flew a kite, and had a limited social life, such as it could be in Pakistan. Amir Jamal Arshad was blind due to a smallpox infection before he was two years old. The disability thoroughly devastated the general when he first learned of it, but he vowed to raise his only son to be a man the very best way he could, regardless. The boy's development tended to favor his other senses, however, to the extent that his hearing was his 'window' to the world. General Arshad had enrolled his son in the Abbottabad School for the Blind so he could maximize his potential, even with such a severe handicap.

At the age of six, Amir heard a violin for the first time at a concert by the famous Pakistani sarod and violin musician Asad Qizilbash. From that moment, he pestered his father to find, beg, borrow or buy a violin for him to learn to play. The general was an extremely practical man in many respects, and argued against his son for the better part of four months thereafter, explaining to him that it was a waste of money and effort for a blind boy to try to learn to play a violin.

General Arshad eventually relented, even if it was only because of the sheer persistence of his son's single-minded and often one-sided discussions with his father about learning to play the violin. He could not give his son sight, but he could contribute to his son's peace of mind, as well as his own by finding a violin for him. Not many people were capable of persuading General Arshad of a position other than the one he had already adopted, but he had to respect his son's remarkable onslaught of discussion, desire and persistence against even his parental authority, let alone his military bearing. He learned that a second-hand violin was available at a school in Islamabad and arranged to have one of his trusted staff go to Islamabad to purchase the instrument for him. The boy taught himself the rudiments of the violin, but his father understood that lessons would be necessary, so once a week, a violin teacher would visit the Abbottabad School for the Blind to teach Amir and guide his progress. General Arshad paid for the lessons out of his own pocket. General Arshad's relationship with his son is what Raj saw as a key to arranging a meeting between General Murray and General Arshad.

With the assistance of The Chancellor Organization, Raj discovered that surgical procedures were available to restore the boy's eyesight. He carefully designed this message and substantiated it with key personalities that Raj and Duke's organization had identified as touching the General's world in a number of persuasive ways. The Chancellor organization also fed the Abbottabad School with information about new techniques in ophthalmic surgery that held great promise in restoring sight under certain circumstances, one of which just happened to be sight destroyed by smallpox at an early age. Raj made sure that information flowed throughout India as well, just to deflect possible appearances of targeted behavior or special propaganda only in Pakistan. He also acquired various medical reports from the Bascom-Palmer Eye Institute at the University of Miami, which had a first-rate reputation for treatment of blindness. With the help of The Chancellor organization, he discreetly distributed them in major cities in Pakistan and India. He included carefully translated copies from the original English to Urdu, just to help spread the story and enhance the prospects for flushing General Arshad out of his carefully guarded world, where The Chancellor organization and General Murray could effectively make him an offer he could not refuse. Along with these activities, Raj coordinated efforts to expose the story in various Pakistani newspapers and magazines, as well as 'public information' spots on the state-run television and radio stations.

This carefully structured operation produced a proper opportunity after slightly more than two months of exposure, when General Arshad noticed a routine periodic communication from the Abbottabad School that included information about new corrective surgical techniques to treat and correct blindness, and drew the intended conclusion that they were available in the Unites States of America. The only problem was money. Although he was a Major General, he was not a wealthy man. The general eventually contacted the school about the information they had sent out, and the school directed him to Raj Sampat, who immediately contacted Duke Chancellor through System 9, and secretly informed him that 'the fish had taken the bait.'

Duke then immediately made a significant 'donation' of $500,000 to the Mercy Hospital and Medical Center in Chicago, Illinois. That subtle ton of bricks earned him a phone call from the administrator of the hospital, Dale M. McConaughy. The Chancellor Organization had learned that a certain anesthesiologist employed at the hospital was Doctor Naved Musharraf, the brother of the former president of Pakistan, General Pervez Musharraf, and that the two brothers maintained phone contact on a regular basis. Duke intended to persuade Doctor Musharraf to tell his brother Pervez in Pakistan about The Chancellor Organization's humanitarian effort to secure the cooperation of General Arshad. They wanted the former Pakistani president to exercise his considerable influence to 'encourage' General Arshad to meet with General Murray and Raj to discuss apprehending Rasheed Shirani. Duke persuaded McConaughy to give him Doctor Musharraf's phone number in addition to preparing the doctor to accept Duke's call. Once Duke had the doctor on the phone, he made sure of his cooperation with the immediate untraceable deposit of a $50,000 'bonus' from the hospital to the doctor's personal checking account. After explaining the nature of his plan without revealing too many specifics, he promised Doctor Musharraf complete anonymity as well as the similarly untraceable delivery of another $50,000 'bonus' to the doctor, one day after the planned meeting between General Arshad and General Murray was to occur. Doctor Musharraf took special note of the considerable persuasive talents of Duke Chancellor, assured him that he fully understood and was entirely in agreement with Duke's plan, the requirement of secrecy and promised to do his absolute best to secure his brother's full cooperation.

While Doctor Musharraf successfully explained the novel plan to apprehend Rasheed Shirani to his brother in Pakistan, the mystery of Sasha's missing memory was about to unfold in Denver, Colorado.

CHAPTER 70

Friday, October 26, 2007
Denver, Colorado

At the request of Henry and Julie, the hotel management provided a relatively small, 1,200 square foot carpeted meeting room for the therapy sessions, but made some basic, easy renovations to take the 'business air,' 'hotel atmosphere,' and typical meeting room echo out of the room and made it appear more like a large living room. It was not a partitioned room, but a single separate solid-walled room acoustically appropriate for the privacy of the sessions, and eliminated noise from outside the room. It also had the more domestically intimate ten-foot ceilings, rather than the typical fifteen-foot ceilings of most of the larger hotel meeting rooms. They removed all of the folding chairs and replaced them with twenty-eight comfortable chairs with blue cushioned seats and backs like those found in the hotel guest rooms. All of the 'business tables' and presentation aids, including computer monitors and projection screens often used for business meetings were removed from the room. They dimmed the typically bright recessed overhead lighting considerably, so they could establish a more comfortable 'domestic' tone with several incandescent floor lamps with stylish light-yellow shades found in some of the more elegant hotel lobby areas.

A large round wooden coffee table with inlaid patterns of different colored wood was in the center of the circle. It had ample room for several pitchers of water and juices, trays of crackers, cheeses, breads and various dips and spreads so people would not feel the need to leave the room for food or liquids, possibly disturbing the productive flow of what could develop from the relatively unstructured session. The hotel staff prepared a typical lunch menu scheduled for a one-hour break around noon, to be served in the room, so the continuity of the session could withstand such minimal distraction. Julie insisted upon having a grand piano in the room. She wanted to be prepared for any form of communication, given the nature of the problem and the exceptionally strong and unusual emotional bond that had been created through music between Sasha and Jake.

Sasha was wearing a conservative dress and flat shoes with a white sweater, effectively obscuring her figure. She was sitting in a small private room with Henry and Julie where Henry started to prepare her for the therapy experience.

"Sasha, you must be aware of certain undeniable facts regarding the process we are about to begin. I want to make sure you understand the foundation from which we will be working. Everyone you will meet during the therapy session actually had at least a small personal exchange or period of interaction with you or someone you cared about very much at some point during the period overlapping the gap in your memory that we will be trying to restore. Therefore, in essence, there are no total strangers out there. None whatsoever. Some of these people have had connections with you from earlier in your life."

"Julie and I will guide the process, but you will be an integral and very important part of how the process develops and progresses. I encourage you to ask questions and express your feelings as sincerely and openly as you can at any time, because we carefully identified all the people out there as important to the process. We specifically invited each of them to come here. Every one of them agreed to participate honestly and sincerely in this effort without any compensation whatsoever because they care about you, and they want you to be able to enjoy your fullest measure of life."

"The therapy will become effective as you start to understand the relationships between what you now know or remember about your life, and what you will learn from the discussions that develop from all of the participants in the room. I am sure you will understand that this effort is sincere and unrehearsed. Many significant details and unique circumstances independently verifiable from more than one person or source support the notion that there is no fabrication or conspiracy possible here. You will know whether the session is helpful better than anyone else will. Although I expect to realize when the therapy is complete, *only you* will know for sure, so I will need you to communicate openly and honestly with Julie and me about your thoughts and feelings as the sessions progress."

"We cannot stop you from terminating the process, but we believe quite strongly that you should follow as completely as possible all of the leads and connections that develop throughout the process. The outcome will very likely be a direct result of your desire and determination to work for the personal sense of fulfillment that Julie and I, and all the people out there so strongly believe you deserve. Ultimately, *you* are the one who must make the connections and understand the relationships among the people and events during this period of your life on the path to understanding exactly what happened to you during this time. We can arrange and present to you what we know to be facts and events and provide opportunities for you to interact with the other people involved in order to provide the 'mental lubricants' we believe are necessary to assist you in making the proper connections among these people, events and feelings."

"You are essentially the same person now that you were during the 'forgotten' period of your life, primarily because it has been a relatively recent and brief period. Therefore, we should expect that you will become fully aware of everything that happened to you during this period to the same extent that each of us carries a memory of who and what we are as well as our experiences, even though all of us have forgotten or suppressed relatively minor details of our lives from time to time. I firmly believe that you have not yet had enough time since this period to develop false and incorrect associations that eventually could 'solidify' or 'bury' this period of your life even further if you postpone therapy, thereby making recovery much more difficult, if not impossible, so I am very realistically hopeful of success."

"Now, we really want you to talk to us before we start the process. We want to know what you feel and what you are thinking about right now. We need to know exactly what you remember, so please include anything else you can think of, regardless of how irrelevant it may seem to you. We want to have the best possible understanding of your thoughts and feelings, regardless of whether you think they are important or not, so we can have an appreciation of any progress or regression during the process."

Sasha looked into Henry's warm hazel eyes for a moment without speaking. She shifted her gaze to Julie and studied her kind green eyes carefully. She waited for what seemed to be a period of several minutes of internal effort, trying to organize her thoughts. Henry and Julie waited patiently. Sasha looked down at her hands, which she had clasped calmly on her lap in contrast to her pounding heart. After about another minute, she looked up and started to share her thoughts.

"For the most part, I feel as normal now as I have ever felt, but with two exceptions—I'm a little nervous and anxious right now, even though I rarely suffer from 'stage fright,' and I am very puzzled by not understanding the origin of that music I wrote the words for, and who those words refer to. I know all the music I sing and where it came from, except that one composition and I must admit that my ignorance is very strange. My Uncle Duke made me realize that I need to understand why that song affects others so intensely the way it does, or at least why I wrote those words."

"I have always been a relatively strong and self-sufficient person, so it is an extremely large leap of faith for me to place my sense of who I am in the hands of other people, but it is primarily my respect and love for my Uncle Duke that has brought me to this point. He is the one who convinced me to take this leap of faith toward self-discovery. It is primarily because of him that I am willing to trust the two of you. The only other odd mystery I think about is the recurring theme in my dreams about a lover, but I never see his face. I suspect that dreaming about a lover may not be unique among women, but dreaming about a lover without a face I believe is quite another matter. Nevertheless, there it is. I do not always dream every night, but when I do, the same theme keeps coming back to me. I do not recall having that experience before—ever."

After several seconds of absolute silence, Julie asked gently with genuine personal, as well as professional therapeutic interest, "When was the last time you had that dream?"

"Last night."

Julie turned her head slowly to look at Henry with an intense mix of trust in him, and apprehension about the untested process they were about to unleash. Once they started, she really did not know exactly where it would lead or how it would end. Sasha sat still for another minute or two. Henry waited a few more minutes until he was convinced she was ready.

After several minutes without further comment from her, he reached out for her hand and said with deliberate hope and optimism, "OK, Sasha. Let's go to the session room and meet your past!"

Sasha gracefully rose from her chair. They all left the room and walked down the dark tan plush carpeted hall to the meeting room with Henry on her right side, and Julie on her left. They were symbolically protecting her, maintaining a sense of security and trust, providing the physical and psychological 'walls' she could lean on if necessary.

Henry reached for the meeting room door and pulled it open wide enough for Sasha and Julie to enter side by side, and he followed, making sure the door was properly closed and latched behind him. The casual friendly banter among the 'guests' quickly tapered off into silence as the three of them walked past a well-polished black baby grand Yamaha piano on their way to the three adjacent empty comfortable chairs in the circle in the middle of the room. They sat with the same protective arrangement with Sasha between Henry on her right and Julie to her left, facing into the circle in the middle of the room and away from the piano behind them. Sasha was beginning to appreciate that this was going to be an unusual session, to say the least, when she saw how many people were in the room, as well as the piano. She also noted the décor and atmosphere in the room. It was not a typical hotel meeting room. It was more like a rather large, but very comfortable living room. Henry and Julie had apparently made significant preparations for her therapy, and her Uncle Duke had obviously gone to considerable expense to make this happen.

She looked quickly around the room at the others, smiling in a way somewhere between her natural fantastic white-toothed professional performance smile and the somewhat muted polite smile of a self-conscious young teenager. From Julie's left, the group sat in clockwise, essentially timeline fashion, starting with 'Stealth' nearest to Julie. In sequential order to his left were the night clerk at the Denver hotel, the 'odd couple' from the elevator, Doctor George Stevenson, Rocky Mason and Tommy Ventura from FTM Studios, Eddie, Marie, 'Dirty Blonde' and 'Dark Hair' from Eddie's Place that Monday evening, the married couple from Eddie's, 'Cooperstown' without his 'Cooperstown' sweatshirt, 'Red Tie' without his red tie, 'Green Skirt' wearing a similar green skirt, Bill Trent, the night desk clerk at the motel in Las Vegas, Patrolman David Fleming of the Colorado State Police, Jennifer Roth, RN, from the Reading Hospital, Tanya Wilkinson and her husband Randy, Ramon Raphael from the Fresno Rescue Squad, Doctor Jonathan Caldwell from the Saint Agnes Medical Center, and Rob Reynolds, the soprano saxophonist from the new 'Autumn Dream' group. These were all of the most critical people Duke's organization could find with information from Jake and some very thorough, intense and creative detective work.

Conspicuously absent from the circle of people were Jake, Joe and Duke. Duke did not want to interfere, nor in any way be tempted to insert his two cents into the process and possibly risk ruining what he was paying Henry and Julie a considerable amount of money to accomplish. He had returned to the Plymouth Building to await progress reports from Kenny, and keep himself occupied with business matters and other projects, like the pursuit of Rasheed Shirani. Joe knew his presence was not necessary, and he did not want to risk unintended results from his presence. He needed to keep himself busy with his restaurant as a way to diffuse the tremendous energy he had put into his efforts to help organize the therapy session. Jake was waiting in a business 'internet room' just off the main hotel lobby for a phone call from Henry indicating that it was time for him to enter the therapy session. He brought a book with him to occupy his mind as much as possible, in spite of his intense interest in what he imagined would be going on in the therapy session. Henry and Julie emphasized how critically important it was for him to stay out of the session until they called him. If he were to succumb to temptation and appear before Sasha was ready, he could set the therapy process back significantly, damage it forever, or possibly even do further harm to Sasha. Of course, he understood. He simply cared too much to take any risks with her welfare. He had to trust Henry and Julie completely, which, of course took no effort at all, given his friendship and experience as a psychologist. The professional psychologist in him promised to play by the rules he knew existed for a very important reason—the success of the therapy.

Henry looked at Julie and smiled briefly, took a deep breath, and then turned to look everyone else in the room in the eye one by one, as he spoke.

"Ladies and gentlemen, I am Doctor Henry Winslow, and this lovely young woman to my immediate left is Sasha Chancellor. The other lovely woman to her left is my wife and partner in this process, Doctor Julie Winslow. You are all here because each one of you has within you a piece of Sasha's lost memory that Julie and I have asked you to present during an experimental therapy session designed to restore a certain portion of Sasha's memory, so that she will be able to continue her life in as rewarding a way as possible. You will all come to understand exactly what that means as the session progresses, and she will as well. I do not know how long we will need to conduct this type of therapy session or just how many sessions we will need because, to my knowledge, it has never been tried before. The professional journals are not particularly helpful in terms of the procedures we will use or their effectiveness, or how much time will be required before we reach a point of resolution."

"What we would like to accomplish here is actually a little more than the specific goal of restoring Sasha's memory. I believe that we will also send a message to the world of terrorism that their views of the human spirit and the value of life are misguided, to say the least. It is our firm belief that Sasha was injured during the Fresno terrorist incident in a manner that interfered significantly with her memory of that general period, and unfortunately, also interfered with a very strong and intense personal relationship. So you see, there is at least one other casualty among the living after the Fresno incident, let alone the hundreds or even thousands of others living with only memories of lost loved ones. I believe that all of us are more capable of achieving our fullest potential in life *with* love in our lives than we are *without* it."

"To the extent that we as a society respect and encourage love, we contribute to the strength of us all and fight back at extremist social philosophies that ultimately strive to limit the fullest human experience and our individual sense of freedom to pursue and explore personal fulfillment and consequent individual and social health, if not world peace and stability. This process will require each of you to share with all of us exactly, and as completely and honestly as possible, what your interaction was with Sasha or with people important to her. You will thereby contribute to her ability to understand exactly who *you* are, and what happened to her during the period of lapsed memory, as well as to understand the timeline of events during that period, so she can reestablish or recreate the memories that make her as whole and as complete a woman as she deserves to be. It is obvious to me that without certain memories of her past, she is somewhat limited in experiencing as much of the future as possible."

"Think about your own lives for just a moment. Do you not seek future experiences similar to the ones in your past that you enjoyed or that gave special meaning to your life? Without the memory of those experiences, you would be unable to seek out or fully appreciate similar experiences that enhance your enjoyment of life in the future and maintain the search for or process of maintaining your sense of identity, purpose and meaning in life. Without the memory of *un*fortunate experiences or pain, you would be less able or less likely to avoid that pain again in the future. Now, think about what it would be like not to remember a loved one. How many of us would give anything to have a lost parent, or a spouse, or another significant family member or friend here with us to share our joy or comfort us in sorrow? Just as we can all give blood to someone who has lost too much of it to sustain life without replenishment, thereby increasing his chances of survival, we can give of our shared experiences with Sasha in a manner that restores her memory of a certain part of her life that I think we would all agree is certainly worth restoring. I am entirely convinced that even if any of you might not completely understand exactly what I am talking about right now, you *will* understand at some point before the therapy sessions are complete."

The people in the circle looked around at one another with hope and rich anticipation and quite a few raised eyebrows of realization, agreement and understanding, eventually looking at Sasha, projecting toward her their hope for and anticipation of her complete recovery.

Henry said with daring and infectious hope, "All right, let's begin! Please introduce yourself, and explain as completely as you can what your interaction or association with Sasha's life is or was so we can all understand. You are all critically important people to this process, so don't be bashful or ashamed of anything. Complete honesty and sincerity from *each one* of you is essential to the success of *all* of our efforts here. Each of you is a link in the chain of understanding that we are attempting to recreate in Sasha's life. Therefore, the best understanding we can convey to her or enable her to comprehend requires a strong and sincere effort from each one of you individually in order to make the entire chain of understanding as strong and as meaningful as possible."

'Stealth' was the first to speak in the timeline arrangement Henry and Julie had constructed, taking his cue from Henry to begin.

"My name is Alex Thornton. I am one of the servers at Eddie's Place in Denver, where Sasha sang with her band. She was there for five days in early September. On Friday, the fifth day, or evening, actually, this handsome professional-looking guy was sitting at the table for two nearest the stage. I saw him watching Sasha with obvious interest. He never ate the hamburger I brought him until it was probably cold after the show. Everyone in the room was enjoying the show, but this guy actually had tears in his eyes from time to time. I figured if he was sad, he would have left, so I thought he was crying because he was happy. I remember that Sasha came down from the stage after the show and sat down in the chair across the table from him as he started to eat his hamburger and they talked for a while—you know, like a guy and a girl talk when they're interested in each other, I guess. Then she took him backstage to the piano Eddie keeps back there, and he played some really nice music for her. We all liked it, of course, the few of us who were there cleaning up for the night. Then I saw the two of them leave the bar holding hands."

"I saw the same guy come in the bar a week from that following Monday, which would have been exactly one week after the Fresno bombing, and sit at the very same table he sat at the first time. He brought with him a pretty white rose in a pink vase, and he put some kind of CD jewel case on the table with the vase. You remember stuff like that because it just doesn't happen every day, you know. *Everyone* in the place noticed! It was pretty obvious to me that something made him really happy between his holding her hand while leaving the bar that first night and bringing in that flower the next time I saw him!"

A round of polite chuckles flowed from around the circle as people became more comfortable with the process that Henry was using.

"As the evening moved on, he kept sitting at the table, not ordering anything but water, I think, and he said his 'friend' would be coming soon. I had to think he was waiting for Sasha. Well, as it turns out, she never came, and he looked really sad. Eventually everyone in the bar was looking in his direction not knowing what to do or what to say, because he was right up there in front of the stage where everyone could see him. Everyone else seemed to notice exactly what I noticed. It was obvious that he was being stood up, since he was wearing his heart on his sleeve with that flower and all. It was like he got shot by cupid, and was still bleeding a lot from the arrow. Eventually, he just gave up and left the bar. I guess any guy can take only so much emotional pain, and then he just . . . folds. I really felt bad for him, but I really didn't know what to do. I really don't remember much more than that right now."

"Thank you, Alex. That was very helpful. Please feel free to speak again at any time if you remember anything else, or if you would like to add to the conversation. Next, please," said Henry with a commanding professional gentleness.

"Hi. My name is Jimmy—Jimmy Jones. I'm the night clerk at the hotel she stayed at in Denver. I saw Sasha and this nice-looking guy come into the hotel and head for the elevator bank. They were looking at each other the whole time! Lucky they didn't walk into a *wall* or somethin'! I see couples like this all the time, as you might guess, but this gal was in high gear, if you know what I mean. I could see it in her eyes. She had this guy in her *sights*, man! He was one done dude! Then I saw this other couple over here next to me kind of rush to the elevator, you know, to beat the closing doors? They got in and the elevator went up. I never saw Sasha or the guy she was with again, 'cause I went off duty at seven that next morning. Saw these folks right here get off the elevator and then get back on again, though. That's about all I can actually say I saw that night regarding Sasha."

He looked at Sasha, smiled weakly and shrugged with a mild apologetic facial expression. Sasha actually smiled back at him.

Was I that obvious?

"Thank you, Jimmy. Next, please," Henry coaxed.

"Hello. My name is Gloria Pittman, and this is my husband Jeremy. We are indeed the couple this young man just described as hurrying to the elevator. I must say, however, that my impression of Sasha today is quite different from the impression I had of her that night! I'm really very sorry, Sasha, but that night I thought you were a hooker, taking this man up to your room, or he was taking you up to his room—whatever!

I remember that he asked you something like 'How much for all night' and you said something like, he 'couldn't afford you for that long.' I was rather shocked at the way you two were carrying on and touching each other and such in the elevator! You caused quite a stir in my husband, the way you smiled at him and blew him a kiss when you left the elevator on the sixth floor. The reason I remember the floor number is that we didn't push a floor button, because we were so befuddled by the scene you and your boyfriend were putting on in the elevator that we just forgot, so the elevator just stayed there at the sixth floor! When the doors finally closed again, the elevator just automatically went back to the lobby!"

More polite, but less restrained laughter spread around the circle. Gloria had broken a little more ice, and then her husband spoke.

"I would like to add to what my wife so honestly admitted a few moments ago. Yes, I was quite impressed with this young woman. I admit it! I still have a memory of my younger days, thank God! And I still remember what young women are like! Sure! I knew perfectly well that she was just teasing me, but a guy my age needs to have that every once in a while, and appreciates it, *believe me!*"

This admission just brought the house down with unrestrained laughter for the next several minutes, as the entire tenor of the group gradually changed to that of a more open, familiar, friendly and intimate atmosphere. Sasha smiled as she looked carefully and kindly at Jeremy Pittman.

I blew you a kiss?

She admitted to herself that it was not out of character when she was in the right mood.

"Thank you, Jeremy," Julie said warmly.

Henry glanced at Sasha for just a moment, and then nodded at Doctor George Stevenson.

"I am Doctor George Stevenson, Jake Lewis's physician. My involvement in this whole situation is rather limited, but also very peculiar. I responded to the invitation to be here because I thought what little I have to offer would be for a good cause. It just so happens that I was giving an electrocardiogram to Jake as part of his annual physical examination the evening of the Fresno attack. I actually have a record of his heartbeat at the reported precise moment of the explosion, or close enough to it to get my attention."

"At the time, I didn't know what to make of it beyond what appeared to be a relatively mild cardiac abnormality. However, as I learned more about the explosion later, and specifically *when* it occurred, I remembered Jake's somewhat unusual facial reaction at almost precisely the same reported time as the explosion and the recorded heart murmur. Looking back on it all, knowing what I know now, and learning more about Jake and Sasha here, I cannot help but marvel at the *extremely odd* coincidence of Jake's facial behavior and cardiovascular response at about the same time as the explosion, even though he was almost 830 miles east of it. I started to think about the controversial psychic aspects of the human experience in general. Could Jake have 'felt' the injury to Sasha at the exact time that it occurred *because* of his relationship with her? I honestly don't know one way or the other, and I have yet to come across convincing professional medical or scientific literature about the subject either way. However, I suspect that some elements of the human experience are not yet revealed through medical science. It is simply a point of curiosity to me, and I offer this observation primarily as an extraordinarily unusual coincidence within the larger picture, and I sincerely hope that it helps what you are trying to do here."

The group listened to Doctor Stevenson with rapt attention. Sasha sighed deeply as she was starting to lose more of her innate skepticism. The doctor's description of the apparently simultaneous occurrence of the explosion and his patient's physical reaction was a little too coincidental to dismiss altogether, and she made a special mental note of it.

"Thank you, Doctor Stevenson. That is indeed *very* interesting!" Julie said and then nodded to the next guest.

"My name is Rocky Mason. I am one of the owners of RTM Studios. We record music for various musicians, both professional and amateur in the greater Denver and surrounding areas. I met Jake briefly in the afternoon of the day of the explosion, when he dropped by my studio to look at the piano I have before he committed to making a recording. He played the instrument for about fifteen minutes, and was really quite good. He obviously was talented, but he also was playing with a lot of emotion, to an extent rather rare among the amateurs I have heard and seen. He asked for an appointment for a recording session, and we agreed on the next day. He asked what the cost would be, and I told him $100 an hour for the piano, plus another $100 for tuning it right before the recording session. He wanted it tuned right before the recording session I think because it was going to be a particularly special session for him. He didn't flinch at all, so we confirmed the appointment for six o'clock the next day, Tuesday. That would have been September 11, the day after the Fresno incident. I was going to be out of the studio that day because of a prior commitment, so I missed what I have since come to understand was quite a nice performance that he recorded on the CD."

Henry waited for just a moment and then nodded to the next person to contribute.

"Hi! My name is Tommy Ventura. I am one of the recording technicians at RTM Studios. I was on duty that Tuesday evening when Jake came in to record his piano music. I remember thinking that this guy was really good, and that he had a rather intimate relationship with the piano that I had never seen before. After he was finished playing, I asked him about what he had played, and he said it just came to him, basically out of thin air. I was a little dumbfounded, but who was I to question a musician? I made the final master CD recording for him, wrote his name and the date on the CD with a magic marker, put it in a jewel case, handed it to him and took his check for $200."

Now Sasha knew where the CD came from that Alex had described. It was a gift of Jake's music to her. It was something he created, a sincere and unique gift from the heart. No one else in her life had ever given her such a special personal gift of any kind. Slowly but surely, she was being drawn irretrievably into the hidden story of her life. The story was apparently real enough to all these people, and yet she had no recollection of it. She began to realize that Henry and Duke had been right all along. She needed to have this part of her life restored, or forever suffer the uncertainty of who her lover was. She started to open up her mind and felt a little more comfortable with the process.

"Eddie, you're up," Henry coaxed calmly.

"My name is Eddie Barringer. I own and run Eddie's Place in Denver. It's a restaurant and bar. I first met Sasha during one of her performances in New York City a little over a year ago, and I was so impressed with her voice and her music that I decided right at that moment to hire her and her band, regardless of the cost. I wanted them to come to my place in Denver and stay for as long as they could be there—turned out to be only five days, unfortunately. I knew the word would get around town after the first night she was there, and I would have more business the next four nights because of it. I paid a little high to convince her to come all the way to Denver, but I would do it all over again. She's one of a kind, and a rare talent! If you have not yet heard her voice—I mean her real *singing* voice—then you have not yet lived, my friends. I really don't care whether that sounds like a plug for either her or my bar, but it just happens to be the truth. Sasha is one of those people you care about from the get-go. I can verify just about everything Alex said, obviously, because we were both there at the same time."

"However, when I saw Jake for the second time on that Monday evening, sitting alone for such a long time with the flower and all, I was almost certain that Sasha was dead. I knew from earlier discussions with her that Fresno was next on her tour after my place, and that it would take her two days to get there. That meant she would have been performing somewhere in one of the nightclub areas in Fresno within the same timeframe as the explosion. I was completely devastated by what I thought was the very high probability that she was killed in the blast. I was almost physically sick with worry, and at the same time, I was extremely angry at whoever was responsible for that explosion. I wanted to lash out and strangle with my own bare hands whoever did that, but I had no target and no proof. I was really, *really* upset!"

Each of the others was practically holding his breath listening to Eddie's increasingly emotional recollection. Sasha had tears in her eyes. Gloria's mouth was hanging open in astonishment as she was working that former 'harlot' image of Sasha out of her system with less effort and more enthusiasm and conviction, practically castigating herself mentally for having perceived her that way in the first place.

After absorbing Eddie's presentation, Henry gestured to the next person to speak.

"Hi. I'm Marie Mangiano, manager of the bar and Eddie's 'right hand woman.'

I tried to be the counterbalance to Eddie's emotional hurt that evening. I tried to make him believe that we had no direct evidence that Sasha had died in the blast, but he eventually was rather convincing that Monday evening, and so I also began to have grave doubts about Sasha's safety. The papers and TV had the story—what it was anyway—without all of the details, and it was easy to draw the conclusion that Sasha could have died in the blast. It could have been a disaster for the business that night, because everyone in the bar was affected by Jake's apparent rejection, and that's not the kind of atmosphere that makes people order beverages and food. After all, he was sitting right up there next to the stage where everyone could see him. Even the band we had that night stopped in mid-performance because of the spreading realization that something was very, very wrong somewhere in the bar. Everyone was looking at the young man who was sitting alone at that table for two with the white flower on it, feeling his hurt, whatever it was. When he left the bar, he also left the pink vase with the white flower in it on the table. Then Eddie took the two chairs from that table and put them in storage backstage. He said no one would sit there as long as that white rose lived, and he vowed to leave it on the table and water it as long as necessary. He said he really didn't give a damn whether he had two fewer seats in the bar because of it. He even changed the overhead spot lighting to focus on the vase. It was really quite touching. Everyone who came into Eddie's Place from that night on asked about the flower. We told them it was a symbol of love and hope for someone lost in the Fresno incident. The really amazing thing is that our business kept increasing over the next five days as more and more people heard about the white flower and apparently wanted to see it for themselves. It got to a point where we really didn't have enough room for people!"

Marie stopped talking abruptly, as her emotions choked her off. She could not continue, and just looked with trembling lips at the woman next to her. She felt she would break down completely if she looked into Sasha's eyes.

Tears were streaming down Sasha's cheeks. She had no knowledge of any of this, but what these people were saying was apparently too real to them to ignore. What she had heard so far was entirely too complex to have been orchestrated or contrived by so many different people who could not have been expected to know one another apart from the obvious relationships. Regardless, they all clearly knew who *she* was! There was absolutely no possibility of mistaken identity!

They all really are talking about me! If what they were saying is not actually true, then they are all going to be up for Oscar awards!

Henry looked briefly at Sasha and then nodded to 'Dirty Blonde' next in the circle.

"Hello! My name is Danielle Shemansky."

She stopped for a moment and sighed, waiting for her courage to return. She steadied herself, and then continued.

"I was at Eddie's Place that Monday evening when this very handsome young man put the pink vase with the white rose in it on the table and sat down."

She stopped again for several seconds, dabbing her eyes with a tissue.

"I remember remarking to my friend how sweet it was of him to do something so special, expecting someone we all thought was obviously a girlfriend, since he came in alone and was sitting alone. I also remember making the excuse of going to the ladies' room so I could circle around the main room inconspicuously on the way back to my table and take a sneak peek at the flower and the vase on his table, instead of deliberately walking up to him without pretext. As I walked past him, I noticed the CD case on the table, and the note near it. It said 'For Sasha, With all my love. Jake.' I'll never forget that as long as I live because it was so sweet. I'm quite certain I have never received that kind of treatment from a man, certainly not in my presence, so it really made a lasting impression on me."

Sasha was hanging on every word. She was now convinced that the lover in her dreams was a real person out there in the real world somewhere, and not just in her imagination. However, she just could not dredge an image out of her memory. She repeated in her mind Danielle's recollection of what was on the note with special attention to the names—*'For Sasha, With all my love. Jake.'*

Henry again waited patiently for a short period to be sure Danielle was finished then glanced briefly at Sasha, and then nodded to the next person in the circle.

'Black Hair' introduced herself as Anne Velimoore.

"I was sitting with Danielle that evening, and can verify everything that she just said. I remember thinking how incredibly lucky some girl was to have a man think of her in that way. I also remember seeing how upset Eddie was, and feeling that something was really not quite right in the bar that night. A rumor was spreading around inside the bar about the guy with the white rose waiting for a girl who was killed in the Fresno incident but did not know she was dead. I knew I couldn't always believe everything I hear, but this rumor definitely caught me by surprise, and I could not help feeling just awful, almost sick with sadness about this guy obviously waiting for his missing girlfriend, not knowing that she was not going to show up, *ever!*"

The rest of them could see the emotion in Anne's face as she just barely kept her feelings in check.

Sasha was beginning to feel the pain of the young man waiting for her with the white rose, not knowing whether she was alive or dead, and not knowing whether she loved him. Henry was trying to gage the group's stamina and the momentum of the session so far. He decided that there was enough to continue without a break, at least not right at that time. He did not want to break the continuity of the process up to that point and the consistency of the message to Sasha as well as any 'connections' that he believed were surely forming in her memory paths. He felt that she was definitely being drawn into the process. He motioned with his outstretched hand to the married couple next to Anne to continue.

"Hi! I'm Max Gentry, and this is my wife Judy. We were also in Eddie's Place that Monday evening, sitting near these two ladies who just spoke. We exchanged a few comments with them at the time about how obvious it was that the young man sitting at the table up front with the flower was in love, big time, and apparently did not care one whit who knew it! It was really unusual, and kind of special, if you know what I mean. You just don't see men openly broadcasting their feelings for a woman like that every day of the week! Actually, I had never seen it at all—ever—until that night, so I figured whoever this gal was, she must have been really pretty special."

Judy looked from her husband directly at Sasha and said, "I was really touched and saddened by what I saw that night, especially after the rumors started going around in the bar. It was all I could do to hold back tears. I absolutely could not recall having experienced such sadness about another person before, especially a perfect stranger, ever! I remember I was so immobilized by this unusual concern for someone I didn't even *know!* It's really . . . really a very unusual feeling . . ."

Henry waited for her to continue, but she apparently did not have anything further to say, or could not say anything more, so he nodded to the next person in the circle.

'Cooperstown' introduced himself next.

"Hi, I'm John Wellington. I am a landscape architect here in Denver, and I show up at Eddie's Place rather regularly. My contribution here is small, but I can honestly say that I have never had the experience of seeing another human being in such pain as I saw in that man with the white rose that evening. The way I remember it, this guy with the white flower was waiting for his girlfriend, who was actually already either dead or injured in the Fresno incident, but he obviously was not aware of that, so I figured he must have thought he was being stood up."

Then, he turned to look directly into Sasha's eyes.

"Now that I have heard everything from these other people who spoke before me, it is crystal clear to me that you, Sasha, are the woman he was waiting for. Like I said, I am a regular at Eddie's so I heard you sing there earlier that prior week. I can understand completely his falling really, *really,* hard for you. That's all I have."

He wiped tears from his face with his hands three times.

'Red Tie' was next.

"Hi. I'm Mickey Morningstar. I'm a freelance photographer here in Denver. I was also at Eddie's that Monday night, but it was my first time there. What I remember so vividly is that this guy everyone was talking about walked by me on the way out of the bar. I saw a man with tears and a really big hurt in his eyes, but walking tall. Everyone made room for him so he could leave, like he was some kind of injured god. It was the kind of situation that you can't look away from, but you can't help the guy either. It was simply a tragedy, in my opinion. It's not very often that I don't know what to do in any situation, but that night I was absolutely helpless. I felt awful that I couldn't even try to make the guy feel better, or say something comforting when he so obviously needed someone to help . . . help him with his heavy . . . burden, whatever it was."

Sasha was listening very carefully. The whole experience was absorbing her. She could no more stop the process than she could stop breathing. 'Green Skirt' spoke next.

"My name is Ginny Ventano. I teach art at Montclair Academy here in Denver. I was at Eddie's that evening also. I can't really add that much to what has already been said, other than to point out that I am obviously a woman, and I saw the same hurt in this man's eyes as well. I heard the rumors going around the bar that others talked about here. This was not a male or female tragedy. This was a *human* tragedy."

Henry waited a few moments, in case she decided to continue. He noticed that she was having difficulty holding back tears, so he nodded to the man next to her.

"My name's Bill Trent. I'm the night clerk at the Las Vegas motel Sasha and her group stayed at. The guys stayed two to a room, and she had her own room. When you see a girl like Sasha, you remember! I can tell you that she did not go with the rest of her group in their van into Vegas that night, Saturday, October 8, when they stayed at my motel. I overheard the guys saying what they wanted to do that night—go to a few casinos. She stayed behind in her own room, I believe, apparently not interested in gambling. They stayed only that one night, so I guess they hit the road again on Sunday. That's all I can say, really. She came through Vegas that weekend, and apparently did not go downtown with the guys she was with."

Henry said, "So that night was obviously a stop on her way to Fresno, since it is west of Denver, right?"

"Yeah, I believe that's where they said they were going."

The next man looked directly into Sasha's eyes as he spoke.

"I am Officer David Fleming of the Colorado State Police. I must say that this is the first time I have ever participated in a therapy session for anyone, but I felt it was important for me to be here because of the experience I had with the man we all apparently agree is completely in love with you, Sasha. I am equally impressed with the ease with which I was made available for this therapy session by my superiors. Someone with very unusual influence obviously thinks that this process is very important. My part of the story is about someone I was going to stop for speeding on the Coal Creek Canyon Road up in the mountains just west of Denver on Tuesday, September 25. By the time I caught up with this vehicle, the driver was no longer behind the wheel of the car, which was parked in a pullout with a beautiful view east toward the city and beyond. The driver turned out to be a man lying on his back on the ground next to the driver's door in some kind of very serious medical or physical difficulty. I resuscitated him and after I was satisfied that he would survive, I called in for an ambulance and started to gather some information. He said his name was Jake Lewis. He told me that he was distraught because he believed that his fiancé had been killed in the Fresno incident. He said he drove too fast up into the mountains to vent his anger at those responsible for the explosion and purge his mind and body of what I thought was a lot of very serious anger and emotional distress, rather than stay home and possibly upset his neighbors with his rage."

Sasha noted the word 'fiancé' as she thought her heart must have skipped a beat as the officer continued.

"I have had a lot of experience with liars in my work, as I suppose you might imagine, but I can tell you with absolute conviction that this man was no liar! I saw the result of his unbridled fury, and in spite of my training felt his emotional pain, and I decided on the spot that getting him some medical help was far more important than giving him a speeding ticket, so I called in for an ambulance."

Sasha finally spoke up, "You're sure he said '*fiancé?*'"

"Yes Ma'am! Positively! He used the word 'fiancé.' Absolutely!"

Oh my God, she thought to herself. *There really is someone!*

The delicate Jennifer Roth, RN, from the Reading Hospital was next.

"My name is Jennifer Roth. I am a registered nurse at the Reading Hospital in Reading, Pennsylvania. This story is getting more and more interesting, the more I hear about it! Since I am obviously from a rather distant geographical location, you may wonder what I have to contribute, but I believe I now fully understand what is going on, and why I was asked to be here. You see, I was on duty when Jake Lewis came to the Reading Hospital to see his mother after we admitted her to emergency care in critical condition from injuries sustained in an awful automobile collision with a tractor-trailer rig north of the city. From what I understand so far, this accident obviously occurred just one day after the Fresno incident, but before Jake had any knowledge of the explosion in Fresno or of Sasha's fate. His mother was unconscious, barely hanging on to life in the intensive care unit, and by all medical knowledge and evidence I am aware of probably could not have heard him but I honestly cannot say with absolute certainty that it would have been impossible. Jake was obviously in significant emotional pain confronted with his mother's critical condition, but he was also obviously very much in love, because he chose to talk to his mother about why he wanted her to live. Since the intensive care unit is not soundproof, I could not avoid overhearing what he was saying to his mother from my nearby station. It was such a heart-rending story that I simply could not ignore it, and I knew I would never forget it. He was coaxing his mother with pure faith and hope to understand the happiness he had found. He told her that he had met the woman he would marry and provide her with beautiful grandchildren. He said her name was Sasha and that she was a singer, and that his mother would love her. He even apologized for the fact that he had met Sasha at a bar, because he knew his mother did not have a high regard for bars. He said to her that the feelings he had for all of the other women he had ever met in his life that he thought he was in love with were insignificant in comparison with the love he felt for Sasha. He said that he did not know whether she could cook, but that it didn't matter anyway. He said that although he didn't have 'the ace and jack of spades,' he was holding 'the ace and jack of hearts,' and was going to 'bet the farm' on Sasha, regardless. That is essentially what I have to offer here—what I would certainly call rare and completely bullet-proof and sincere evidence of a man's most intense and total love for a woman."

Sasha was weeping openly.

Is Jake the lover in my dreams? How could it possibly be anyone else? All of these people are talking about someone named 'Jake!'

Henry was in uncharted waters, but still steering the ship, or so he thought. He concluded that the session was having an important effect far sooner and far more significantly than he had ever expected, but he was inclined to push forward, getting by with the snack food and delaying the planned lunch. Tanya Wilkinson spoke next.

"My name is Tanya Wilkinson, and I live in Fresno. Sasha and I were roommates at Smith College in Northampton, Massachusetts over eight years ago. She called me the day of the explosion, around one-thirty in the afternoon, and wanted to come out and visit, since she had some free time before her singing engagement that evening. I said it would be great to see her again, so she said she would be at my house in about twenty minutes. Almost exactly twenty-five minutes later, she drove up to the house in her van. I invited her into the house and talked her into taking a splash in the pool as we caught up on old times. She confided in me that she had a lover, and had administered to him by herself an extremely serious dose of intense erotic excitement similar to what the two of us did together in college in our sorority house attic to a guy from Yale who we lured out of a mixer."

Sasha interrupted with an innocent quizzical expression, *"I did?"*

The men in the group were all holding their breath, particularly Henry, concerned about what Tanya might say next.

She continued, "You certainly did, Sasha! And you explained quite clearly to me that you had found the love of your life, and were prepared to give up your singing career for this guy! You actually said you met the man you would *marry!*"

Henry stepped in to try to control the increasingly unpredictable Tanya.

"So you can verify that Sasha was at your house at least up to around seven thirty or so, was apparently in a very significant love relationship, and was not yet at the location of the explosion, right?"

"Yes, that's correct."

"Randy, you're next," Henry said, effectively preventing any further potentially 'direct' or 'graphic' comments from Tanya.

"As you may have guessed by now, I am Tanya's husband, and I must say that I also am rather surprised by the ease with which I was given the time to participate in this session. I am a lawyer, and I work for people who equate time with money rather seriously, so I must conclude that someone with major league influence was involved with persuading my superiors that it was important enough for me to attend. With that in mind, all I can do right now is verify the fact that Sasha was at my house until about seven twenty-five or seven-thirty in the evening before the explosion, and that according to my wife, she apparently had a singing engagement at Club One in Fresno that evening. I met her for the first time as I brought my two little girls home from their soccer practice earlier that day. She left our place roughly a half hour before the explosion was reported to have occurred, I believe."

"Thank you," Henry said as he nodded to the next person.

"My name is Ramon Raphael. I am an Emergency Medical Technician with the Fresno Rescue Squad."

With that announcement, everyone in the room focused much more intensely upon him as it became evident that they were all about to hear from someone who was actually at the scene of the explosion or close enough to it to have what could very well have been the last glimpse of Sasha's life.

"I got the emergency alert about the explosion on my pager during my supper and had no difficulty finding the location, because anyone could see the dark smoke rising into the sky from all over the area. As

I tried to drive closer to the explosion, I had to backtrack and find another route, since the street I had turned onto was basically gone at the scene of the explosion. As I looked for another route to get closer to the center of the damage, I came across an overturned GMC Savana van in a bank parking lot near the bulk of the devastation and saw this beautiful lady, Sasha, unconscious and half way out of the driver's side of the vehicle. I examined her quickly for vital signs and any evidence of fractures or bleeding, but found no evidence of broken bones, although she had several bruises, abrasions and cuts. She must have been one *very* tough lady! Her blouse was torn and I covered her up. I could not make a definite determination of her injuries, but she was alive—apparently, just barely alive—so I called in for an ambulance and stayed with her until it arrived. I helped get her out of her overturned vehicle, then onto the stretcher and into the ambulance, and then went on to help another woman nearby, who, unfortunately died . . . right there in front of me."

Sasha slowly rose from her chair and went to Ramon, who stood as she approached, reaching out for him. Everyone in the room was transfixed as the two of them stood together in respectful embrace.

She was crying again, as she whispered in his ear "Thank you! Thank you! Thank you . . . for saving . . . my life!"

Ramon was more than a little flustered in such close proximity to a tall, shapely and beautiful woman, but managed to blurt out, "I . . . I was just doing my job, Sasha."

She kissed his cheek, smiled at him and then hesitated slightly before she turned to go back to her seat. Ramon's face turned cherry red before he sat back down in his seat. Everyone was watching him, smiling in admiration and genuine appreciation. Then one by one, they all stood and clapped for several minutes in tribute to his obvious role in saving Sasha's life.

Doctor Jonathan Caldwell spoke next after everyone stopped applauding and sat down.

"My name is Jonathan Caldwell. I am a physician at Saint Agnes Medical Center in Fresno, where Sasha arrived in that ambulance. I watched over her every day as she barely clung to life in a severe coma for more than two weeks. It was apparent that she had sustained a head injury during the explosion that overturned her vehicle, which is most likely the cause of her recent amnesia. It is further apparent to me from the discussions so far today that the reason no one knew whether she was alive or dead is quite simply that we did not know *who* she was, until after she regained consciousness and could talk. She had no identifying information with her when she arrived, and the EMT crew had absolutely no information about her either. The emergency workers and facilities throughout the city were stretched to the extent that typically thorough searches for identification were not always possible. So when the ambulance personnel looked through her van they did not find anything identifying a woman, although they found registration information for a male, probably one of her backup musicians who all apparently perished in the blast."

"It is now painfully quite obvious to me after having heard all of the prior discussion here that it was during this period of her coma that Jake expected to see her at Eddie's Place for their first reunion. Her comatose condition also explains why she did not answer her phone. First of all she was unconscious, and second, we never found a phone among her personal belongings."

"After one of our nurse's aides eventually discovered that she had regained consciousness and called to inform me of that, I immediately went to her room and talked with her. While speaking with her, I learned that she was a professional vocalist from New York, and concluded that she was the missing woman pictured in all the posters around town and on the internet at that time. I explained to her that she had suffered a relatively severe head injury near the site of the explosion, and that she was taken by ambulance to Saint Agnes Medical Center. She seemed to understand and accept that. When I asked her where her home was, she said Union City, New Jersey. When I asked her what she was doing in Fresno, she said that she didn't know. Although I was definitely concerned about that, we found no other evidence of memory loss beyond what typically occurs in such traumatic situations, which is what she seemed to be experiencing, because we had so little evidence of her life in general, let alone her identity and specific recent personal history."

"All of the area hospitals were quite busy with patients from the disaster area in critical condition on top of their normal workloads. We simply had no context within which to appreciate the extent of her memory loss. She seemed to display essentially normal body function, sensation and balance after she came out of the coma. Her appetite appeared to be normal, and she seemed to be in good spirits, considering what she had apparently suffered through. She showed no *unusual* evidence of confusion or emotional distress. When I asked her where she wanted to go, she said she wanted to go home. When I asked her how she was going to get there, she said she would fly home. I told her I wanted to monitor her for another few days anyway, just to make sure she was healthy enough to do that. I could not discover upon further examination any relapse or other evidence of trauma during that time, and her balance and movements were all completely normal. All of her blood work data came back from the lab within normal ranges, most of her visible wounds were well on their way toward complete healing and her mental, psychological and social functioning appeared to be normal, so I discharged her from the hospital."

"It's a cardinal rule that medical professionals should not become emotionally involved with their patients, but I must admit that I never rooted so very hard for anyone to pull through in my entire professional career as I did for Sasha. For weeks, all I knew about her was that she was beautiful and in critical condition. It seemed so unfair and tragic that such a beautiful young woman was so close to death well before her time. I had absolutely no idea how talented she is until after she recovered, when I finally heard one of the recordings of her voice on the internet search for her. I might add that I thought it was extremely odd—actually amazing and almost like magic—that an overnight FedEx package arrived at the hospital addressed to her the day before I discharged her. We had just discovered who she was only two days prior to that, and yet someone else obviously also knew who and where she was."

"Thank you Doctor Caldwell," Julie said and then looked to the man to his left.

Rob Reynolds was next and last. He played the soprano sax in the 'new' Autumn Dream.

"At first, I really had no idea why I was asked to be here, but I also had an undeniable intuitive feeling that I *should* be here, and now I know why."

"I first met Sasha at the Fat Black Pussy Cat in Manhattan on September 28. I remember the date, because Sasha made a really positive impression on me, and you can see why. We talked a little and soon discovered that we both had musical interests. She said she was a singer, and I told her I played horns of all sorts in college, used to have a band, but was out of work. She said she needed work also, and suggested that we put a group together and see how we sounded. I told her that it would be no problem for me to find the other musicians she wanted. She came across like she knew exactly what she wanted, and asked whether I could play the soprano sax. She was all business. I said, 'no problem' and she smiled a little."

"I got some of my friends together with the other instruments she said she wanted—a keyboard, drums and guitar—at my place the next day. I didn't have a soprano sax right then, so I borrowed one from a friend. After we did our first number together as a group, I was absolutely dumbfounded that she was not working somewhere already! It never even occurred to me that she was suffering from amnesia! Even so, I was not particularly interested in her past, because the presence of her voice and her stunning beauty were all I needed to know. By the time we finished that first song, it was like, '*WHOA!* Where has *this* lady been hiding?' I could tell immediately that the sound of her voice and the soprano sax fit really well, so I decided to switch to the sax as my main instrument from that point on."

He stopped speaking long enough for Henry to conclude he had nothing further to say at that point.

"Well," Henry said, looking around at the group, and ending with a kind look into Sasha's eyes, "I believe this has been a rather thorough presentation of much of what we have been able to learn about what happened to you, Sasha, including or during this period of amnesia. Now, I would like to hear from you about your reactions to what you have heard here, or anything else you may want to say, while your thoughts are fresh."

"Well . . ."

She hesitated, obviously trying to control her emotions, looking down at her hands clasped together on her lap. Everyone else in the room was watching her intently, expecting, wishing or hoping for signs of a breakthrough.

"I . . . I'm a little . . . I'm really overwhelmed . . . right now . . ."

She waited for over a minute, rubbing her arms as if trying to quell a chill.

"I don't remember ever . . . having felt so much intense emotion . . . coming from so many different people within such a relatively short time!"

She was obviously having trouble maintaining her composure, but tried to continue anyway.

"I'm so very appreciative of what all of you have shared with me today about what happened during this hidden period of my life, and what you have tried to do for me here. On the one hand, I feel an enormous relief, like a heavy burden that I didn't even know I had has been lifted from my shoulders, but I also feel a little like a broken doll that has been put back together, but the glue has not hardened yet, and I still have this unresolved emptiness inside me. The doll's hands, arms and legs all work, but the heart . . . is still broken. Before today, I merely had a dream about a lover who had no face, and no identity. Now I have this . . . this vast emptiness in me. I need to meet this man, Jake, who so many of you spoke so eloquently about, but I have mixed feelings. On the one hand, it would be absolutely wonderful if he were the one who possesses my soul and can fill that emptiness in me. On the other hand, if he is not the very special person I hope he is, the man in my dreams . . . if I do not recognize him, then I have great fear that I will . . . that I might die. I'm sorry, but, I am at a desolate crossroad, and I am hopeful but very frightened and anxious . . . all at the same time."

She stopped talking and bit her lower lip for several seconds. Then she inhaled deeply, filling her lungs for several moments, and then exhaled slowly, trying to maintain control of her emotions, while most of the group inhaled and held their breath as if they were one organism suspended in apprehension. After a brief pause, she continued.

"I cannot go backward after having heard all of your beautiful thoughts and very personal experiences about the part of my life that was missing, and yet I do not really feel completely 'put back together' yet."

Henry was concentrating on her with unaccustomed focus, as was everyone else in the room, and took special note of her words '*was missing.*' However, he knew the process was far from complete. She sat quietly, struggling to hold back her tears, but they streamed slowly down her cheeks anyway.

Henry and Julie looked directly into each other's eyes, and the two of them registered identical personal and professional fear about Sasha's condition and the enormous risk they had taken. The oblique reference to dying caught them by surprise. Henry's mind was running in overdrive, and Julie was racing through recollections of her professional experience and intuition from her very first days of psychotherapy, case by case, all the way to the present, trying to think of a plan or technique that could work under such enormous stress. They both looked at Sasha. Henry would never forgive himself if he pushed her over the edge, never to regain her life, even to the apparently lightly damaged extent she had been able to live with since the Fresno incident. He felt he was in the worst professional uncertainty of his career, believing on the one hand that he would eventually be successful, but on the other hand, he was also intensely aware that he had no immediate traction. He was not accustomed to this kind of therapeutic '180-degree turn.'

Everyone in the group was acting as though he sensed alarm bells going off somewhere, but no one was willing to speak up in front of the entire group. No one apparently had a specific clear thought to share in public. They all just started whispering to the person in the next seat to the left or right. Henry and Julie simultaneously agreed out of almost convenient desperation that it was time for lunch.

Julie addressed the group with controlled, veiled urgency.

"OK, everyone! I think we all should take a break now, have some lunch and then resume our discussions in half an hour from now."

She wanted a break, but without losing the essential continuity of the session. She felt forced to make the decision. The emotional engines in the room had been 'red-lining' for far too long to justify continuing at the recent intensity without a break.

Then a rush of increased whispering and low voices spread throughout the group. Julie noticed that people were not dispersing, as she would have expected. They still acted curiously like one organism, almost like a school of fish in the ocean, staying rather close to each other. They were constantly whispering and exchanging facial expressions, and nodding with apparent conviction or agreement about something. She had never seen anything like it in her entire professional career, even outside of a therapy session.

Usually a group of almost complete strangers like this might assemble in separate groups of two or three, particularly where they may have had some prior association, like the employees at Eddie's Place or the recording studio. Some would go off to be alone and not interact with anyone else, maybe as might be expected of the Colorado State Policeman, but the behavior she was witnessing was quite different. *Every* person in the group was within arm's reach of at least two others from minute to minute, and they were all essentially mimicking what struck her as 'bee hive' activity as everyone appeared to try to communicate with every other person in the group. Something was 'brewing' and she did not know what it was, and that bothered her, both personally and professionally.

Lunch arrived within seven minutes, and the 'bee hive activity' eventually dispersed somewhat into the more formal, but still relatively intimate grouping of the chairs they had been sitting in during the presentation of experiences. Henry was huddling with Julie and Sasha, taking advantage of the opportunity to relax somewhat, or at least try to, and satisfy his need for food and liquids. Sasha let out a huge sigh, and addressed Henry and Julie quietly with a very gentle, determined voice, but with obvious halting effort.

"I want . . . Jake Lewis . . . here in this room . . . as soon as possible. Someone wanted . . . this piano here . . . today. It didn't just . . . roll in here . . . all by itself. I admit . . . that I am very curious . . . about this man . . . everyone has identified . . . as Jake Lewis. I believe in my heart . . . that if we had . . . a musical connection once . . . then it is possible . . . that it still exists . . . or is still available within . . . within me to recover . . . under the right circumstances. If . . . If your theory is correct . . . about massive stimulation . . . of my memory capacity . . . from all of these people . . . with all their stories . . . and feelings they talked about . . . as a way to reestablish connections . . . in my memory gap, then I . . . I would have to believe . . . that further stimulation . . . of my 'musical self' by . . . by someone more familiar with . . . with that part of me . . . could only help . . . achieve the ultimate goal. That may not . . . may not be psychologically correct . . . but it is . . . it is what I believe."

Henry was quite relieved to hear her say that and responded with the unadorned truth. He quite plainly had no other choice either personally or professionally.

"Sasha, you are absolutely right! That piano *is* here for a reason. I was going to have Jake come and play for all of us, but for you in particular as part of the therapy process. The fact that you just expressed the desire to have him here tells me we are on the right track. He is here in this hotel, and will be right here in this room shortly after I call him, but I'm not quite ready to do that right now. I want to make sure I have gotten everything from the group that I can get at this stage before I take that next and very important step."

"OK, but he *will* be here . . . right?" she said with an almost child-like request for assurance and hope.

"Yes, Sasha. He *will* be here. *I promise! You have my word!*"

After about thirty seconds of silence, Sasha started softly humming the tune that Jake played for her that first night at Eddie's Place, and then she started actually singing the words she put to his music. She was in effect conducting her own therapy with music. The room became absolutely still with the exception of her beautiful voice. Everyone froze in place and looked at her in complete and absolute astonishment. There was clearly nothing wrong with that part of her memory. She knew the music, and she knew the words. Those who had heard her sing before divided their attention with deliberate concentrated effort between watching Sasha and watching those who they knew were hearing her for the very first time, knowing the kind of rare aural thrill they must be experiencing.

Marie looked over at Ramon, who swallowed hard, thinking back to how vulnerable and still she was when he first saw her, in contrast to this beautiful live person actually singing with such an unbelievable voice. She noticed that Jennifer Roth was transfixed, yet smiling in absolute delight. She saw Randy Wilkinson, the lawyer, just gaping openly at Sasha. He was having trouble reconciling the profound emotional sensitivity he was hearing now with his memory of her nearly naked and absolutely luscious female figure dripping pool water on his patio that afternoon before the explosion.

Eddie glanced at the Colorado state trooper, who actually had tears in his eyes, now understanding so much more of the pain he had witnessed in Jake's behavior that night high in the Rocky Mountains just west of Denver. He watched Doctor Jonathan Caldwell unabashedly staring at Sasha with his jaw hanging down, considering the enormous contrast between what he remembered as basically a comatose unknown woman in need of constant medical observation and this very exciting, vibrant and remarkably talented young woman.

Alex Thornton saw Gloria Pittman dabbing her eyes with tissue. She was remembering her first impression of Sasha in the elevator, thinking she was a prostitute and how terribly and *completely wrong* she was. He noticed that her husband Jeremy was simply glowing with obvious delight from the sound of Sasha's voice, and undoubtedly her physical beauty, thinking that somehow, he had been right about Sasha all along.

Jimmy Jones just gaped at her.

Then someone knocked at the door. Julie got up and went quietly to the door, opened it just a few inches and saw Kenny obviously breathing hard from what had to be an urgent rush to get to the therapy session.

"Julie, you really must see this!" he said in a controlled breathless, but hushed voice, realizing that he might be interrupting something important. His look of victorious accomplishment hit her full force as she carefully entered the hallway and left the therapy session as inconspicuously as possible and closed the door quietly behind her.

"See *what*, Kenny?"

"One of my people in Fresno did some extra detective work, and manufactured an opportunity to comb through that Savana van Sasha was diving when the explosion knocked it over, and found this wedged underneath the dashboard! He called last evening to tell me he had sent it to the hotel via Federal Express and that I should be expecting it today. I picked it up at the front desk just a few minutes ago. It's Sasha's cell phone!"

Kenny's obvious enthusiasm started to fan Julie's embers of realization rapidly into a full fire of understanding what this could do to help the therapy.

"Are you *sure* it's hers?"

"Yes! Absolutely! Just page through the voicemail list. What do you see?"

"I see one phone number. So . . . ?"

"What's the area code?"

"303." Julie still could not make the relevant connection.

"What's the time and date?"

"Four fifty p.m. September 17, 2007."

"303, Julie, happens to be one of two area codes for Denver, Colorado! And that is about the time Jake was to meet her at Eddie's, given the one hour time difference, and September 17 was the first Monday after the explosion in Fresno! I will bet heavily that there is a message from Jake hiding behind that number. It *is* Jake's phone number. I checked—303-525-6101. The immediate challenge we face is that only Sasha knows how to access her messages—hopefully she still remembers that—and we don't know what that message is, or even whether there is a message. It might be just a hang-up. I would bet, however, that there *is* a message! What we *do* know is that Jake called her. I believe we should let her listen to that message!"

"I agree. Give me the phone, please, and go inside and tell Henry to come out here right away. I want you to stay inside and make any excuses you believe are necessary until we return, hopefully in less than a minute or two. I don't want to draw any attention to this inside right now. Henry and I need to come to the same understanding and agreement before we do anything with the phone."

"Will do!"

Kenny did as she told him, and a few moments later Henry slipped through a minimal opening of the door into the hallway as quietly as possible and quickly closed the door behind him, leaving Kenny with their guests, who were still thoroughly transfixed under the spell of Sasha's captivating voice. Kenny was dumbfounded. He could see that no excuses were necessary, because everyone was concentrating upon Sasha. He was rapidly appreciating much more of the whole drama, as her voice enveloped and soothed him so completely. He now understood with complete conviction what all of his prior understanding of this incredible story was all about. This was the first time Kenny had seen Sasha in person. The actual sight of her explained a lot more, in addition to just having heard her very unusual and beautiful voice for the first time, about why Joe had been so passionate at the meeting with Duke in Maryland, and why Duke would put forth so much effort and expense.

Out in the hall, Henry quickly asked, "What's going on, Julie?"

"Look! One of Kenny's people found Sasha's phone, and it has a message on it that we believe is from Jake on that Monday evening they were to meet at Eddie's Place. We need to agree right now about whether to let Sasha have the phone and access that message!"

He gushed as quietly as possible, "Jesus! That's wonderful! *I can't believe it!* This firmly puts some kind of relationship with Jake within the timeframe of her memory loss. She will *have* to *see* that! She won't be able to avoid the connection!"

A look of apprehension fell over her face as she said, "Wait a minute, Henry! I just thought of something. How do we know that she will remember that it's her phone or how to access the message?"

Henry was stunned for just a second, but quickly recovered.

"Well . . ." He was stalling. "We'll just *tell* her it's her phone, because we believe it is. Kenny *said* it was her phone. We have to accept that, and then do whatever is necessary to convince her that it really is *her* phone. If she doesn't remember her message access routine, then we'll go directly to the phone company and do whatever is necessary to get that message. I'm sure that Kenny can do that if his people could find the phone in the first place! And if he can't then I'm sure either Joe or Duke *certainly* can!"

He had already experienced a dose of Joe's 'persuasion' techniques, so he had no doubt that Joe could get that information. Julie was regaining her hope again, and she agreed with him.

"We've gone so far with this Julie that I want to try everything that even remotely *smells* like it will help Sasha! Let's do it!"

"OK! Let's do it!" she repeated with renewed conviction.

They entered the room again quietly and as inconspicuously as possible as Sasha was apparently just ending her song. They noticed the array of emotions evident in the faces of all the people around the room. They understood immediately, as they sustained an internal emotional 'double-take' at the richness and clarity of the last part of her impromptu performance. About fifteen seconds after her voice fell silent, they all stood and applauded with smiles of genuine appreciation. After they all settled down and returned to their seats, Henry was just getting ready to make an announcement about the cell phone, which he had hidden in his pocket. Then Gloria Pittman stood up with the look of determination from a woman who had seen almost everything in this world and was not the least bit shy about saying what was on her mind.

"Doctor Winslow—both of you—we had been talking among ourselves earlier, and have come to the conclusion that it is time for Jake Lewis to make an appearance, and play that piano. We've figured out why it's here, and we understand very well what you are trying to do here."

She looked around her for reaffirmation of what she said they had all collectively agreed upon, and received nods of decisive agreement from each and every one of them. Henry was a little surprised, because he had never read or heard about a therapy session guided by people other than the therapist and the patient, but then the total immersion technique he was trying to use with so many people had never been used before either. It was a risk in the process that he would have to remember. This was the closest thing to 'mutiny' that he had ever experienced, and enriched his understanding of the concept. Fortunately, what they wanted was consistent with his therapeutic game plan in the first place. However, he was not accustomed to losing control of his own therapy session.

"Thank you, Gloria, for your suggestion, and all of you for your agreement. I was about to get to that, but something unanticipated has just come up."

He was trying to re-characterize her little speech and at least maintain or reestablish some appearance of control, and gestured to indicate that they should take their seats. They were all very curious, watching him intently, particularly Sasha, as they all sat down again, wondering as one what could possibly have trumped their unusually insightful conclusion. He looked at Sasha with renewed faith in his conviction that the therapy would eventually succeed, and smiled at her.

"Sasha, we have just recovered your cell phone that was apparently lost on the day of the Fresno incident."

The group inhaled as one in an audible expression of genuine surprise, as they all exchanged looks of anticipation, curiosity and hope with a new flurry of unintelligible murmurs and whispers among each other, and then quickly quieted down and looked at Henry.

"Only one message is identified in your phone message menu, and we would like you to listen to that message. If you would like to have some privacy for that, Julie will take you to another room."

Sasha looked at him with an intense mixed expression of surprise, curiosity and hope, and held out her right hand as Henry reached in his pocket, retrieved the cell phone and gently handed it to her with a kind expression on his face and a genuine smile of encouragement. She obviously recognized it as her phone, and did not feel the need for privacy, because she stood up and immediately opened the phone to its operating position. She tried to temper her growing curiosity and anxiety by pacing while she pressed the keys necessary to retrieve her messages. Her cell phone was such an integral part of her everyday life that it apparently was not hidden by her amnesia. She quickly found her message function and then pressed the key sequence to retrieve the only message there, then tilted her head while she combed her hair away from her ear with the fingers of her other hand and looked up without focus into nowhere. They all riveted their attention upon her eyes when she was pacing in a direction that allowed them to see her face, searching for even a small sign of promise or hope. Randy appreciated the opportunity to admire her upright form again, even though she was not 'dressed to kill.' She stopped pacing suddenly, gently closed the phone and turned around to face Henry with tears streaming down her face. Everyone was watching her intently, waiting for her to speak and break the suspense. She waited for a few moments to compose herself, obviously with some difficulty, and then turned toward the group.

"There was a . . . a voice message. It was from Jake, calling from . . . from Eddie's Place at ten 'til six . . . telling me he was getting a little worried . . . and asked me to call him. I now firmly believe that Jake . . . has been an important person . . . in my life . . . but oddly enough, I don't . . . feel that I really . . . know him personally."

Henry noticed that everyone in the group was looking straight at him, as if telling him it was time for Jake to appear. He turned to Sasha.

"Sasha, would you like to call Jake and ask him to come in here to play for us?"

He thought of doing it himself as he had previously planned to do, but at the last minute thought that Sasha would benefit from making the call herself if she wanted to. It was *her* life he and Julie were trying to put back together, and he wanted her to have more and more control over it, rather than do things for her that she could and should do for herself.

"Yes, actually . . . I would."

Gloria Pittman smiled immediately, as if she knew something the others did not know, and surreptitiously clasped her hands together in front of her chest as if she were about to pray. All she had that the others did not have, was a generous dose of wisdom-enhanced female intuition. It comes with age.

Sasha pressed the redial button that held in memory the last phone number registered as an incoming call, flicked her beautiful silky hair away from her ear and began to pace again. Max Gentry quietly smacked his right fist into his left hand and whispered to himself, "Yes!" like he might have been at a baseball game with the bases loaded in the bottom of the ninth inning and his team behind by three runs, watching a fly ball hit by his favorite player about to sail over the center field wall.

"Jake? This is Sasha . . . I want you to come to the conference room where the piano is and play for me. Will you do that please?"

"Yes, Sasha, I will. I'll be there in just one minute!"

He closed his cell phone, dashed out of the internet room, mentally did about a dozen cartwheels and hurried recklessly like a lovesick teenager down to the conference room, ignoring several stares of wonder, surprise or concern from a few hotel patrons along the way. He arrived within one minute, and knocked on the door. Kenny was closest to the door, and opened it, welcoming Jake with a handshake and a genuinely friendly smile while simultaneously firmly clasping his upper right arm.

"Hi Jake! It's good to see you again! Come on in!"

Jake recognized several of the people with a cursory glance around the room as he stepped farther into the room, but he stopped cold when he saw Sasha. She turned toward him and brightened somewhat, but rather slowly, as she appeared to recognize him.

"You're the man I met after the show at Club 46 in Manhattan recently," she said with only mild evident surprise. "You said you missed me. I remember that."

Henry immediately noted that statement as a rough approximation of the most recent end of her memory gap. However, there was still no recognition of a 'long lost lover' in her tone, just like that night at Club 46, and no invitation to embrace. Henry looked directly into Jake's eyes as Jake approached and clearly closed his eyes and moved his head twice from side to side, signaling to Jake not to embrace Sasha or do anything other than what they had specifically discussed and agreed to. He was simply to play the piano as a way of opening up the possible connection between her blank 'personal' memory and her 'musical' memory, and Henry and Julie would deal with her response. Sasha would embrace him when and if she was ready, and not one second before.

Emotionally, Jake had one foot on the accelerator pedal and the other on the brake at the same time, simultaneously trying to steer his emotions and keep them in balance on a winding slick country road. He was mentally grinding gears, leaking oil and transmission fluid and burning rubber all at the same time, while pushing his emotional tachometer past the red line in his overwhelmingly intense desire to hold Sasha in his arms again. Henry knew Jake would be tempted to go to Sasha for an embrace and probably try to kiss her, so he continued to guide Jake with his demeanor, walking toward the piano between him and Sasha. He held his hand out as if inviting him to sit on the piano bench, effectively blocking a potential 'rush over right tackle' by Jake to get to Sasha. As he approached Jake more closely, he shook his hand very firmly, leaned closer to him and whispered firmly as if he were an accomplished ventriloquist.

"Keep it under control, cowboy!"

Jake immediately summoned more discipline than he was born with or learned in his twenty-nine years, and chose the expected path, just barely overcoming raw emotion. He sat on the piano bench and made himself as comfortable as possible under the emotionally severely strenuous circumstances. Everyone else in the room found a seat as the invited guests all looked around at each other again with expressions of solidarity, purpose, anticipation, wonder and hope. Not one of them readily would have left for the rest room at this point, even if the body demanded it. They were determined to absorb every instant of this amazing real-life adventurous drama in which they all had created such an intensely personal stake. Oddly enough, Sasha was the only person in the room who had ever heard Jake play a piano besides Rocky, Tommy, Eddie and Alex, and yet she was the only one who could not remember that or much of anything else about Jake beyond that last brief encounter at Club 46.

He put his hands on the keyboard, searching for a starting phrase or melody, but he just was not ready. Nothing was coming to him. He was emotionally too wound up. The room was like a theater where the lights had already dimmed and the pre-performance hubbub of the audience had diminished to utter silence and anticipation, but the curtain was not going up when it should have. Jeremy Pittman clasped his hands together and started to pray. Ramon crossed his chest and tried to will Jake to find the right keys. Patrol Officer Fleming took a deep breath and leaned forward on his seat with his elbows on his knees. Max was mentally chanting, *Go Jake . . . Go Jake . . . Go Jake . . .*

Sasha sensed his difficulty, and suddenly arose gracefully from her chair, shot a facial expression toward Henry that meant '*I'll handle this,*' and walked up behind Jake and innocently leaned into his back while reaching over his shoulder to touch the keyboard. She played the first seven-note phrase of the introduction to the song she had just sung. Since Jake had not been in the room, and since almost everyone else had just heard the song for the very first time, this would be the most crucial test of whether Jake was indeed the man in her dreams if he could play that same music. She already suspected that this was going to be the ultimate showdown, but she was ready for a final resolution to her newfound fear and anxiety, one way or another. Jake was still electrified by the very familiar feel of her breasts pressing into his back as she played the same six keys. He knew what to do. He continued the melody, adding the proper harmony to the best of his memory. No one would be able to know the difference if it was not *exactly* the same as he played that first night on Eddie's Yamaha, or to which Sasha had just sung the melody. It was important only to get the song right enough to prove to her that he was indeed her lover. He had the melody down pat. He knew that much. No one else in the whole world could offer her that kind of solid proof. No one else could have just walked into that room and played the music to the song he could not know that she had just sung in front of everyone else in the room. Each of them knew this could be the deciding act, the solution, the restoration of Sasha's memory, her life, and her future . . . their future.

If ever he was required to repeat an improvisation exactly, this was the time. It was the first time in his life that his music would actually *determine* his fate. Sasha's heart started to race in anticipation as she returned to her seat and faced toward Jake. His heart was racing as well. The music was coming back to him quickly, but he was playing it with a new passion and hope. He was increasingly comfortable and gaining confidence as he focused on the music, losing awareness of everyone else in the room except Sasha. After the introductory phrase, she knew he was starting with, Sasha stood up again and went to the piano beside Jake, put her hands on his shoulders and started singing the words as only she could. They were, after all, *her* words, coming from *her* memory and from *her* heart.

Everyone else in the room was spellbound and scarcely breathing. The suspenseful attention could have been like watching Tiger Woods try to sink a sixty-foot putt on the 18th green for a championship win. They were enduring the almost agonizing microsecond-by-microsecond, heartbeat by heartbeat actual pace of reality, unable to move or leave, not wanting to blink, imprisoned by the present and oblivious to all but the drama unfolding before them, and indeed within them. All human biological functions in the room seemed to cease in deference to the demands of the mind and the heart. The atmosphere in the room was as electric as one might imagine at a horse race where everyone's favorite 'come-from-behind' horse was just now in the lead by a nose for the first time after having been behind by ten lengths since the start of the race. Jake had only to continue, now with the potential to pull away with only half a lap to go to the finish line and victory!

Jake and Sasha ended their impromptu performance as if they had rehearsed it 100 times. The final vibrations of the piano and the gentleness of Sasha's voice simultaneously faded into complete silence. No one in the room moved or dared to make a sound for the next twenty seconds.

Jake was the first one to move. He stood up and turned around to face her, looking into her eyes. With renewed resolve, he was determined to let her make the first move as he promised Henry he would, if indeed she was even so inclined. He summoned every ounce of discipline and self-control within him with the determination of a lifetime. He wanted, indeed *had* to know that way anyway. After several very long and agonizing seconds, she slowly began to smile at him the way he remembered from that first night in the hotel as she stepped toward him, and then leaned closer and gently pressed her lips against his, reached around him and held him the way he remembered. He knew. He wrapped his arms around her with unrestrained passion and held her tightly. Everyone else in the room suddenly burst into applause, stood up and cheered. Henry and Julie looked at each other, almost astonished, wondering whether it was truly over, whether they had succeeded in restoring Sasha's memory. Only Sasha would really know for sure, but her behavior and the collective wisdom of the group appeared to offer the maximum proof possible.

Henry eventually found a proper opportunity to speak after what seemed like more than five minutes of continuous joyful applause and cheering, and addressed everyone in the room.

"I think it's rather obvious that we can adjourn for the day, but I would like all of you to stay at the hotel this evening, get some rest and be prepared for one more session tomorrow morning in this same room for about an hour or two. I think we all need some time to let this day settle into perspective. I hope you all understand that this has been an experimental technique. Because no one has any experience with what the outcome of such an intensive session should be, I believe it would be wise to take a step back and think through everything we have experienced, said and done here today. We will discuss our thoughts and feelings tomorrow morning after breakfast when everyone has been refreshed with nourishment, a good night's sleep and the advantage of perhaps some added reflection. There are no guarantees in life, especially in therapy sessions, let alone experimental ones like this. We will not know how successful our efforts have been today until they have withstood the test of time. That is the only way I know how to assess the value or effectiveness of therapy. I believe we have all done our best so far, and there is no reason whatsoever for any of us not to take at least some measure of satisfaction from today's experience. Julie and I want to thank you all for your generous and sincere assistance in this relatively daring effort today, and look forward to working with you all again tomorrow morning in this room at nine o'clock."

With that, Henry dismissed the group, but he knew that the therapy was not really over. He was satisfied that he could now actually initiate the next part of the experimental therapy technique. He went to the corner of the room to a telephone on a small table, lifted the receiver to his ear and dialed '0' for the front desk. It took less than a minute for him to convey his intentions, and then he replaced the receiver and turned to walk back to Julie as if nothing had happened.

He and Julie joined hands between them, face to face, as she said to him, "I hope the next part of the therapy works as well as the first part appears to have worked."

She could sense his exhaustion and saw the intense anxiety in her husband's eyes. He had been sailing successfully in uncharted waters, and did not know how long his 'luck' would hold out, but they had agreed upon a plan, and they would see it through until there was nothing else they could do.

That is how we all face even the simplest uncertainties of the future every day, Henry thought to himself.

That evening the whole group ate in the hotel's premier dining room, getting to know each other a little better and sharing their thoughts about the therapy session so far. Although they arrived and departed at different times throughout the late afternoon and early evening, they mingled with one another, moving from one table to another, pulling up empty adjacent chairs and making more room where necessary, even though they finished eating at the table where they started. From an outsider's perspective, it could have been some kind of small wedding reception, but without all the decorations and an orchestra or band. One couple in particular seemed to be the focus of much of the activity as people seemed to go to their table and sit for a while, and when they left, other people were right there waiting for their turn to sit and talk for a while.

Then a cute little girl with a long blonde pony tail held in place with a white bow, wearing a bright blue dress and what appeared to be brand new white shoes walked up to their table. She could not have been more than six years old, but brazenly sat down in an empty chair, just as she had seen so many other people do during the last twenty minutes or so. Jake and Sasha looked at her with some surprise and curiosity, since they had no idea who she was or where she had come from. She had simply been observing the periodic parade of people to this particular table from the lobby on the other side of the room and decided to go see for herself what all the excitement was about.

She looked Sasha directly in the eye and blurted out with all of the innocent sincerity of a young child momentarily away from her parents' supervision, "You're very pretty. Are you a movie star?"

Sasha adapted instantly to the unusual interruption and looked at the little girl with a warm and adoring smile, and said gently with obvious sincerity, "No, honey, I'm not a movie star."

"Well, you *look* like a movie star! May I please have your autograph?"

Jake was struggling with great effort against the urge to laugh as he reached into his coat pocket for his pen and casually handed it to Sasha looking directly into her eyes with a broad grin on his face.

Sasha took the little piece of paper the little girl offered her, and wrote 'Sasha Chancellor' on it and handed the paper back to her. The little girl looked innocently at Jake and appeared to study him for a few seconds with a quizzical expression on her face, and then looked back to Sasha.

"Who's he?"

Jake was almost ready to explode with laughter, but wisely kept a lid on it.

"He's . . . he's . . . ummm . . . well, he's my . . . boyfriend."

"Oh."

Jake's building urge to laugh dissolved instantly in the utter joy of Sasha's admission in simple terms that even a child could understand, even though he realized that she was dueling wits with a six-year-old.

Then, apparently out of nowhere, a woman who was obviously the girl's mother hurried over to the table.

"Oh, I'm so sorry! Has she been bothering you?"

Jake said, "No, actually, she has been extremely helpful!"

The woman gave Jake a strange look, took her daughter's hand and said, "Come on honey, we must leave now."

Then she looked apologetically at Sasha and Jake as she turned to leave. They both smiled at the woman and her daughter as they walked through the dining room and into the main hallway. Within a few more minutes, Jake and Sasha retired to the main lobby and sat on a large leather sofa in a secluded corner. Sasha was exhausted, and leaned into Jake, putting her head on his shoulder. He was afraid he might lose his composure as he felt the delightful pressure of her female contour against his arm, but put some effort into remaining on an even keel. She closed her eyes, and within two minutes, was fast asleep.

After the day had long since given way to darkness, Jake was wrestling with the possibility of spending the night with Sasha in her room, but he thought it would actually be best to hold off for a while, maybe days, but he feared a complete 'psychosexual Chernobyl' if he had to wait weeks for her intimate attention. Given his memory of how many times she acted as though she could practically read his mind, he fought off even his current thoughts out of respect for even the remotest possibility that she was 'reading him.' He was determined not to do anything to damage or hinder what he had seen as very good progress during his presence at the therapy session. If this was as close as he was going to get to her this evening, he decided it would be enough. It was certainly better than nothing! However, his reluctance to change positions to be more comfortable was giving way to the very real and growing necessity of restoring the flow of blood to his arm, which was beginning to tingle and 'fall asleep.' He remembered that he had yet to pick up his room key at the front desk and very gently awakened Sasha.

"Sasha? Sasha, I need to pick up my room key. Will you wait here a few minutes while I go to the front desk?"

"OK," she said sleepily with her eyes closed. "I'm not going anywhere tonight."

"I'll be right back," he said.

He reluctantly left her on the couch and strode across the almost empty large lobby to the main desk on the far side, as the evening clerk noticed his approach.

"Good evening, sir! How may I help you?"

"My name is Jake Lewis. I would like to have my room key, please."

The clerk said, "OK," and retrieved a plastic card from a drawer under the counter and typed several commands on his computer keyboard while he stared at the monitor.

After verifying Jake's registration, he placed the card in an electronic reader, which also recorded on the card all of the relevant information for unlocking the electronic room lock and capturing the charges for any services throughout the hotel.

He then retrieved the card from the reader, handed it to Jake and announced with a smile, "Room 614."

Jake looked at the clerk in disbelief as his throat instantly went dry and he felt the blood drain from his face as his heartbeat started racing.

"Is something wrong, Mr. Lewis? Are you OK? You look rather pale."

"No! I mean yes! I mean . . . are you *sure* this is the right room?"

"Sure am, Mr. Lewis!" he said in veiled bewilderment with a blank expression on his face.

Jake's mind lurched into high gear, as he pondered the whole concept of coincidence and fate, but he shook it off after a few moments and said, "Thank you," as he felt his composure returning.

At least I could have some pleasant memories tonight, he thought to himself.

He returned to the couch on the far side of the lobby to discover that Sasha was already sitting up and awake. She stood up as he approached her, and the two of them walked to the elevator bank side by side but not holding hands. She did not offer, and Jake did not want to risk even the slightest possibility of some kind of rejection by reaching for hers if she was not ready. Maybe she was just tired. He reached for the elevator button instead, still thinking about this latest room 'coincidence' and wondering about the permanence or durability of what appeared to be her long-awaited acceptance of him in the therapy room. They waited silently for the elevator to return to the lobby. The doors parted quietly, and they entered the elevator, stepped to the rear and both leaned against the back wall forgetting to select a floor destination, and silently stared at the floor numbers above the door for a few moments. The door had not closed yet when Gloria and Jeremy Pittman suddenly entered the elevator and looked at them with surprise.

"Well! Good evening!" Jeremy gushed.

"Well, hello there! What a coincidence!" Gloria added pleasantly.

"Yes, it is indeed!" Sasha responded.

Yes, it is indeed? Jake's mind was basically nearing a 'short circuit' as he smiled politely, wondering whether he had outwardly betrayed his reaction.

This is not possible! I don't believe what's happening here! This can't be part of the therapy! Can it? No way! Henry's good, but he's not a magician! Jesus! Does she know what's happening here? Oh My God! Does she remember?

The doors had stayed open because all four of them had neglected to press a floor destination button on the interior control panel while they were exchanging pleasantries. Jake's brain was overloaded with analysis against emotion as he recognized increasing similarities to their first night together. No one pressed a button!

The doors finally closed slowly after Gloria pressed '6.' She turned to them and said effusively, "Your performance today was just *heavenly,* both of you!"

She pressed the '6' button! Heavenly?

Jake responded, "Thank you, Gloria," just to see whether his voice still worked, since his brain was absolutely sizzling with the real meaning of Yogi Berra's uniquely famous statement, '*This is déjà vu all over again!*'

They all exited the elevator at the sixth floor. Jeremy and Gloria both said, "Good night" to Sasha and Jake as they walked in the opposite direction down the hall from Sasha and Jake, who echoed "Good night!"

Sasha laced her arms around Jake's right arm as she walked close by his side down the plush hallway. Jake was still not sure what was going on. He knew that 614 was the next room on the right. He did not know whether she was going to visit with him in his room for a while, stay all night, or kiss him good night and continue to some other room on the sixth floor, go back to the elevator, or just go to another room without a kiss, or shake his hand, or what! However, he still did not believe he should make the first move. He was back in the pinball machine, not knowing where the next '*ka-ching*' of reward or '*buzz*' of disappointment would come from, bracing for the next possible emotionally propelling '*whack*' from a flipper.

They arrived at room 614, and Sasha got her key card out of her purse, much to Jake's profound astonishment, and inserted it in the reader in one swift and smooth motion. Henry had specifically instructed the hotel manager before the beginning of the therapy session to be prepared to provide both Sasha and Jake with key cards for the same room on the sixth floor, room 614. He had called the front desk to confirm that decision after the first session.

She said softly, "Ladies and gentlemen, start your engines!" looking at the lock light as it changed from red to green, knowing that Jake could hear her. Then she turned to him, looked deep into his eyes and said point-blank in her most inviting and sensuous manner, "Heaven is on the sixth floor, Jake" as she pushed the door open.

Jake just barely sustained all three psychological 'punches' in rapid 'rope-a-dope' manner. First, *her* key operated the lock to room 614, the *same* room he had been given. Second, she actually expressed verbally *his thoughts* from that wonderful and unforgettable first night together, '*Ladies and gentlemen, start your engines.*' Third, she repeated (remembered?) *her own* special words from that night: '*Heaven is on the sixth floor.*'

He knew she was back. *All* of her, including her memory and the part of him that she unwittingly harbored in lost memory for far, far too long, was now available to him. She had deliberately calculated the most convincing way of confessing her love for him, proving to him that she was finally whole, that she knew the man in her recurring dream. Jake just let himself go. He embraced her and kissed her lips gently, nibbling them tenderly, and she responded eagerly. They both succumbed immediately to their accelerating reflexive need for more oxygen, as they started breathing heavily, quickly giving in to unbridled passion and tearing at each other's clothes as the reservoir of pent-up emotion and desire cascaded out of each of them. Both of their faces were wet with the ultimate joy of the victory, of restoration, of being reunited, and of the most complete love either of them had ever known.

CHAPTER 71

Saturday, October 27, 2007
Denver, Colorado

Jake woke up first. It was six forty-eight. Sasha was still sleeping soundly. He slithered carefully out of his side of the king-size bed, found his jacket on the floor, then took the ring out of his pocket and quietly slipped back into the bed without waking her. He lay there on his back, just waiting for her to wake up on her own. He wanted her to know he could plan a few tricks as well. Within a few minutes, she stretched and sighed while turning to him with eagerness in her eyes, basking with ultimate pleasure and satisfaction in her renewed sense of self.

"Good morning!" he said brightly. "Did you sleep well?"

She just laughed, as she slid her right thigh over his abdomen and patiently encouraged his inevitable reaction. When she knew he was ready, she drew herself over him and enveloped him, looking down at him with her disheveled beautiful hair flowing down over her face. She leaned forward and brushed his face with her hair. Within a surprisingly short period she stiffened somewhat and shuddered over him, letting out an urgent series of high-pitched moans for several seconds, relaxed, and then smiled, knowing Jake had yet to finish.

"Give me your hands," he said, smiling up at her.

She looked quizzically at him with the beginnings of a smile, but innocently complied without hesitation. Jake gently took her left hand in his and deftly slipped the expensive reset diamond on her ring finger as if he had practiced the move for days. He was simply lucky, in more ways than this. The ring appeared to fit perfectly. She sat motionless on him, staring at the surprisingly large, brilliant diamond for several seconds longer than long enough.

"Is that a question?" she asked seriously, subtly taking a deep breath, as she focused her beautiful clear eyes on his with urgent expectation.

She wanted to hear him say the words that she longed to hear from him and no one else.

"Will you marry me?" he said after several seconds of contrived suspense.

"Yes! Yes, Jake! I *will* marry you, and love you for the rest of my life!"

She then made *absolutely* sure he was completely satiated and relaxed. They lay together for several minutes, quietly enjoying the most peaceful moments of the 'therapy.' Jake mulled over the perfectly astounding brilliance of what had to be Henry and Julie's 'experimental' therapeutic plan. Within seconds, he started laughing uncontrollably.

"What's so funny?" she asked, somewhat unsure of why he was laughing so hard.

"Nothing's funny, Sasha. I'm just so happy that I have absolutely no control over myself! I can honestly say I have never been happier in my entire life!"

He then told her the amazing story of the history of the diamond as he understood it, so she would have just that much more appreciation of how special it was to him and therefore how special it would be to her as well.

They playfully prepared for the day with a quick shower together, got dressed and went downstairs to have breakfast in one of the small restaurants in the hotel before going to the meeting room for the second day of the therapy session. During breakfast, they talked about their future, where they wanted to live, what plans Sasha would make in her singing career, and what Jake would want to do for a living. He had not told her of his recent financial security yet, however. He wanted to keep that for later. For the time being, he just wanted to know that she cared for him as a human being, as a musician, and as a man. She also had not informed Jake of her future financial security. She just wanted to know that he loved her for the same kinds of reasons—pure love for her as a person, and particularly as a woman.

They finished their breakfast of pancakes, sausage and fruit juice to satisfy their bodies' accelerated hunger after their periodic intense physical activity during the last ten hours, and walked down to the conference room. Everyone else was already there, standing in several groups, eagerly discussing every topic people typically want to learn about in getting to know each other a little better. With Sasha's entrance, they all settled into their seats, quietly anticipating the resumption of the process.

Sasha was wearing a white sweater over a mid-length dress with small diagonal stripes of white and dark blue, effectively hiding most of her shapely legs and not accentuating her well-proportioned figure. She held her right hand over her left hand on her lap as she took her seat. Jake was wearing his tan casual 'office' sport coat and complementary brown slacks with an open-collar cream-colored shirt. He sat to Sasha's left next to Henry, and Julie was to Henry's left. The others sat essentially in the same positions they occupied yesterday. Everyone looked fresh, rested and well fed.

Sasha 'inadvertently' smoothed her dress over her thighs, slowly pushing her hands from her waist to her knees, thereby deliberately exposing the diamond for about ten seconds as she admired it briefly. She then slowly repositioned her hands as she had them before on her lap, again hiding the ring, and looked toward Henry with an inscrutable, but warm expression, morphing into a mischievous smile as Henry started to speak.

"Good morning everyone . . . I hope you all had a good night's sleep! This morning, I would like to review the essential elements of yesterday's experience as a way of solidifying the value and truth of what we all learned yesterday. In this manner . . ."

An unexpected murmur of hushed voices interrupted Henry's delivery, causing him to stop, looking somewhat bewildered. He looked at Julie with a 'Now what?' expression on his face, and she responded with a blank look, turned her palms to the ceiling and shrugged her shoulders in ignorance. The murmur was accelerating from the right side closest to Sasha, counterclockwise around the circle to the left like a wild fire, as Sasha let the slightest smile begin at the corners of her mouth. This time Jake was immediately alert to what was happening, and he too, could not suppress a grin. He saw what she did and knew why she did it. It reminded him of the audience reaction after he performed his first successful magic trick at a school assembly when he was just ten years old—a slow but growing appreciation of how he did it. Henry and Julie were still befuddled, as the entire group rose as one and started clapping. The applause accelerated and slowly grew into a round of cheers and chanting.

"Sa-Sha! Sa-Sha! Sa-Sha! Sa-Sha! Sa-Sha!"

This went on for about twenty seconds before Henry finally stood up and held his hands up in the air in an effort to get the group to calm down so he could understand what was going on.

After everyone was quiet, Ramon yelled to Henry, "She's wearing a diamond engagement ring, Henry! The therapy worked!"

Henry and Julie looked at each other with expressions of shock and amazement, and then they both looked to their right, where Sasha was again proudly displaying about $77,500 worth of nature's brilliant crystal-clear carbon beauty, easily sparkling even in the artificial light of the conference room from her left hand resting on her knee. For the first time in years, Henry wept with joy as he released some of the pent up intensity of his personal and professional hopes and sense of personal responsibility for restoring Sasha's memory. His theory worked! Not only that, but it worked in what he thought had to be record time, much less than what he had been prepared to expect. He had completely underestimated the intensity of the process, or possibly the nature of the people involved, or even the unusual social context of so many potential strangers who had unknowingly participated in the same story one way or another. Perhaps it was the special 'social energy' of this *particular* group of people in combination with the incredible story of Sasha's brush with death. Maybe it was because of the intense love relationship that facilitated the proper connections in her memory much more rapidly than he ordinarily could have imagined. Regardless of the real reasons, it worked, and he would have only one report to deliver to Joe: Mission accomplished!

Sasha and Jake stood up together holding each other's hands between them with irrepressible smiles and then faced the group. Everyone sat motionless as she turned toward them and spoke so clearly and confidently.

"I cannot thank you all enough for what you have done for me and Jake. I want all of you to attend our wedding ceremony, so be prepared to get an official invitation shortly!"

Cheers erupted again, this time with Henry and Julie joining in the celebration. They knew the therapy was complete. There was nothing more they could do but wait and watch over the weeks and months to come.

CHAPTER 72

Saturday, October 27, 2007
Attock, Pakistan

General Murray and his group flew in civilian attire via United Airlines from Washington to Dubai and then via Emirates Airlines from Dubai to Benazir Bhutto International Airport, just south of Islamabad in just over fifteen hours of total flight time. The plan called for as little official United States symbolism and identity as possible, hence the commercial aircraft. Raj Sampat met the group at the airport, and arranged for a private bus to transport them west to Attock, which would take at least another one and a half to two hours, depending upon road conditions and traffic. A helicopter was not available, suggesting something less than full Pakistani hospitality.

The group finally arrived at the front gate of a small artillery army base in the city of Attock, with five very capable bodyguards, specifically chosen because they were well-trained experts in the martial arts since they would not be carrying weapons anywhere in Pakistan. Raj Sampat brought along a portable CD player that operated on 220-240 volts.

The sun was already sinking lower toward the western horizon, just above the distant mountains. Six Pakistani soldiers met the bus at the gated entrance to the small Army base at Attock, made sure the five bodyguards understood that they were to remain with the bus at that location, and escorted General Murray and Raj several hundred yards to the relatively small command headquarters building. The soldiers 'wanded' the two men and then frisked them in a respectful, efficient, but thorough military manner before ushering them into the rather narrow dull tan internal hallway and through the full length of the building to a general purpose meeting room big enough for about sixty people. A large, visibly well-armed sentry stood at attention by the entrance to the room, and inside waited Army Major General Raza Arshad, dressed in his duty uniform. Raj and General Murray entered the room as General Arshad stood up to his full six-foot, two-inch height and moved away from the table placed in this room for this particular meeting and greeted them.

"General Murray, welcome to Attock! I know who you are, and I think I know why you are here."

He glanced politely at Raj, took note of the CD player he was carrying, and then faced General Murray again with a well-crafted expectant facial expression across his dark and weathered, but handsome and intelligent face.

General Murray sensed his question and announced, "This gentleman is Raj Sampat. He serves as my interpreter, personal aide and researcher."

Raj recognized the impromptu creative characterization of his identity, but betrayed no outward response as all of them then sat in chairs at the table. He was playing a rather cool hand, as Duke would have admired.

Indeed, the Pakistani general mused to himself.

"General Murray, I will be completely candid. Some people of respectable influence in Pakistan 'encouraged' me to meet with you, but I must admit to you that I do not have patience with such influence beyond the essential 'requirements' of my position, as I am sure you will understand, so please get to the point of your visit."

"Very well General Arshad. We both know how the world works, so I will give you the short version. Undoubtedly, you are aware of the Fresno incident in California on the west coast of my country."

"I am aware," he responded evenly.

"General, my organization has discovered who is responsible for transporting the explosive components and constructing the very powerful device that killed 419 innocent people and injured another 1,647 in that terrorist attack. His name is Rasheed Shirani, a Pakistani national. We have very good information that recently places this individual within the province of your command, General. The United States government does not wish to employ military means to capture him, which could risk injury to innocent Pakistani citizens and inflame relations between our two countries or others in the process. However, my government is very committed to finding new and effective ways to combat terrorism, which I am sure you will agree, does nothing to enhance the lives of the majority of Pakistanis, Muslims living here and elsewhere, or anyone else. Whether you or I like it or not General, many people throughout the world, rightly or wrongly, generally associate terrorists with Muslim extremists. The sooner we demonstrate effective responses to terrorism, the sooner we will all be able to limit its growth, correct the unfortunate association between extremist behavior and the worldwide Muslim community and increase world stability . . ."

General Arshad interrupted with his natural 'command voice,' "That all sounds like nice politics, General, but what does it have to do with me?"

"General Arshad, I have very good reason to believe that you are the only person in an effective position right now to assist the United States by capturing this individual, and, shall we say, 'limiting' his ability to continue conducting terrorist activities."

General Arshad paused with emphasis for a few seconds before responding, "Suppose I *am* actually in such a position, General Murray. Why should I search for, no less capture or arrest this Rasheed Shirani person?"

General Murray easily shifted into his professional 'wing it' mode and looked into General Arshad's eyes with intense anticipation.

"Among other reasons General, you must be aware that a regime change in Pakistan might affect your future. As I am sure you know by now, former President Pervez Musharraf has been interested in returning to power in Pakistan, and my sources inform me that he has considerable backing among your countrymen and your fellow senior officers. Perhaps you would receive a promotion if your 'activities' were 'sympathetic' to General Musharraf's well-known progressive social philosophy."

General Arshad sat just slightly more upright in his chair. General Murray subtly motioned to Raj to play the CD, and in so doing gained control of the discussion by altering it in a way General Arshad had apparently not anticipated. Even though the portable CD player was relatively small, and had somewhat limited high fidelity characteristics, the beautiful voice of Sasha Chancellor filled the room with a quality that readily penetrated through culture, time and style.

Raj was watching the general very carefully. He was going to 'translate' his body language into diplomatic negotiating language. He saw his pupils dilate. His eyes blinked more rapidly, but not too rapidly. Raj had been counting his blink rate from the beginning of the meeting. He saw the general's nostrils widen slightly as he inhaled a little more deeply than he had prior to that time. General Murray glanced innocently toward Raj, who responded with a very subtle affirmative nod of his head, indicating that General Arshad was about as receptive to the next argument as they could expect him to be. They all waited and listened to the single recording of Sasha's beautiful voice to the end of the track. General Arshad watched the CD player. Raj and General Murray watched General Arshad. After a little more than five minutes, her recorded voice faded into silence and Raj turned the player off.

General Murray and Raj sat quietly, patiently waiting for a response from General Arshad. The Pakistani sentry outside the room also heard the music. He smiled to himself in a very private moment of departure from expected military demeanor with a respite of joy he had never experienced before. General Arshad shifted in his seat in an effort to camouflage his having been drawn into non-military thought and reminiscence, somewhat softened by this woman's voice.

He finally returned to 'full General composure' and asked, "Exactly *what* are you trying to say, General Murray?"

"The woman whose voice you just heard was a victim of the Fresno bombing."

He paused for effect, to let that thought sink in for just a moment.

"She did not die, fortunately, but she was very seriously injured, suspended between life and death for several weeks. You, General Arshad, would not have had the pleasure of hearing her beautiful voice had she been killed in the Fresno explosion, nor would countless others, including your son, who I am quite sure would have an even greater appreciation of her talent than most people would. Isn't that part of the meaning of life, General Arshad, to experience joy, pleasure, personal fulfillment and achievement? Isn't that part of what we all ultimately want for ourselves, our children and their children?"

General Arshad's eyes narrowed somewhat as he looked intently into General Murray's eyes and interrupted.

"Exactly what does *my son* have to do with our discussion, General?"

Raj took a deep breath as subtly as he could in a controlled effort not to detract from what he knew to be the perfect development of their progress up to this point.

It's now or never, he thought to himself.

General Murray continued with his uniquely persuasive confidence, "I can arrange for your son to *see* this young woman in person, and hear her beautiful voice in a private concert."

General Arshad immediately stiffened somewhat as he announced with some force, self-important assurance and evidence of growing impatience, "That is *impossible*, General Murray! You disappoint me! My son is *blind*, General! He cannot see *anything!*"

The sentry outside the room felt the reflexive warmth of fear welling up inside him with that familiar incipient evidence of General Arshad's impatience and potential outbreak of his well-known and very explosive temper. General Murray continued evenly with no change in his diplomatic confidence or demeanor.

"I fully realize that General. He attends the Abbottabad School for the Blind. I also know that Amir plays the violin, even after your reluctance to purchase a violin for him when he was just six years old. I know that he is now twelve years old. Surely you must realize that if I know that much, I also know what I am saying when I say I can arrange for your son to *see* this young woman perform in person."

General Arshad was speechless for the first time in decades, and thrown slightly off guard by General Murray's referring to his son by name, as well as his obvious knowledge of extremely private details about the violin as Raj noticed his increased blink rate and slightly widening eyes.

After a moment, he recovered somewhat to say respectfully and cautiously in something slightly less than his habitual senior commander's voice, "I stand corrected . . . You are . . . quite unusually well informed . . . General Murray."

He glanced briefly at Raj once again with increasing suspicion that this man was probably more than he appeared to be, while General Murray continued to apply subtle gentle pressure.

"Specifically, General Arshad, I can arrange *privately* for the latest ophthalmic surgery and treatment for your son, Amir, to restore his sight in the United States, at any time of your choosing from this moment forward. My offer includes proper post-surgical care for as long as is medically required, as well as all necessary transportation, food, clothing and housing, at no cost to you or the Pakistani Army, or the Pakistani government." General Murray paused once more for emphasis, and then continued, "I repeat . . . this is a *private* offer, General, between *you* and *me alone*."

For a moment, General Arshad was not sure whether he was meeting with a completely insane man or a messenger from Allah. Surely, a United States Army General did not get to that position by being insane, or stupid for that matter. Yet he believed that all people, with or without high rank, are susceptible to some degree of ignorance, mistake or misinformation from time to time, regardless of which God they believe in or what country they live in or serve. General Arshad sat in silence as his agile brain carefully processed this entire bizarre scene. He, SSG Army Major General Raza Arshad, is effectively 'persuaded' by a former Pakistani president to have a meeting with a certain rather knowledgeable United States Army General, who comes to Pakistan with some kind of civilian Indian or Pakistani sidekick, to meet with him specifically about capturing a 'terrorist.' He is being asked to capture *a single terrorist* in his own country for the Government of the United States of America, and in return, this man promises to give sight to his only son. *Really?*

He was suspicious of Raj. Exactly *who* was this man who could very well have been unnoticeable on the streets of Islamabad, Lahore, Peshawar or even Attock, and yet appears to have the personal trust and confidence of a United States Army General, highly positioned in the CIA, no less?

General Murray opened his attaché case and pulled out a copy of the near-photographic quality computer-enhanced sketch-artist image of Rasheed Shirani's face.

"This is the man I want, General Arshad. I *know* he is in Pakistan, and I strongly believe he is currently located within your official geographical military responsibility."

General Murray ever so slowly and subtly held it closer and closer to him across the table without actually 'handing' it to him, until

General Arshad finally reached out and grasped the image. He studied it carefully for about twenty seconds, but betrayed nothing of his thoughts that either General Murray or Raj could detect.

"And what if I refuse to betray one of my countrymen by arresting him? And, furthermore, General Murray, what if you are *mistaken* about the identity of this person? What then, General Murray?" he added with a renewed and challenging air of superiority.

"Then, General Arshad, I fear we all will have lost a golden opportunity to control the spread of terrorism. The world in general, and this man in particular, will learn that he is beyond punishment, that his behavior does not have serious consequences, which will very likely, if not inevitably become known and contribute to the boldness of other terrorists. I believe that boldness will lead to the senseless deaths of more and more innocent people anywhere in the world, including Pakistan, who do not agree with the philosophy of the people who commit these acts of terrorism."

"And, like it or not, General Arshad, large numbers of people in my country, and most likely elsewhere as well, tend to associate terrorist activities incorrectly with the Muslim religion, if not with Pakistan in particular even though no Pakistani citizens were directly responsible for the 9/11 attacks in my country. I *personally* watched those planes hit the World Trade Towers on 9/11, General Arshad. I watched innocent and extremely frightened people actually jump from at least as high as 100 floors in the air to their certain deaths below. I am sure, General, that you too have witnessed senseless death."

"You and I, or any number of other people in positions of leadership or authority simply do not have the ability or the tools available to change people's ignorant, foolish, selfish, or otherwise misguided social perceptions to the extent necessary to correct those mistaken social impressions and beliefs. We can act most effectively only on a case-by-case basis. I know *you* are *not* a terrorist, General Arshad. I also know you *are* a Muslim. I fully believe you have serious reservations about exercising your military authority against your own countrymen, as would I. And yet surely you understand what is possible, as you and I are meeting here like this without either of us killing innocent Pakistani or American citizens."

"I believe it is my obligation to lead by example, because example provides the most visible, effective and sincere lesson from which others can learn to deal with the many problems we face in the age of terrorism. If we use traditional methods to fight terrorism, then we stand a very good chance of getting *only traditional* results. That is not good enough, in my opinion. If we are daring enough to cooperate deliberately in new and creative ways in the interest of the greatest common good for the greatest number of people, then we stand a very real chance of accomplishing something better than what has been traditional behavior, like wars and collateral damage from sophisticated, but still somewhat less than precise and very expensive surgical military strikes. Surely, if we do nothing, then we at least maintain, if not increase the probability of further terrorist activity."

"There are no easy answers, General Arshad, as I am sure you are well aware. Let's try something new, the two of us, and see what happens! My proposition regarding your son still stands. Neither of us would be threatening innocent lives unnecessarily by following this plan. If you are willing, General, I would be happy to accompany Amir on my trip back to the United States and personally take responsibility for his safe return to Pakistan when he is able after the surgery."

"In anticipation of your rightful concern about whether we have identified the wrong man in this case, I have brought some of the critical evidence with me. General Arshad, we have sequential satellite photographs of the truck we believe was used to transport the explosives to Fresno from what we believe to be its starting point somewhere around Miami, Florida. At the point of transfer in California, another driver took over the truck to deliver the explosive device and detonated it in Fresno, and died in the explosion. The image you hold in your hand is a computer enhancement of a police sketch artist's drawing from the instructions of the man who accepted payment from Rasheed in Mobile, Alabama for fuel, a candy bar, bottled water and No-Doz, which is commonly used to maintain wakefulness during long periods of driving. This transaction occurred at a small convenience store at an Exxon gasoline station. Two of our agents visited that store and interviewed the manager, who gave a physical description of Rasheed's approximate height and weight, as well as his clothing and facial characteristics to an experienced, well-trained police sketch artist. This man just happens to have an eidetic memory, General. We have already verified without question that he possesses almost perfect total visual recall. The few images of Rasheed Shirani that we were able to produce from satellite photographs are entirely consistent with the height, weight and general appearance of the man whose facial image you hold in your hand. The timing of our photographic evidence is entirely consistent with Rasheed Shirani's presence at various locations according to interviews with eyewitnesses at gas stations, motels and convenience stores along the route we believe he followed from Miami to Wheeler Ridge, California, where the transfer of the explosive device occurred. We have both local camera surveillance and confirming satellite photographic evidence of that transfer site, as well as evidence that Rasheed did not continue on to Fresno in the truck, but mounted a bright green Kawasaki motorcycle at Wheeler Ridge and left the area, eventually to appear in Mexico City. A Mexican private detective gave us the serial number of that motorcycle, which we traced to a certain Khalid Kayani, also a Pakistani native, living in San Diego at the time, who we believe drove the truck from the transfer site at Wheeler Ridge to Fresno, where he detonated the device. We have eyewitness evidence from that private detective in the Mexico City International Airport where Rasheed boarded a flight back to Pakistan. That detective actually flew in the same airplane with Rasheed back to Pakistan, where he unsuccessfully attempted to follow him before he was obligated by Pakistani authorities to return to Mexico. Furthermore, General Arshad, we do not have any evidence of any *other* person or occurrence consistent with the known facts to identify any other person or persons who could possibly have been involved in the construction, transportation, transfer and detonation of the device. However, we believe that the explosive material used in the bomb was manufactured either in the United States or in Iran and some of it possibly in England and was delivered to Rasheed somewhere on his deadly route by people we have not yet identified."

"I have put my commission on the line to the President of the United States, General Arshad. If I am mistaken, then my career is over. I have given my word. Furthermore, General, if I am mistaken, then I am fully prepared to *rot in hell!*"

General Murray opened his briefcase, and withdrew a large manila envelope with no external markings and spread the contents over the table between them. He had removed all official annotations, titles and labels from the internal contents to prevent identification of the electronic methods of their production or the official departments or locations that produced the information, assessments and annotations. He arranged across the table a series of photographic images of a large GMC two-axle truck with the U-Haul logo or portions of it clearly visible on several images. Each image included date and time stamps with longitude and latitude along the bottom, and each image was numbered in sequential order with a red magic marker for easy organization. The envelope contained fifty-eight such images taken at various locations along the analyst's assessment of the most logical route from Miami to Fresno. The packet also included several images of the stationary truck at the truck stop at Wheeler Ridge, California, including the image of the van with a small single-axle flatbed trailer holding what was obviously a bright green motorcycle. The time gaps in the series of photographs were consistent with the local periods of darkness from when the truck left Miami to when it arrived at the Wheeler Ridge truck stop. Furthermore, the series of date and time stamps did not allow for much idle time or deviation from the routes included in the photographs. Therefore, the vehicle was obviously on a deliberate course with only minimal slippage in time and distance that could easily be accounted for with meals, lodging and fuel stops, and possibly as many as two or three cargo transfers en route. Notations in the attached reports included the conclusion that only one individual was driving the vehicle because of the time taken to travel the approximately 2,379-mile distance between the two locations. He explained to General Arshad that had there been two or more drivers, the distances calculated along the way could have been traversed in significantly less time than indicated from the date and time stamps, assuming that one driver could sleep while the other drove. Given the specific nature of the trip and the need for secrecy, there was no reason to assume that more than one person was traveling in the truck. He then arranged another set of a dozen photographs from an Air Force reconnaissance jet, showing Rasheed Shirani in much greater detail, along with the infrared images including the overheated truck engine and drive train in the Arizona desert just east of Tucson with independent time and date stamps entirely consistent with those from the first set of photographs.

Then he produced a separate series of reports from the detective in Mexico City, Cordera Alvarez, who identified a man with a bright green motorcycle entirely consistent with the one seen in the photographs.

The reports confirmed that Alvarez had followed this man to the airport, where he discovered that the man was listed as a passenger on a flight to Rawalpindi in Pakistan, and that the detective purchased a ticket on the same flight with remarkable ease, considering the relatively short time until departure, and flew in the same airplane with the suspect all the way to Rawalpindi.

Alvarez led a double life. He was also a member of The Chancellor Organization, but General Murray kept that fact to himself. The report also included a simple photograph of the man in the passenger gate area of the airport terminal, taken by Alvarez. That photograph appeared next to the computer-enhanced sketch artist image and was compared with several computerized facial identification algorithms. The report included an analyst's written conclusion that the two images were of the same man with greater than ninety-nine percent certainty. It also included a copy of the flight manifests, both arriving in and departing from the United States, clearly showing Rasheed Shirani's name on the lists dated entirely consistent with the timeframe before and after his journey across the United States.

General Arshad sat motionless for another thirty seconds, looking deep into General Murray's eyes. Then he shifted his attention back to the evidence on the table and then back into General Murray's eyes several times. Raj was trying to quiet his pounding heart and avoid at all costs disturbing General Murray's efforts.

General Arshad finally concluded that General Murray would not rot in hell, and he spoke slowly with a civil tone of personal sincerity in spite of his habitual military bearing.

"You are a very persuasive man . . . General Murray."

He thought about his blind and only son, Amir. He thought about how much successful surgery would enrich Amir's life. If the surgery were unsuccessful, he would not have to honor General Murray's request. This particular terrorist could easily have 'disappeared' into the complex obscurity of northern Pakistan in the meantime. He sat motionless for about thirty seconds, studying General Murray, carefully weighing the importance of what this man wanted, the extremely unusual effort he had obviously put into arranging this meeting, and what he was willing to give in order to get what he wanted, and then spoke deliberately and sincerely.

"I will have my son brought here tomorrow to meet you. After he returns from the United States, I will ask him about his private concert with this woman singer you have told me about."

CHAPTER 73

Sunday, October 28, 2007
Attock, Pakistan

After a rather sleepless night at a local hotel and a minimal and tasteless breakfast, General Murray and his bodyguards and Raj arrived back at the same military building in which they had their meeting with General Arshad. Pakistani guards again escorted them to the meeting room. General Arshad was already there, and with him a thin, but handsome teenager, slightly taller than most twelve-year-old boys, with wavy jet-black hair covering the tops of his ears, down the back of his neck and hanging down in the front almost to his eyebrows. He was dressed in khaki trousers and sandals, and a lightweight short-sleeved white shirt with a dark blue tie. He smiled, sensing the entrance of General Murray and Raj, facing almost directly toward them, but only slightly to the side. His sense of sound was obviously superb, and no doubt accentuated after almost a decade of compensating for his lack of sight.

General Arshad proudly introduced his son, "General Murray, Mr. Sampat, this young man is my son, Amir."

The boy had obviously learned manners that were evident across cultures as he held out his right hand in the general direction of General Murray in a gesture of expecting a handshake. General Murray met his expectation with a firm, but not crushing military handshake, as he would have offered a grown man. General Murray spoke first.

"Amir, I am General Murray from the United States of America. I am very pleased to meet you!"

Amir corrected his slightly misdirected facial direction almost precisely at General Murray's face.

"I have with me my personal assistant Mr. Raj Sampat."

With that, Amir amazingly turned *toward* Raj, and not the other way. The boy seemed to have an extremely unusual personal 'radar.' Still smiling, he held out his hand for another expected handshake, in remarkably accurate general placement for Raj to accept. Raj reached out with a much softer, but friendly and firm handshake.

"It's a pleasure to meet you, Amir."

"I am very pleased to meet you, sir!"

General Arshad smiled at his son briefly in an expected proud paternal manner, and then looked General Murray straight in the eye as his smile disappeared.

"General Murray, I have agreed to take this step in the direction you indicated yesterday after having explained to Amir the availability of surgical procedures in your country to correct blindness. I must insist, however, that three of my best bodyguards accompany you for your comfort and Amir's, as well as 'facilitating' solutions to any possible difficulties that may arise. They will have direct communication with me during the entire time."

The General's eyes had a language of their own. They made it clear that this was a requirement well beyond the implication of 'insisting.'

"I trust that you will be able to accommodate their presence throughout the journey and return to this location," he said with a degree of confidence that General Murray knew meant that there was no deal without these three men.

"General Arshad, you have my word. I assure you that your representatives will be with Amir and me for the entire period."

The meeting was over, and General Murray, Raj and the soldiers returned to their hotel. General Murray was extremely relieved that he did not have to play the 'British jail' card. It would have been far more difficult and time-consuming, and the longer his negotiations persisted, the greater the chance that Rasheed would learn of his discovery and go much deeper into hiding. He prepared a thorough summary of the meetings with General Arshad and sent it immediately through System 14 back to Duke just after he informed Director Miles of the same information through normal CIA channels. He immediately ordered an unmarked long-distance chartered aircraft to be available on October 31 at Rawalpindi, which is the location of Pakistani military headquarters, for the long flight back to Homestead Air Force Base near Miami. His time schedule allowed Amir to be transported back to the Abbottabad School for his clothing and return to Attock for a final visit with his father before he left for Miami.

Duke dispatched Joe immediately to Mercy Hospital in Chicago to make another significant 'donation' to the hospital. While he was there, Joe made a special point of meeting with Doctor Naved Musharraf to inform him of their progress up to that point and to thank him for his efforts to help. Joe conveyed the personal gratitude of Duke Chancellor and the entire Chancellor Organization for his part in making this plan work, and asked him to make sure to tell General Pervez Musharraf that The Chancellor Organization was extremely appreciative of his assistance in the next phone communication between the two famous Pakistani brothers. Duke sent a personal note of appreciation and gratitude to both Doctor Musharraf and General Musharraf, and offered his services in the event that either of them might find The Chancellor Organization useful to them in the future. The promised untraceable 'bonus' deposit of $50,000 mysteriously appeared in the doctor's business checking account.

CHAPTER 74

Monday, October 29, 2007
Miami, Florida

"Doctor Fuller, there's a Mr. Joe Czarzhynenski on line two for you."

"Who?"

"He said his name was Joe Czarzhynenski. I had to ask him how to spell his last name."

"What does he want?"

"He wouldn't say specifically, Doctor Fuller. He said he wanted to speak with you directly about something very important. He was *quite* insistent! This is the fourth time today that he called, so I think he is likely to continue to call if you don't speak with him."

Doctor Fuller was the Chief Executive Officer of the Bascom-Palmer Eye Institute at the University of Miami. He was a very busy man, and in no mood for games. However, he also knew that he should take a call from someone who had obviously defeated what he learned over the years were Sherry's considerable talents of controlling or deflecting unwanted intrusions into his very busy schedule.

He sighed with his greatest exasperation of the day so far and said, "All right, Sherry, I'll speak with him." He reached for his desk phone and pushed the 'Line 2' button. "This is Doctor Fuller. I understand that you have something important to tell me. What is it?"

"Good afternoon, Doctor Fuller. My name is Joe Czarzhynenski. I am prepared to make a significant unrestricted contribution to the general fund of the Bascom-Palmer Eye Institute if you will secure for me the services of Doctor Stanley Jensen within the next several days to restore the sight of a certain Pakistani teenager who has been blind since a very early age due to the effects of smallpox."

"What did you say your name is?"

"Joe."

"And your last name?"

"Czarzhynenski. C-Z-A-R-Z-H-Y-N-E-N-S-K-I."

"What is your relationship to this young man, Mr. Czarzhynenski?"

"Doctor Fuller, I am calling you from my cell phone in my car. I am in Miami right now, and I can be in your office in about a half hour to give you a complete explanation. My guess is that it would be in your best interest and the best interest of the Bascom-Palmer Eye Institute if you permit me to come to your office with an offer you can't refuse."

"Mr. Czarzhynenski, with all due respect, I don't care for your manner and I do not have the time right now to disrupt my very crowded schedule to meet with people I don't know. Now if you will please excuse me, I have a great deal of work to do. Please call my secretary to schedule an appointment."

Doctor Fuller ended the connection before Joe could explain his urgent time schedule.

OK, Doc. We'll do it my way, Joe thought to himself.

He terminated his blue-tooth connection in his Corvette, and entered the parking lot near NW 9th Avenue and NW 17th Street, diagonally across from the Bascom-Palmer Eye Institute. He read the sign at the corner near the entrance to the parking lot that indicated 'Patient Parking' and mused to himself, *How odd that I can park 'patiently' here.* After pulling into a parking space, he plugged his laptop computer into the accessory power outlet and logged on to System 8.

Sammy, I need an appointment with Doctor Raymond F. Fuller, Chairman and Chief Executive Officer of the Bascom-Palmer Eye Institute at the University of Miami within the hour. Please arrange ASAP and prepare for transfer of funds per my instructions to come, and stay on the system. I have a lot of ego to plow through down here and I have no time to waste. Should be fun!

Joe knew that General Murray would be leaving Pakistan soon with Amir, and he did not have any time to spare with slow or uncooperative people. He also knew that he could not afford to waste any time in the effort to find Rasheed and get him into custody before he could learn of his possible discovery or attempts to apprehend him, and possibly retreat deeper into the obscure terrorist world of northern Pakistan.

Within thirty seconds, Sammy replied through System 8, *Roger, no problem. Will notify you ASAP.*

Sammy went to work. He started one of his special internet search routines, found the Bascom-Palmer Eye Institute's intranet and casually broke through its relatively weak security system, quickly found Doctor Fuller's appointment schedule, and noted the two names occupying his time for the next two hours. He then created fictitious e-mails, which he sent to Doctor Fuller's e-mail address, one from each of them, both with apologies for last minute change of schedules preventing their meeting with Doctor Fuller today, delivered in different styles from untraceable sources to avoid suspicion beyond the obvious and very curious narrow timeframe within which they arrived at their destinations. He then made two separate calls to Sherry's telephone number, disguising his voice each time and offered sincere apologies in each call for having to reschedule the meeting with Doctor Fuller today. Then he called each of the two people to apologize for Doctor Fuller's unfortunate request to postpone their meeting until an unspecified later date. Although he could not confirm that each of his e-mail messages had been read, he could determine exactly when each was received and opened. He was satisfied that the scenario he needed to create had been put into action, and that Joe would have a chance to apply his unique personal version of persuasion before the ruse could be discovered. He waited for the e-mail receipt confirmations to appear. Within seventeen minutes, he received both confirmations, and sent a message back to Joe's computer on the secure System 8.

I have apologized to Doctor Fuller's secretary for the unfortunate cancellation of the next two hours of appointments with Doctor Fuller, so I hope you have enough time to do what you need to do. Please advise if you need more time. I am standing by for your instructions.

Joe's computer chirped in acknowledgement of the message, which he then read, and replied with affirmation that he would have enough time, terminated the connection, and put his computer in its sleep state and put it back in its case. He left his Corvette, and walked over to the eye institute and found Doctor Fuller's office location in the lobby directory, and took the elevator to the fifth floor, walked down the hall to the door with Doctor Fuller's name on the outside and entered Sherry's outer office with his signature friendly confidence.

He announced in his most gracious and professionally pleasant manner, "Hi! My name is Joe Czarzhynenski. I would like to see Doctor Fuller, please."

Sherry looked up in stunned amazement as she recognized his voice, but could not understand how he would just show up after Doctor Fuller had clearly rebuffed his earlier efforts to meet with him.

"I believe he has some time to see me now," he said in his most ingratiating and pleasant manner.

"Oh? As a matter of fact . . . he . . . does!" she said, looking at her computer monitor, still utterly bewildered that this coincidence had occurred.

"Please have a seat and I'll let him know you are here," she said with cautious courtesy and no 'Plan B.'

"Thank you!" Joe said as he pleasantly beamed back at her to keep pushing her 'be pleasant' buttons.

She entered Doctor Fuller's spacious office, strode to his desk and said in her best apologetic tone, "Doctor Fuller, Joe Czarzhynenski is actually here to see you."

"I thought I had a meeting with the sales rep from the Lumenis laser company about new equipment! What's going on here?"

"The sales rep called not long ago to cancel at the last minute due to unforeseen developments. He said he would reschedule within a day or two," she offered, still in her best apologetic role.

"Oh, all right! Send this guy in and let's get it over with, whatever he wants!" he said with marked impatience.

Joe had heard enough to invite himself into Doctor Fuller's spacious office, stepped around Sherry while he delivered his best flashy smile at her, intending to remind her that she might still have some appeal to men, even short balding ones, then extended his hand to Doctor Fuller and introduced himself in his characteristic socially adaptive manner.

"She's really a gem!" he continued with even more charm. "Just call me Joe. Everyone else does! Besides, it takes too long to pronounce my last name!"

He chuckled to himself, intending to put Doctor Fuller a little more at ease as the two men shook hands.

"All right . . . Joe. What's on your mind?" he said impatiently with no smile, as he sat back down behind his desk, subconsciously and slowly softening to Joe's magnetic personality.

"A Pakistani teenager needs to have his sight restored, Doctor Fuller, and I believe this is the best place to have that done. Furthermore, I believe Doctor Stanley Jensen is the best surgeon to perform the required operation. I am prepared to pay all costs involved, but I would like to have this procedure done within the next several days, if that is possible. This young man will be in the United States within two days."

"Now hold on . . . *Hold it just a minute!* Exactly who are *you*, and *who* is this teenager?"

"I like to think that I am a facilitator of good works and destroyer of red tape . . . among other things," he said pointedly. "Do you remember telling me on the phone to schedule an appointment for later with your secretary?"

"Yes, I do."

"How do you think I got this opportunity to meet with you today, Doctor Fuller?"

"I . . . I don't . . . really know!" he replied, stepping a few rungs lower on his ladder of imagined superiority.

"The short explanation is that my organization is very efficient and effective, Doctor Fuller, and it is my job to be both persuasive and effective."

Doctor Fuller sat motionless for several moments staring at Joe with no further reaction from him, and then said cautiously, "I see. And exactly *what is* your organization . . . Joe?"

All pleasantries disappeared from Joe's demeanor as he continued, "I work for The Chancellor Organization. From this point forward, Doctor Fuller, our conversation is strictly confidential. *Understood?*"

Doctor Fuller nodded in affirmative capitulation, as he continued with almost dignified self-justification, "And exactly *what* is The Chancellor Organization?"

Joe answered immediately with his 'don't make me repeat this' tone.

"We are a worldwide information network that assists people and organizations in times of need when others are too selfish, bureaucratically immobilized, unwilling, unaware, unable, incompetent, or apparently devoid of any historically common sense of human decency. Obviously we are extremely busy."

After several moments of stunned silence, Doctor Fuller responded, "So, why haven't I ever heard of your organization, Joe?"

Joe responded in a manner that told Doctor Fuller that was his last question.

"Because we operate in *secrecy*, and we're *very good* at what we do."

Doctor Fuller felt strangely chastised, but he was hooked and began to realize that he should take this man very seriously.

After another thoughtful moment, he said, "Of course. Please continue."

"Have you heard about the Fresno incident, Doctor Fuller?"

"Of course I have!"

"I expected as much. Now, how do you *really* feel about that incident, Doctor?"

"I'm deeply saddened by the tremendous and senseless loss of life, obviously, and I'm extremely angry because of the heartless and evil manner in which I understand it was carried out!"

"That's about what I thought, Doctor Fuller. Many people feel that way, including my employer. We provide assistance to individuals or other organizations that are not in a position to help themselves under certain circumstances for any of a variety of reasons. However, with our help such organizations could contribute meaningfully and constructively to people's lives, or various social needs. In this case, unfortunately, the United States Government is not in a position to hunt effectively for the perpetrator of this terrorist act inside a foreign country, let alone Pakistan, for at least political if not logistical reasons, but my organization *is* in such a position, and has been working toward a solution for several weeks. I believe that the sooner this individual is brought to justice, the better it will be for all people targeted by terrorists, particularly in this country. The terrorist organizations around the world need to understand that we will get to their *leadership* quickly and efficiently, that there is no place to hide and that consequences will be swift, sure, and effective."

"The young man I have described to you is the only son of a rather powerful Pakistani Army Major General, who is in a position to capture the primary organizer of the Fresno bombing. In order to secure the General's cooperation, my organization has assured him that the sight of his only son can and will be restored at no cost to him or the Pakistani government. My organization is working 'in the background' to make sure that happens. That is essentially the short version of the plan."

Doctor Fuller sat motionless, trying to make sense of this incredible story so foreign to his everyday world, profession and experience.

"Please forgive me for what I hope you understand to be honest doubt, but . . . exactly *how* are you going to make this rather incredible plan work?"

"I got this opportunity to see you in spite of your very efficient and dedicated secretary out there didn't I?" Joe said evenly, as he motioned with his right thumb over his right shoulder as he spoke.

"Yes, Joe, I must admit you did."

"Look in your general operations bank account at Bank of America, Doctor Fuller. You will notice an 'extra' one million dollar credit. It is there to use for the Bascom-Palmer Institute as you see fit."

Doctor Fuller was completely dumbstruck. He sat quietly staring at Joe, as he slowly started to reach out to his left for his computer keyboard without looking, and accidentally knocked over a picture of his family, and then slowly turned his body as well toward his computer and typed several commands. After several seconds, he was in the hospital's general ledger report and scrolled down slowly until he got to the credits. Indeed, there was an 'extra' credit of exactly one million dollars that had not been there before, and had no identifying description beyond 'Other' and today's date. He could not help rapidly imagining all the projects he could use that money for at the institute. He logged off his computer and turned slowly back toward Joe, deliberately stalling, as he picked up the fallen picture frame while trying to think of a reason to doubt him but simultaneously hoping he would fail.

"Exactly . . . *how* . . . did you know . . . that money was there?" he asked evenly with a hint of incredulity.

"I put it there. That is the answer to all of your questions, Doctor Fuller. Now, do I have your full attention and cooperation or do you require further persuasion, or shall I look elsewhere for the assistance I require? I am running out of time."

Doctor Fuller was deep in thought, and no longer wanted to doubt Joe's sincerity. Joe was approaching the outer limits of his patience. He reached for his cell phone.

"Doctor Fuller, I can make a simple phone call to make that million-dollar credit disappear from your ledger. Would you like a demonstration?"

"OH NO! NO! That will not be necessary! Please excuse me. I'm a . . . little . . . bewildered at the moment!"

"Then may I assume we will have the services of Doctor Jensen to perform the required procedures whenever my patient arrives?"

Doctor Fuller hesitated only slightly as he rapidly processed as many of the 'pros' and 'cons' as he could within what appeared to be a situation over which he had much less than his customary control. He decided that the money would absorb a host of expected questions and possible unknown objections from the people he would have to answer to, as well as Doctor Jensen.

"Yes . . . Yes! Absolutely! I'll see to it myself!"

Joe smiled his special '*I thought so*' smile and said, "Then I will assume we have a firm gentleman's agreement, and that the deposit will be adequate compensation?"

"Yes! Yes! Absolutely!"

Doctor Fuller did not doubt for a moment that the deposit would disappear very quickly without his full cooperation, and he knew he was not in a position to ask for even more. He would never doubt Joe's word again.

Joe stood to leave, extended his hand to Doctor Fuller and said, "I will be in touch with further details as soon as they develop."

They shook hands amiably, and Joe turned to leave.

CHAPTER 75

Tuesday, October 30, 2007
Miami, Florida

Doctor Stanley Jensen was clearly impatient and irritated by having to meet with the Chairman of the Institute after a very busy day of surgery. He was only thirty-nine years old, a product of Columbia College and the Stanford School of Medicine, handsome, but still single, and already had a reputation for being one of the best ophthalmic surgeons in the United States. He was entirely too busy with his profession and his reputation to take the time out for social relationships that might lead to marriage. He had published many articles about surgical techniques and lectured at the Miller School of Medicine at the University of Miami, as well as other medical schools periodically throughout the country. He was widely acknowledged as an extremely accomplished, creative and brilliant surgeon, but also had a reputation for impatience and egotistic dominance at the relatively few social events he did attend that contributed to general recognition of him as typical of many 'type A' personalities.

"Doctor Fuller? Doctor Jensen is here to see you," Sherry said as she walked into Doctor Fuller's office with several documents for his signature.

"OK," he said, rather exasperated. "Send him in."

Doctor Jensen marched into Doctor Fuller's office with his usual air of superiority.

"What's this about my having to operate on an adolescent Pakistani boy out of the clear blue?"

"Sit down, Stan."

"I have three procedures tomorrow as it is with my own patients! How am I supposed to squeeze another one in that I know nothing about?"

"I have transferred those three cases to other surgeons, Stan, because of extremely unusual circumstances. I want you to be alert and rested for the Pakistani boy. You have already done at least five procedures very similar to this one, so it's not completely 'out of the blue.' You will have complete surgical team support from those who have the proper experience. Besides, some very influential people have specifically requested that *you* take this case, and have already forwarded all of the relevant clinical details from the Abbottabad School for the Blind in Pakistan."

"Oh? Who?"

"I'm quite sure you wouldn't recognize any names, and I am obligated not to disclose any details anyway. Let me just say that this procedure has *very important* international implications, so I want it done to the best of your ability—the way you always operate. That is why I have taken the admittedly unusual liberty of transferring your procedures tomorrow to other surgeons so you can have proper rest and preparation prior to his arrival, which could be within a day or two. We have a sufficient number of very well qualified people on staff here, so your patients are not going to suffer any inconvenience or lack of proper care and treatment."

"But those are *my* patients, not *yours!*"

Doctor Fuller knew he could no longer effectively control his impatience and mounting frustration from Doctor Jensen's imperious personality, as he continued with an uncharacteristically loud voice, "*And I am the Chief Executive Officer of this institute, responsible for making some very difficult decisions you are fortunate enough not to have to make!* Our future is not always of our own choosing, Doctor! Sometimes we are obligated by circumstances beyond principle and intent to cooperate with independent forces and real life developments beyond our control! You should at least take some personal comfort and satisfaction in knowing that some very influential people have recognized *you* as the best surgeon in the country for this procedure!"

"Well, I'm not doing it without knowing who is pulling the strings!"

"I figured you would say that," he snapped, and then continued with exceptional self-control. "Obviously, I cannot force you to perform any surgery, Doctor Jensen. All I can do is provide the services necessary for our patients under sometimes difficult circumstances. If you absolutely refuse to do this, then you had better be prepared for the consequences. Among those, you will not receive a rather significant bonus for the successful completion of this procedure. You will forgo likely meaningful professional recognition to add to your resume of significant accomplishments, and those accolades will go to someone else of my choosing, or perhaps of *their* choosing. And, quite honestly, I don't know what to tell you about the potential response of the people who have asked *specifically* for *your* services. My best guess is that they don't tolerate disappointment very well. I *can* tell you, however, that the principal who brought this subject to my attention arranged to see me without an appointment by clearing my schedule in less than thirty minutes. You *do* know what is necessary and how difficult it is to see me outside of Sherry's management of my time, do you not?

"Yes, I do," Doctor Jensen admitted with evident restraint.

"Well, then, think also about the quality of influence that persuaded two—not one, but *two*—reasonably important people not to keep previously sequentially arranged meetings with me yesterday, *in less than thirty minutes!* Think about how the bottom line of this hospital was instantaneously improved *significantly* as an incentive to have *you* perform this particular procedure, as soon as possible. The people behind this 'request' do not play games, and they are obviously very well informed, well connected and influential. Am I making myself *clear*, Doctor Jensen?"

"Yes, I believe you are," he said with a sigh of petulant capitulation.

"Well, then! Do I have your permission to confirm to the principal I described that you will commit to doing this procedure?"

"Yes," he said, after a few thoughtful seconds in the only apparent admission of defeat that Doctor Fuller could recall in his five-year association with the 'superstar' surgeon.

CHAPTER 76

Tuesday, October 30, 2007
Rawalpindi Airport, Pakistan

Amir, General Murray and his five bodyguards and the contingent of three Pakistani guards boarded a chartered Boeing 777 airplane at Rawalpindi Airport just south of Islamabad at six o'clock in the morning after spending the night at the Best Western Regency Hotel near the airport. General Murray had arranged the chartered flight capable of the non-stop distance from Pakistan to Miami specifically to avoid unnecessary commercial airport security checks as well as any unwanted publicity, leaks or delay. All of the military people had changed into civilian clothing to help maintain as much of a low profile as possible upon disembarking at Homestead Air Force Base and later upon entering the hospital. Although the Pakistani guards were obligated to relinquish their weapons, they would remain with Amir as the two generals had agreed.

CHAPTER 77

Tuesday, October 30, 2007
Miami, Florida

Joe had advised Doctor Fuller about security measures and how many people he should expect on security detail because of the nature of the agreement and the purpose of the entire mission. He called Duke to report the time schedule within which Sasha should plan to be in Miami at the Bascom-Palmer Eye Institute to fulfill General Murray's promise that Amir would see her as well as hear her sing.

The group from Pakistan arrived around one o'clock in the afternoon at Homestead Air Force Base, about twenty-five miles south of Miami, Florida with an auspiciously rather smooth landing. General Murray reviewed the plans for the day and reminded the Pakistani and American soldiers that they were expected to maintain security for Amir and the entire operation and throughout the entire period at the hospital and the return trip to Pakistan until Amir was again with his father. General Murray noticed that after the long flight, the soldiers from both countries had begun to form a workable camaraderie that undoubtedly would make the entire security operation more effective, efficient and easier for all of them. They all bypassed airport security beyond a simple head-count according to advance orders from General Murray. He produced his military identification and a printed copy of his own 'top secret code word' advance orders for the sentry on duty. They were all cleared to proceed and entered a waiting blue air force bus outside the terminal that would take them directly to the Bascom-Palmer Eye Institute. The soldiers would rotate through observation and guard duty on two-hour shifts, always with one Pakistani soldier per shift, so each of the three Pakistani guards would be spending more time per day near Amir than each of the American soldiers would. The Institute provided sleeping and dining accommodations for all of them as General Murray had requested.

The group arrived at the institute just before four o'clock, where Joe met them and escorted them to a meeting room, where he introduced Doctor Fuller and Doctor Jensen to all of them. The meeting would serve as a way to familiarize the soldiers with the entire hospital complex as well as the institute and their accommodations. The meeting would further allow the institute staff to understand the most important unclassified elements of Amir's visit and to become familiar with the faces of the military people who would be around them almost all the time. At the same time, Doctor Fuller explained the limits of the soldiers' presence in and around the actual surgery and recovery areas to assure proper sanitary conditions and not interfere needlessly with the general operation of the hospital. General Murray explained the need to maintain absolute secrecy about the entire process, including keeping Amir as insulated as possible from learning the secret events and original reasons behind the operation. He had to assure that his operation would not be a source of political shenanigans in this country, or in Pakistan, and he needed to keep The Chancellor Organization influence completely out of the picture. He also carefully guarded against any media exposure of any kind. Prying eyes or other unanticipated investigative efforts from the media were doomed to provoke some of the most effective 'persuasive techniques' of the Chancellor Organization. General Murray was satisfied that sufficient intent to cooperate had been established at the meeting, and that he would not have any problems that either he or Doctor Fuller could not handle personally in short order.

After some further minor discussion and a few normal or expected questions, the group was ready to go to work. Doctor Jensen took Amir to his room with two of the guards and approached him to establish the trust he knew Amir would need at this rather frightening and potentially major turning point in his life. He wanted Amir to recognize and remember his voice, and to understand what would be happening to him. Doctor Jensen was genuinely drawn to the tall, but slightly built and gentle boy, and recognized his intelligence and awareness, in spite of his blindness. They entered the room, and the two guards remained outside the closed door.

"Amir, you must understand that although I am a very good doctor, I am only a doctor. I am not God. I cannot work miracles, but I honestly believe I can restore at least some of your ability to see. Your condition is not unheard of, and other people have regained their sight with treatment similar to what I will give you. First, I need to know some important things about you. One of the nurses will ask you quite a few questions in order to understand your medical history. She will draw some blood, and you will have to give a urine sample, so we can understand your body chemistry to make sure any medication we may use will be effective and not harm you. After that, I will examine you, especially your eyes, and I will be using some special electronic equipment designed to take pictures of your eyes, your brain and the optical nerves between your eyes and your brain. It will not hurt you, but you will wear earplugs to block the loud noises it makes. I will also conduct some tests designed to assess exactly what your optical ability is. Although I understand that you cannot see anything at all, I need to discover exactly what parts of the complex process of seeing are not working properly, so I can repair them. After I have done all I can do, then you must rest for several days. I will put bandages over your eyes that the nurses will change periodically, but we will keep your eyes bandaged only for as long as they need that protection until the natural healing process is progressing sufficiently to allow for their removal. That could take up to four weeks, possibly longer, but might be as little as two weeks. Mother Nature will take over after I have done my work, and she will enable you to see something, or she may enable you to see a great deal. There is also a very remote chance that the procedure will not work at all. However, there is also the chance that it will give you completely restored sight, just the way God intended that it should be. Do you understand everything I have told you, Amir?"

Amir spoke gently with an effort of subtle bravado far beyond both his fear and his maturity, "Yes, I understand, Doctor Jensen."

"You are indeed a very brave young man, Amir. It is quite normal to be afraid, but you have come a very great distance for this treatment. This is a special hospital where very skilled and well-trained people work to repair and restore human sight. That is all they do. They are specialists. The people who work here are very good at what they do, and they will all care for you the same way they have cared for many other patients, both old and young, who have come here before you. Our success rate is very good, so I am quite optimistic. I have already treated conditions like yours several times before."

"Doctor Jensen?"

"Yes?"

"I am afraid."

"I understand that you are afraid, Amir. Fear is a normal part of life. I have been afraid also during my life. When I operated on a patient for the very first time, I was afraid precisely because I had never done it before. However, I had studied very hard in college and medical school and learned everything I could about what all the special parts of the body, especially the eyes and the brain are like and how they work, so I could know how to proceed. I watched experienced surgeons perform various procedures many times before I actually operated for the first time. I had another doctor with me at my first operation who was very experienced, and I learned from him as well, standing by my side during the operation, guiding me and talking to me all the time, so I would do all of the right things and not make any mistakes. After that, I performed many other operations, also with other experienced doctors watching over me, so I learned more and more, and with that knowledge, controlled and reduced my fear to a point where I have no fear today, and operate by myself with others helping me, although I have respect for a variety of possible outcomes. When we are afraid, Amir, it is usually because we are facing something we have never faced before—something completely new, unknown or unfamiliar. That fear is entirely normal. But, when we are with someone who has faced that same thing before, particularly someone we trust and respect, then we can feel better, more confident and less fearful about the future."

He let that sink in for a minute.

"Doctor Jensen?"

"Yes, Amir?"

"I feel better."

"I'm very glad to know that, Amir. I will do my absolute best for you. *I promise!*"

"Doctor Jensen?"

"Yes?"

"Do you know that I can play a violin?"

Stanley Jensen was caught completely off guard by Amir's sudden leap to another subject, but recovered quickly.

"You can? That's *wonderful!* I must hear you play after the operation when you are ready! Will you play for me?"

"I did not bring my violin, though," he said with obvious disappointment.

Jensen replied immediately, "Don't worry about that, Amir. We will *find* one for you to play! I *promise!*"

Stanley Jensen had both surprised and out-done himself. When it came down to his patients, they were more important than he was, and Amir had reached his heart rapidly in a very special way. All of the prior irritation and argument with Doctor Fuller had fallen by the wayside, and it really did not matter as much whether there were some very important people pulling the strings, or that his other patients had been shuttled off to other surgeons for this relatively brief period. He would soon go to them individually and carefully explain the very unusual circumstances. Doctor Jensen was satisfied that they could now proceed with the medical history and all of the laboratory tests he wanted and then complete his examination. Doctor Fuller assured him that this procedure would have top priority and that everyone and everything would be ready for surgery Friday morning at eight o'clock sharp.

By early evening, Joe had left to find a motel, since his presence at the hospital was no longer necessary. However, true to his word, General Murray remained at the hospital with his guards and the three Pakistani guards, who started their rotation of watching over Amir with one U.S. guard and one Pakistani guard outside Amir's room, while the others settled into their assigned accommodations. Everything was proceeding as closely as possible to his basic plan.

CHAPTER 78

Friday, November 2, 2007
Miami, Florida

The hospital staff and Doctor Jensen's surgical group completed all pre-op preparations in time for surgery to begin just before eight o'clock that morning. The anesthesiologist prepared to administer general anesthesia intended to put Amir into a deep sleep for the surgery. Just a few seconds before the liquid combination of three drugs would start to flow into the tube inserted in the back of his left hand Amir spoke with obvious apprehension lying on his back on the operating table.

"May Allah guide all of you well . . ." and then the drugs entered his body. Within seconds he succumbed to a deep sleep.

Shortly after three o'clock, an orderly wheeled Amir into the recovery room on a gurney with a pair of plain-clothes military guards close behind, one Pakistani, and one American. They maintained their station outside the only entrance to the recovery room. Doctor Jensen was waiting to examine Amir's bandages and check all of the post-operative notes. He was satisfied that he had done everything humanly possible to reverse Amir's blindness. He thought about Amir's last words before he succumbed to the anesthesia, took a deep breath and let it out slowly as he left the room to make a very important phone call.

Amir's recovery had already begun with the natural forces of the universe adapting to the surgical changes made by a relatively young, outwardly brash and egotistical but inwardly sensitive and caring physician. The subtle damage inflicted upon the optical pathways of a talented young Pakistani Muslim boy by an early unfortunate battle with smallpox, now unwittingly a pawn in a novel plan to reduce the threat of terrorism, began to change. He often dreamed of being able to see like every other twelve-year-old boy. At this point in his life, he was neither Pakistani, nor Muslim. He was simply a twelve-year-old boy with hopes and dreams. Doctor Jensen hoped for the ultimate success of his efforts after years of intensive study and practice at the frontiers of his profession, in spite of his rather overwhelming ego. General Murray anticipated the success of the operation and closure of the other end of the bargain he had struck with the boy's father, a politically and militarily uniquely positioned Pakistani Major General. Joe still hoped for ultimate world peace, perhaps enhanced with this unusual and daring effort. Those hopes would carry them through the next three weeks until the bandages would come off for the last time.

CHAPTER 79

Thursday, Thanksgiving Day, November 22, 2007
Miami, Florida

Doctor Jensen smiled at the two guards outside Amir's private room as he opened the door with an optimistic air and strode briskly over to Amir's bed and announced, "It's time, Amir. It's time to take the bandages off for the last time. We will know the answer to your prayers—to all of our prayers—very soon. I am going to turn the lights down so your eyes will not sustain excessive strain or shock when you open them, so the room will be relatively dark. You may feel some pain or discomfort in or around your eyes, but this is to be expected. If you have a severe headache, however, you should tell me immediately. Do you understand everything I have told you, Amir?"

"Yes, I do, Doctor Jensen."

"Do you know what day this is, Amir?"

"I'm . . . not sure . . ."

"This is Thanksgiving Day. It is an annual American holiday started early in the development of our country when we celebrate our good fortune. Many people thank God for providing abundant food, shelter, friends, good health and hope for the future, among other things, so this is a very special day indeed for us to remove your bandages."

"Then I will be especially thankful for all you have done, Doctor Jensen. I hope for the best."

"You are indeed a very special and brave young man, Amir. Tomorrow, I understand we will have a very special treat for you, but I'm not sure I know what it is."

Joe had just arrived outside Amir's room along with General Murray. All of the military guards were outside the room, regardless of how much sleep they had or which shift they had been on. Doctor Fuller was also there, in spite of his normal day off and the endless parade of other pressing hospital matters he usually had to address. Several nurses from the surgical team also ignored their customary day off, and waited anxiously nearby for Doctor Jensen to remove the bandages.

Doctor Jensen pushed the rheostat slider down adjacent to the room light switch, as the overhead lights gradually diminished in intensity to a dim light. The recovery room was an interior room, so there were no windows admitting the intense Florida sunlight to interfere with the process. He walked deliberately over to Amir and removed the tape from the outermost gauze strip around his head. He started to unwrap the seemingly endless length of gauze, carefully rewrapping it around his left hand for easy disposal. Amir felt the gradual release of the mild pressure on his eyes and around his head as each layer of gauze fell away. After he was finished, Doctor Jensen discarded the ball of gauze that was around his left hand, and reached for the two remaining cotton pads, one over each eye.

"Amir, I am going to remove the last part of the bandage next, but I want you to keep your eyes closed until I tell you to open them, and do not rub your eyes, even though you may feel the urge to do so. Do you understand that?"

"Yes. I understand, Doctor Jensen."

He removed the two pads and discarded them as everyone behind him in the hall tried to peer into the room through the window in the door, straining to see the boy's eyes. He looked carefully at Amir's eyes to assess the degree of temporary swelling or any signs of possible trouble before continuing. He saw nothing adverse and smiled to himself. It was *perfect*, at least on the outside! He waited for several seconds, and then spoke.

"Amir, you may now open your eyes—very slowly."

With palpable apprehension and anticipation throughout the room and in the hallway outside his room, Amir opened his eyes slowly and saw the off-white ceiling with four dim recessed lights of a dull whitish-yellow color. He saw Doctor Jensen's flesh-colored face and dark brown hair above him, but it was a little fuzzy and distorted, as tears welled up in his eyes. Doctor Jensen was leaning over Amir, watching him carefully.

"The tears are normal, Amir. They will help wash out your eyes and clear them of any remaining loose cells from the surgery."

More and more tears streamed down Amir's cheeks—tears of joy and gratitude in addition to his body's natural self-cleansing reaction.

"I can see! I can see! *I can see!*"

The usually quiet hospital halls filled with cheers and applause. Even the tough military guards smiled openly, cheered and a few wiped away their own tears of joy revealing something of the unusual bond they had formed with Amir during what would otherwise have been a simple routine assignment of escort, protection and guard duty. They knew he was special because they were providing very unusual protection for him, but they did not know the intricate background of 'the deal' or the connection between the Fresno incident and 'the deal' that was struck between General Arshad and General Murray that had now acquired more momentum toward fulfillment of General Arshad's end of the bargain. They certainly knew nothing of the secret events since the Fresno incident and the unusual intrigue leading up to the agreement between the two generals.

"Amir, the hard part is now over. However, you must stay here in the hospital for another several weeks, while we conduct tests to assess the progress and durability of the recovery process and the quality of your sight. We will need to determine the extent to which you can see colors, and if you can see colors, you will need to learn the names of those colors. You will also need to begin to learn how to read basic printed words and signs, so you can learn to become comfortable with the printed language and social behavior patterns of the normal sighted world. We will get you started with that learning process, but you will continue to learn more after you return home."

"OK," Amir said with cautious determination.

The senior Pakistani guard then walked down the hall to a secluded spot near a stairwell and called General Arshad on his cell phone to inform him of the success of the surgery and the coming timetable of several weeks of testing, assessment and education before Amir would be able to return to Pakistan.

General Arshad listened carefully and then inquired, "How have they treated Amir and you?"

"Everyone here has been quite helpful, courteous and professional. You should have no concerns at all. I can assure you completely that General Murray has indeed been a man of his word. The surgeon is apparently the best in his field of expertise in the United States, if not the world."

General Arshad thanked his commander and broke the connection. He thought about his early doubts in sharp contrast to what General Murray had accomplished. He thought about his own honor as a General, as a man, and as a father. He would not carry the personal guilt of not fulfilling his end of the bargain. He would not bear personal failure of this magnitude for the rest of his career or the rest of his life. He knew that the truth eventually presents itself, sometimes under the most unexpected circumstances or in unusual forms, and where it is deliberately hidden dishonestly or dishonorably it eventually burns through the soul with tragic and sometimes devastating consequences. He started to organize his troops and plans to fulfill his promise to General Murray with determination, confidence, a clear conscience and an honest heart.

CHAPTER 80

Friday, November 23, 2007
Attock, Pakistan

General Arshad gathered a select group of forty-eight soldiers in the same meeting room where he had met with General Murray. He held up a copy of the computerized image of Rasheed's face.

"Your mission will be to arrest this man and bring him here to me, alive and uninjured, and as soon as possible! We know he has lived in this military district in the past, but he may have moved farther north. You are to exercise the *utmost secrecy!* Is that *clearly* understood?"

He noted nods of agreement as he looked into the eyes of each man before him, one by one.

"Major Wasim Ahmed will be my field commander in charge of the entire operation, and will keep me informed on a regular basis. Are there any questions?"

There were no questions. There rarely were questions after General Arshad had given an order. He again showed the men the computerized image of Rasheed Shirani that General Murray had left with him.

"Memorize this image. This man's name is Rasheed Shirani. He is the man you *must* capture."

General Arshad left the room in charge of Major Ahmed, who took the image of Rasheed and studied it very carefully, and had each of the soldiers under his command study it as well. He had already made fifty pocket-sized laminated copies of it, one for each of the soldiers to keep with him to refer to, and handed them out, and kept the remaining two in reserve in his pocket.

"We will operate in twelve groups of four to remain as inconspicuous as possible, sweeping from the south to the north across the western provinces for as long as it takes to find this man. The pictures you now have will not leave your possession *under any circumstances!* We do not want our intentions known among the locals. I will arrange for communications, logistical support and manpower assistance with all military bases throughout the western provinces. When we have located Rasheed, we will close in with sufficient numbers to assure his capture *alive.* No one is to attempt to capture him alone, and no one squad is to attempt to capture him without all necessary assurance of success! *Is that perfectly clear?*"

Unanimous acknowledgment came from the forty-eight soldiers in the room, but Major Ahmed looked out over the faces before him, assuring that he made eye contact with each one of them in a way that persuaded each soldier that he would be held personally accountable for even the slightest violation of his orders. Major Ahmed knew the assignment would involve a 'cat-and-mouse' game as his forces would have to search in areas that had distinctly extremist leanings, and the locals would be alert to a military search and could make it as difficult as possible to locate whoever they thought might be the subject of possible arrest. His men had to be exceptionally subtle and clever in order to outwit consistently the 'interference' or possible collusion from the locals. He would need some luck and perhaps some outside help.

General Arshad had already anticipated that possibility, and contacted General Murray, who immediately sent a message to Duke on System 14 about the need for some 'extra' help. Duke forwarded his message to Raj on System 15 and explained the need for some undercover work in the western provinces to find Rasheed, and to contact General Arshad. Raj responded immediately with excitement and enthusiastic willingness to help. He was excited to be part of the field effort in a real and meaningful way, and not just looking in from the outside, particularly after having put so much effort and energy into researching the entire plan and guiding the effort as much as he had. He knew he could move easily and comfortably among the locals in an effective way because he was obviously not military, not American, and had presented no apparent threat to anyone during his research. Nevertheless, he wanted to use a disguise to assure his anonymity. He decided to make himself look much older by using some makeup and wearing the common clothing typical of many of the remote villages.

He arrived in Attock and met with General Arshad the next day, and offered a plan of what he thought he could do to help. General Arshad approved of his plan with minor modifications by providing him with a tiny transmitter securely inserted inside a common, tan, but otherwise non-descript canvas backpack that he was to carry with him at all times. It would transmit a signal every ten seconds, identifying its exact location with a signal that General Arshad's commanders would see on their field computers. He also gave Raj a cell phone to reach him directly, which they would also track on their portable computers. If the two signals separated too far without a phone call, they would know that Raj might be in trouble, and would send armed soldiers to both signal locations immediately.

CHAPTER 81

Friday, November 23, 2007
Miami, Florida

Doctor Jensen entered Amir's room with a gift-wrapped box, approximately three feet long by eight inches high, by twelve inches wide.

"The color of this wrapping paper is blue, Amir."

"Blue!" he repeated with building anticipation.

"Very good, Amir. And the color of this bow wrapped around it is red" he said, as he touched the bow, looking at Amir for evidence of his understanding.

"Red!" he continued with almost irrepressible anticipation.

"Okay, Amir. And what do you think is printed on the card?"

"Is it my name?"

"Yes, Amir. That is what your name looks like in print in English. Excellent! Now you may open the box. It is a gift from all of us at the Institute to you!"

Amir accepted the box with what could easily have been equivalent to the sum total of all of the glee and anticipation of every twelve-year-old boy in the state of Florida. He eagerly untied the red ribbon and ripped the paper away to reveal a plain light brown box of thick corrugated cardboard. He carefully opened the cover of the box and experienced his first 'peek' with his new visual capability, and saw with the shock of a lifetime something he almost could not believe. Inside the box, carefully cushioned over the entire surface with thick bubble-wrap, was a well-crafted violin case. He virtually shouted with joy, looking at the case and then up at Doctor Jensen, and then back at the case and just stared at it for more than half a minute. Then he slowly removed the plastic bubble-wrap and then the case and placed it gently on his bed. He drew a deep breath, released the four shiny brass metal latches and carefully opened the case. He virtually yelped with joyful surprise as he started to admire the instrument from end to end, nestled in a deep red felt-covered form-fitting bed of thick foam rubber.

Aware of his extra compensation for the successful surgery he had performed, Stanley Jensen felt it was only fair, and an honor to present Amir with a brand new Stradivarius violin built by Rigidio Riva in Sardinia, Italy. He had ordered it with special express delivery from Fein Stringed Instruments in St. Paul, Minnesota in the phone call immediately after the surgery was complete. It cost him a 'mere' $4,500, which he easily and gladly paid.

Amir admired the instrument with the combined memory of what a violin should look like from having played one, his 'tactile memory' of his own second-hand violin in Pakistan, and his restored real vision. The connection between his imagination and reality stunned him both with the realization of how limited his life without sight had been, and yet how much more absolutely miraculous and wonderful it would be from now on with the gift of sight, new to him, but commonly accepted as normal by most of the world's population. He would forever cherish his ability to see.

"I want to hear you play your violin, but not here. All of us who have been taking care of you want to hear you play. Actually, the whole institute and many of the other patients would like to hear you play, so we are going to go down to the auditorium now where there is enough room for everyone to listen to you! It will be a statement of hope to others, both here and around the world, that if we work diligently together for what we want and believe in, we can achieve almost anything we put our minds to!"

Doctor Jensen and General Murray walked with Amir and the two guards on duty. Amir held his precious violin case carefully in front of him with both hands, looking around at everything he could see as he walked down the hall. He was also learning to coordinate his already well-developed sense of hearing with his new visual life. They all took the elevator to the first floor, where they exited and walked a short distance to the institute's general-purpose auditorium that held only about 300 seats in a relatively steep curved configuration facing a rather small center stage. The remainder of the guards had taken the stairs to the first floor. The auditorium, designed for academic lectures and general institute meetings, would now serve as a small, but adequate concert hall. General Murray and the guards walked with Amir down to their seats in the middle of the front row. The auditorium was already almost completely full.

Amir asked Doctor Jensen "Is this where you want me to play?"

"Yes, it is, Amir. Remember, you do not have to be perfect, and you can play anything you want to play. All of us will be thankful to hear anything you play!"

Doctor Fuller walked onto the stage and spoke briefly.

"Thank you all for coming down here. Most of you know why we are here today. For those of you who have not yet heard, we have just recently completed the successful restoration of full sight to a very special young Pakistani boy, who just happens to be a talented violinist. I believe we owe him the opportunity to express his gratitude the best way he knows how. Let's all give Amir Arshad a very warm welcome!"

Everyone clapped appreciatively as Amir rose from his seat and walked up the two steps to the stage with his new violin, turned around and announced in his quiet voice, "I will play for you The Partita for Violin Number Two, by Johann Sebastian Bach, written sometime between 1718 and 1722 in memory of his first wife."

The audience definitely was not prepared for this degree of musical sophistication, and none of them had any idea of what this performance would be like, as they all looked to others seated nearby with expressions and hushed comments of surprise and wonder. Amir spent a few minutes tuning his new violin to make sure the strings were at the proper tension and relative pitch, and then adjusted and secured the tension on his new bow to his satisfaction.

Amir had played only in his school in Abbottabad, and never really appreciated what it would be like to play in front of a live audience that he could actually *see*. His new sighted world presented some new and uncomfortable feelings of intimidation or 'stage fright' in a way that he had never known before. However, he had also developed an acceptance of performance as a blind boy at Abbottabad that his new feelings of 'stage fright' did not completely defeat. The entire auditorium gradually fell completely silent in anticipation as Amir brought the instrument up to his chin.

Amir began to play, actually watching his fingers instead of just feeling them, although he was so accustomed to the music that he often closed his eyes anyway while he was playing. He made the violin sing with feeling, as he believed both the composer and the builder of the instrument intended. By the end of Amir's almost thirty-minute performance of the five movements, the spellbound audience had at least a mild appreciation of the composer's feelings for his first wife. Those in the audience who had little appreciation of classical music nevertheless developed an appreciation of Amir's talent and passion for the violin. The piece was complex and long, often requiring simultaneous string expression and several difficult interval sequences and transitions with precise fingering. They all sat stunned for a moment after Amir finally brought his new violin down from his chin and bowed graciously at the end of his performance. Even those with no musical ability or experience could appreciate his special talent. Members of the audience then stood one by one at first, and then the whole audience stood, clapping and cheering in appreciation of his passion and talent as well as the near miracle of his restored gift of sight. Doctor Jensen did not regret one single penny of the cost of the violin. Had he known more about Amir's considerable talent, he would have bought an even better one. After over two minutes of continuous applause, Amir stepped down from the stage and returned to his seat, basking in the greatest joy of accomplishment of his young life. He carefully placed his new violin back in its case and closed it, then sat down in the front row again with a broad smile of pride, joy and profound gratitude.

Then General Murray stood and mounted the steps to the stage.

"Thank you very much, Amir, for sharing your very special talent! We all wish you continued success in your musical life! I hope you all will forgive me for this extra part of our impromptu program, but I made a promise to this young man's father in Pakistan that he would see and hear a very special young lady sing before he returns to Pakistan. I decided that this was the best opportunity to fulfill that promise, and at the same time provide some rare entertainment as further expression of my personal gratitude to all of you for a very difficult, but very important job well done under very unusual circumstances."

Everyone in the audience looked around, whispering to one another nearby in genuine surprise, curiosity and anticipation. The day had already become one of the most unusual in the history of the institute, and yet they felt even more anticipation.

General Murray walked to the left side of the stage and opened a door for the four male members ofThe Autumn Dream dressed in their signature black outfits to assemble on the stage with their equipment, instruments and wooden stools. All of this impromptu preparation occurred in less than fifteen minutes, as the audience continued to buzz periodically with anticipation and curiosity. Amir sat in the front row, watching everything very carefully with his new gift of sight, glancing occasionally up to Doctor Jensen next to him, who was equally as curious as everyone else.

The men finally appeared to be ready to start playing, as Rob Reynolds nodded to the others with the beat of the first song. They started to play one of their traditional introductions while Sasha was still backstage. Although they were somewhat limited in producing their customary nightclub introduction of Sasha, she started singing their first number behind the stage, and then walked through the door on the left, wearing her signature white sequined dress, flooding the entire auditorium with her unique, rich and exciting voice as she approached the middle of the stage. They had no need for voice microphones in the relatively small room. Doctor Jensen took note of her visual allure immediately, as was apparent in his open-mouthed stare. Amir was overwhelmed by his first sighted appreciation of exceptional female beauty. His well-tuned sense of hearing during most of his life up to that point absorbed every nuance of her unusual and very beautiful voice. He more than all the others in the room felt the quality of her voice and appreciated her remarkably broad vocal range. This simultaneous sensation of visual beauty and virtual vocal seduction was practically an incendiary assault on a young teenage boy with developing male hormones. Sasha made a permanent impression on the young Pakistani musician that would assure his very sincere and truthful report to his father of having *seen* and heard the woman General Murray had promised he would see and hear.

As the music ended, the audience stood as one, applauded and cheered in generous heart-felt expression of their enjoyment of the group and their music. The Autumn Dream would perform another five songs before they left the stage, leaving everyone in the relatively small auditorium thoroughly refreshed, overjoyed, and at peace.

CHAPTER 82

Monday, November 26, 2007
Miami, Florida

Doctor Jensen examined Amir carefully, looking for continued proper healing as well as sight quality, including tests for normal differentiation of light intensity and color. He noted with great interest that Amir's vision was almost twenty-twenty. He was seeing what most people are able to see clearly and unaided at various standard distances. Amir passed all of the tests, indicating to Doctor Jensen that further care at the institute would not be necessary. His job was finished, so he called General Murray to inform him that Amir was ready to go home. Then he turned to Amir.

"Amir, you are ready to go home! You are a very special young man, and I will miss you very much."

"I will miss you also, Doctor Jensen. I cannot thank you enough for what you have done for me. Maybe someday I will be able to thank you properly."

"Amir, I understand what you are saying, but I want you to understand that you have already thanked me more than enough. However, I would be very pleased if you would write to me occasionally to tell me how you are doing. If you ever have any difficulty with your eyes, then I want you to tell me, so you can come back and let me take care of you. Will you do that, Amir?"

"Yes, Doctor Jensen, I will."

Amir hugged Doctor Jensen as the two bid each other farewell.

General Murray arrived just in time to see Doctor Jensen leave Amir's room. The Pakistani guard outside in the hall smiled in recognition of both the successful completion of the surgery and knowing he would be going home as well.

General Murray said, "OK, Amir. Let's go home! Don't forget your violin!"

The contingent of eight tough-looking soldiers in common civilian attire, a U.S. Army General out of uniform, and a twelve-year-old Pakistani boy left the Bascom-Palmer Institute for the last time, but with a sense of friendship and familiarity far different from the unusual circumstances of their arrival just twenty-six days before. The same blue Air Force bus was waiting in front of the institute, as the entire military group boarded the bus with Amir for their return to Homestead Air Force Base, and the chartered plane that would take them non-stop back to Pakistan.

CHAPTER 83

Wednesday, November 28, 2007
Attock, Pakistan

Amir arrived at the Army base just after noon for his first sighted reunion with his father. General Arshad was waiting at the main gate to the military compound as the military van carrying his son, the three Pakistani guards, one of General Murray's bodyguards and General Murray arrived. The other four United States Army guards were in another van behind the first one.

The guards got out of the front and the rear of the van first, and opened the middle doors for General Murray on one side and Amir with his violin on the other. General Murray met Amir at the front of the van and escorted him for the remaining thirty yards to his waiting father, and then stood away from the two to allow suitable privacy.

General Arshad looked intently into his son's eyes at arm's length, and saw for the first time the life and visual enjoyment for which he had all but given up hope for most of the last decade. He felt for the first time in over ten years the *visual* bond taken for granted in most families and all of its subtle nuances that would enrich their relationship. General Arshad smiled broadly as tears of joy developed slowly and fell from his eyes for the first time since he first learned of his son's blindness. Amir put his violin case down just before his father hugged him and held him tightly in a long and warm embrace that elevated him from a mere Major General to a proud and loving father. Amir cried as well, enjoying actually *seeing* his father after years of having only a vague mental picture of him. He reached up to touch his father's face, connecting for the first time in his memory the tactile and visual image of him. After what seemed like a full five minutes of embrace, Amir pulled back from his father and picked up the precious violin case for his father's approval, almost as if he were presenting it as a gift.

"My doctor was wonderful! He gave this violin to me, Father! It is a Stradivarius, one of the most famous violins in the whole world! I played it for the first time after my surgery in an auditorium full of people from the hospital! Then I heard a very beautiful woman sing after I played my violin! I have never heard, nor ever imagined such a beautiful voice or such a beautiful woman, Father! I felt almost as though she was singing *just for me!* I felt a musical connection with her! I am so overjoyed I cannot speak any more!"

General Arshad thought for just a moment of how the young woman *actually had* sung *just for Amir*, but he also realized that she had sung for a better future for many other people as well.

"Amir, I am also overjoyed that you can now see. I will enroll you in a regular school where you can continue to learn with the advantage of sight taken for granted by so many young people, and you will have continued violin lessons, as well!"

General Arshad then slowly turned away from his son, and strode over to General Murray and said in a subdued, but firm commander's voice, "And you shall have Rasheed Shirani, General Murray. I will call you when he is in my custody."

"Thank you, General Arshad. I will return to the United States, and await your call on my private number."

He then handed General Arshad a card with his contact information. He noted that General Arshad did *not* say '*if I can find him.*'

General Murray then turned to Amir and said, "Amir, you have been a very brave young man, and you have done more good than you can imagine. I am honored to have been a part of your life-changing experience, and truly wish you continued success with your education and your violin. If you would like to visit the United States again, you will be more than welcome. I promise you that!"

Then he turned and walked back toward the van and got in along with his contingent of soldiers. One of General Arshad's soldiers drove them back to the airport for their return trip to the United States.

CHAPTER 84

Monday, December 24, 2007
Wana, Pakistan

Major Ahmed and his troops had been scouring the Pakistani countryside for weeks in search of Rasheed Shirani, and his men were approaching the very rugged northern part of the western provinces with no success. They would probably have searched the western and northern provinces for many years if an informant had not suffered the torment of conscience.

It was Christmas Eve. Hamid Salim saw soldiers moving through Waziristan, obviously looking for someone. Hamid and Rasheed were the same age, but had parted ways years ago when Hamid started exploring Christianity. It was actually more of Rasheed disapproving of Hamid than the other way around. He was a devout Muslim, but had an intellectual curiosity about Christianity that he could never satisfy one way or another, and was therefore not a 'pure' enough Muslim for Rasheed's friendship. He read what little he could get his hands on, and kept his curiosity about Christianity hidden even from his family, because he knew he would suffer extreme disapproval, if not being cast out from his family completely if they were to discover his interest. He knew the kind of evil Rasheed was capable of when he set his mind to something. In spite of his initial boyhood friendship with Rasheed, he saw Rasheed slip further and further into extremist Muslim philosophy and the two saw less and less of each other over time, until they became almost completely estranged. As a young boy, he had personally watched Rasheed kill insects and torment small dogs and cats and other animals with almost a perverse glee and vicious sense of power when no adults were around. He had also watched Rasheed mercilessly tease and bully some of their friends while he stood by helplessly, afraid to challenge Rasheed or stand up in support of his friends.

Raj was sitting in a small teahouse in Wana, Waziristan reading a newspaper, just off the east side of the Wana Road, taking a well-deserved rest from his search. Wana is a small town about 200 miles west-northwest of Faisalabad, and about 160 miles southwest of Peshawar. He adopted the persona of a silk merchant, which he could play rather comfortably, given his life experience and his family's business. However, he deliberately kept his Indian heritage hidden as best he could with his disguise because relations between Pakistan and India were still generally far from friendly in the remote politically unorganized areas, and he could not always be assured of acceptance in the Pakistani tribal regions he was traveling through, which were home to more than seventy different tribes. The internal social structure of Pakistan itself was weak, held together primarily by the dominance of the military. However, several extremist militant groups were still active in Punjab, Pakistan's most populous province where Raj had been traveling, and some apparently still had ties to Al Qaeda. Raj was aware of rumors that they had trained militants who participated in the London bombings on July 7, 2005, so he knew he was in essentially hostile territory and did not want to take any unnecessary chances.

Raj left the teahouse to walk down the street, and stumbled as he accidentally stepped into a small pothole in the road and fell to his knees with enough pain to remain in that position for several seconds. He lost his grasp of his backpack, which he had been carrying at that point with the photo of Rasheed inside, both of which fell onto the road in front of him. Shortly thereafter, a young man approached him, offering assistance.

"May I help you, sir?"

Hamid saw the photograph that had slipped out of the backpack onto the ground and inhaled with a quickened heartbeat and surprise in his widening eyes. Raj looked up at the young man, noticing that he was staring down at the image of Rasheed with obvious recognition.

"Thank you, but I will be all right. I just stumbled in that pothole and lost my balance."

The young man said nothing as he continued to stare at the image on the ground. Raj swallowed hard and took a deep breath before speaking again.

"Do you know the person in that picture?"

Hamid slowly turned toward Raj, studying him carefully, while offering his hand for Raj to grasp and helped him stand up, and responded with guarded and then gradually undisguised suspicion, "Yes. I know him . . . Who are you?"

"My name is Raj. I am a silk merchant looking for new business in the western provinces" he said evenly, but with a quickening heartbeat, fearing that an intelligent person would detect his lie, but hoping this young man would not betray him.

He was gambling with his cover story and identity for the first time with potentially negative consequences, and he felt caught completely off guard by these unanticipated circumstances. He could have fallen anywhere, but he wondered why he had to fall in the first place, let alone near someone who could challenge his identity and intentions.

Hamid knew that Rasheed could have absolutely nothing to do with a silk merchant, and immediately suspected that Rasheed had again done something serious enough to attract the unusual attention of other people, and in this case, those other people could very well be the police.

"Why do you have this picture?" Hamid asked cautiously, convinced that Raj was not a silk merchant.

Raj felt very vulnerable but gambled with a partial version of the truth, "I am trying to find this man."

Hamid was apprehensive, but pressed further with continued suspicion, "Why are you trying to find him?"

Raj hesitated with a dearth of excuses or credible stories, unable to escape the other man's simple and expectable logical question.

He looked around and then took a deep breath while trying to settle his racing heartbeat, and said almost desperately, "Because I believe he is responsible for killing over 400 people in Fresno, California with a bomb on September 10 of this year."

He waited with increasing apprehension for some kind of reaction while his heartbeat raced within him, almost holding his breath in preparation for the worst consequences of his ill-planned behavior during this unanticipated encounter. 'Undercover' fieldwork was indeed far more challenging than he had ever anticipated. Hamid's eyes widened, and Raj noticed, relieved for the moment that his gamble so far had not cost him either personal injury or real fear of failing in his mission—*yet.* Every passing second without adverse consequences helped settle his anxiety to some extent. Hamid hesitated for a moment, as if recounting a lifetime of experiences with Rasheed, realizing that his former friend might indeed be capable of such treachery. He stooped down, picked up the backpack and the picture and handed them to Raj.

He knew about the Fresno incident. Even the closed societies of the world could not completely prevent the steady spread of the story through the internet or long-distance phone conversations and subsequent word of mouth. It had reached even the most remote corners of the earth in one form or another, just like the news about the 9/11 attacks had a little over six years before. The two men continued to stare at each other, each mentally groping for release from his mounting anxiety. After what seemed like a minor eternity to Raj, Hamid finally spoke evenly without his prior tone of suspicion.

"Come with me, my friend. I know where to look for him."

Raj looked at Hamid with stunned disbelief as the pain momentarily disappeared from his leg and he began to realize that Hamid would probably not be a threat to him. Raj followed slightly behind Hamid as the two men walked down the street for several blocks toward another teahouse. Approximately 150 feet from the teahouse, Hamid hesitated in front of Raj, effectively halting their progress, and turned around to face Raj. He spoke in a quiet confident voice.

"He is sitting outside at that teahouse at the end of this block. Do you see a man sitting alone outside that teahouse?"

Raj looked carefully in the direction Hamid indicated, and hesitated for only a moment before answering, "Yes."

"Then I must leave you, my friend. I cannot help you any further. May Allah guide you and keep you well."

Raj felt relieved that his mission was still intact, but he also felt abandoned as Hamid turned and walked away, leaving him without the only semblance of real human support he had had since he left

Attock. He understood that Hamid had probably just suffered through a very intense personal moral decision.

Then he walked down the street to the teahouse and took a seat at a table about fifteen feet from the man Hamid had pointed out. His heart was racing. Raj subtly checked his computerized image of Rasheed inside his backpack. Now he was sure. Rasheed turned and glanced blankly at Raj for a moment. Raj almost vibrated with anticipation and anxiety as he looked at his paper, and feared betraying his mission. He knew he could not physically attack the man, and had no weapons to use as 'persuasion,' and he certainly had no experience in physical violence. Yet, he also feared that this would be his only opportunity to accomplish something constructive in the larger effort to arrest Rasheed, and if he failed, then Rasheed could very well disappear for a very long time to come, free to invent and implement further havoc and evil. Raj then casually arose from his seat, left his backpack under the table as an electronic marker, circled around the table and then walked out into the street again in an innocent but honest effort to find some privacy to use his cell phone, but he did not want to move so far away as to lose sight of Rasheed. He stepped behind a wall, just enough to obscure his behavior from Rasheed, and called General Arshad, who answered his private number on the second ring.

"Yes?"

"General. Raj Sampat here. I have Rasheed in my sight at a teahouse near a bazaar on Wana Road. I have left my backpack under a table near him, and I have moved away from the building."

"We have your signals now. You should continue to move farther away from there, but try to monitor his location and call me if he leaves. If he does leave, remember to go back to pick up your backpack. I will have troops at your backpack location very shortly. My men will have a description of your appearance, as well as a signal from the cell phone you are using, so you should be in no danger as they approach. Nevertheless, you must find a safe place to observe Rasheed from a distance so he does not become suspicious of you. I will establish road blocks around the entire town shortly, effectively preventing anyone from entering or leaving the village."

Raj said with unaccustomed and daring confidence, "I'll do my best."

Raj walked farther down the road to find an inconspicuous observation point and sat down on the curb and rubbed his sore leg, but kept an eye on the teahouse. Rasheed had not moved. He was still busy reading his own paper.

Raj looked furtively from side to side for some evidence of General Arshad's troops, but he saw no such evidence. People looked at him occasionally, but without what Raj could detect as unusual interest. He still blended into the culture well enough, he thought, with some relief. However, he was becoming unsure of himself. Thinking about how to act in a field operation was one thing. Actually *doing* it was quite another reality altogether! He developed a sudden hunger, and his mouth was getting dry. His body was beginning to betray him.

Where are the troops?

Then he heard something unusual, and turned his head from side to side to try to identify exactly where the sound was coming from, but still could not recognize the sound. Then he understood. He heard the rapid but muffled 'whop-whop-whop' sound of at least one helicopter apparently behind the distant hills. He was concerned that Rasheed had heard it also, and would leave, or hide. He could not see anything at all unusual. Then the sound stopped. His apprehension increased. Rasheed still had not moved. His cell phone rang, shocking Raj into the intensity of the developing reality of his situation with such a jolt that he yelped.

"Yes?"

"This is General Arshad. I am monitoring the location of your cell phone. I have men down the street from you wearing local clothing so no one will recognize them as soldiers. I want you to cross the street, stoop down and scratch your ankle before you get to the opposite side of the street, so my men can identify you. Do it now."

Raj complied, and innocently stooped to scratch his left ankle, still holding the cell phone to his ear, and then continued across the street.

"My field commander sees you, but you will not see him. He and his men are blending into the community as you are. However, uniformed soldiers are standing by outside the village, guarding all roads in and out of the village, as well as some of the open areas. We are now going to apprehend Rasheed at the location of your backpack."

That must be why I heard helicopters! Raj thought to himself.

"You have done well, Raj. Now keep walking away from Rasheed, and do not show any unusual interest or lack of interest in anything that happens around you during the next fifteen to twenty minutes. I will call you back when we have captured Rasheed."

"I understand, General. I am continuing to walk northeast on the main road."

"OK. We will have him in custody shortly. That is all."

General Arshad continued to follow the cell phone signal very carefully everywhere Raj went. Special troops not wearing uniforms were already infiltrating the town, and some were approaching the teahouse from every side street around it, thereby blocking any escape from that small area as they tightened their 'noose' around the teahouse where Rasheed was seated. The residents of the village closest to the teahouse could sense something in the air. Something unusual was happening, but they were unaware of anything obvious at first. They could not see General Arshad's uniformed troops outside the village, and they could not see anything suspicious in the main street, but they had a collective unspecified intuitive awareness of danger, like many animals sense danger completely outside of human perception capabilities. The 'plain-clothes' troops moved in slowly, steadily, toward the teahouse in pairs from all four sides. Rasheed was still visible outside at a table, reading his paper. Suddenly, he looked up, sensing the same air of apprehension wafting through the village nearby, but it was already too late for him to try to escape. Eight men quickly surrounded the table in front of the teahouse, three from each of the side alleys on both sides of the teahouse as each of the two soldiers coming from the rear took opposite sides of the building, and two from the front. Rasheed panicked in place and dropped his paper while pushing himself away from the table.

"Rasheed Shirani!" called a deep commanding voice from the man approaching behind the loose circle of eight soldiers.

Rasheed stood quickly, but immediately froze as eight automatic rifles appeared from under eight robes around him, pointing directly at him. He looked warily at the muzzles of the guns and back into the cold eyes of the men standing around him. He knew they were serious. He was still not prepared to die. Major Ahmed parted the circle of troops from the street and faced Rasheed.

"You are under arrest for causing the deaths of 419 people in Fresno, California, in the United States of America. We will not kill you, but we will transport you to a holding cell in Attock, and eventually to the American authorities in Rawalpindi for extradition to the United States to stand trial for your crime. If you do not cooperate fully, we will sedate you! Do you understand everything I have told you, Rasheed Shirani?"

Rasheed pleaded with all of the intensity of a thoroughly depleted conscience, "I am not this Rasheed Shirani person you speak of! I have done nothing wrong!"

He was effectively denying his own existence in an ironically prescient manner.

Major Ahmed rushed abruptly forward to within inches of Rasheed's face holding the photographic image of Rasheed rendered from the police artist's sketch right in front of his eyes. Rasheed stepped back reflexively, completely stunned by the extremely persuasive likeness of himself that he could no longer deny. He had not allowed anyone to photograph him during the last fifteen years, and had no idea where this picture had come from. He could not even begin to comprehend how this image had been produced. He just entered the world of known terrorists from the world of obscurity.

"Is this picture not of you, Rasheed Shirani?" the Major demanded sharply with the weight of his complete conviction.

Every subsequent second of Rasheed's shocked, confused and fearful silence convinced the commander that he had the right man.

"Secure the prisoner!" he ordered sharply.

Two soldiers then grabbed Rasheed's arms firmly, one from each side, and secured him with vice-like strength while two other soldiers bound his hands and legs with rope, assuring that he would neither try to injure himself nor try to escape.

"Search him thoroughly!" Major Ahmed demanded.

The platoon sergeant gave his weapon to one of his soldiers, and approached Rasheed with a cold, determined glare into the back of his eyes and began a thorough, impolite body search. He found and removed a small moneybag with typical contents. He removed a small hunting knife. Then he found and grasped a cell phone, and removed it. The remaining search yielded nothing of significance. The sergeant handed what he found to Major Ahmed and then retrieved his weapon.

Major Ahmed called General Arshad on his field telephone while keeping his eyes fixed on Rasheed's.

After only one ring, he said, "I have Rasheed Shirani in custody, General! There was no shooting and there are no casualties."

"Excellent, Major! Now bring him to my command prison in Attock as soon as possible, *alive and unharmed!*"

General Arshad then called Raj to confirm that Rasheed Shirani was now in custody, and that he was relieved of his assignment. Relieved both officially and emotionally, Raj started to look for a taxi for his trip back to Attock. He had absolutely no intention of being near Rasheed again even by joining the military guards for that trip.

CHAPTER 85

Wednesday, December 26, 2007
Attock, Pakistan

"General Murray, this is General Arshad. I promised you a call when I have Rasheed Shirani in custody. He is here in my command prison in Attock under guard. He has been held under restraint to prevent suicide, and he has been fed as well as can be expected under the circumstances. I suggest you come and pick him up as soon as possible, because it appears that he has recently decided to starve himself to death. I will minimize all security procedures for your convenience, and have him at Rawalpindi Airport by the time you arrive, ready for your immediate custody. And incidentally, we have his cell phone, which I believe you will find quite interesting!"

"Thank you very much, General Arshad! I will leave for Rawalpindi Airport, arriving sometime tomorrow to pick him up with the same squad of soldiers as before who are already familiar with the situation, to keep security procedures as simple as possible."

"Understood, General. I will have him taken to the airport, where I will await further confirmation of your arrival. We will hold him at the southeast end of the main runway to maintain as much privacy and security as possible. Have your pilot taxi to that location for transfer. I will see that the relevant airport operations personnel are aware of my requirements for this mission and will not interfere. I will also ensure that a fuel truck is available at the transfer location."

"Thank you for your assistance, General Arshad. I will keep you informed of our arrival schedule."

Both men broke the connection, and General Murray immediately alerted his troops and prepared to leave for Pakistan.

CHAPTER 86

Thursday, December 27, 2007|
Rawalpindi Airport, Pakistan

General Murray stepped down from the custom-configured Army Gulfstream V C-37 twin-engine jet in his tan fatigue uniform with his contingent of five uniformed guards, also in fatigues. They walked quickly to the prearranged location at the end of the main runway far from the airport terminal where there would be no observers or unwanted interference while the aircraft was refueled. General Arshad was waiting by a military truck similar to a two-and-a-half-ton U.S. Army vehicle with a squad of eight uniformed armed guards, two on each side and two in front of and behind Rasheed Shirani. Rasheed was shackled in chains with just enough slack to allow him to walk and prevent extension of either his arms or his legs beyond minimal requirements for balance and movement. A fuel truck was standing by near the transport truck, exactly as General Arshad had promised. General Murray and his soldiers approached the men near the truck.

The two generals saluted habitually without further formality as General Arshad proclaimed, "Now he is yours, my friend. Here is the cell phone we found in his possession when we arrested him. Good luck!"

With that, General Murray accepted the phone and put it securely in his pocket, and said simply, "Thank you General. He will have a trial in a civilian court of law, and then the will of the people will prevail."

General Arshad nodded briefly, and then the two generals shook hands.

After a brief pause, General Arshad said with genuine sincerity, "Thank you again for what you did . . . for my son!"

General Murray smiled briefly, nodded silently with an appreciative focus directly into General Arshad's eyes, and then turned away to join his men. The five tough U.S. Army soldiers knew very well who they would be guarding, and they replaced the encirclement of the Pakistani guards smoothly, watching him with expressions threatening immediate and effective harm if he did anything but walk as expected to the stairs of the waiting Gulfstream jet. General Arshad and his men returned to their truck and sped off away from the sleek jet as the stairs disappeared into the plane, and the door closed and locked for the long flight back to Fresno, California, via a prearranged stop in Tokyo for refueling.

Within twenty minutes, the plane was fully fueled and ready to leave Rawalpindi. The big Rolls Royce jet engines roared to sufficient power to move the plane into a turn to point down the longest runway for take-off. It hesitated for only twenty seconds, and then the engines roared to full power once again as the sleek jet rumbled quickly down the runway with rapidly increasing speed. The plane easily lifted into the clear sky and quickly climbed to its cruising altitude. Inside, General Murray sat facing his prisoner next to a window in the specially reconfigured interior five feet from him and securely fastened to his seat with a guard in the seat across the aisle, one in the seat behind him, and one in the other seat facing him from the front.

"I am aware that you have refused to eat, Rasheed. That is of little consequence to me, because I am going to get you into a United States courtroom as soon as possible. You will have an attorney appointed by the court, most likely, unless someone else feels compelled to come to your defense. Your fate will be decided according to the laws of the United States of America."

"*My fate will be decided by Allah!*" Rasheed retorted with venomous rancor.

"*Allah is not flying this airplane, Rasheed!*"

The highly disciplined guards looked straight ahead, as if they heard nothing. Their orders were to see that Rasheed left that plane and entered the courtroom alive. They would also serve as a second security force working with the sheriff's deputies during the entire trial, including transportation to and from the courtroom and his confinement between court sessions, protecting the public as necessary, and generally maintaining order. General Murray specifically ordered his troops to do whatever was necessary to see that the trial came to its proper conclusion.

General Murray opened up his laptop computer and logged on to System 12 to notify Duke that he was en route to Fresno via Tokyo with Rasheed Shirani in custody, and indicated that his prisoner was apparently intent upon starving himself to death as soon as possible. He communicated the same message to Director Miles via CIA channels, assured that the President of the United States would get the same message very shortly thereafter.

CHAPTER 87

Thursday, December 27, 2007
Cambridge, Massachusetts

Duke informed Professor Michalik that the trial of Rasheed Shirani had been scheduled in Fresno for January 4, 2008. The professor immediately contacted each of his seminar students, offering them an opportunity to attend the trial at no cost to them during the optional winter session. All of his students accepted, and individually found their way to Fresno after New Year's Day at the expense of The Chancellor Organization.

The upcoming trial received broad media coverage over the airwaves, in print and through the internet all over the world, including the frigid beauty of Alaska, where one very large, angry truck driver broke a long-standing practice. He purchased a first-class round-trip seat on Alaska Air to Fresno, California for $750.

General Murray sent the cell phone to Langley by special currier as soon as possible after his plane landed, and called his communications analysis group leader to tell him to expect the phone. It would be there within the hour.

"Captain Martin, you find every bit of rat shit, every electronic bit and byte in that phone and prepare an assessment of every goddamned thing you find—every memory content, every call incoming or outgoing, times, dates, locations—fingerprints included. This is of the highest priority, twenty-five hours a day! If you need personnel help, take it on my authority. No one—I repeat—*NO ONE* is to interfere with or delay this assignment for any reason whatsoever, or I will have his neck on the chopping block! Contact me with your results on a secure channel immediately when you are through. If you encounter any flak of any kind whatsoever, call me *immediately* and I will make whatever is necessary happen for the most efficient and timely accomplishment of this assignment! Is that perfectly clear, Captain?"

"Yes sir! Clear as a bell! I'll be on it as soon as it arrives!"

CHAPTER 88

Friday, December 28, 2007
Fresno, California

By this time, the federal prosecutor in Fresno, William H. Mensch knew that he would be prosecuting the case of his lifetime. He was a 1972 graduate of Middlebury College and the Yale Law School. The trial would be at the 9th Circuit, Eastern Division of the United States District Court in the Robert E. Coyle Federal Building at 2500 Tulare Street, Room 2401, barely four and a half blocks from the actual site of the explosion. By this time, workers had already replaced several hundred broken windows, the only major damage to the Federal Building. However, the damage from the blast was still evident throughout the downtown Holiday Inn and Casino One location, as well as the Fulton Mall. Mensch had all of the relevant information from the CIA and the FBI, including the flight manifests with Rasheed Shirani's name on them and the time-stamped satellite photographs of the journey of the U-Haul truck at various locations across the southern United States. He had the photographs of the man and the U-Haul truck and trailer and infrared imagery from the Air Force jet that flew over Rasheed's location in the desert east of Tucson with the classic infrared signature of intense heat coming from the overworked truck engine and transmission from the long journey. The Mexican private detective Cordera Alvarez would testify about Rasheed's activities in Mexico, including the fact that Rasheed had arrived with Khalid's bright green Kawasaki motorcycle at the Mexico City airport after the Fresno explosion and left it there before returning to Pakistan. Juanita Morales would testify that Rasheed was indeed the man who checked into her motel on Saturday, September 8 near Tucson, Arizona. He had the computer-enhanced sketches from the Mobile police sketch artist, Sylvia Amoretti. He had the testimony of Trooper Vince Robertson of the California Highway Patrol about a suspicious Toyota van abandoned on the east side of the northbound lanes of Route 99 south of Fresno. The FBI would confirm through the serial numbers on the engine block that Khalid Kayani was the owner of that van. Farah would identify the FBI pictures of the van and the motorcycle, stating that they belonged to her husband. He had the circumstantial evidence of the blast site, including evidence of the explosive material used, nails, truck fragments and expert military and scientific witnesses to testify about the nature of the blast, the approximate location of the center of the explosion behind and between the Holiday Inn and the casino, and the extent of the blast damage. He also had the time-line story about Khalid, the alleged final driver of the explosive-laden truck and trailer, including his sudden and unexplained complete disappearance the day of the explosion. He had a list of statistics, including 419 dead, 1,647 wounded, at least fourteen of whom would never walk again, at least a half dozen of whom lost their sight, and at least 128 of whom would not be able to afford medical care for their injuries. He had official assessments of $1.35 billion of physical building and infrastructure damage, along with 196 automobiles destroyed or damaged by the blast. He did not have evidence of the source of the C4 or the PE4 explosive material, and that bothered him a great deal, but he thought he could work without it. He did not know the identity of at least one obvious accomplice, or several other suspected accomplices between Miami and California. He did not have evidence of other vehicles that may have been used in transporting the explosives from their point of manufacture to Rasheed. He did not yet know about the cell phone. However, he did have public opinion and outrage on his side, which he knew would define justice in the end if he did his job correctly, and he knew that there was no location in the United States where that pervasive outrage did not exist. The entire case would come precariously close to the boundaries of fairness and correct application of accepted circumstantial legal principles on the one hand, and the law of the jungle on the other.

However, up to this point Rasheed was dictating the pace of justice, while at the same time he was indirectly confirming his guilt with his continued refusal to eat. He had instilled terror in the hearts of innocent United States citizens. In his heart, he had taunted the United States authorities for not capturing him immediately after the event. Now he was intent upon robbing his victims, their loved ones and the country of the rather limited satisfaction of punishing him, even as inadequate as that 'punishment' would be.

CHAPTER 89

Saturday, December 29, 2007
Langley, Virginia

At precisely nine forty-seven Saturday morning, General Murray's secure computer in his office was recording a message from Captain Martin. That event in turn generated a signal to General Murray's private cell phone. He immediately drove to his office to retrieve the information. When he got to his office, he retrieved the following message from his computer:

'The following individuals are associated with the phone numbers in the cell phone identified as belonging to Rasheed Shirani. Role identification was derived in part from the date and time of the phone contact:

NAME: Mohammed Abdul-Muqtadir
Location: Detroit Michigan

We believe he was the first driver of the U-Haul truck to the initial location in Miami.

NAMES: Faiz Anas and Marid Abdul-Aziz
Location: Washington, D.C.

We believe these two men are responsible for the delivery of the C4 load in Mobile, Alabama.

NAMES: Muhammad Kazmi and Kamran Shah
Location: Philadelphia, Pennsylvania

We believe these two men are responsible for the delivery of C4 in Houston, Texas.

NAME: Hatem Magdi
Location: New York City

Most likely delivered the trailer load of PE4 in Ozona, Texas.

All of these individuals have had some association with Jamaat al Fuqra, a terrorist organization founded by Sheik Mubarek Ali Shah Gilani, the Islamic cleric Daniel Pearl was attempting to interview when he was kidnapped and killed by Al-Qaeda in 2002, and a group that may be linked to over two-dozen murders and fire-bombings inside the U.S.'

General Murray immediately contacted the FBI to relay this information verbally and electronically, and made sure they understood the significance of who these people were, and would arrest them, get them into custody, and then transfer them to Lemoore Naval Air Station as soon as possible.

CHAPTER 90

Friday, January 4, 2008
Fresno, California

Only a few fair weather clouds floated in the otherwise sunny morning sky above the city of Fresno, as people arrived at the courthouse wearing sport coats, jackets and light sweaters. The courtroom filled to capacity, but with only one television camera and one operator allowed by the judge. All the major national wire services had reporters in the courtroom, and at least two dozen foreign correspondents made their way to Fresno and managed to find seats in the crowded courtroom.

Judge Howard J. Keller had a reputation throughout the judicial community in California and most of the 9th Circuit jurisdiction in the western United States as a tough, but brilliant jurist. He took complete control of the courtroom and would not tolerate much 'creative' legal procedure from the lawyers who appeared before him. He was a young fifty-eight years old, thin, just over six feet tall, and fit from years of jogging and playing squash. He still had all of his original adult teeth and most of his dark brown hair. He always commanded the attention of everyone in his courtroom with his clear, penetrating and solid bass voice, which was even more effective when he looked out at the gallery over his wire-rimmed glasses.

Among the crowd in the courtroom were the entire group of participants in Sasha's therapy session in Denver, as well as Joe, Kenny,

General Murray, Cordera Alvarez, J. Davis Harrington, Lou Bishov and Steve Markham, Professor Teodor Michalik and his seminar students, Doctor Naved Musharraf, Raj Sampat, San Diego Patrolman James Dennison, Hector Johnson, Farah Kayani, and various public officials of the city of Fresno and the state of California. Duke Chancellor was not there.

The public defender of Rasheed Shirani was G. Mitchell Rushman, a thirty-four-year-old graduate of Stanford College and the Stanford Law School, first in his class, but with no significant professional triumphs up to this time. He had little more than about ten days of preparation, and an obviously hopeless case, but he was obligated to provide the best defense his considerable intellect could muster.

"All rise!"

Everyone in the courtroom stood with a collective rush of anticipation.

"The United States 9th District Court is now in session, The Honorable Judge Howard J. Keller presiding!"

Judge Keller walked through a doorway behind the modern, but still imposing bench and ascended the two steps to his seat.

"Ladies and gentlemen, please be seated" he boomed.

Within seconds, the crowd of spectators sat almost as one with the dull rush of the sound of many bodies coming to rest upon the wooden benches, and settled in for what promised to be an exciting and emotionally charged trial. Judge Keller proceeded.

"Ladies and gentlemen, this is a court of law. This is where we try to contribute to resolution of the never-ending struggle for order and peace in our society through a concept we usually define as justice. It is not a perfect concept, but it is the best we have to work with, and it is much better than the alternatives. It has withstood the tests of centuries. We will strive to arrive at justice in this case through discovery and recognition of the truth, but we will not tolerate disruptions. Because of the widespread publicity of the events at the foundation of this case, we will expect strong beliefs and emotions to come to the surface, but we will maintain order and respect for the process of understanding the facts and arriving at a determination of the truth and the associated disposition of justice. There is no justice without truth. Anyone who chooses to attempt to disrupt these proceedings will be removed immediately from this courtroom, and will not be permitted to return.

The case before us is that of the accused mastermind of, and active participant in the Fresno explosion of Monday, September 10, 2007, Mr. Rasheed Shirani, a Pakistani citizen."

He then turned directly toward Rasheed.

"Mr. Shirani, you are accused of masterminding or otherwise planning and successfully executing that plan to detonate a powerful explosive device in the city of Fresno, California, on Monday, September 10, 2007, with the sole intent of killing or injuring as many people as possible and causing as much property damage as possible in violation of Unites States law. Do you understand the charges filed against you?"

Rasheed was silent.

"Your Honor, my client respectfully refuses to respond. He has informed me that he is responsible only to Allah."

"I *noticed* that he did not respond, counselor! Mr. Shirani, How do you plead?"

Everyone in the courtroom stared at Rasheed as Rushman leaned toward his client and whispered something into his ear. He then turned to face Judge Keller as Rasheed continued to stare at the judge with evident disdain.

"My client pleads 'not guilty,' Your Honor, and he has informed me that he will not recognize or accept these proceedings."

A minor murmur of collective disbelief flowed through the courtroom. Judge Keller fixed his stare over his glasses on and into Rasheed and bombarded him with the deep, penetrating steady voice that was a signature of his personal identity and professional reputation.

"Mr. Shirani, this court will proceed with or without your consent. Your conduct will be noted for the record. Is the prosecution ready?"

"Yes, Your Honor!"

"Is the defense ready?"

"No, Your Honor. I have not had sufficient time to prepare my case!"

Judge Keller rose from the bench and boomed evenly, "Chambers, gentlemen!"

The military guards and Sherriff's deputies closed in around Rasheed, as Rushman and Mensch left the courtroom for the judge's chambers behind the bench. The courtroom buzzed with the beginnings of what would recur as anticipation and suspense built to almost unsustainable levels, threatening to incur Judge Keller's quick execution of his threat to remove disruptive people from the courtroom.

The prosecutor and defense lawyer joined Judge Keller in his chambers. The judge closed the door quietly behind him and turned immediately to face Mitch Rushman.

"Let's get something straight right now, Mr. Rushman. You have had two weeks to prepare for this trial, and you have been given every scintilla of evidence available to the prosecution. We do not have total control of this case, and you know it! The accused refuses to eat, and if he persists in that behavior, he will die before we complete this trial if I have to continue to entertain your well intentioned, but clever academic interruptions and other delaying tactics. I will conduct this trial with utmost speed but also with due respect for the process of justice, as well as the very real public need for *perceiving* justice in this particular case, in spite of a timetable so far dictated by your client. You will therefore conduct yourself with proper respect for this set of admittedly difficult circumstances and do your level best within the law to provide the best defense for this man your considerable academic credentials and personal talents will afford *without delaying tactics*, or, God help me, I will cite you for contempt! Have I made myself perfectly clear, Mr. Rushman?"

"Yes, Your Honor, I believe you have! However, conscience compels me to point out for the record that my client is facing a jury that is not comprised of his peers! I noticed during the vois dire that there were no Muslims or people of Pakistani heritage in the jury pool, Your Honor. Surely, you will have to consider the possibility of a mistrial on that basis alone!"

In spite of Judge Keller's reputation for fairness in the legal community, Mitch Rushman was dancing foolishly at the edges of creative legal maneuvering that would eventually invite Judge Keller's wrath. The judge started with a surprisingly mild head of steam.

"May I remind you, Mr. Rushman, that justice resides somewhere between chaos and the ludicrous application of picayune academic legal drivel. In my courtroom, we will concentrate upon the application of legal principles that do not insult the common sense of our profession and the essential fabric of our republic, our history and the greatest common good for the greatest number of legal citizens of this country, and, I would hope, all of humanity! I know where you are going with this line of reasoning, Mr. Rushman! This is a United States court of law, not a house of worship or a law school academic bullshit session! We will *apply* the laws of the United States of America, not *make* them! If you want to make laws, then get yourself elected to Congress! Your client is accused of a crime committed in *this* country, not *Pakistan,* and will be tried under *our* laws and cultural values, *not theirs!* When people from other countries chose to come to this country, they are obligated to conform to *our* legal system! Mr. Mensch, do I need to clarify any of this for you as well?"

"No, Your Honor."

"*Questions*, gentlemen?"

The two lawyers responded in atonal duet, "No, Your Honor."

"I still expect this trial to move fairly and expeditiously to its proper completion, gentlemen. Now let's get back to work!"

The three men returned to their seats in the courtroom, and the process once again appeared to move forward.

"Mr. Mensch, you may proceed."

William Mensch pushed his chair back from the prosecutor's table and stood confidently without notes.

"Thank you, Your Honor. The people will present clear and compelling evidence that the accused planned, arranged for and participated in the transport and delivery of a significant amount of deadly C4 and PE4 explosive material in a large rented U-Haul truck, which he drove illegally from Miami, Florida to Wheeler Ridge, California. The evidence will show that he picked up a load of C4 somewhere in Mobile, Alabama, another load near Houston, Texas, and a U-haul trailer loaded with additional explosive material in Ozona, Texas. That truck and trailer eventually arrived at the site of the Fresno explosion defined by the rectangular area between the Fulton Mall and Van Ness Avenue, and between Fresno Street and Tulare Street on Monday, September 10, 2007 shortly before eight o'clock that evening. We will present evidence of the extremely powerful and deadly explosive characteristics of these materials as evidence of Mr. Shirani's intention to conduct a deadly, massive, premeditated and sinister attack upon completely innocent human beings and property. We will show that another driver we believe to be Khalid Kayani, also a Pakistani citizen, took over the truck at Wheeler Ridge, drove it to Fresno and detonated the explosive device in a suicide mission. We will show that the accused mounted a motorcycle and proceeded south from Wheeler Ridge to Los Angeles, and then to Mexico City, where he boarded an airplane bound for Rawalpindi, Pakistan."

"We have evidence of Mr. Kayani's life up to the date of the explosion, evidence of his intent to travel to Fresno on the date of the explosion, and absolutely *no evidence* of his life thereafter. We have evidence that none of the boot orders found in his boot shop in San Diego were filled after September 1, 2007. The paper trail of his personal and business activities ended completely and abruptly on September 10, 2007, the very day of the explosion. We believe Mr. Shirani was the original mastermind behind the design and execution of this plan to detonate a powerful explosive device in a manner that would produce maximum loss of life, personal injury and property damage in the city of Fresno, for the sole purpose of instilling terror in the lives of ordinary citizens of the city of Fresno, the State of California, and by implication, citizens of the entire United States of America, if not all of western civilization."

He returned to his seat, as the courtroom remained distinctly silent.

Judge Keller looked at the defense lawyer with the clear intention of reminding him of their session in chambers at the slightest provocation.

"Mr. Rushman?" he said, with an implicit '*don't push me!*'

"Your Honor, I move for a change of venue."

A rush of whispers and unintelligible comments wafted through the courtroom, prompting the unmistakable sound of Judge Keller's gavel, and his clear warning, "*Order!*"

He then turned his attention to Rushman.

"That is a purely academic request in this modern age of instant and widespread communication, where it is almost a certainty that there is not one location in these entire United States where people have not heard of this tragedy. *Denied!*"

"Your Honor, my client refuses to participate in his own defense. I will need time to make him aware of what is going on here!"

"I believe your client knows *exactly* what is going on here, Mr. Rushman! He understands and speaks English quite well as one of his native languages! *Denied!*"

"I have nothing else right now, Your Honor."

Judge Keller looked at Mitch Rushman as if to say, *I thought you would come to that conclusion!*

The trial proceeded with the sometimes interesting and sometimes boring detailed clinical presentation of evidence and testimony from various experts in the fields of explosives, logistics, satellite imagery, airborne military reconnaissance, and various witnesses along the route traveled by Rasheed across the United States and eventually to Mexico City, including Roger Benson, Juanita Morales and Cordera Alvarez. Professional testimony about eidetic memory, including dramatic and remarkably effective demonstrations, and its validity along with experts in police sketches and computerized image enhancement droned on, including testimony from Sylvia Amoretti from the Mobile Police Department, as well as the two CIA investigators. The prosecutor entered Sylvia's original sketch into evidence, as well as several examples of the computer enhancements of her sketch.

Sasha looked intently at Rasheed sitting at the defense table with Rushman. He was still shackled, but not with chains. The chains were a little too barbaric for the sensitive tastes of the California public, so he was sufficiently restrained with sturdy plastic bands around his wrists and ankles, and was closely guarded by a pair of very fit, obviously muscular sheriff's deputies, and not the usual overweight and out-of-shape members of the department. The military guards were nearby. She thought about how very close she had apparently come to death because of what this man had done. She never knew anyone who would kill another human being—not even a policeman or a member of the armed forces. She could not understand the man's reasons for killing so many innocent people—people he could not even know or appreciate in any way whatsoever. She just could not understand his behavior with or even without a 'reason.'

Jake looked at Rasheed with the growing, burning desire to choke the man with his bare hands. He had suffered the very real belief that Sasha had died because of his treachery. That was not a forgivable act in Jake's mind. Rasheed had put Jake through an agony he felt was worse than death.

Joe stared at Rasheed with unaccustomed hate as well. He saw a man undeserving of a trial, but he understood why the trial had to proceed.

He thought to himself, *you were born somewhere. You had a mother. She must have held you and given you milk, warmth, affection and love. Where did you go wrong? Where did you get the idea that killing Americans is the right thing to do? What kind of perverted logic tells you that you have done something honorable or good?*

Hector Johnson looked at Rasheed with the unbridled hatred of a big kid who still thought the world should be fair. He was no longer interested in having the boots or his deposit. He would never wear them under any circumstances whatsoever because he now knew what kind of despicable person had made them. He wanted personal justice for the death of his only sister because Rasheed destroyed the natural progression of his sister's life and his life. He imagined how he could simply crush Rasheed with his obviously superior strength, weight and size advantage, but it gave him no satisfaction whatsoever.

Cordera Alvarez looked at Rasheed and saw the presence of the man as considerably less than that of the man he had followed to the Mexico City Airport and subsequently to Rawalpindi Airport. He too wanted to kill Rasheed, even though he had not suffered immediate personal loss. He felt insulted as a member of the human race that the man had carried out such an evil plan, enabling its deadly conclusion.

And for what? For WHAT?

He almost yelled aloud, but caught himself, just in time to avoid Judge Keller's wrath.

Professor Michalik looked at Rasheed and saw the same evil that killed his parents so many decades ago. The only difference was the personal philosophy and the politics of the time. The 'righteous' evil capability of man had not changed in the last sixty-three years according to his personal experience, nor during the prior several thousand years, according to his deep understanding of human history.

General Murray felt as though he had been through almost all but the explosion with Rasheed after his intense research and investigation, and saw Rasheed as a man he could actually try to strangle with his own bare hands. What he hated even more was that this vermin of a man had reduced him from an extremely well-trained, intelligent and disciplined military general to his most basic human animal instincts in spite of his lifelong efforts to make himself fit the mold of his ideal honorable man and professional soldier. Yet he had succeeded to a certain extent in carrying out his personal vow to himself after 9/11.

He had participated meaningfully in bringing a terrorist to some point of justice.

Sylvia Amoretti looked at Rasheed, still struggling with the feeling of having profoundly soiled her hands with the pencil she had used to create his image from Roger Benson's descriptions, and yet she felt some pride in having played such a critical role with her unique talent in helping to bring Rasheed to this point of reckoning. This trial would probably not be happening at this time if her artistic ability were not as good as it was. She wondered whether her early art teachers would have been proud of her. No one could have known at that time that a little girl from a common, struggling family would eventually grow up to play such a critical role in a major historical event.

Roger Benson looked at Rasheed with the self-incrimination and Monday-morning quarterbacking logic that convinced him that he could somehow have prevented the carnage in Fresno. He was angry at the 'forces of the universe' for putting him in such a position without the knowledge, ability or foresight to prevent such a tragedy. If he had only known what his unspecified intuition at the time really meant, he would have done something to stop Rasheed, or would have called the police. However, what would he have told them? That he had a 'bad feeling?' He probably would have aroused suspicions of prejudice. Nevertheless, he was only human. He could not know the future. He would suffer the extended torment of knowing that he had failed where fate had intended that he should fail, and yet he was blessed with the unusual ability to remember the intricate details of Rasheed's appearance so critical to the coordinated efforts to bring him to this point of reckoning. He would suffer only inadequate and partial vindication for a long time to come.

William Mensch looked across the room at Rasheed with the ultimate frustration of realizing that there was really no legal remedy or punishment available in the United States judicial system, or probably anywhere else in the world that was even close to what he could imagine as adequate or appropriate for the 'crime' he had to prosecute. The gap between what the law allowed and what he personally needed to accomplish as a statement of justice was absolutely huge.

If he succeeded in getting the death sentence, what would that mean, really? In this society, it would mean Rasheed would never again commit an act of terrorism—a pathetically inadequate result, from Mensch's perspective. Rasheed probably would still learn to enjoy minor episodes of satisfaction, even during a long prison term if it came to that, and probably even with certain prison 'privileges.' In his special culture of extremist beliefs, it would probably establish him as a martyr and encourage others to take his place, continuing the terrorist effort to bring down western culture. There was to be no difference between the punishment for killing one man and the punishment for killing 419 men, women and children and injuring 1,647 others. He would be prosecuting what he saw as an act of war as if it were a mere common street crime.

How absurd!

Officer Dennison looked at Rasheed with unfamiliar rancor, as he thought back over his initial role in bringing his early suspicions about Khalid Kayani to the attention of the San Diego Police Department and eventually the FBI. He was absolutely dumbfounded by how it was possible for someone to succeed in a terrorist attack of this magnitude after 9/11. He too was struggling to stifle enormous and deadly animalistic rage.

A tall middle-aged black man in the back row of the jury box stared at Rasheed with a furrowed brow. The older woman with unnatural silver hair sitting next to him looked over her spectacles at Rasheed with an expression that could have meant that she just bit into a sour apple. The fortyish gentleman next to her who looked like a business executive, sat with his arms crossed in front of him, watching Rasheed as if he were preparing to meet him outside for a dose of personal justice. Another juror grimaced as he stared at Rasheed, as if he were fighting an unwelcome and substantial reflux of stomach acid. The young woman to his left was also staring at Rasheed, but with the completely blank expression of ultimate disbelief. A rather large older gentleman in a short-sleeved shirt barely containing his abundant abdomen sat with his fat arms crossed in front of him staring at Rasheed with wide accusing eyes amplified by his thick wire-rim glasses. Next to him, a man of Chinese heritage with only the beginnings of grey forming in his otherwise uniform black military-style crew cut hair leveled an inscrutable steely stare at Rasheed. A short, thin fiftyish woman in a flowery dress with incipient grey hair, close hawk eyes and two vertical creases in her brow just above her nose stared intently into Rasheed's eyes. A thirtyish trim black woman dressed like a bank executive shot

Rasheed a challenging '*try me!*' expression on her face as she raised one eyebrow higher than the other on her flawless, but serious face. Another older man with the residual physical evidence of a former athlete leaned forward with his elbows on his knees looking intently at Rasheed. A sandy-haired middle-aged man with a rough weathered face and neck and bulging biceps, dressed in a sharply contrasting fashionable shirt, trousers and bright red tie squinted at Rasheed thoughtfully. A young woman of Japanese heritage wearing a blue dress with small white polka dots just stared blankly at Rasheed.

These twelve people comprised the 'jury of his peers' who would carefully evaluate the evidence, and decide whether he was guilty or innocent of a deed he felt honorably duty-bound to commit according to his self-righteous religious conviction.

Had Rasheed been accused of robbery or even involuntary manslaughter, the jury would have considered dispassionately all of the points of view, all of the nuances of the evidence and subtle persuasion of the attorneys, and would even have argued among themselves along minute gradations of emotion and even the letter of the law in their deliberations. However, this man was accused of committing an act that had no subtle nuances of emotion or gradations of guilt according to the essence of humanity that could ultimately supersede the law. The jury could just as easily have been a small herd of a dozen 'water buffalo,' menacingly approaching the accused 'lion' that had injured their 'offspring,' the fabric and future of their social order and culture.

The legal process continued throughout most of the rest of the day, with Prosecutor Mensch carefully and persuasively telling the entire story according to direct and indirect evidence, facts and suppositions, opinions, expert testimony and as much of the borderline assumptions, innuendo and implication that he could get away with in Judge Keller's presence. He meticulously presented evidence in the form of the sequential satellite photographs along with the Air Force reconnaissance photographs and laced it all together with compelling logic and time-line evidence that told the convincing story of Rasheed's deadly and sinister journey across the southern United States from Miami, Florida to Wheeler Ridge, California.

Around four fifty, Judge Keller decided that it was time to take a break and continue on Monday, and said, "Mr. Mensch, I believe we should break it up here, and continue Monday morning, unless you have a strong objection to that."

"No, Your Honor. I have no objection."

"Mr. Rushman?"

"No objection, Your Honor."

"Very well, then. This court is adjourned until nine o'clock Monday morning."

He still used the traditional gavel to add aural punctuation to the closure of court events for the day, and quickly disappeared from the bench into his chambers. He sequestered the jury because of the enormous public interest and potential for various attempts to influence or pester them with public opinion on either side of the issue. He was also concerned about possible extremist efforts to threaten or harm them. Judge Keller would allow none of that, and made sure of it by sequestering them.

The crowd started to mill about in the courtroom, engaged in vociferous conversation and discussion, as the media correspondents attempted to interview people in the gallery, hoping for some kind of sensational statement or remark. However, the mood of most of those in attendance would not tolerate any typically shallow or insipid media questions, so they kept their responses brief and uninformative, if not terse or only slightly civil.

The two 'over-muscled' sheriff's deputies and the military guards escorted Rasheed from the courtroom on their way to an unknown secure location. Judge Keller did not want any kind of disturbance or potential cause for a mistrial to develop, so he made sure Rasheed's non-court location was as secret as possible, and variable. He had arranged for three separate holding cells and four identical black GMC SUV transport vehicles to obscure his location or confuse potential followers as much as possible. His primary plan, however, was to house Rasheed at Lemoore Naval Air Station just south of Fresno. There certainly would be no disturbances of the prisoner there.

At five twenty-three that afternoon, General Murray received a call from the FBI indicating that they had tracked down and arrested all six of the individuals identified in the summary analysis report about Rasheed's personal cell phone. He called William Mensch and arranged to meet him at his home, where he delivered the information to him in person that evening.

CHAPTER 91

Monday, January 7, 2008
Fresno, California

Court resumed on Monday morning promptly at nine o'clock. Prosecutor Mensch informed Judge Keller in his chambers in the presence of Mitch Rushman that he had identified six co-conspirators from information extracted from Rasheed's cell phone by the CIA, and that they had been incarcerated at Lemoore Naval Air Station on Sunday, and were just now arriving at the courtroom. He wanted to include them in the proceedings as co-conspirators.

Judge Keller decided that the co-conspirators would be tried in a separate trial, but their testimony would be allowed in Rasheed's trial. The six co-conspirators took the witness stand one by one, with almost identical responses to every question from Mensch by pleading the fifth amendment. Rushman was completely frustrated because these responses merely had the effect of confirming his client's guilt to the jury.

Judge Keller sighed with only mild sympathy for Mitch Rushman's predicament. He had no credible realistic defense. He almost desperately claimed mistaken identity, and that drew visible evidence of going nowhere with the jury in the form of facial expressions of exasperation and disgust. It occurred to prosecutor Mensch that the lack of any credible defense simply highlighted the futility of what he was trying to do, and of the inadequacy of the legal system as a forum for resolution in this series of tragic events. The defense possibilities were all pathetic and mindless political and legal posturing in the face of overwhelming evidence of guilt, in his opinion.

"Mr. Rushman, do you have anything else to offer?"

Mitch Rushman felt completely defeated for the first time in his young and promising career. His growing reputation as a sharp defense lawyer seemed to crumble right there before him as he realized the utter futility of trying to deny what the prosecutor and the evidence so overwhelmingly presented or implied as accomplished fact. He wilted at the thought of the hopeless maze of negotiation and legal maneuvering possible within the judicial system to mitigate Rasheed's punishment, petition for a new trial or reduced charges, or to attempt any other legal tricks that the judge or Mensch certainly would either not allow or easily defeat. The prosecutor did not like having this trial in the first place, and he certainly was not going to allow any watering down of its capability, regardless of how inappropriate he thought it was.

"No, your honor. I have nothing further."

Judge Keller stared at him for another moment, just to make sure he was finished, and then he turned to the prosecutor.

"Mr. Mensch, do you have anything else to add?"

"No, your Honor. The people rest."

"Very well, gentlemen. This case is now in the hands of the jury."

He turned toward the jury and calmly reminded them of their duty to deliberate according to the evidence and the law. He finished speaking, but still looked at each of them, one by one, with a fleeting sense of mental discomfort—an almost imperceptible tinge of unfamiliar apprehension. He dropped his gavel once more, almost completely by habit.

The jury returned after only about four hours of deliberation. The bailiff notified Judge Keller in his chambers that a verdict had been reached. Word quickly spread within the courthouse, as well as outside where several people were still stretching their legs and getting some fresh air without straying too far from the potential excitement of the conclusion of the trial. Speculation wafted throughout the courtroom about what took the jury so long to return. With electric urgency in the air, people rushed back into the courthouse. Those not already back in the courtroom dropped whatever they were doing, finished snacks, closed their cell phones and notebook computers, abruptly terminated conversations and hurried back into the courtroom. The jury had already reconvened and Judge Keller dropped his gavel at the bench.

"This court will come to order. Ladies and gentlemen, please take your seats."

He turned to look at the jury over his spectacles.

"Foreperson of the jury, have you reached a verdict?"

The heavy older man with the thick glasses responded with confidence, "Yes, Your Honor, we have."

Judge Keller indicated to the foreperson that he should hand the verdict to the bailiff, who was already approaching the jury box. After the bailiff handed the verdict to Judge Keller, the judge took more time than might normally have been expected to read the verdict. He continued to study the verdict for several seconds with no outwardly visible evidence of his thoughts, and then slowly turned his head to face the jury.

After another several thoughtful seconds, he turned away from them as if he had made a decision, and looked directly at Rasheed and said, "The defendant will please rise."

The courtroom was remarkably silent, allowing only the minimal sound of two chairs moving at the defense table as Mitch Rushman and his client, Rasheed Shirani stood together as if they had choreographed and practiced the move to be perfect. Someone's muffled cough echoed briefly through the otherwise silent courtroom. The sheriff's deputies and the military guards moved closer to Mitch and Rasheed with initially subtle, but then quickly obvious preparation to maintain order. Judge Keller handed the verdict back to the bailiff, who returned it to the foreperson.

The judge addressed the foreperson, "You may read the verdict."

"We find the defendant, Rasheed Shirani, guilty of committing a terrorist act that killed 419 innocent people and injured 1647 others on Monday, September 10, 2007 in the city of Fresno, California in violation not only of United States laws, but in violation of the common social order, human decency and respect for all of humanity."

The ensuing buzz and whispers of surprise started to increase throughout the courtroom, as people took note of the foreperson's statement and focused their attention upon this unusual departure from what they had come to expect as normal courtroom behavior, language and procedure.

Judge Keller accepted the minor departure from the norm, and tried to continue with legal protocol, "So say you all?"

"Yes, Your Honor."

Mitch Rushman spoke up out of desperation, "Your Honor, I wish to poll the jurors."

Judge Keller allowed the poll, which was completed quickly, simply, and without hesitation from any of the jurors.

"Very well, Mr. Rushman, do you have any other motions?"

Mitch Rushman hesitated, surprisingly without words, and offered weakly, "No . . . Your Honor."

"Mr. Mensch, do you have anything further before I pronounce sentence?"

"No, Your Honor."

Judge Keller continued, looking directly into Rasheed's eyes, "In the matter of the people versus Mr. Rasheed Shirani, case number A9-136684 in the state of California, United States District Court, 9th Circuit, this court has found you, Mr. Rasheed Shirani, guilty of 419 counts of murder as acts of terrorism, committed on Monday, September 10, 2007, in the city of Fresno, California. In conjunction with other acts of terrorism, including the deliberate destruction of life and property, as well as inflicting unspecified injuries to 1,647 other people in the city of Fresno, State of California, this court hereby sentences you to death in a manner to be determined by the jury."

A loud chorus of unintelligible verbal expressions of surprise and astonishment, as well as cheers of approval rose from the gallery, prompting Judge Keller's gavel to fall harshly upon the bench several times.

"Order! Order in this courtroom!"

After about a minute of unusual patience from Judge Keller while the courtroom simmered down to quiet whispers, he turned his attention to the jury, "Have you determined the manner of death?"

The foreperson answered, "Yes we have, Your Honor."

Sounds of increasing anticipation and surprise broke the tension once more, as Judge Keller dropped his gavel again. The gallery apparently concluded that the reason the jury took so long to return was not the determination of guilt, but the determination of the manner of punishment.

"Proceed."

"We the jury have determined that the convicted terrorist, Rasheed Shirani, shall be bound to a fifteen-ton 'bunker-buster' bomb or other device of comparable destructive force and be released with that device from a suitable aircraft to be exploded within a target identified by the United States Military authorities as a terrorist training camp located within Afghanistan."

The courtroom immediately exploded with spontaneous exclamations of shock, shouting, cheers and angry protests in a cacophony of increasingly unintelligible expressions as Judge Keller's gavel practically pleaded to be heard in the midst of developing potentially riotous conditions. Cries of extreme and unusual punishment collided with equally strong and loud rebuttals and fresh charges of how the crime itself was fundamentally far beyond extreme and unusual in the first place. The verdict and manner of punishment had already escaped into cyberspace with instantaneous communications via cell phone texting and surreptitious calls in spite of the din of shouting and argument that prompted Judge Keller's almost inaudible order to secure the courtroom. Two dozen deputies quickly appeared out of nowhere from every entrance to the courtroom, and efficiently removed the most obviously active protestors in the gallery as those not yet rudely hustled out of the room or with enough self-discipline or common sense not to challenge Judge Keller's authority sat back down in their seats and wisely kept their mouths shut.

Judge Keller's deep and commanding voice ripped through the remaining, but diminishing minor chaos in his signature penetrating voice, "Anyone who chooses to disrupt this court again will be arrested on charges of disorderly conduct and contempt of court!"

After a short period of relative quiet and collective recognition of judge Keller's warning, during which the remaining crowd in the momentarily stunned gallery had apparently chosen to respect the power and authority of the court, Judge Keller continued addressing the foreperson while anticipating Mitch Rushman's thoughts.

"Is your determination of the manner of death unanimous?"

"Yes it is, Your Honor."

"Very well, then. Anything further, Mr. Rushman?"

Mitch Rushman felt defeated professionally, psychologically, and personally, in spite of his innate competitive and fighting personality. He saw the futility of further legal maneuvering and protest as merely postponing the inevitable. The jury and almost the entire gallery had clearly stated their sentiments in a manner that in his estimation even an appeal with full review by the Supreme Court of the United States might not overcome. The jury had in effect stated the mood of the country, and he knew it. He imagined for a moment that the jury had just written an amendment to the Constitution. The Fresno Incident had clearly redefined the legal framework and punishment that the public was willing to tolerate in dealing with the age of terrorism. They had verbalized what so many other people apparently had been unwilling to release from their most private thoughts. This jury had defined the law of the jungle that would apply in response to terrorist behavior. 'Justice' or 'social satisfaction' was no longer a matter of taking the 'civilized' moral high road versus the low road. The jury had admitted that they were willing to recognize their basic animal tendencies as best they could to meet the challenge of the animalistic behavior of terrorists. The argument that the country had stooped to the low moral standards of terrorists would no longer hold water, and gave way to the law of the jungle—*we will live, and they will die*.

The country did not have the masterminds of at least a decade of terrorism attacks in custody, but the members of this jury had the planner of the Fresno incident firmly in their grasp, and they had made a statement to the world about how they wanted to deal with him. The determination of the manner of execution reminded Rushman of the O. J. Simpson trial, in which the jury had asserted itself by essentially ignoring the evidence and acquitting the accused. In this case, the jury had asserted itself by inventing a manner of execution heretofore not available within the judicial system.

"Mr. Rushman?"

"Nothing further, Your Honor."

"Mr. Mensch?"

In spite of what he had just heard from the jury, Mensch stifled his urge to express his dissatisfaction with the verdict and punishment. The punishment still was not adequate to the crime. To him, the very concept of punishment was almost irrelevant in this case. He wanted to vaporize and permanently eliminate Rasheed and all thoughts and memory of him from every person in the world. How else could the social order respond to such unspeakable evil?

He could almost understand and tolerate tragic death from the ravages of natural forces beyond human control, but he could not accept death due to the deliberate evil behavior of human beings that almost defies expression. He had learned to live with one person murdering another. He could almost accept the sick behavior of serial killers. He had never prosecuted such a case, but he had read about and studied several. As a student of history and son of a Vietnam veteran, he understood war and all of its profound ugliness. However, he could not tolerate the behavior of a small group of people without even governmental sanction who executed innocent men, women and children just because they thought they had an obligation to do so. The inadequacy of the punishment relative to the crime continued to burn through every fiber of his being.

This man's personal evil imagination had become reality without any meaningful peer or social review or external evaluation whatsoever! Even the brutality of war has rules of conduct! This man has none!

"Mr. Mensch . . . Are you with us?"

Judge Keller's voice interrupted Mensch's thoughts as if it echoed from the other end of a long tunnel, and brought him back to the courtroom.

"Uh . . . Yes, Your Honor . . . I have . . . nothing further."

"Very well then. The sheriff will secure Mr. Shirani. Sentence will be carried out as soon as possible within the next ten days, and confirmation of its execution from the responsible military authorities will be reported to this court immediately thereafter."

Rasheed Shirani finally spoke up with a much stronger voice than his deteriorating physical condition might have appeared to allow, *"Allah will have his revenge! Many others will follow me to punish the American infidels! You do not know the truth and power of Allah! All of you will be destroyed!"*

The courtroom started to boil again with expressions of protest, contempt, cheers and taunts of satisfaction.

"Sheriff! Take him away! This court is now adjourned."

Judge Keller's gavel officially slammed into the bench with at least some personal emphasis. He stood, turned around and quickly returned to his chambers.

He sat down at his desk, shut out the outside world for a few moments, rested his head in his hands and settled into deep personal reflection. He knew that he had just presided over what had to be the most unusual and creative exercise of criminal 'justice' in the history of the United States of America. In spite of his legal education, experience, judicial position, reputation and responsibilities, he had taken this daring and creative step outside of tradition and allowed the inner conscience of the public to express itself and take its course through the jury in *his* courtroom. Unknown to all but a handful of people, Judge Howard J. Keller was a member of the Chancellor Organization.

CHAPTER 92

Monday, January 11, 2008
Lemoore Naval Air Station, California

Arianna Lamington, the egotistical Botox-laden and overly made-up forty-seven year old free-lance investigative news correspondent for ABC television had 'discovered' the location of Rasheed Shirani with her extensive network of informants, using favors, bribes, and manipulation of malleable public servants with various degrees and shades of the truth and whatever outright lies she thought she was entitled to use. She arrived at the main headquarters building at Lemoore Naval Air Station with Lester, her handsome and beefy 268-pound, six-and-a-half foot tall black 'personal assistant' and camera man, and an equally imposing Japanese-American driver, who stayed behind the wheel of her sparkling white 2008 Cadillac Escalade. Lester escorted her to the entrance to the building and inside to the information desk where Petty Officer Third Class David Raker greeted them.

"Welcome to Lemoore Naval Air Station. How may I help you?"

"My name is Arianna Lamington, as I assume you know. I am here to interview Rasheed Shirani."

Raker responded with only mild surprise, "I'm sorry, Ma'am, but he's not here."

"Don't lie to me young man! I know he is being held under guard at this facility!"

"Again, Ma'am, I'm sorry, but your information is incorrect."

"I wish to speak with the base commander, please—immediately!"

Raker did not want to make a bigger scene than she was apparently already quite prepared to create by telling her with military adjectives what was on his mind and what he thought of her.

Nevertheless, he managed to utter a polite "Please wait here for a moment, Ma'am."

Raker picked up the telephone receiver on the desk before him, dialed an internal number, and after several seconds said, "This is Raker. I need to speak with Commander Anderson." After about half a minute he continued. "Sir, Arianna Lamington from ABC television is here with a cameraman requesting an interview with Rasheed Shirani. I told her he is not here, but she insisted upon speaking with 'the base commander,' sir."

"Very well, Raker. Show her to my office."

Raker replaced the phone receiver in its cradle on his grey metal desk with well-disguised exasperation and arose from his seat.

"Ma'am, please follow me."

Lester followed Arianna with his camera on standby. She followed Raker down the hall to Commander Anderson's office. He was in full dress military uniform, standing before his desk by the time Raker entered his open office with the visitors.

"Welcome to Lemoore Naval Air Station, Miss Lamington! How may I be of assistance?" he said with practiced official demeanor he reserved for people for whom he had no personal respect.

He glanced at Lester's camera, and then into Lester's eyes with the implicit visual command not to raise his camera to its operating position.

Gesturing toward Raker, she said, "This young man told me that Rasheed Shirani is not here. My information is otherwise, Commander. I wish to interview this man as soon as possible for a television program that will air nationwide this evening!"

Commander Anderson's initial facial expression of friendly hospitality slowly changed into the serious expression of his military bearing as the base commander with official rank, personal self-assurance and pride. He glanced at his watch and then looked into her eyes with his 'no tolerance for fools' expression that he reserved for people he perceived to have too much self-importance.

"Miss Lamington, Rasheed Shirani left this facility very early this morning. I imagine that he is about 35,000 feet up in the air somewhere over the Pacific Ocean right now in a B1-B aircraft, heading west on a special strike mission."

"But . . . but . . ."

Commander Anderson glanced at Lester again with a visual message that told him it was time to leave, and then returned his official bearing toward Arianna.

"Miss Lamington, is there something else I can help you with?"

Raker was holding his breath just inside the door to Commander Anderson's office, realizing that it would be unwise of her to persist.

She just looked into Anderson's eyes with the slightest hint of rare defeat, completely speechless, in spite of her well-practiced 'TV personality' and customary dominance of any situation, as she said, "I . . . I have . . . I believe we should get back to my studio . . . Commander Anderson . . . Thank you for your time."

Commander Anderson extended his hand to her, turned and smiled briefly at Lester and then turned back toward her and said, "I'm sorry I could not be of more help, Miss Lamington."

Raker escorted the two visitors out of the building. They returned to her Cadillac and left the base. Her program that evening would be a harangue of commentary and opinion from 'experts around the world' about 'due process' and 'cruel and unusual punishment.' Her show's initial Nielsen ratings showed a noticeable decline.

CHAPTER 93

Friday, January 11, 2008
22,000 feet above Pakistan

The pilot of the B1-B aircraft announced through his intercom, "Prepare for target alpha with single fifteen-ton ordnance. Attach and secure the prisoner now! Manual drop will be in fourteen minutes. Bombardier, set the fuse for ground impact. Target bravo will be in nineteen minutes with normal automatic delivery."

Three men secured Rasheed to the bomb with eight high-grade three-inch wide canvas straps around the circumference of the bomb, firmly secured through special brackets specially welded onto the bomb case itself. The bombardier also secured a pulse-monitoring transmitter to Rasheed's left arm to transmit his heart rate during the entire drop. Two of the crew then secured a separate canvas tarp around the entire body of the bomb, encasing Rasheed so the flight of the bomb would not rip his head or extremities off. The initial pulse transmission registered 113 on the pilot's receiver.

Exactly nine minutes later, the bombardier manually released a single fifteen-ton 'bunker-buster' bomb with Rasheed Shirani securely strapped to it to assure that he would remain with the bomb throughout its entire trajectory of descent to the training camp below them, just a few miles northeast of Khost, Afghanistan. They had made only minor adjustments to their trajectory calculations to accommodate the altered aerodynamic characteristics of the bomb package enveloping

Rasheed. During the next approximately forty-six seconds, the pulse receiver registered increasing numbers up to 186 before stopping with the enormous explosion.

Rasheed did not die of fright on the way down. He had approximately forty-six seconds just prior to his death to contemplate his entire life and his relationship with Allah. He died immediately upon impact as the explosion completely obliterated his body. The pilot reported to his base commander that target alpha was hit with the specified ordnance in the prescribed manner as he continued on to target bravo. Within the hour, satellite reconnaissance images revealed twenty-nine bodies on the ground in or near the compound away from the impact site, and confirmed that damage to the physical camp was severe. Judge Keller had the report within the hour, as did the President of the United States.

CHAPTER 94

Saturday, January 12, 2008
Early evening.

Sasha was singing at The Algonquin in Manhattan with The Autumn Dream, still transporting her audiences to the most joyful and peaceful extremes of their imaginations. Jake was enjoying the show from the table closest to the stage. Occasionally she would look his way, and they would both smile at each other. No one who might have noticed could have understood the significance of those smiles.

Joe was cooking mushrooms for a new and exciting recipe. His dining room was full of satisfied customers engaged in their own lives, and he would have a late night cleaning up. There was nothing urgent on his agenda for the Chancellor Organization.

Kenney was out on the town at a restaurant in San Francisco artfully resisting the charms of a young socialite with a clear amorous message in her eyes.

Paul and Sarah Jepson were sitting in their warm living room with logs burning in the fireplace on a cold night with their new golden retriever that they unwittingly named 'Duke.' Sarah was working on a crossword puzzle. Paul was almost asleep, thinking about Wesley Simpson and the unusual events since the auction. He was also feeling great pride in his son, imagining what Mike was doing that night.

Michael Jepson was taking a break from studying and enjoying a relaxing evening, eating a pizza with Gaye in Cambridge. Her smile was rich and inviting, if not deliciously compelling, in spite of the tomato sauce on her lips.

Professor Michalik was relaxing at his home with his wife. He was reading a book about Islamic history, and she was crocheting. He wondered which of his seminar students would chose to accept his eventual invitation to join The Chancellor Organization.

Lights illuminated only one corner office on the top floor of the otherwise dark Plymouth Building in the cold and quiet evening in Maryland. Duke Chancellor was working late. He did not have the luxury and comfort of a personal love relationship. He still wondered what his father would think of what he had accomplished and what he was doing with his life.

Bertha and Willie had moved to Chicago with some assistance from an anonymous benefactor in Maryland, and Willie was taking night courses in computer programming at a local community college while working at a local warehouse during the day. Bertha had found a job in a hat factory. She felt much more secure than she had felt in Baltimore, and enjoyed a new and refreshing sense of optimism and faith. She still wondered why Detective D'Anatoli had been so kind and helpful to her and Willie.

Detective Mike D'Anatoli was on another drug case, waiting in his unmarked car in western Baltimore for an opportunity to remove another drug dealer from this planet.

Ramon Raphael was coaching at a basketball clinic at the local YMCA in Fresno, persistently correcting the boys' English after every instance of misuse.

"*Don't* give me all that 'dude talk!' If you want me to teach you how to play basketball, you speak to everyone here in proper English! There's no free lunch here!"

Sammy was taking a break from developing new encryption systems by playing spider solitaire in his new home in San Francisco. He did not have any urgent tasks to accomplish for The Chancellor Organization. Occasionally, he would retrieve the image of Janice Smith that he had stored in his computer and admire it.

Henry and Julie Winslow were out dining together in Cheshire, Connecticut. Their practice had simmered down to normal after the exhausting experience with Sasha and Jake. They were still reviewing the case, still wondering whether Sasha was permanently and completely as whole as she could be. They admitted to each other that she probably was. They were co-authoring a case study in 'total immersion' amnesia therapy with a theoretical discussion of talent-related neural pathways for publication in the professional journals.

Raj Sampat was relaxing during a visit at his father's home in Mumbai, India, thinking about what might be in store for him within the Chancellor Organization. He had not told his father about his exciting experience 'in the field' during the search for Rasheed in Pakistan.

Doctor Stanley Jensen was at a dinner in Miami with friends and some professional associates with noticeably subdued evidence of his formerly abrasive and overwhelming ego. He was in an animated intellectual discussion about whether sight was a necessary component of artistic expression and appreciation.

General Arshad was considering the significance of his remarkable experience with General Murray, and how he now considered him to be a true friend, a person to whom he would be eternally grateful for Amir's gift of sight. He eventually learned of the sentence meted out to Rasheed, and thought about his role in bringing Rasheed to that horrible end, but it did not disturb his conscience at all in the light of what General Murray had done for Amir. He sensed a refreshingly new sense of commitment to use his power and influence for good. He enjoyed a renewed sense of self and hope.

Three teenage youths in a small village north of Wana, Pakistan were having an early evening bullshit session while kicking a soccer ball around in a vacant dirt field. They were discussing how they would someday start Jihad as they had been encouraged to do by one of the village elders. They were unaware of the arrest and death of Rasheed Shirani. They did not know how his life ended. They boasted to one another about how much they hated Americans because they were infidels. It was so plainly obvious to them. None of them had traveled more than twenty miles from their village. None of them had ever even seen, let alone talked to an American. Nevertheless, that did not matter to them, because each one of them understood the ultimate and necessary truth of Allah that they learned in the village school at an early age.

From a small rise in a vast quiet rolling grass-covered vista somewhere in Uganda with several acacia trees in view, the world appeared to be at peace near the end of another day as a mild breeze ruffled the tall grass in periodic waves, highlighted by the early evening sunlight piercing a blanket of reddish orange clouds near the horizon. In the tall grass not far from a lone tree, a lioness and her two cubs were feasting upon the remains of a water buffalo she had just killed.

ACKNOWLEDGEMENTS

I hope you enjoyed reading "THE FRESNO INCIDENT" at least as much as I enjoyed writing it. As is certainly the case with all fiction, the author refers to many aspects of reality in efforts to make a story realistic and interesting, and in so doing understandably presents certain errors of interpretation, judgment, 'artistic license' or description of detail that may be different from more knowledgeable or professional opinion or actual reality. That is part of the nature of fiction and of life itself. I take full responsibility for any such errors of description or fact that may have diminished your enjoyment of this story.

I am grateful for the assistance of several people, who provided certain insights and appreciation of portions of this story that I probably could not have rendered as well without their help. Any errors of interpretation are mine alone, not theirs. Michelle Adessa, a former 'little girl next door' who blossomed into a very talented opera singer, helped define Sasha's voice. Larry Gorrell provided insights into and understanding of the Midwest auctioneering business. Patricia Ashley and Ellen Welsh, both registered nurses, gave insights into some of the medical, hospital and nursing facets of the story. Dr. Bruce Clark enabled better understanding of some of the medical conditions I attempted to portray, and Philip Decker clarified aspects of the insurance industry.

I especially appreciate the encouragement of friends who showed interest in my effort during the nineteen months it took me to write this story. Furthermore, I want to thank my older son Marc for being the first to edit the early draft of the story and make important suggestions, and my other son Jeff for his encouragement and interest throughout the effort. I especially thank a very special friend of more than forty-four years, Bill Kiser, for taking extra time and effort to offer suggestions and comments from the unique perspective of both broad intelligence and long-standing personal friendship. Finally, I would like to thank my wife LeAnn for putting up with the sometimes exclusively dedicated concentration I required at various times to complete this project.

Phil Rettew

Made in United States
North Haven, CT
14 October 2023

42762602R10321